Torn

Also by Anne Randall

Riven
Silenced

Torn

Anne Randall

Constable • London

CONSTABLE

First published in Great Britain in 2017 by Constable

1 3 5 7 9 10 8 6 4 2

Copyright © Anne Randall, 2017

The moral right of the author has been asserted.

A CIP catalogue record for this book is
available from the British Library.

ISBN: 978-1-47212-276-6

Typeset in Palatino by SX Composing DTP, Rayleigh, Essex
Printed and bound in Great Britain by CPI Mackays

Papers used by Constable are from well-managed forests
and other responsible sources.

MIX
Paper from
responsible sources
FSC® C104740

For Don

THEN

Sunday 27 June, 2004

The Search

It was stoking her own hope, trust, and sure and certain knowledge that Amy was alive, which exhausted her. If, in some unguarded and unarmed moment, she let a splinter of doubt pierce her resolve then she would be defeated and something dark, something sticky and awful would bleed into her consciousness. No, better to keep herself armed with certainty until the city and the cruelty of its river told her otherwise.

Rachel Dawson stood on the bridge and watched the police divers search the River Clyde.

A softly spoken family liaison officer had informed her gently that the police had specialist resources, that they would follow up every lead while uniformed officers would continue to conduct city-wide inquiries. But Rachel knew that the combined time, money and resources of the special support units screamed quietly that they were looking for a body. They were convinced that Amy was gone. Rachel knew that they were not looking for her bright, vibrant daughter, but for an empty vessel. They weren't searching for Amy, they were looking for a corpse.

Rachel had passed a reporter staring into a camera lens, had heard him confidently tell the television audience, 'Amy Dawson was last seen leaving her flat at 7 p.m. on Friday 25 June.' Rachel knew that he would show the grainy CCTV image of Amy's car travelling along London Road at 7.23 p.m. She heard him continue, 'The last confirmed sighting of Amy's car suggests that it was heading towards the Campsie Fells. Detectives from Carmyle Station are working on building a picture of Amy's last movements after she left her flat in Prosen Street in the East End of the city. Amy was last seen wearing a white cotton summer dress and black sandals.'

Rachel knew that the picture she'd given the police was a good likeness. Amy smiling into the camera, brown eyes, short, dark hair, a silver nose stud which glittered like a talisman.

Sometimes it is better that the city gifts us her secrets, however dark and unpalatable they may be.

The Trial

'DARK?'

'SUBVERSIVE?'

'DEPRAVED?'

I watched the defence. Mark Ponsensby-Edward, QC, allowed a lengthy pause between each word. He was six foot four of sinewy muscle and sarcasm. After the first day of the trial, I'd googled him. He was from a prominent family, had excelled at rugby as a youth and had chosen his career path to sate a desire for adversarial debate rather than from financial necessity. His hair and moustache were prematurely white, the result of a teenage skiing accident which had left him temporarily paralysed. He'd recovered but had been left with a pronounced limp.

When he stared at me, I believed that he saw straight through to my bones and, given his sour expression, he didn't like what he saw. His nails were long, his bony hands, claw-like. His teeth were small and perfectly

5

straight apart from the two incisors which tapered to unusually sharp points. A modern-day Dracula, he sucked the life out of his opponent's argument.

'I want you to consider the thrall that bondage and discipline, dominance and submission and sadism and masochism, held over both Marcus Newton and Amy Dawson.' His voice echoed around the silent courtroom. 'Marcus Newton openly admitted that he took pleasure in disciplining Amy Dawson but Ms Dawson was a very willing participant. Remember that it was Ms Dawson who first made contact, she was the instigator of their relationship. Remember too that she had been an active member of the BDSM community for many years. We have heard evidence that she regularly demanded the use of leg restraints, handcuffs and erotic asphyxiation to satisfy her craving for submission, a fantasy that my client and Ms Dawson explored together. A fantasy that she continued to explore with a great number of partners, long after she split from Marcus Newton. The prosecution's case is severely flawed, there is no concrete evidence that Marcus Newton was with Amy Dawson on the night she died.' Ponsensby-Edward waited, poised, a magician expecting applause. As if the court were a stage and he had magicked the brutal, enticing images from a dark abyss.

Previously I'd listened to the prosecution, Advocate Depute Duncan McConnell, QC. Google hadn't had so much on him. He was a bit of a hermit. Lived for his work. Unmarried. No scandal. He'd spoken in a voice that was full of outrage, had appealed to our humanity. It was a pity I had none. 'It was a torture chamber, nothing less. Despicable acts of sadomasochism were repeatedly inflicted on Amy Dawson, until that fateful night when Marcus Newton decided to act out his murderous fantasy and finally kill her in cold blood.'

Lacking Ponsensby-Edward's passion and charisma, McConnell had stumbled over his words at one point. 'Amy was a sexually adventurous woman who joined the BDSM community looking for fun. What happened next was that Marcus Newton preyed on her and exploited her for his own pleasure. In effect, he denied her the oxygen of self-esteem and continued to control her in increasingly barbaric ways.'

I and my fellow jurors listened as the evidence was presented. We accepted the graphic, explicit photographs that were circulated to us and the judge. In the first one, a naked woman was bound, the ropes around her wrists attached to a hoist. A bar between her ankles ensured that her legs remained open. Around her neck, a thick leather collar. I was enthralled and listened, fascinated, while McConnell fed us the tantalising details. 'This image was recovered from Marcus Newton's mobile phone and shows a woman in the act of strappado.'

My heartbeat quickened.

'As part of the BDSM community, Marcus Newton would have been familiar with this practice. Strappado has its origins in medieval torture and the bar fixed to the woman's ankles, known as a spreading bar, would have been placed there with the express intention of keeping her off balance. Whoever held the rope had total control over her. This physical control was a precursor to the psychological control Marcus Newton used to dominate and exploit women.'

My mind was in turmoil. As the trial progressed, I

became aware of the difference in my and my fellow jurors' reactions to the images. I heard deep sighs, saw hands being wrung, an uncomfortable shifting in seats. I'd tried to mirror their actions but was acutely aware that I was aroused. I had to be careful. I recalled how a psychology lecturer at college had once explained how easy it was to reveal our true selves through body language. I dutifully stared at the photographs, resisted the desire to lick my lips and trace a finger over the images of the naked women. Instead, I calmly folded my hands on my lap, forced myself to remember what the lecturer had said, that the usual response, when confronted with images for which one feels distaste or repulsion, is that the pupils of the eyes become constricted. I knew better than to meet the gaze of either QC; I was certain that my pupils would not be constricted, but instead would be dilated, the common reaction when one is excited. My mind became a fantastic kaleidoscope of disturbingly thrilling images and, as I tuned out of what was being said by the defence, I allowed these images to loop and play endlessly in my imagination. Bliss.

Finally, the closing statements were delivered and the judge made a short speech. Then, we, the jury, were taken from the court and led to a cramped, airless room. I desperately wanted to be back in my flat, alone with my thoughts and the dark sexual images. Instead, I hovered around a table set with tea, coffee and biscuits. Busied myself pouring coffee, listened to John, the foreman, speak. Heard the disgust in his voice as he asked, 'Well, everyone? What are your thoughts?'

'Such shocking images,' said one juror. 'And the poor mother sitting in the room, having to hear all of it.'

'The photographs are seared into my mind,' replied another.

And so it continued.

'How can I ever forget?'

'Dreadful.'

I sipped my coffee, thought of the women in the photographs, felt a rush of excitement and desire. Kept my voice neutral, emotionless. 'Appalling. Just appalling.'

That night in my flat, I'd turned on the news, heard a reporter state what I already knew – Marcus Newton had been found guilty. A few seconds later, he finished by stating that, 'the murder of Amy Dawson was a cruel and unforgivable act.'

I flicked through the channels, another reporter mid-sentence: '. . . and in this case, role play, at the hands of depraved Marcus Newton, led to something far more sinister.'

I opened my laptop, found the website and downloaded the video. Strappado. Just like in the photographs at the trial, the women were naked, bound to hoists, their legs forced apart by bars. I felt my heartbeat quicken, my palms become moist. I was instantly hard. I knew that the trial had been life-changing, that I was not the same person who'd entered the courtroom a week earlier. For me, the exquisite carnal journey was only just beginning.

NOW

Chapter One

Tuesday 8 July, 2014

The Actress

Forty-five minutes in this heat, thought Karlie Merrick, and she'd be basted like a fucking turkey. The temperature was building steadily and there was no air con but she still couldn't face the motorway. Couldn't trust herself. Not today. Not the way she was feeling.

Once she was clear of Glasgow, she turned the silver Volkswagen Golf towards Strathaven, kept her speed on the low side, switched on the radio, heard the Kill Kestrels, 'Death of an Angel'. Turned up the volume. Tried to ignore the anxiety that gnawed in the recess of her mind. It had begun last night after she'd spoken with Steve Penwell. His paranoia had been infectious as he'd warned her, 'What I've told you is gold. You need to be careful.' For a moment she'd had hope, then he'd ruined it all by seeing faces in the curtain and talking about pirates. 'Fucking pirates,' she muttered. 'I don't know what to believe.' But the old man had her so freaked that by the time she'd left the care home she'd checked the back seat before getting in the car. 'Nuts,' she'd muttered, 'I'm going crazy.' But, hands shaking, she'd made the call. He'd told her that he'd take care of it. They were meeting up later that evening, after she'd finished at the farm.

Last night, when she'd been going to bed, she'd crossed to the window to draw the curtains and could've sworn that there was someone standing in the shadows across the road. She forced the image to the back of her mind, indicated and pulled out to overtake a lorry, accelerated. Just as she passed it she saw the turn-off for the farm. 'Shit.' She swerved left, barely made it in front of the lorry, shot off the road, skidded onto the dirt track, braked fiercely as she heard the squeal of brakes behind her, the rasp of the horn, as she made her way down the farm track, past the crumbling outbuildings. The whole place was a decrepit sore on the landscape and the old boy who owned it was so cash poor he'd been pathetically grateful for the opportunity to diversify. She felt the car bump down the track, on towards the huge, windowless, metal barn. She pressed a button and the car windows closed, keeping out the stink from the hundreds of battery hens shut up inside. She drove past another field before the three metal shipping containers came into sight. They were surrounded by junk, bits of old cars decayed beside a crooked crane, ancient farm machinery tilted against piles of building detritus, broken bricks and concrete slabs slumped next to rubble. Dirt and decay, the whole place was rotten. Again, images of a lone figure standing across from her flat curled and wove its way around her imagination, whorls of fear and sinister shadows. 'Cut it out,' she told herself as she parked beside a battered pickup truck, 'You're paranoid.' She stepped out into the fierce heat.

14

Ahead of her, a short, skinny man, whose face was set with deep lines, was leaning against a container. He was engrossed in watching a movie on his phone. He might have been watching a classic perhaps, or a favourite musical. If it wasn't for the screaming. Then the voice pleading for it to stop. Her voice sounded tinny, it always did. She knew that Johnny Pierce was watching a film of her. Strappado. It had been shot at one of the empty hotels Gary Ashton had access to, shit places mostly.

'Hey, Johnny.' Heard her voice sound different in the sunshine, the wide open space. How normal it sounded in contrast to the voice on the recording. He looked up. She heard herself scream and beg for forgiveness. Then the silence when a ball gag had been stuffed into her mouth. She knew the video ran for another twenty minutes. The spreading bar had been removed and leg restraints had been put on, then the whip had been used. Her legs had been sore for days after the shoot. Not just her legs.

'This is shit-hot, Karlie.' Pierce held up the phone. 'Talent like this, you're wasted here.'

'You don't need to convince me.'

'You still looking to relocate to the States?' he asked.

'If I can.' She saw him glance at the video again, knew in it nipple clamps were being fitted. 'You never fancied going out there?'

'Not sure I'd get in, small matter of a holiday I took a few years ago.'

'Go on.'

'I was a guest at that big hotel Barlinnie for a while. Her Majesty's pleasure.'

She walked to the container. 'What for?'

'Assaulting my ex-partner. Long time ago. I've moved on.'

'You think Gary might give me a rise?'

'Gary Ashton's a tight bastard.'

She watched him pull the door wide. Inside were rails of clothes, a row of cheap shoes. The outfits. On a white plastic table were handcuffs, whips, nipple clamps, ball gags, chokers and rope. The props.

'But you can always ask.'

'Does Gary's partner knows about this little venture?' she said.

'Lisa? Doubt it.'

'Because?'

'The profits from this hobby are solely for him to fund his coke habit, the wedding stuff he shares with her and the kid.'

'You think I could use it to get a bit of leeway for a rise?'

'If you're looking for trouble, that'd certainly be a short cut to it. From what I hear, Lisa's mother bought them the house. Any upset and he's scared she'll chuck him out.' Pierce picked up a whip and ran the tip of it gently against her cheek. 'You still seeing that shrink of yours? What's his name – Bellerose?'

'George's not a shrink, he's a life coach but yeah, he's helping me get focused to relocate.'

'Still offering cut-price sessions?'

She nodded.

'He's got a thing for you, he wants to get into your knickers.' Pierce paused. 'Is he in with a chance?'

'Not a snowball's in hell but as long as he gets me out of here, he's welcome to his fantasies. The Studio open?'

'Christ, I've just arrived, give me a sec.'

16

She waited while he dragged open the door of the second container Gary Ashton insisted they called the Studio. Ashton was deluded. Without air conditioning, the heat inside was intense, and more than once she'd felt the sweat run down her back and pool in the waist of her outfits. 'This whole place is fucking unhygienic,' she muttered.

Five minutes later, she had put her hair up and had slathered on thick make-up. She kicked off her sandals, stripped off her clothes and walked across to the rack of clothes. Sexy secretary. Couldn't be more clichéd. She heard a motorbike come to a stop outside. A couple of seconds later, Gary Ashton's bulk filled the doorway. He was thirty-two, wore his long blond hair in a ponytail. He dumped the crash helmet on the table. 'Hey.'

Karlie pulled on the leather pencil skirt, buttoned the white shirt, kept her tone friendly. 'How's the wedding photography going?'

He shrugged. 'Pays the bills.'

'Glad to hear it.' She drew a slash of red lipstick across her lips. 'Does Lisa know about your little outfit here?'

'She doesn't need to, seeing as it's got fuck all to do with her.'

'Why's that then? You reckon she wouldn't approve?'

'I'm not interested in asking her opinion. So, what's with all the questions, Karlie?'

'I'm just saying, this is your little secret and I'm sure you'd like to keep it that way.'

'Go on.'

'What say you up my wages?'

Ashton crossed to her, his face inches from hers. He was too close; she could smell the coffee on his breath. Practically taste the nicotine.

17

'Or?'

She tried for a smile, failed. 'I'm worth more than I'm getting paid.' Heard the tremble in her voice.

'Go ahead, talk to Lisa. I don't mind.'

'Really?'

'Honestly, I'm not that bothered. My only concern would be for you and your work prospects.'

'Because you'd fire me.' More of a statement.

'After I'd broken your fucking neck.'

Pierce called from the doorway. 'Everything's set up next door guys and Will's ready.'

Ashton waved him away.

She tried to move forward. Ashton blocked her.

Her voice small, she said, 'I was only joking.'

He smiled down at her. 'Of course you were and now that you've had your fun, put on the fucking shoes.'

She reached for the stilettos, knew they were a narrow size four, she was a five. She crammed her feet into them. 'These are tiny.'

His fist missed her face by a fraction. 'Another fucking woman nagging me. I don't want to hear it, OK?'

She nodded, said nothing.

'That's it, you just need to be a good girl and get on with it.'

She hobbled across to the second container, felt her toes cramp and a sharp pain shoot up her right calf.

Inside, it was set up as an office, with a wooden desk and chair in the centre. In the corner sat a smaller desk with a telephone, computer and a stack of folders. In the absence of a generator, Ashton had rigged up battery-run lights.

'The camera's on the far wall, above the desk, so mind

18

you face it and for God's sake try to get some action going, this stuff's supposed to be a turn-on.'

Will Reid edged his way into the container. 'All OK, guys?'

'Get into place,' muttered Ashton.

They took their positions.

'Action.' Ashton backed out of the container.

Same old, same old, thought Karlie, she could do this in her sleep. 'You wanted to see me, sir?'

'You've made mistakes, Miss Samson, too many mistakes.'

'I can only apologise, sir. I'll redo these reports and get them to you first thing in the morning.'

'That isn't good enough. I'm afraid the board and I have decided that you need to be punished.'

'I can explain, sir.'

'Enough, Miss Samson. You were warned not to continue to make mistakes. You didn't listen. I have no other option. You know what to do.' He sat back in his chair, loosened his tie. 'Strip.'

The same old routine, different outfits, different props. Varying degrees of pain and violence. One theme. Men in power over women. The way of the world, thought Karlie, but she wasn't going to be exploited, she was going to exploit them. She thought of her other job – it paid well, but again, the same themes. One guy got off washing her mouth out with soap while he called her Jean. Perverted fucker. Plus, she'd only had two shifts there and, well paid as it was, she needed more.

She leaned palms down on the desk. After a few minutes they changed tempo and position. Karlie lay on the desk and groaned as he tried and failed to improvise dialogue. She heard him repeat his usual refrain, 'I hope you are learning your lesson, Miss Samson.' Another couple of changes of position and it was over. She eased off the shoes and rubbed her toes.

'OK, let's keep going,' said Ashton. 'We don't have all day.'

She traipsed back to the container, changed outfits. When she returned, Ashton had placed a thin mattress over the desk, draped the makeshift bed in nylon faux fur throws and satin cushions. He'd added a couple of steel chains to the head and foot of the bed. 'A budget dungeon,' muttered Karlie as she squeezed her feet back into the too-tight shoes.

'Action.'

Will Reid gripped the leather collar in his right hand and beckoned to her. She had been scripted to be *fearful but compelled*. Ashton had underlined 'compelled' twice. Reid had been instructed to *be seething* and *rough* when he fastened the collar around her neck and led her to the bed. Erotic asphyxiation. She waited while he attached the collar, then the lead. She lay on her back. As they filmed, Karlie thought of the recent developments. Three things. When she'd told her friend Maureen about the old man who had contacted her about the night her father had died, she'd been sceptical because he was in a care home, suffered from schizophrenia and had seen faces in the curtains. Two, her cousin Beth had sent through a box of old papers belonging to her father, mainly a jumble of old letters but there were some pho-tographs. It was good to have them, she had so little belonging to her parents. Three, she had emailed one of the Kill Kestrels. He'd been two years above her in school and now he was famous. Things were about to happen; she could feel it.

'Can you feel that, bitch?' asked Reid. 'You enjoying it?' He tugged the collar and she knelt. She checked that she was face on to the camera. Felt herself being rocked back and forward. Heard the old desk creak. She wanted out of this shit hole and fast. Rumour had it that regulators wanted porn made in the UK to exclude spanking and strangulation. She saw Reid reach for the whip, adjusted her position, closed her eyes and moaned and writhed on the mattress. The collar around her neck dug into her skin, she felt it chaff. Thought of the article about the earnings of the top porn stars in the US. Anything between $50,000 and $95,000 a year. Plus, public appearances. She was certain that the lifestyle would suit her. She knew that she was going places, had always known it. Even at school she'd created drama when she'd accused the bitches in her year of bullying. She'd taken it as far as she'd wanted, then dumped it. They'd been her first audience though. Now she wanted something bigger, she wanted LA, the big house, the pool. She whiled away the time deciding on the décor of the house and choosing the colour of the tiles in the swimming pool.

When it was done, she made her way back to the container, pulled a packet of facial wipes from her handbag and began sponging herself down. Saw Ashton in the doorway watching. She took off the collar, rubbed her neck. 'Bloody hell, that was rough. I need a shower.'

'You complaining again?'

'Just saying we need to get some kind of a shower rigged up in here or even a basin. It's manky not being

21

able to have a rinse.' She binned the used wipes and pulled on her jeans and T-shirt.

'We make it big time in the States and you can get what you want.'

'We?'

'If you make it, I'd manage you. End of story.'

'What will happen with Lisa and Ewan?'

'They'd stay here. No point in upsetting their routine. You'd be making enough for both of us.'

She grabbed her bag, made for her car. 'You're all heart.'

Outside, she waved to Pierce as she drove off. Switched on the radio, heard Pharrell Williams' 'Happy' being played. She waited until she had driven past the stinking chicken shed before she wound down the windows.

A car was parked in the lay-by. As she passed, it inched its way out on to the road. There was no need to rush, the driver took it easy, kept two cars between them. He knew that Karlie was a cautious driver. Used her seat belt every time. Clunk click, every trip. Stay safe, Karlie. But all the care and caution she'd used to keep herself alive would be in vain. He'd been pleased when she'd called him last night after she'd left the care home and now he was looking forward to their meeting later that evening. Clunk click, every trip, Karlie. Stay safe. For now.

/

Chapter Two

The Manager

Take your pick, he thought, from a billboard of sordid delights. Sex with an underage prostitute (Skye), two accidental overdoses when he'd been discovered shaking uncontrollably (Skye), when an argument had got out of hand, a glass had been smashed into a face, resulting in a photographer being given a substantial bribe not to press charges (Josh). He could go on, the list was, if not endless, then definitely lengthy. The Kill Kestrels manager Dougie Scott sat in the lounge nursing a double vodka and tried not to think too hard about the length of the list. He wore his usual uniform – a loud Hawaiian shirt which strained around his bulk, grey chinos and a pork pie hat. In winter he added a grey cashmere overcoat. He was fifty-five and had managed bands, with varying degrees of success, all his life. His previous two – the Stations of the Cross and the Grimsdales – had done reasonably well for a while, but the Kill Kestrels were by far the most financially successful and he was not about to let them fuck it up. Like every good manager, he made sure his band turned up and got the job done. Of course, there had been times when he'd had to manage the extent of their partying, but he'd been in the business long enough to know which substances fuelled creativity and which killed it. For his part, he let the Kill Kestrels indulge themselves, but Dougie made sure that they followed the three Ps, that they knew performing, promotion and producing new songs were their priorities.

The Braque Hotel had been chosen because of its solid history of accommodating the excessive lifestyle of rock bands. Dougie knew from previous experience that the staff were loyal and had been employed partly for their skill of steadfastly ignoring indiscretions. Over the years, the antics of the Kill Kestrels had never even been remarked upon by the staff, or, worse, leaked to the press. There were no shots of Skye returning to his room, stumbling and disorientated, his eyes glazed. Or of the girls being discreetly ushered in and out of the side entrance. No shots to incriminate Josh, Joe or Lexi in any way. The hotel staff understood that the band was a product and that sometimes that product had to let off steam.

Dougie glanced at his watch; the guys were supposed to have checked in with him fifteen minutes ago. He gulped the remainder of his drink and started for the lift, let his finger rest on the up button. A few seconds later, the doors opened and the four of them piled out. 'My boys—' Dougie grinned '—I knew you wouldn't let me down. Fresh as a daisy,' he lied, 'a credit to bands everywhere.' He followed them back into the lounge, scrutinised them as they grabbed menus and clustered around a table, noted Skye's bloodshot eyes, his grey pallor. At five foot eleven, twenty-eight-year-old Skye

24

Cooper was the tallest of the group and also the lead singer. His dirty blond hair framed his face, his jeans were ripped, his shirt was clean, but wrinkled. His already dark eyes had kohl smudged around them, giving him the look of a fallen angel. Tattoo ink snaked across most of his body, curling around skulls, daggers and a complicated series of hieroglyphs which only Skye knew the meaning of but had once hinted that they were records of sexual encounters. Skye wanted to be a Rock God. Dougie knew that their fan base was growing fast and, if they stayed on course, he'd get his wish. His female fans wanted to be with him and his male fans wanted to be him, and over the years Skye had worked hard to perfect the persona of the sensitive artist. The outsider always had a cachet. Dougie knew it and more importantly Skye worked it. But the real money came from the royalties; whoever wrote the songs got the cash and that honour was shared fifty–fifty between Skye and Josh. But there was a darkness to Skye that troubled Dougie. It was as if he'd had an emotional bypass. Skye had no empathy when anything went wrong for the rest of the band, it was all about him, his ego sat at the centre of the band and was the most likely to explode.

To Skye's left was Josh Alden. He was thirty, slim and wore expensive jeans and a box-fresh T-shirt. His head was shaved and heavily tattooed and he had piercings through his nose and eyebrow. His ears had been gauged, held open by silver rims from which hung silver skulls. Josh had grown up in a home and later on the street and knew how to handle himself. An early bit of trouble with violence but all that was behind him now. He was the bass player and also the most methodical of the group.

He turned up on time to every rehearsal and sound check and did the job like clockwork. Just like his playing, the deep throbbing bass, always on the beat, hooking in with the drums. That was the point, Dougie thought, there was something routine about Josh's approach to being in the band, he showed very little real passion for the process of making music. Dougie worried that the band was only a means to an end for Josh; he just wished he knew what that end was.

Next up was Joe Edgewood. Five four and a confirmed introvert, he was twenty-five and played guitar and keyboard. He kept his hair short and neat and wore cotton shirts, in a variety of quiet tartan and plaid. Joe had his future planned, he was going to relocate to the US, to Athens, Georgia to be precise, the place he most associated with the group who had first inspired him. Joe had looked at California, with its beaches, the glamour of LA, but he had always returned to Athens. And this wasn't fantasy – as the son of an accountant, Joe had already costed it and reckoned that it was very doable given what the band was earning. He wanted an expensive house, he had ambition.

Next in line was Lexi. Small, dark haired and energetic. At twenty-two, Lexi MacGowan was the baby of the group. On stage, he crackled with nervous energy, his hands flying as he drummed, in a world of his own. Off stage, he wasn't that interested in the groupie scene and only occasionally got plastered. He craved the company of other musicians, he'd go see new bands, or hang out in recording studios with friends. Lexi only wanted to play music. It was his obsession, he practised way more than the others, but his was the least requested photograph by

26

the fans and he got a lot less attention from the media too, but that was the way Lexi wanted it and Dougie knew that was the way he intended to keep it.

Dougie joined them at the table. 'Remember, guys, we have our photo shoot tomorrow with the two lucky winners and you all need to be there. It's over in the West End.'

'Remind me what this is again?' said Lexi. 'Dougie, tell me this isn't the VIP package shit you were trying to sell us?'

'No, it's not. I heard you loud and clear on that front.'

'Only, if it is some back-door way of going about it, I'm not showing up,' said Lexi.

'I told you, the *Glasgow Chronicle* ran a competition, first prize being a chance to meet you four and two tickets to the gig on Saturday.'

'And?' Lexi studied the menu.

'And some wee lassie called Ellie something, from Dennistoun, won the tickets and her and her pal are coming along to a photo shoot at the Golden Unicorn Hotel. Christ, but you're suspicious, Lexi.'

'I just don't want our fans to be ripped off, I hate all that corporate bullshit. You know that, Dougie.'

'Which is why we don't do it,' said Dougie. 'You need to trust me.'

Josh waded in to the argument. 'Fuck's sake, Dougie's not bullshitting you. I remember seeing it in the paper he brought to rehearsals. I had a quick read through it at the break, it was a free competition, nothing dodgy about it. Straight up, send in your name and address and someone would be picked at random from the pile.'

'Fine then,' said Lexi.

27

'So you need to be there' said Dougie. 'The prize was for the winners to meet all of the band, not just the ones who can be arsed turning up.'

'I just didn't want it to be the VIP charge-a-fortune-to-meet the Kill Kestrels package,' said Lexi. 'Way too lacking in integrity.'

'I think you already mentioned all of that in our discussion last time,' said Dougie.

'Which hotel is it again?' asked Skye.

'The hospitality room at the Golden Unicorn. I've invited a few of the press boys for publicity. And Paulo Di Stefano's dropping by to take a few snaps, he'll be shooting the cover for the next album.'

But Lexi still wasn't happy. 'Can't we just meet our fans, you know, person to person? Keep it real.'

Keep it fucking real? Dougie could have slapped him. 'It will be real and the girls will love it. Plus, they'll get their picture in the paper. You don't want to deny them the opportunity, do you?'

'They'll have mobile phones; they could take their own pictures.' Lexi sounded peeved. 'The meet-up doesn't have to be part of the press circus.'

'It's not a circus,' muttered Joe. 'Fuck's sake, Lexi. This is our job. It's what pays the bills. It's what'll eventually buy me my place in Athens. You need to grow the fuck up.'

'And maybe you try to keep it real, Joe. Our fans aren't there to be ripped off.'

'It was a free fucking competition!' said Joe.

'OK. I was just nervous about the VIP stuff.'

'How is a VIP package to meet us even a fucking rip-off?' said Joe. 'The fans want access to us and we can supply it. It's the usual business model, supply and demand, and right now we're in demand. I don't know how you cannot see that. You are so full of bullshit. Do you know what I think? I think this is inverse snobbery. You don't like the fact that some fans can pay for the VIP package and would be absolutely fucking delighted to pay for it, when others can't. You're actually a snob, aren't you? You despise our fans who have a bit of money and you delude yourself that somehow this isn't a business, that it's some kind of superior art form and—'

'So for you it's just a financial transaction?' asked Lexi.

'That's more realistic than your shit.'

'I don't fucking think so.'

'Guys!' Dougie clapped his hands loudly. 'Enough! We discussed it and ultimately decided that the VIP package wasn't a goer. I'm disappointed as anyone, but let's just move on.'

But they wouldn't, and Dougie observed the band returning to type by sniping at each other; they were four young men, who resorted to teenage behaviour when under stress.

'Lexi, you're negatively affecting my earnings.' Joe then turned on Josh. 'And it's OK for you and Skye, you two are quids in because you get the royalties. I don't.'

Skye waded in. 'And that's not by some kind of fucking fluke, Joe, it's because we write the songs. If you want more of the cut, then maybe you should try writing something? Oh, wait! That's right, I remember now, you did try to write some and what was it that happened? They were shit, absolute, fucking bollocks.'

Joe stood. Skye mirrored him.

Christ, thought Dougie, talk about handbags at dawn. 'Guys, calm it down. Come on, keep it civilised, we're all in this together. Eat. Get some food inside you and you'll feel better.' But he spoke to Joe's back.

'I'll order room service, Dougie. I'm not sitting here with this prick.'

Dougie watched Joe leave, reminded himself to breathe, just breathe. He knew to let it go, sometimes they each needed to go to their respective spaces and come back later in a calmer mood. He'd had enough experience of bands to know that a difficult or adversarial relationship could actually work in the overall dynamic and feed the creativity. It was a critical balance, though, allowing just enough bitterness and rivalry to give the band energy but not to let it spill over and split them up. Dougie needed to keep them going, they were his pension. And by God, he thought, I'm earning it.

'Right.' He addressed the remaining three as if the argument hadn't happened. 'You lot have a hearty meal and get yourself set up. I'll join you for another drink.'

The young waitress, who'd tried to enter the room in the midst of the argument, then retreated, came back. She smiled nervously. 'Are you guys ready to order?'

'Just a double vodka for me,' said Dougie.

'Make that two,' said Josh.

'Three,' muttered Lexi.

Skye held up four fingers.

'Four doubles it is then. And food?'

There were no takers.

Dougie saw a man in the doorway. He was five-five, skinny, shaved head. Hands balled into fists, looked like he was spoiling for a fight, but it was his eyes Dougie noticed most – they were dark pinpricks of violence. Dougie scrambled to his feet, knocked over a chair.

'You've taken a wrong turning, mate. This is a private party.'

The man ignored him.

Dougie raised his voice, 'Listen pal, I said—'

'It's cool, Dougie, he's my guest,' said Josh. 'Hi, Cutter. Good to see you. Cheers for coming over.'

'Not a problem, Josh.' The man stabbed a finger at Dougie. 'Who's this prick?'

'No worries, he's good. He's our manager.' Josh smiled. 'Dougie meet Cutter Wysor.'

The manager and guest glared at each other.

The waitress returned with the drinks, Josh grabbed his. 'What are you having, Cutter?'

'Absinthe.'

'Oh for fuck's sake,' muttered Dougie.

Josh ordered for his guest. 'Welcome to the party.'

Dougie watched Josh lead the guy to another table, saw the waitress bring a glass of the green liquid, wondered just who the hell Cutter Wysor was and what shit Josh was getting mixed up with.

Chapter Three

The Gang

Owen

He had fucked up. He was a loser. A fucking tosser. Everything that he already knew. Everything that had already been said about him was true.

Owen McCrudden crawled into the back of his white van. He'd roughly bandaged his hand with an old rag and washed the painkillers down with a beer. But it wasn't the pain in his hand that scared him, it was the fear of what Mason Stitt would do. Owen needed Mason and was terrified that he was going to expel him from the gang. That must not happen, couldn't be allowed to happen. The gang were family. They were all he had. Mason was all he had, they were like brothers but Mason had said it was all his fault, that he'd fucked up and now Davie and that wee shit Chris were dead. Fuck. Fuck. Fuck.

Owen refused to let the images of the gang fight into his mind. Instead he let himself drift.

He'd been five when his dad had left and his mum had told him, 'The minute you're sixteen you're on your own.

Till then you're good for nothing except child benefit.'
He'd lived in a crumbling caravan in her shitty back
garden. No electricity meant no heating or hot water. The
place was almost unbearable. In winter, when he'd stolen
enough money, he'd gone to the local swimming pool for
a hot shower. Everyone in his class had laughed at him.
Arseholes. Then finally he'd moved out. Slept rough for a
couple of years. Got a key worker who'd found him a flat
and a job. At eighteen he was doing OK. When he could
afford to feed the meter, he had hot water and heating.
He could wash properly. But people still took a detour
around him. It was if the stench of his filthy childhood
clung to him. He'd tried to be friendly but the response
was always the same: 'Fuck off, perv.' 'Who are you
smiling at, cunt face?' He'd lost the job, then the flat, then
eventually had landed a job cleaning. Night work.
Solitary. No need for other people. He'd been paid cash in
hand and bought the van. He lived under the radar. He
cleaned a couple of factories and eventually got to sweep
out the Cockroach, back when big Ronnie ran it like it was
his home from home. That's when he'd first come across
Mason and it had felt good to be near his strength. There
was something about Mason's confidence. He was sure of
himself and Owen had badly wanted to be on his radar.
Beside him, Owen had felt himself expand, had boasted
about having a pal. A first. Then he'd been allowed to join
the gang. Finally, he had become a person with some
respect, instead of the weirdo fuckwit who lived like a
tramp. But now what was going to happen?

Owen lifted the cracked mirror, combed back his greasy,
sandy-coloured hair. He had the pale blue eyes of a husky
and his stained T-shirt had a rip on the left shoulder

exposing a large expanse of anaemic skin. He lay down on the filthy mattress and stared at the card. Mrs Hinds had given it to him when he was seven. She had given every child in her class a card on their birthday. It was the only birthday card he'd ever had. Not that he'd ever had a party either. But he had asked once. His stepfather had slapped him so hard he'd lost the hearing in his right ear for a week. He hadn't asked again. On the card, three fairground horses were alone in a dark forest. The only light came from the fairy lights of the carousel. A white horse in the foreground, three golden stars on its rump, a pink saddle. A large horse in the background, striding out, a blue saddle on its back, a series of small circles on its rump. And a tiny horse to the side, its short legs trying to keep up. A family.

He looked at the horses and went into the familiar darkness, strained to hear the music in the forest but it was silent as a grave. He watched the horse with the three stars prance. Its legs were high. It was so proud and certain and sure of itself. He bet it had never fucked up.

As he stared, the lights above the horses seemed to flicker and fade, the forest grew darker and more oppressive. He willed the lights to get brighter. To blot out the darkness. The fear. The unknown future. It had always been unknown, his life. Membership of the gang had been his only real certainty. Owen felt the painkillers and beer hit his stomach, the acid reflux kick in. He yanked open the door and vomited an arc of sour liquid onto the sweet-smelling grass.

Chapter Four

The Performer

'Smells like sweeties.'

In her tenement flat in Tollcross Road, Holly Lithgow poured the sticky liquid into a plastic bottle. Her sister Nikki watched her. 'What's in it, Holly?'

'It's a mixture of saltwater, honey and a wee secret ingredient. Once I rub this on my hands and a bit of chalk, my grip will be fantastic.'

'I'm not happy about this new job of yours. Angie says—'

'Angie who?'

'Angie Burns, she works at the café on London Road.'

'That skinny wee lassie? She looks like she needs a bag of chips inside her. Way too thin. I hope you didn't tell her anything?'

'No. Just that you got a new job and I was concerned about the hours. I lied about that bit. Besides, what would I tell her? Anyway, I don't think she was paying attention, she's started seeing some guy name of George Bellerose, he's a life coach but I think he's messing with her head. I'm worried about her.'

'You're worried about everyone and everything, Nikki. You need to cut it out and think of yourself. You're going off to Blackpool for a break. Relax and enjoy yourself.'

'I mean, Angie denies it and everything but I think he's got her on some kind of starvation diet.'

'Then she's off her head listening to him.'

'I think you're making a mistake.'

Holly saw the furrowed brow of her younger sister, knew that she was genuinely concerned. 'Stop worrying, I know what I'm doing.'

'You were doing OK at your last job.'

'I was on the minimum wage, had a pervert for a manager who hit on me constantly, and when I knocked him back, he put me on permanent shelf-stacking. Then I was threatened with redundancy, remember? For the second time in my short working life. Anyway, this pays far better.'

'So, why can't you tell me about it or let me come and see you perform?'

'I told you it's a private club.' Holly combed out her long blonde hair, sprayed a halo of hairspray around it, let it settle.

'But you're not allowed to tell me where?'

'No, but I already told you, it's all very legit. These are very fucking professional people. I mean really posh shit; you should hear their accents. They don't talk like you and me or normal folk, they talk like they're in the government or royalty.'

'Is it all guys at this place?'

'Stop asking questions, Nikki. I told you, it's confidential. I've signed a contract. I'm a performer, that's it. End of.' She packed the chalk into her bag and made sure the lid on the honey water was screwed tight shut; she didn't want it dripping over her bag. It wouldn't be professional rolling up at the McIver Club covered in slime. She glanced at her sister, saw her struggling not to say whatever was on her mind. Knew it would out, Nikki never could keep her mouth shut. Holly checked her bag: towels, chalk, ointment, painkillers, purse, phone, car keys. She grabbed her make-up and began applying it.

'Do you strip for these guys?'

Holly ignored the question, expertly applied a thick layer of foundation, then heavy liner around her green eyes. Two coats of mascara. She stood back, surveyed herself in the mirror. She looked the part.

Nikki's voice was quiet, her tone sour. 'Mum would turn in her grave.'

'Stop it, Nikki. I'm an erotic dancer. I perform for money; just like they do in clubs all over the world. Including Vegas. Christ, there's no shame in it, so don't even start to go there. It pays the rent on this flat and the food you pack away when you visit. And, as for Mum, she's not here to see me, is she? She's not here to judge. Besides, you're an adult now and you need to be thinking about what you're going to do with your life.' Holly heard the whine in her voice, knew that it sounded like she was nagging, but Nikki needed pushing away from her childish ideals and towards something more realistic. She watched her sister pick at a rag-nail on her thumb and worry at it until she pulled a thin strip of skin from her finger. A tiny pool of blood formed in its place. Holly watched her stick the finger in her mouth and suck the blood away. Nikki had been doing it since she was a kid; it was a sure sign of stress.

37

Finally, Nikki spoke. 'I'm never going to do anything like that. When I leave college, I'm going to get an apprenticeship at the salon.'

'Good for you, you'll make a great hairdresser.' Holly tried for enthusiasm but her tone fell short. Anton Cousins salon – Anton's Style & Smile – was a tiny, local hairdresser in the housing scheme. Anton was going nowhere but he had a thing for Nikki, despite being twenty years her senior. It was a dead-end place but he had told her she could start there and build up her client base. For what? thought Holly. For a lifetime of perming old dears' hair and listening to them complain about their corns and how the operation to have their hip replaced had been delayed and wasn't the NHS in a shocking bad way? It wasn't a life Holly could contemplate, she just couldn't bear the thought of it. She turned to face her sister. 'It's not like in the films, you know. Prince Charming isn't going to come along and rescue you. You have to make your own luck in this world, you have to look out for yourself.'

'I know.'

'This way, I'm in control of my finances. Give it a couple of years and I'll have enough saved to get a mortgage. I want the security of having my own place. Is that too much to ask?'

'You're on the game, Holly, aren't you?'

That was it. 'I'm not on the fucking game. I'm a performer. Remember I did that circus skills course? Remember how good I was at gymnastics at school? I use these skills every fucking time I perform. And don't you forget it.' Holly heard herself rant, knew that she was revealing herself, knew that her sister knew. Still she denied it.

'When we were growing up, you told me you were going to perform in some big, international circus. You said you'd be in the Cirque du Soleil.'

'I still might, someday.' Holly calmed herself, took the sting and hurt out of her tone. 'But, in the meantime this pays very well. Can't you be a little bit pleased for me?'

'I think it's dangerous.'

'It's not dangerous, it's complex. You have to move and pretend like you're in pain but the mechanism's rigged so you don't strain yourself. It's a bit like trapeze only not so straightforward. It's more like I'm being a stunt woman. Remember all those video games? The Lara Croft stuff? Well, what I do is a bit like that.'

'Then it is dangerous.'

'It's rigged. I told you, I just need to fake the pain. OK? Happy now?'

'And afterwards?' Nikki persisted. 'Do you sleep with them?'

'You don't get it, do you? It's confidential.'

'I'm scared, Holly.'

'Of what?'

'I think when you signed that contract, you signed away your life.'

'We're done here.' Holly picked up her lipstick, drew a slash of red over her lips. Frowned at the tiny scar above her lip, dabbed on more concealer. Once she was satisfied, she sprayed herself liberally with perfume, checked her reflection in the mirror and turned to her sister. 'I'll drop you back before I head off to work. And no more talking about me to that skinny wee freak Angie Burns.'

Chapter Five

The Waitress

Angie Burns stretched to her full height of four foot eleven. She was so small and slight that she bought her clothes and shoes from the children's section of her local supermarket. Her short red hair was sparse and stuck up in spikes around her head. She stood at the window of her flat and gazed out. She was thinking of him again.

She'd been thirty-four when she'd met George Bellerose in an online chat room. Dating was to have been a fresh start for her. She'd split up with her last boyfriend three years previously and hadn't met anyone since. Then she'd met George and she'd felt like he was her reward for being patient. Angie knew that she'd been flattered by his attention but George was definitely keen. Soon after they'd chatted, he suggested that they begin seeing each other. Things had moved very quickly, and when he'd told her that he loved her, she'd been delighted. He was a good man who, as a life coach, spent his time helping others to achieve their potential. In the first few weeks of their relationship, George had even made references to an engagement ring and venues and suggested countries where they might honeymoon. His job took him away on business a lot, but each time they reunited it had been special, although he'd never taken her out or invited her to his house, preferring instead to come to hers. 'Cosying up together' was how he'd described it.

After a few weeks she'd felt that they'd told each other just about everything. Then one night he said he had a secret he had been wanting to talk about. That's how it had started, innocently talking about their needs and desires.

George had been his usual gentle, loving self as he'd explained that he'd tried to keep the secret from her, but it was putting a distance between them, and if she *really* wanted them to continue, he needed to tell her. Later, he would claim that she forced it out of him, but she hadn't, she knew she hadn't.

He'd told her that, before they'd met, he had been active in the BDSM scene in the city. 'My job is so full on. Look, I help people all day, every day. I'm a very caring type of a guy, but sometimes I need downtime, a fun way of unwinding. You understand?'

She'd nodded.

'It was a great scene and I loved that kind of role play. It was fun and I got an incredible rush from it.'

She'd listened while he'd told her about all the excitement and thrills he'd had with other women.

'Well, it was before we met, so you can't really complain, can you?'

She'd supposed not.

'I mean, what we have is fine, but the other stuff? It's like a drug. And it's a drug that's pulling me back. A few times, I had the master/servant relationship going and it was a complete mental trip. I mean I'm getting hard just thinking about it.'

She'd seen that for herself.

Eventually, he'd blurted it out. 'Would you be interested in going along with me to one of the clubs?'

She had felt a pain in her chest, as if the air had been kicked out of her lungs. She'd struggled to formulate an answer. Finally, she'd told him the plain truth. 'No, George, it's not my kind of thing. I'm really sorry.'

But he hadn't given up. 'Just try it? For me?' Until finally, his tone hardened. 'You wouldn't do it for me? To save us?'

'I'm so sorry.' It had been more of a whisper and she'd watched his expression move from excitement to anger. She had tried to explain. 'You know I'm so introverted and I'm on my feet all day in the café. I'm exhausted in the evenings. And the thought of going out to party, in that kind of a way, with complete strangers, just doesn't do it for me.' She'd reached for his hand, held it tightly. 'Besides, if we love each other then surely that's enough?' She had waited for the response she craved, but George had said nothing. He had merely disentangled his hand from hers and walked into her bedroom and begun to pack. His trip to London had meant that they would be apart for a week. He'd ignored her attempts to continue the conversation. By the time he was ready to leave, she'd relented.

He'd been delighted, 'That's great, Angie, just give it a try. Entry level, master and servant. Just you and me, I promise. No club. I am willing to give up the club for you, if you want me to? I'll do it because I love you. It'll only be psychological, nothing physical at first. We can do it by Skype. It'll be fun.'

That had been the beginning of their new 'special rela-tionship', as George began to refer to it. Today was her birthday and he'd told her that he had a present for her. Angie crossed from the window, switched on her com-puter and waited for the familiar Skype icon to appear. George was leaving for London again the following day, for another conference, this time something about Carl Jung's archetypes. She trembled with anxiety. Lately, he'd been getting angry with her and had accused her of not being committed to the relationship. She wondered if it was the stress of his job.

Suddenly, he was online. 'Master.'

'Have you eaten yet?'

'No, nothing at all. Just as you ordered.'

'Good.'

Angie relaxed.

'Since it's your birthday, I want you to do something special for me.'

'Yes?'

'I want you to wear your nipple clamps. All night.'

'I can't tonight, Master.' She swallowed.

'It's an order.'

'I—'

'No refusal.'

'I need to be at work tomorrow.'

'Not my problem.'

'I can't do it.'

'Silence. Now, I want to see them on you. Do as you're told.'

She waited.

'Move.'

Angie crossed the room. She took off her T-shirt and

bra, opened the drawer. She reached for the clamps and took a deep breath before she put them in place. She felt the familiar, dull pain as she made her way back to the monitor.

'Good. Wait there.'

She heard him leave the room, the door close behind him, the lock fall into place. Knew she was required to wait until he returned. Fifteen minutes later, she heard the door slam behind him, saw his face come into view on the screen, watched him position himself in front of the monitor, making sure that the takeaway was visible.

'Tonight, it's beef and pork meatballs with tomato sauce and spaghetti.'

Angie felt saliva gather in her mouth.

'Are you hungry?'

'Yes.'

'Yes, what?'

'Yes, Master.'

'Excellent.'

She watched while he slowly and methodically worked his way through the meal, stopping now and again to wash the food down with a glass of red wine. When he'd finished, he peered into the monitor. 'The clamps stay on all night.'

'I can't, George—'

'Master,' he corrected her.

'I can't, Master. I have to be at work in the morning.'

She watched his face contort, his anger obvious. She shivered. She wanted more than anything for them to go back to the way they had been at first. When he had told her that he loved her.

'Do you want this relationship to work?'

'Yes, Master.'

'Then do as you're told. I'll leave the connection on, so that I can watch you during the night.'

She knew then that she couldn't go to work. She thought fleetingly of removing the clamps, but George had explained that the rules had to be obeyed. She knew in her heart that he loved her, otherwise why tell her? She crossed to the unit and picked up her mobile and punched in the numbers. Texted her friend at the café, Jenny McLoughlin.

> Jenny, I am so sorry but I won't be coming in tomorrow morning. I just don't feel well.

She pressed 'Send'.

A minute later she heard a reply come through.

> What's wrong, Angie?

> Stomach upset.

> Maria's going to be pissed with you. You've been skiving off a lot recently. You sure you can't drag yourself in?

> Positive.

> Shit.

> Sorry. Can you do my shift for me?

> It's not what I had planned, OK. But you owe me :)

> I know I do. Sorry :(

Angie put her phone on the table. She knew that she was in danger of losing her job at the café, but she was

45

more worried about losing George. But she had obeyed him, that was what was important. He'd see that and go back to his old ways and they would be fine. Every relationship had its ups and downs, she chided herself. They'd get through it. She thought of her parents and their marriage. Shuddered. Remembered her dad's cruel and casual violence towards her mum. They hadn't set a great example.

Chapter Six

The McIver Club

The clubhouse, a very fine example of Scottish baronial architecture, was set in fifty acres of park land and woodland. There was also a walled garden, manicured lawns, peacocks and a lily pond. The windows of the grand old building glowed.

Inside, they were seated at a table in the bar. Paul Furlan, head of security, was on one side, Skye Cooper faced him on the other. Furlan was six foot three, 230 pounds of muscle and had a boxer's nose. His face was tanned and relaxed but his jade green eyes were shrewd. Skye thought that Furlan had a restless energy and his bulk made him even more expansive. Even the way he walked was authoritarian, he led with his shoulders. Beside him, Skye felt like a boy. A boy who had just signed a contract agreeing to the terms and conditions of the McIver Club. He pushed the contract across to Furlan. 'Why are you doing the admin? I thought you were security?'

'Jeffrey's on holiday. Besides, we like to keep things within the family, it keeps it nice and confidential.'

'Streamlined,' said Skye.

'Yeah, that too,' said Furlan. 'Now you can celebrate your membership.'

'My platinum membership,' Skye reminded him. 'It cost enough.'

'It's well worth it, I can assure you. Everything, and I mean everything, can be supplied here at the McIver. In the meantime, another drink?'

'Same again.'

Furlan called a waiter. 'Two vodka Martinis.' He stood. 'You relax while I go file this.'

Skye looked around the bar area, recognised Thom McClure, the Premier League footballer; Gil Varela, a prominent journalist. At a table at the back, Ronald McMasters. McMasters had recently won a ten-million-pound court case and was famously quoted as declaring that he 'had such extensive experience of law, that it was pointless calling for anyone else'. Skye watched McMasters debate with other club members. Saw him flick back his shoulder-length hair, gesture wildly to make a point with elegant hands.

Skye thought of the last club he'd frequented. It had been in Amsterdam, before the band had made it big. It hadn't been in the same league or nearly as upmarket as the McIver. In fact, it had been a shitty dive of a place. The services and prices had been chalked up on a board above the bar. Breast bondage. Nipple clamps. Clamps with weights. Ball gags. Strappado. There had been nothing classy about it. Purely a financial transaction. Partying in such a downmarket club with ugly, scarred women had only reinforced his feeling of desperation.

Furlan returned.

'How many women do you have?' asked Skye.

'Over twenty on call-out.'

'All here at the club?'

'Not on site but they can be here in half an hour or so. We tend to rotate them; it keeps them fresh.'

'You have photographs? Only I know what I like.'

'We all do. Sexual attraction is in the first instance visual.' Furlan slid a thick leather folder across the table. 'It's like choosing a cocktail, it depends on the night and how you're feeling. What we need can change daily depending on our mood. The McIver can accommodate all of these needs.'

The waiter brought their drinks, as Skye flipped through the photographs. Each woman had been photographed naked, then in various outfits and finally in full bondage. Their age, height, weight and nationality were listed underneath their pictures.

'No names?'

'Not used by either party. That's not what we do here. It's a clean deal. Names are too personal, they blur the boundaries and where does it lead? Do you start talking to each other, trading life stories? All that shit? What's the point? You're a member of the club. The women are here to work.'

'She'll need to be blindfolded,' said Skye. 'The band, you know – I can't have her recognising me and talking to the press. My manager would kill me.'

'If you insist, but there's no need. They've all signed in-depth confidentiality contracts, and I mean in-depth. Our lawyer has them just about sign away their lives. Nothing leaves here, no information, no names. And that includes you, Skye. Whoever you recognise here at the club, however connected or famous they are, it stays right here. That's why we have such an exclusive clientele; they know that whatever happens at the McIver is completely confidential, they know they're safe.'

'Yeah, I just saw Ronald McMasters. Very high-flying guy.'

'No one is ever publicly recognised. Our members come here, without judgement, without titles and, more importantly, without restraint. Just like yourself. Here at the McIver you are a club member first and Skye Cooper second.'

Skye finished his drink.

'Another?'

'Why not? I'm starting to relax.'

Furlan ordered two more drinks and then stood. 'Let me attend to another guest for a sec and then we can get you organised.'

While he was gone, Skye watched a man leave the bar. He was laughing with a companion. Skye recognised the white hair and moustache, the pronounced limp. Mark Ponsensby-Edward, QC, had been the defence in the Amy Dawson/Marcus Newton case a decade earlier, the trial which had kick-started Skye's carnal journey. Ponsensby-Edward looked even more gaunt than he had at the trial, but his hands were still claw-like and, when he smiled, the incisors were still as sharp, still as pointed. Skye remembered that at the trial he'd thought of the QC as a modern-day Dracula. If anything, he looked more the part now. 'Vampiric' was the word that came to mind.

Skye smiled. He was among friends here at the McIver. He scanned the bar, noted another two Premier League football players. He relaxed. Thanks to Paul Furlan, this place was watertight. Skye knew that he badly needed release from the tensions of his life and that whatever he needed to do, he could do it at the McIver, secure in the knowledge that it wouldn't get out. He trusted Paul Furlan. Everything about the man suggested business. Skye took in the polished oak of the bar, the huge mirror behind it. He glanced at the food menu, saw that it included beef heart stuffed with mushroom and spinach, ox heart with buttered potatoes. Steak tartare. Skye tossed the menu aside; raw meat wasn't what he was looking for. Well, at least not of the animal variety.

He took a long drink; he was where he wanted to be in his life. The Kill Kestrels were going well, their fans loved them. The group was on an upward trajectory. It was just the sex. After jury duty a decade ago, he'd started on a journey and over the months that followed the trial he'd got high almost every time, but over the years, the highs had dissipated. He craved the hit he'd had the first time he'd seen the photographs, but that experience had become more and more elusive. Skye looked around the room, thought about the options at the club, 'without restraint' Furlan had told him. Well, perhaps the McIver would be his salvation after all.

Chapter Seven

The McIver, Moroccan Room

The large, windowless room was in the basement. The only light came from seven lamps with glowing brass bases and intricately carved leather shades. They cast a gentle, warm light around the room. The walls had been painted in dark blue hues and the floor was tiled with brightly coloured mosaics. On one side of the room there were low, leather sofas, plump cushions and side tables. When she'd first started at the club, Holly had reached for the bowls containing the macadamia nuts, but her hand had been quickly slapped away. 'The food is for the guests, Holly, not for the likes of you. Besides, you don't want a bloated stomach. Not a good look. Get into position.'

Now she knew better. She stood naked and waited while she was tethered and her wrists secured to the hoist. The spreader bar was affixed to her ankles, preventing her from either closing her legs or balancing properly. Strappado. Holly knew that if the client demanded it, she would be blindfolded. Despite knowing that they'd all signed confidentiality contracts, she'd been told that some of the clients were paranoid about being recognised.

She'd heard that a few of them were high-up lawyers. A rumour was that one of them was a judge, who liked having someone sit on his face. To her they were all just punters, she'd no desire to recognise them for who they were outside the club. Besides, what would she do with the information? Then there was the staff member who'd washed her mouth out with soap while calling her Jean. At the thought of him, Holly shivered.

'You cold?' Jimmy Weightman, one of the doormen, sounded solicitous.

'No, I'm fine, Jimmy, thanks. Just raring to get started.'

'He'll be here in a sec.'

A few minutes later, he limped into the room. She saw that he was tall and slim and both his hair and his moustache were white. She watched while he sipped from a champagne glass, the opened bottle placed on the low table beside him. His too long nails tapered from bony hands. The man ignored her until he had made himself comfortable on one of the leather sofas, then he looked up and clapped his hands together softly. Jimmy started the hoist. The mechanism rolled and the cuffs tightened around her wrists as she was lifted towards the ceiling, until she was suspended high above the floor, splayed like a spatchcock. She would be lowered soon enough.

As the evening continued, a second bottle of champagne was brought to him. Holly waited, tethered, as he drank. The client raised his glass to her. 'Ravishing. You look absolutely ravishing.' She heard a cultured voice, vowels pronounced like he was on the BBC, she'd heard it all her life. How posh folk talk, was how her mother used to describe it. This guy was certainly that. She watched him signal for her to be hoisted and then released. She

53

dropped quickly, felt the mechanism abruptly halt before she hit the ground. Holly writhed and turned, moaned quietly. Made it look painful. At the very least it was bloody hard work.

The man watched for a few seconds before signalling for Jimmy to suspend her again. He crossed the room and peered up between her legs. Holly was glad she'd gone before the performance; this wasn't the time to need a pee. Although she'd heard that some punters wanted that and more. Fuck, but these guys were a bunch of perverts. She swung gently, contented herself by doing the maths in her head. In her previous job, she'd been on £6.50 an hour and had been standing all day in the shop or stacking shelves, when she wasn't dodging the creep of a manager. That meant that, less tax and National Insurance, she'd earned around fifty quid for an eight-hour day. Here, she was paid cash in hand. OK, it meant that she was self-employed and so had no holiday entitlement, or sickness pay. But for an hour's shift, she cleared £150. Three shifts a week and a doubler, and she'd be earning over three grand a month. Add extras, and she was made up. She reflected on what her sister Nikki didn't understand. That it was all about hard cash. Nikki was having sex with her pimply boyfriend Kyle for free. Here Holly was, carving out a career for herself. Her sister might think that she had the moral high ground, but she would be on minimum wage at the hair salon for the rest of her days. And as for that wee freak Angie Burns at the café, she'd be on the same or even less. And besides, before Angie should bother judging her, she should try to remember to feed herself. Shit. Holly felt the tiniest amount of gas escape. Fuck. Fuck. Fuck. She waited. Had he noticed?

Beneath her, he cleared his throat and swayed drunkenly back to his seat.

Holly improvised, she'd been told what his particular interest was. Pain. She began to cry quietly, then to whimper.

'To the exquisite beauty in agony—' he raised his champagne glass again '—to our shared pain.'

Our shared pain? thought Holly. *My pain and your fucking money would be more realistic.* But she said nothing and continued to writhe. Later, when she was on the floor, she cried out in pain and pretended to faint. When she came round a few seconds later, he was standing over her, peering into her face. 'Dirty girls like you love all this, don't you?' Again the accent. She'd heard it called 'received pronunciation'.

'Don't you?' He smiled. A row of small, perfectly straight teeth, except for the pointed incisors.

She nodded.

'I thought so. I've heard many debates and closing arguments over the years suggesting otherwise. But I knew I was right. You're all the same. Filthy little bitches on heat.'

She watched him leave. Saw him turn left, meaning that he would leave by the side entrance, no doubt to be picked up in a chauffeured car.

Once he'd gone, Jimmy grabbed a robe from behind one of the sofas, quickly crossed the room and began to unhook her. 'You did well, Holly. All that crying and moaning. He was loving it.'

She pulled the robe around her. 'Bloody hell, though, that was a tough call. All that fucking peering up at me.'

'It's obviously just one of his things. You know the

score.' Jimmy removed the bar. 'That's what the big bucks are for. What made you think you wouldn't need to work for it? Anyway, you get plenty of free time.'

'I'll need the bloody time off to recover. I felt like my shoulder was going to dislocate.'

'You'll get used to it.'

'Still hurts though.' She rubbed her neck.

'Safety's built into the system. Nothing's going to happen to you. Paul Furlan knows what he's doing when he constructs these things.'

'Looking at the client's response when I was dropped, I thought he wanted me to fall completely.'

'Then that would be snuff.' Jimmy laughed. 'And I don't believe even Paul Furlan would go that far, do you?'

Holly looked at the floor, said nothing.

Chapter Eight

The Cops

He was late. Either that or he wasn't coming. Detective Inspector Kat Wheeler glanced at her mobile. No message. She arrived at the café, took a seat outside in the shade. Two days off stretched ahead of her and she'd woken up with a serious headache, had started the day with a black coffee and two painkillers. She scanned the park for him, nothing. So much for him buying her a celebratory breakfast. You beat them at snooker in front of their pals, Christ, in front of the whole fucking pub, and then they renege on the promise of buying breakfast. Sore bloody loser. She took a scarf from her bag, tied her short blonde hair back with it. Scrolled through the local news. A new exhibition 'GANGS. VIOLENCE. GLASGOW. THE DARK SIDE OF THE CITY' had been given a five-star review. Great, let's celebrate gang culture as art. She'd heard about a gang fight in Queen's Park in the Southside the previous evening. Two dead, others in hospital, fighting for their lives.

She read that a report with the crime stats for 1971 to 2013 had just been published. It suggested that crime in the city had peaked during the early 1990s so people should feel safe. Wheeler scrolled down, read that despite the fall in crime, some institute had ranked Glasgow as the most violent area in the United Kingdom. Fantastic, she thought, on the one hand telling folk that Glasgow's safe, but on the other?

She heard a scream from the park opposite. Glanced across, only a small child playing water pistols with a friend. Their squeals of excitement carried across the park. She watched a crocodile of small children, laughing and chatting, make their way towards the Kelvingrove Art Gallery and Museum. She knew that, later, there would be a queue to enter the cool of the spacious building. Glasgow was teeming with tourists, many clutching cameras, smartphones, iPads. Click. Click. Click. Memories frozen in time. The city sweltered in the sun. A group of teenage boys ambled by, all shirtless. Three teenage girls, wearing Kill Kestrels T-shirts, trailed behind them, their voices loud, animated.

'. . . no but Skye said in an interview that . . . "My Desire for You" is really about . . .'

'I know, but "Death of an Angel" is really about unrequited love and Josh said that . . .'

'No way!' argued the third, almost dancing with excitement. 'Josh said in that interview on YouTube that . . .'

'I so wish I'd won that competition to meet them face to face. Can you imagine it, being in the same room as Skye Cooper? I think I'd die on the spot.'

'I know, what a nightmare not winning it, I was absolutely gutted.'

The girls passed by, squabbling about who knew the most about the Kill Kestrels and the meaning behind the song lyrics and what utter hell it was to have missed out on the chance to meet them – the pain of teenage infatuation. Wheeler at least knew the group were in town. You couldn't miss them, posters everywhere and their songs constantly rotated on the bloody radio. She knew that they were playing the final gig of the tour at the O2 Academy on Saturday. The press had been full of the band all week, moody shots of the four young men peered out of the *Chronicle* on a regular basis.

Wheeler felt a welcome breeze as she watched a group of joggers in Day-Glo outfits snake their way through the park, while cyclists overtook them. Glasgow had changed over the last few years. Maybe it was the effect of the Commonwealth Games but there was a new excited commitment to exercise in the city. She checked the menu; lunch options included quinoa salad with peppers, cranberries and flaked almonds or salmon with broccoli, watercress, pumpkin and pomegranate seeds, all listed with a little smile motif as superfoods. Wheeler remembered growing up in the city, when broccoli and watercress were just plain vegetables. She glanced up, saw DI Steven Ross dart across the road. A few seconds later, he stood in front of her, took off his sunglasses, glanced at the menu. 'Morning, Smiler, what are you having?'

Wheeler grinned. 'Thought you had reneged.'

'Slept in.'

'Egg sandwich and iced coffee.'

'Since we're on holiday, I'll have the large iced coffee, waffles and syrup.'

'The healthy option then?'

'I'll run it off later.'

'Well, you can start by running inside and ordering at the counter.' She ignored the harrumph.

When he returned with the tray of food, she heard the inevitable. Ross complaining.

'The whole city has gone nuts,' he said, starting on his waffles. 'A bit of sunshine and it's like we all have heatstroke.'

'Because?'

'The radio was on inside, there's been two fatal stabbings over in the Southside last night. A couple of guys lost their lives. Rival gangs. Community's gone quiet. No one saw a thing.'

'So I heard.' She started on her sandwich, felt the band around her skull tighten like a tourniquet.

'You OK?' said Ross 'Only you look pale.'

'I'm fine.'

Her mobile rang. She checked the number – Carmyle Police Station. 'Wheeler.'

She listened to the scant detail. A woman's body had been found in the East End.

'Let's go. I'll fill you in on the way.'

'So much for a couple of days' holiday and a bloody leisurely breakfast.'

Wheeler was already ahead of him. 'Runners discovered the body in the undergrowth up by Sandyhills Road.'

Ross drove through the city. When he accelerated to overtake a bus, she saw another poster advertising the exhibition. 'GANGS. VIOLENCE. GLASGOW. THE DARK SIDE OF THE CITY'.

Twenty-five minutes later, they parked up. 'Given it's

such a busy area, maybe we'll get lucky with CCTV,' said Ross. 'What do you reckon are our chances?'

'We might,' said Wheeler. She knew how valuable closed-circuit television could be, both as security and surveillance. A recent case in the Southside had been solved within forty-eight hours when a local shopkeeper had handed over his CCTV. Luckily, he had invested in a top-of-the-range, 360-degree system, but she knew that across the city CCTV quality was variable and there were the inevitable blind spots. She saw the press grouped together, heard a reporter call out, 'Can you tell us if the body found this morning is female?'

'At least confirm if it's a murder?'

Wheeler ignored them. Walked on. She heard the nasal whine of Graham Reaper, chief crime reporter with the *Chronicle,* call after her, 'Can you confirm if the victim was sexually assaulted?'

'Fuck,' muttered Ross, 'we haven't even had a chance to see the body yet.'

She heard the whine close behind her. Reaper had peeled off from the press pack. 'DI Wheeler, can you confirm reports that a woman's body was discovered in the undergrowth earlier this morning?'

She tut-tutted. 'When I know what's happening, Grim, I'll let you know. Thought you'd have grasped that by now.'

''Mon, Wheeler. Give me a wee bit of info about the body?' he persisted.

'As I said, Grim, when there's a statement prepared for the press, you're welcome to report it. Until then . . .'

'All I'm sayin' is—'

Wheeler cut him off. 'In the meantime, get out of my way.'

The reporter stayed put.

'Shift,' she growled.

He stepped aside. 'Bloody police cooperation is zero in this city. It's all cosy when you lot want us to help you publicise a case but when it comes to a heads-up there's never any help. Christ, I can actually see the crime scene from here, yet not a bit of info.'

Wheeler ignored him but Ross rose to the bait. 'Just because you can see a part of it, Grim, doesn't mean you get to wade your size tens through it. You'd sell your granny for a story.'

The reporter didn't contradict him.

Wheeler strode on towards the police tarpaulin, on past a group of parked vehicles, saw a red BMW car with personalised number plates which meant that her friend Callum Fraser was already on site. She ducked under the cordon and spoke to the uniformed officer. 'What do we have?'

'Morning, DI Wheeler. A woman's body was discovered this morning at—' the young officer glanced at her notes '—eight-fifteen. It was partially concealed in the undergrowth in the wooded area over at the back there. Four men from a local running club were following their usual route around the perimeter of the golf club when they saw her.'

'Where are they now?'

'After the paramedics checked them over, they were taken to the station. One guy in particular was desperate to get away from the scene, said he couldn't stand to be here any longer. He'd already thrown up.'

'Now the SOCOs have to eliminate their DNA,' said Wheeler. 'Not a lucky break. Any identification on the body, tell me we have a name?'

'Nothing I'm afraid, no bag or purse has turned up yet. No credit cards or phone either.'

'Car?'

'Not parked nearby. We're still searching the wider area.'

'OK,' said Wheeler. 'So, other than the body, we've nothing?'

'Looks that way.'

Wheeler walked on. 'We're quite close to a pub, the Coach House. It's a bit of a dive, isn't it?'

'Known as the Cockroach,' said Ross. 'Bikers' bar. It's had its fair share of trouble.'

They made their way towards the forensic officer waiting to hand out the overalls, bootees and masks. Everyone on site had to be swaddled in appropriate clothing. Wheeler could see a group of scene-of-crime officers already working the scene. She hoped that they would be fastidious about maintaining the integrity of the site. There had been a recent case where DNA evidence had been contaminated by a newly qualified SOCO. The crime-scene manager had erupted in anger. Wheeler noted the CSM directing the SOCOs a short distance from her – some of the SOCOs were searching the ground, others were taking photographs of the scene, while another was videoing it. Tread plates and markers had been placed in specific areas. The body would have already been photographed. Wheeler knew how helpful it was to see pictures of how the body appeared in situ and the layout of the crime scene. Later, the images would be pinned to the board, so everyone at the station would be familiar with the information.

'Morning, DI Wheeler.'

She recognised the strong Aberdonian accent; she'd worked with Jim Watson on other cases and knew him to be one of the most experienced SOCOs in Glasgow. A man who lived for the job, he'd once told her. 'This here is not what I do, this here is who I am. It defines me.' Never the most cheerful of men, Jim was, however, the consummate professional. At least when he was on the job – she'd heard rumours about the excessive drinking. 'Anything so far, Jim?'

'Nothing of any great interest. Yet. At the best of times, reducing background DNA from the site is difficult. Add to the mix the bloody runners who came over and stuck their noses in,' he grumbled. 'So a load of different footprints contaminating the place. Have they never even seen an episode of *CSI*? You'd think they would have had more bloody sense. And then one of them threw up. Can you bloody believe it?'

'I heard.'

'It must have been a bit of a shock for him,' said Ross.

'Damn right it must have been, but it meant we had to get samples from all of them, including their sodden footprints, in order to eliminate them. And anyway,' he muttered, 'it's not good for the joints.'

'You've lost me,' said Wheeler.

'All that running, senselessly pounding the pavements and roads. I don't understand folk. But as usual I'll be thorough and I'll let you know if I get lucky.' He sounded doubtful.

'Let's stay positive.' Wheeler walked towards the clearing, saw the bulk of the forensic pathologist, Professor Callum Fraser, crouched beside the body. Two mortuary attendants waited in close proximity.

The pathologist glanced up. 'Beautiful morning,' he said by way of introduction. 'Glorious weather.'

'For us, yes, it is.' Wheeler looked at the corpse. 'But not, I'm afraid for this poor soul.' She saw that the woman was of slim build, with dark hair. She was wearing a pale blue T-shirt, jeans and gold sandals. Her toenails were painted a dark red to match her fingernails. There was a rose tattoo on her ankle. 'Looks to be in her mid to late twenties and those ligature marks around her neck are pretty dramatic. What can you tell me, Callum? Was our victim strangled?'

'You'll get my report in good time but preliminary findings suggest that the cause of death was strangulation. 'Look here—' he pointed to the bruises '—these are not manual chokeholds. The marks weren't made by fingers.' He put his fingers close to the woman's throat. 'It's too broad an outline,' he continued, 'perhaps a belt or some kind of collar?' He gestured to the chafing. 'When someone is strangled by hand, it can leave an exact outline of their fingertips, certainly their shape, which can be most useful.'

'And if they're a really helpful killer, they'll leave DNA traces in the slight hollows of the flesh,' added Wheeler.

'Indeed.'

'Could she have been hanged?' asked Ross.

'If she had been hanged these imprints would be raised.' Callum pointed to the bruising. 'And these would be heading in an upwards direction.'

'Because?' asked Ross.

'Gravity would bring the body down, so the imprints would point in the opposite direction. I'll have a better opportunity to examine the larynx and tongue during post-mortem. If they are enlarged, it will indeed confirm strangulation, but I won't know for sure until I examine her.'

'Did she have a chance to defend herself?' asked Wheeler quietly.

'No defence wounds. Our killer, whoever he or she was, made a clean job of it.'

'Estimated time of death?'

'Difficult to know for sure.'

'But if you had to hazard a guess, Callum?' said Wheeler.

'I've taken a reading of her temperature and lividity is present in the back of the body, so I'd suggest that she's been dead for roughly six to eight hours and was killed elsewhere and her body brought here.'

'Somewhere between midnight and two o'clock in the morning?'

'Around about then.' He stood back and gestured to the two attendants who had been patiently waiting to transport the body back to the mortuary.

Wheeler watched as the corpse was placed in the bag and then loaded into the van. She looked around the area. 'What do we have, Ross?'

'A pub, a golf club, houses and lots of wide open spaces.'

'And no identification on her. No clues.'

'Or witnesses,' Ross added. 'Looks like it's business as usual for us then. Just as well I hadn't made any plans for my time off.'

'We had plans for this evening,' said Fraser. 'My new husband and I had booked a table at Rogano's for dinner, thought we would treat ourselves to lobster. We've had to cancel. I've had a bit of a day. There's our girl here and there was bit of a mash-up by rival gangs over in the Southside last night.'

'I heard about it,' said Wheeler.

'A tragic waste of young lives. Four of the luckier ones are in intensive care in the Royal Infirmary. It means that I'll get to our girl here as soon as I can.'

'Later today?' prompted Wheeler.

'I think that might be too tight. I'll let you know for sure, but it's looking more likely that it'll be first thing tomorrow.'

Wheeler watched him leave. There wasn't anything else to be seen. 'Let's get back to the station, Ross.' She headed for the car. 'Uniform are doing house-to-house and the SOCOs are doing their job.'

'So, all we have to do is catch the killer,' said Ross.

'Exactly.'

The man was part of a small crowd of rubberneckers who had congregated beyond the police cordon, all straining to see something of macabre interest. He wondered what they'd like to catch a glimpse of – Karlie Merrick's corpse? Did they want to see the bruises around her throat? He felt his hands tingle at the memory. The belt he used was floating in the River Clyde; it may wash up somewhere, part of the flotsam and jetsam. But this did not trouble him. He watched the two detectives leave. The tall blonde spoke briefly to her dark-haired partner. She walked on quickly, he struggled to keep up. The man wondered if she was any good, if she would track him down? He doubted it. He adjusted his sunglasses, decided he would head into the city centre. Glasgow was full of tourists, eager to see the sights. There, he would join the throng of shoppers, visitors, buskers and street performers who milled around the mall and the cafés, bars and restaurants of Buchanan Street. There he would be invisible. And safe.

Chapter Nine

The Life Coach

Safe was never how he'd played it.

The hotel was in the centre of London's Covent Garden and a myriad of attractions were on his doorstep. George Bellerose could have gone to the Courtauld Institute of Art, viewed the paintings of Renoir, Cézanne, Degas, Monet and Manet. He could have dropped by the London Film Museum. Or he could have hung out in one of the trendy cafés in the area while watching street theatre. He could have spent the time before the conference on Carl Jung's archetypes being a tourist. But these attractions held no interest for him. Instead, George spent his free time in hotels in much the same way as he spent his time at home – fantasising about, watching or actually having sex.

In his room, he watched the Skype symbol disappear before he closed his laptop. His relationship with Angie Burns was slow. OK, he conceded that it was moving in the right direction and she'd kept the nipple clamps on overnight, but, Christ, she was dragging her feet. He constantly had to dangle the wedding carrot in front of the daft cow. Surely she knew deep down there was not a chance in hell that he'd settle down? It was all part of the script. He'd used it before on various women. Maxine had lasted two years before the penny had dropped that there would be no happy ending. He had been progressively grooming her, had made some inroads. Then one night he'd pushed it too far and one of his trusty props had let him down. The smooth, slender neck of the beer bottle had long been a favourite; there was something enticing about using it. Finishing his beer and knowing what was coming next. That night he'd found the downside; she'd ended up in Accident and Emergency at two in the morning. Good luck that she'd told them she'd done it herself. After her, Marta had been a beauty but had ditched him after two weeks, leaving him in the lurch and so desperate for sex that he'd played nail the whale and had targeted Jojo, the fat waitress who'd served him in a downmarket city-centre pub. He was way out of her class. They both knew it. She had an arse the size of a bus and a filthy mouth on her, but she was flattered by his script. She took him back to her flat that first night and let him hurt her. He'd dumped her a week later. Better like that. He couldn't be seen out in public with a porker. 'Always fish at the bottom of the pool,' his dad had told him, and he'd been right. A lot of women over the years had given him the brush-off. Thought that they were out of his league. Feminist cunts. George ignored that level of woman, stuck to what he knew. With his girlfriends, he'd let them know subtly and gently that they were too ugly, too fat, too stupid, too wrinkly or just too much of a loser to be attractive. He'd gradually worn them down until they hadn't known their own mind and they'd had to lean on him, had to depend on him to tell them what to do.

70

He flipped open his laptop again and began streaming. Settled himself comfortably on the bed. Watched a naked woman on her knees being dragged around a room on a lead. A thick leather collar sat tight around her neck. A group of men were watching her, one left the group and bent over her, extinguished his cigar on her thigh. The other men laughed. The woman kept moving. George wondered about Angie, how far he could take it? Right now, the pain was only psychological, but if he broke her in slowly, broke her spirit completely, how far could he take it physically? He'd need to take it gently, though, no point in moving too fast. He watched while the woman on screen was humiliated again. He wondered about the McIver Club, he'd heard rumours about how good it was, but it was far too expensive for him. The joining fees were astronomical but the place must be heaving with guys at the top of their game. What a turn-on it must be to have money and power and to know that you were untouchable. That in itself would make him hard. The idea of not being accountable, of being able to do whatever he wanted, to be flying high above the law. Throw money and clout at any problem and it would disappear. No matter, George consoled himself, those guys at the McIver were exactly like him. They all needed the same thing. Sure, they did it in luxury, but their endgame was the same. 'There would be no bad men if it wasn't for bad women,' his dad used to tell him. George lay back on his bed, watched the screen. Saw the woman being abused by two of the men, saw the degradation she suffered. Licked his lips. Wondered if he could do that to Angie.

Outside, in the city, preparations were under way for

Neil Young and Crazy Horse to play Hyde Park. The same week the city would host the British 10K London run, but the vibrancy of London was lost on George. He had only one dark focus.

Chapter Ten

The Station

'Super-fucking-efficient,' said Wheeler, pulling into the station car park. 'I've shaved ten minutes off my personal best and eighteen off yours. I have brilliant driving skills.'

'It was bordering on careless.' Ross closed the passenger door.

As usual Wheeler took the stairs to the CID suite two at a time. She turned into the corridor and nearly collided with Detective Chief Inspector Craig Stewart. His grey hair was shorn to a peak, his pink-gold Rolex was just visible under his cuff and his lightweight summer suit was pristine. 'Boss,' said Wheeler, suddenly acutely aware of her jeans and T-shirt. Instinctively, she reached up and took the scarf from her hair and stuffed it into the pocket of her jeans.

'Bit casual for the station, Wheeler.'

'I was supposed to be off for a few days, boss. I haven't had a chance to change yet.'

'I've just finished interviewing the fourth runner, Jeb Milligan,' said Stewart. 'Go through to the Incident Room.'

The rest of the team were arriving.

Although large, the room was badly insulated. In winter, it was cold; in summer, it was airless and stuffy. At the front of the room a noticeboard had been set up. As the investigation progressed, all relevant information would be placed on it. At the moment it was sparse, holding only the barest detail: the day, date and time the body had been discovered, and the location – a photocopied map of the Sandyhills area, the green swathes of the golf course, park, playing field, recreation ground and running track clearly visible. A photograph of the victim had been placed centrally, the ligature marks around her neck clearly visible. Another picture of the rose tattoo on her ankle. Photographs of the crime scene. What was missing, thought Wheeler, was a name, address or any personal information about the victim. The only names were those of the runners who found her.

When they had all assembled, Stewart cleared his throat and began. 'We've now spoken to all four runners.' He glanced at his notes. 'Ray Aitkin was out front and noticed the pale blue of the victim's clothing amid the greenery. He ran over to the opening and discovered the body. The other three, Mike Logan, Rob McKenna and Jeb Milligan, then caught up and unfortunately followed him into the scene. Eventually, the reality of what they were doing dawned on Logan and he herded them off to the side while they waited for the emergency services to arrive. Obviously, their footprints and DNA samples were taken by forensics on site.'

'Are they eliminated from the investigation, boss?' asked Wheeler.

'For the time being. I doubt that they were involved.

All four were in considerable shock and looked visibly distressed. Logan in particular was shaking uncontrollably; poor guy could hardly speak.'

'Was he the one who threw up?' asked a uniformed officer.

'Unfortunately, yes, Mr Logan was sick at the scene.'

'Did they disturb anything else?'

'Aside from leaving their footprints and DNA, nothing stupid like touching the body if that's what you mean. They came to their senses fairly quickly. They all have the same alibi; they were at a friend's house last night gaming until 3 a.m. We've checked with the friend and it pans out. They got up early and were running their usual route along Sandyhills Road, skirting the golf club. Other than a man walking his dog, they didn't meet anyone. The dog walker's already been spoken to – he saw nothing and has also been eliminated from the investigation. I've arranged for the runners to be driven back to their flats in Mount Vernon. They're still very shaken. They were offered psychological support but declined.' Stewart paused. 'Wheeler, what did you get from the pathologist?'

'Callum Fraser suggested the victim was killed somewhere between midnight and two o'clock in the morning. Most likely cause of death was strangulation.'

'Was she killed on site?'

'It looks like she was dumped. There was no sign of a struggle and no car or bike found nearby.'

'Driven there and dumped.' Detective Constable Alexander Boyd drank noisily from a bottle of water. 'Defence wounds?'

'None.'

'The killer surprised her?' asked a young female officer.

'Or she knew her attacker,' said Wheeler. 'Ross and I will get over to the Coach House.'

'I contacted the pub already,' said Boyd. 'The new manager's a guy name of Andy Carmichael. He was at pains to distance himself and his punters from it, said they were a good bunch but noisy. "Rowdy" is how he phrased it. Claims he was at his girlfriend's all last night and she'll back him. He's on his way to the pub now.'

'The Coach House has been recently taken over,' said Stewart, 'but, for those new to the team, it was a notorious place up until fairly recently. Back in the day, big Ronnie Crawford ran it like it was the back room of his house. I hope this new manager's better than him.'

'Big Ronnie still inside?'

'Two years of his sentence still to serve.'

'Didn't someone get knifed on his watch?' asked Boyd.

'Jimmy Shotts was stabbed four years back,' said Stewart. 'It was chucking-out time and the place was crowded but no one could help us with our inquiries, nobody saw a thing.'

'Including Jimmy, if I remember?' said Boyd.

'Difficult to miss someone coming at you with a six-inch blade but apparently he didn't see a thing.' Detective Sergeant Robertson picked an imaginary speck of fluff from his carefully ironed trousers. 'And even when we recovered the weapon, wiped of prints obviously, it still didn't jog his memory.'

'There's no way it wasn't Ian Bunyan,' said Stewart.

'So rumour has it, boss.'

'Ian Bunyan's a grotesque figure,' said Stewart. 'We know he has what's left of his fingers in many pies, including extortion and drugs, but so far he's managed to evade every bloody inquiry.'

'But now a body's been found close to the pub? You think it's him?'

'Bunyan's an evil bastard who loves to inflict pain,' said Stewart. 'Find out where he was at the time she was killed.'

At the end of the briefing, Wheeler issued orders to individuals. 'Uniform are conducting house-to-house in the area. Boyd, you and Robertson get out to the golf club. The rest of you, liaise with uniform, get on to the pitches, the golf club CCTV, everything that was recorded in the area prior to this woman being murdered and immediately afterwards. Establish a 24-hour window. Find out who was in the area last night, which vehicles were driven through Sandyhills. Contact the council for their CCTV of Sandyhills Road and the surrounding area. I know it's shit trawling through CCTV but we need to get on it. Also, check the system and find out if anyone has reported her missing. You have a photograph of her; sift through social media, get me a bloody name.'

The energy in the room increased as the team became animated. Wheeler could feel it become charged as they began the hunt for the killer. 'Right, you and me, Ross, let's go see Andy Carmichael at the Cockroach.'

Chapter Eleven

Family Life

Gary Ashton lived in a Victorian end-of-terrace villa in Tennyson Drive. In the living room the television was on, the sound was turned down. The information scrolled mutely across the bottom of the screen.

'A woman's body has been found in the East End of Glasgow . . . Two gang members were fatally stabbed in an altercation in the Southside of the city on Tuesday evening. The two men, named locally as Davie Ward and Chris Wood . . .'

Ashton was having his morning coffee and a smoke. His computer sat on the table in front of him, his Twitter and Facebook accounts were open and he was pasting links to his website, 'Capture the Dream'. He always asked clients if he could include a photograph from their wedding on his website. It was free publicity for him and most couples were happy enough to agree. He'd only been refused once, there was always one fucking control freak. He selected a photograph from the most recent wedding, Lorna and Robert Maine. She'd worn a full-length silk wedding dress; he'd bought a kilt. 'Waste of fucking money,' Ashton muttered at the image. 'It's not like you'll ever wear that dress or the kilt again.' But he knew the couple, like many others, had convinced themselves that they would. At least the Kibble Palace at Glasgow Botanic Gardens was in the background, which provided the shot with some interest. He'd arranged a few photographs of the couple next to the marble statue of Eve by the Italian sculpture Scipione Tadolini. Lorna had looked awkwardly at the nude, but he'd assured her it was high art. Ashton managed to send a few more tweets and finish his coffee before he heard her getting up. Shit, he should've been away by now. He stubbed the last of his cigarette on the saucer as his partner Lisa shuffled into the room and thrust his screaming son, Ewan, towards him.

'Can you take him? He needs changing.'

'No can do, I'm off out.'

'I'm desperate for a bath.' She sniffed the air. 'You're not supposed to be smoking in the house, Mum wouldn't like it.'

'She's not here. And it's not her house.'

'It's as good as, she gave us the deposit. She warned you about smoking with the baby here.'

'It won't do him any harm. It was just the one, it takes the edge off.'

'What is the matter with you? Why do you need to take the edge off anything?'

The baby cried louder.

'What do you think is the matter, Lisa? You gave up your career. Now our combined income is down twenty grand and you're asking me why the hell I'm edgy?'

Her tone changed to one of resignation. 'I've been up

79

half the night with him. I'm exhausted. I need a bath. Just ten minutes.'

'No chance, childcare is your department. Get your mum to come round. Or Katie. Or Zoe. Christ, you were there for them when their kids were small.'

'You don't even want to change your son.' A statement.

'It's not a case of my not wanting to, it's your bloody job. I see to him in the evenings when I can.'

'You're never here in the evenings.'

'Don't start. I work late. Think back before your mind got addled, surely you remember what work is? The bit where you go out every day and earn money to pay bills?'

Her voice a whisper. 'I thought you wanted to have a baby.'

'I don't remember having much of a say in it. You came off the Pill and neglected to mention it, so don't play the bloody martyr. You got what you wanted and now I have to find the cash for all of us.'

'You could go back to teaching art. We were doing well.'

'I fucking hated teaching.'

'It wouldn't be for long. I'll go back to Tesco once Ewan's a bit older.' The baby began to cry again. She soothed him. 'It's OK, wee man, it's OK, Mummy's here.' She turned back to Ashton. 'You got any more bookings?'

'I told you this kind of work is slow, a few small weddings here and there and a bit of freelance work. I've got a couple of other bits and pieces going on. Why?'

'You're out all the time, I never see you. I wanted us to be a family.'

'Which is why I'm having to diversify to keep us afloat.'

'Ewan needs a stroller.'

'He can't walk yet but he needs a stroller? I bought you the wrap-round sling you kept banging on about.'

'He can't be in the sling all the time, he's growing so quickly. I'm exhausted carrying him.'

'Zoe offered you her old stroller.'

'It's knackered.'

'Then ask your mum.'

'Again? You've got to be kidding.'

'How much are we looking at?'

'The decent ones are around three hundred.'

'Christ, how much?'

'One of your cameras cost way more than that.'

'They're for work. Without them you don't eat.' He gestured to the child. 'Or him for that matter.'

'And your son's not worth it?' she asked quietly.

'I didn't say that. I'm just saying that we need to be careful with money. Unlike your mother, I don't have a spare three hundred quid lying around. How much are the others?'

She sighed. 'They start around sixty pounds but I want one that he can have for just now and then grow into. Otherwise it's buying twice.'

'Sixty it is then.' He peeled three twenty-pound notes from a roll, grabbed his mobile. 'I've got to go.'

'Where?'

'Work.'

'I thought you said it was slow?'

'Slow, not dead. I have leads to chase up and I need to get out there and network; making contacts is half the battle.'

She followed him to the door. 'What about my bath?'

'Not my problem, Lisa.' He picked up his helmet. As he

walked down the path, he heard her call after him: 'What about my needs?'

'Fuck knows about you and your ongoing needs.' He turned back to her. 'And don't wait up tonight. I've got a business meeting later on; I won't be back. I need to make some connections. Network. Hustle. You get the picture?'

He ignored the slam of the door, started the Kawasaki and headed off. Maybe the ride to his office would improve his mood; being with Lisa and a screaming kid sure as hell hadn't.

Fifteen minutes later, he parked outside his office in Duke Street. More and more it was becoming his refuge. Once inside, he closed the door and slipped the small plastic bag containing the white powder from his bag. Took his time to prepare it, savoured the moment before leaning in and snorting. Allowed the intense high to hit him. For a few brief, tantalising moments he felt the surge run through him, like a light flashing through his system. He was on fire. Suddenly life was all good. He sat back in his chair. Shit, it was incredible. But all too soon it was gone and he experienced the unwanted crash and felt the familiar edginess return. Fuck it. He needed to get more. Lisa's constant nagging was bringing him down. It was her fault really. The complaints about money and the blah, blah, blah about her needs. What about his fucking needs? It was Lisa who'd given up her job. Self-indulgent cow. He looked at the photographs he'd taken. He'd shot some of the weddings in sepia, others in black and white, but most of the couples had wanted colour. Brides in draped silk smiled as bouquets were thrown into the crowd. Couples posed hand in hand in front of families. Children grinned into the camera and, on one occasion, a large tri-coloured collie made an appearance with a velvet bow attached to its collar. Pictures of tiered cakes, modern and ancient churches, flowers and registry offices. All expressions of love they'd said. A load of shit is what he'd said when Lisa had suggested they get married. It was all a money-making sham just like Valentine's Day, wedding anniversaries and the rest of it. OK, he was part of it, but he wasn't kidding himself that he'd fallen for it. In his experience, men wanted sex, women wanted kids. He ran through his options. There was no money in the house if they sold. By the time the old witch clawed back her deposit, he'd end up in a grotty bedsit. And there was no way he was going back to teaching. Not that he could. He'd not mentioned to Lisa, or to anyone, the real reason that he'd had to leave the profession. He licked his index finger, traced along the residual powder, put it to his mouth. Reminded himself that the sham was paying his mortgage but the porn supported his habit. Or at least it had until recently. He was now in debt to his supplier, Ian Bunyan. Unbidden, an image of Bunyan flashed into his mind, like the devil being invoked. Bunyan with his clown smile and his deformed hand. He'd heard that he'd lost two fingers, the index and the fourth, in a poker match. When Bunyan laughed he had a habit of covering his mouth with his hand, the splayed fingers, the botched job when they had been severed. Bunyan had finally arranged a rematch and had won, so had taken a pair of pliers and set about his opponent. Christ Almighty, Ashton shuddered, what kind of a man was he? He'd ignored the phone message Bunyan had left the previous day. Bunyan had spoken quietly, had even sounded friendly, but Ashton knew what was coming. He'd heard how, after some punter didn't pay up, he'd smashed her face so badly that she'd needed reconstructive surgery. Another time, he'd stabbed a guy name of Jimmy Shotts at the Cockroach pub. The manager at the time, big Ronnie Crawford, who was a nightmare himself, was too scared of Bunyan to intervene. Fuck, there was no way he was going near the pub until he had cash. The new manager, Andy Carmichael, was a scary fucker too. Maybe he should just keep away from them all? The landline rang and Ashton's heartbeat paused. He stared at the number. A mobile. It wasn't Bunyan's but then the bastard changed mobile phones on a regular basis. Ashton hesitated for a moment before answering, 'Capture the Dream Wedding Photography. How may I help?'

'I need a wedding photographer for Saturday . . .'

He felt his heart settled into its regular beat.

'. . . Our photographer's let us down at the last minute. He's gone. Done a runner. His office had been stripped and everything.'

Ashton heard the desperation in her voice; he'd add a couple of hundred quid to his price. 'I'm so sorry to hear that. And you say your big day's this coming Saturday?'

'Yes.'

Maybe he'd make it three hundred.

'I saw your photographs on your website. I know it's a long shot . . .' The young woman began to cry.

He waited, listened while she talked.

'I am so disappointed; I feel so let down. I mean I booked him over a year ago.'

So what? How the fuck did that guarantee anything? Ashton said nothing.

'How could this even happen?'

Shit happens all the time.

Finally, she sniffed loudly and finished with a tearful, 'I was wondering if you were even available?'

He'd nothing on at all that day. 'Let me double-check.' He kept her waiting for a long moment before sighing. 'It's going to be extremely tight, but I think I might be able to squeeze you in between appointments. It would be very rushed for us and we'd have to charge a premium rate. But we would, of course, include a video.'

'How much will it be?'

He grabbed a pen and notepad. 'Why don't you tell me a little bit about yourself and what you envisage for your wedding including your estimated budget and I'll put a package together for you?'

Twenty minutes later, he killed the call. He'd managed to add over four hundred and fifty quid to the bill for the short notice and had also taken a hefty deposit. He rolled his shoulders. He felt less tense about bumping into Bunyan now; things were starting to come together, although he'd still stay away from the Cockroach. There was something about the place, like a death was waiting to happen. He switched on the radio, heard the Kill Kestrels' 'Death of an Angel'. 'Shite,' he muttered and turned it down low. Heard the buzzer.

'It's me, Terry.'

A few seconds later, Terry McAvoy bounced into the room. 'How did it go last night at the Olde Pilgrim Hotel?'

'Good, except Laura was still feeling a bit shit. She threw up again.'

'She up the duff?'

'Nah, I think the greedy cow just ate too much. Tonight's shoot is where exactly?'

'Old hotel in Auchterarder, called the Albion. It's on the market for over two hundred grand. Here's what I put together for the owners.'

Ashton took the glossy estate agent's schedule. From first impressions, it was one of those old tired hotels which, with the advent of travel lodges and budget hotels, had gone out of fashion. He saw the vividly patterned carpets, the tables set with paper tablecloths. No one wanted to get married in those places anymore and they were being sold off cheap. 'Eight bedrooms. Any of them any good? I'm not driving all that way if they're shit.'

'The honeymoon suite's the one you'll be using. Four-poster bed. Part of the original village inn. Stone floor. Very atmospheric.'

'And it's definitely empty?'

'Of course it's empty. Why are you so jumpy? The owners flew out to Rimini yesterday for a month in the sun. I've to show prospective buyers around. Not that there are any yet. And I reassured them that I'd keep a close eye on the place, maybe pop in now and again, switch on the lights. No point in folk thinking there's no one looking after the place, so we're covered if anyone sees the van outside. You need to remember the throws and other stuff though.'

'I've got a container full of props.'

'I don't want the owners ever catching sight of their hotel in a porn movie. And I don't want any telltale jizz stains on the furniture.'

'There won't be, and I'll shoot the background in soft focus.' Ashton tapped the brochure. 'Looks jaded.'

'Granted, it's traditional,' said Terry. 'But great for one of your period drama pieces, the whole sexy wench stuff. Who's coming? The dark-haired girl?'

'Karlie? No, she was out at the Studio yesterday. Laura's back in tonight.'

'I'll meet you in the car park. Usual time.'

'You're a pal, Terry.'

In the background, the music cut to the news.

'A body was discovered in the East End of Glasgow this morning . . . a police spokesperson . . .

'Police are still investigating the deaths of two men after an alleged gang attack in the Southside of the city . . .'

Terry reached over and switched the radio off. 'You want me to do the last edit of yesterday's cut?'

'Yeah, let's get it finished and shipped.'

Ten minutes later they had the final cut. On the screen, Karlie writhed in pain. 'She can do fear and pain, that one,' muttered Terry. 'No way this is art but it's good enough for me.'

'It sells,' said Ashton.

'There's a lot of competition out there, companies who are making more sophisticated material.'

'They're aiming at a different audience. The folk I sell to are hardly that discerning. Let's just give the punters what they want.'

'Which is?'

'Pain,' said Ashton. 'Plain and simple, they're turned on by pain and suffering. Then again—' he grinned '— aren't we all?'

Chapter Twelve

The Cockroach

'Talk of the devil,' muttered Wheeler. She watched Ian Bunyan pull on a motorcycle helmet before starting up his black Honda. He pulled away from the kerb as they approached the pub. 'I see his usual demonic grin was pasted on for our benefit.'

'Lucky us.'

Ross turned into the car park of the Cockroach. It was deserted save for a gleaming chrome, maroon and black Harley-Davidson. 'Place must be doing well for Carmichael to afford something like that, seeing as he's only the manager of a pub.'

'I can't imagine the Cockroach paid for that machine, at least not through the books.'

'How much do you reckon it would cost? Ten, twelve grand?'

'No idea,' said Wheeler.

'It's bloody gorgeous though, isn't it?'

Wheeler had to agree that the motorbike was a thing of beauty.

Inside, the bar was empty and, from a quick glance, it

didn't look like Andy Carmichael had improved much in the way of interior design. Motorbike memorabilia was all around the place, framed stills of actors from the *Mad Max* movie, the iconic shot of Brando on a motorbike in *The Wild One*, Peter Fonda and Dennis Hopper in *Easy Rider*.

'Christ, they all want to be outlaws, don't they?' muttered Wheeler.

'I could just see myself on a hog,' said Ross.

'In full leathers?'

'Would you like that?'

'In your dreams, muppet.'

'I take comfort in my fantasy world.' Ross feigned hurt.

'It feels like a bit of a theme park, though, doesn't it?' Wheeler turned as the kitchen door swung open. The man was in his late forties, his beard was grey and his hair lay in greasy strands to his shoulders. He wore denims, a black T-shirt and a black leather waistcoat. Black and silver biker boots. Despite the dim of the bar, he was wearing sunglasses.

'Fucking cliché,' muttered Ross.

'Andy Carmichael?' asked Wheeler, as the man approached.

'Who wants to know?' His voice low, unfriendly.

'I'm DI Wheeler and this is DI Ross.' They flashed their IDs.

He ignored them, removed the sunglasses. 'Oh aye, one of your lot called me earlier.'

'We're investigating a murder, Mr Carmichael.'

'So your guy said on the phone. What was his name, Boyd?'

'I believe Detective Constable Boyd rang you earlier.'

'He mentioned that a woman's body had turned up in Sandyhills, so naturally you thought you'd shoot straight over here for a chat.'

'We're trying to piece together the victim's last known movements,' said Wheeler.

'And you're wondering if she'd been in here last night, because that would figure, wouldn't it? Someone got killed and your first stop is the Coach House?'

Wheeler ignored the tone. 'We're scouring the area; you're not being singled out, Mr Carmichael.'

'She got a name?'

'We don't know the victim's name yet,' said Wheeler. 'She was mid to late twenties, around five foot four, slim with dark hair.'

'Was she a biker?'

'We don't know.'

'Then I doubt that she'd have come in here.'

'Non-bikers aren't welcome?'

'It's not that they're not welcome.' Carmichael smiled, revealing a row of steel gum piercings. 'Let's just say that they don't feel too comfortable. They don't speak the same language, if you get my drift.'

She could imagine. 'Do you remember seeing a woman fitting that description in the bar?'

'There were a couple of girls in last night around that age. Both had dark hair, although neither of them was what you'd call slim, so I guess not your victim.'

'Besides yourself, who else was working last night?'

'Just me. Cal Moody dipped in for a bit. He helps out, but he's a clumsy bugger, cut his hand in the kitchen. It was late on, around eleven. Ended up at Accident and Emergency at the Royal Infirmary.'

'I'd appreciate a contact number.'

Carmichael scribbled it on the back of a beer mat, handed it to Ross.

'Was it busy last night?

'Sure was, the place was heaving and a few of the boys got a bit carried away. A wee bit rowdy.'

'In what way?'

Carmichael shrugged. 'A couple of them were just having a laugh, nothing dangerous.'

'Did you notice anything unusual or anyone acting suspiciously?'

'You suspect one of my regulars?'

'I just told you,' said Wheeler, 'we're trying to piece together the last moments of our victim. If she was here, we need to find out who she arrived with, who she talked to and if she left with anyone. It's in everyone's best interest if we can eliminate your customers from our investigation. I'm sure you agree?'

'Fine by me.'

'It would be helpful if we could find out if they saw anything unusual last night,' said Ross. 'Maybe earlier in the evening or when they were leaving at closing time? Perhaps you could speak to your customers, find out if they saw anything?'

'Maybe.'

'I saw Ian Bunyan drive off as we arrived,' said Wheeler.

'Don't know the guy, don't recognise the name. Maybe he was just turning in the car park. Loads of fuckers do that; it drives me nuts.'

'You sure you don't know him?' said Wheeler.

'Just said so, didn't I?'

'I'll also need to look at your CCTV.'

'That's where you'll have a problem: we don't have any. It got busted a while back when a few of the lads got carried away. High jinks. But I'm in the process of getting it sorted.' He grinned at her, revealing the metal gum studs again. 'Top of my list.'

'Right,' muttered Wheeler. She gave him her card. 'Call me if you hear anything.'

Carmichael let his gaze travel slowly down Wheeler's body. 'Any excuse at all, doll, and you'll hear from me.'

Outside, they made for the car.

'I think Carmichael likes you,' said Ross.

'Lucky me.'

'Those gum piercings must have hurt.'

'Guy like that probably loves pain,' said Wheeler.

'You think our victim might have been in the pub?'

'It's the nearest place to where she was found. It might be relevant that she was dumped there, or maybe it was just random. At this stage it's worth keeping an open mind. Even if she wasn't in there, someone might have seen her on their way home. And if Carmichael could speak to his regulars they'll probably tell him more than they would uniform. If he's not involved himself.'

'You think it could've been Carmichael?' asked Ross.

'Boyd checked out his alibi – girlfriend supports him.'

'Very convenient him not having CCTV and the girl-friend being his alibi.'

'What about the golf course?'

'Boyd and Williams are there now.'

Her mobile rang. The station. Robertson. 'I'm listening.'

'We've had a breakthrough.'

She listened while he talked her through it. 'That's got

to be our victim. Send uniform to pick her up.' She ended the call.

'Update?' said Ross, as he edged the car out into the traffic.

'A woman named Maureen Anderson just called the station. She'd been due to meet a friend for coffee. The friend didn't show and isn't answering her phone. Maureen saw the television report about a body being found. Robertson got a detailed description.'

'Tell me it's good news.'

'Sounds like our girl.'

The man was seated in the John Lewis café at the Buchanan Galleries. The coffee was delicious, as was the pastry. Casually, he scrolled down the newsfeed on his phone.

DCI Stewart from Carmyle Police Station has just issued the following statement:

Police were called just after eight o'clock this morning to the East End of the city after members of the public discovered a woman's body concealed in undergrowth on Sandyhills Road. The identity of the deceased is not yet known and we would ask anyone who was in the vicinity of Sandyhills and who saw or heard anything suspicious to get in touch with us at Carmyle Station directly or at one of the numbers listed below. The woman is described as being in her mid to late twenties, approximately five foot four, of slim build and wearing a pale blue T-shirt, dark blue jeans and gold-coloured, open-toed leather sandals. We would ask anyone with information to contact

93

Police Scotland on 101 or Crimestoppers on 0800 555
111 if you wish to remain anonymous.

The police at Carmyle had a dead body to play with but
they had no name. They were slow. Pathetic.

The man flicked off his phone, sipped his coffee. Here
he was invisible. He was safe. He was free.

Chapter Thirteen

The Friend

Wheeler heard the door slam behind her as she approached the desk sergeant. 'Has Maureen Anderson arrived?'

'A few minutes ago. I put her in Room Two, and I've arranged for tea to be brought through.'

'A couple of biscuits might be an idea,' said Ross.

'Last time I looked you weren't bereaved,' muttered the sergeant.

Ross followed Wheeler into the interview room.

Maureen Anderson was sitting at the table. She looked up, gave them a weak smile.

Social niceties and politeness in the face of darkness, thought Wheeler. She kept her voice soft. 'I'm DI Wheeler and this is DI Ross. I want to thank you for coming in, Ms Anderson.'

'Maureen.'

'Maureen. We'd like you to tell us a little bit about your friend and why you're concerned about her. Starting with her name.'

'Karlie Merrick.'

Ross quietly took out his notebook. Began writing.

Wheeler already had a rough description from Robertson, but she needed the crucial information that would confirm if Karlie was their victim. 'Can you describe her in as much detail as you can?'

'My height, five four, shoulder-length dark hair and brown eyes.'

So far so accurate.

'And she has a tattoo.'

It was her. Had to be. Wheeler waited.

'She has a rose tattoo on her ankle.'

'Do you have a picture of Karlie?'

'Not with me. I've got some at home.'

It was important to get the information while Maureen could concentrate. Once she knew her friend was dead, she would go to pieces, which would be a whole lot less useful. 'What age is Karlie?' Wheeler, careful to use the present and not the past tense.

'She's twenty-eight.'

'And when was the last time you saw her?'

'Last Thursday. We went for a drink at Jinty McGuinty's, over in the West End.'

Wheeler knew the bar. It was located in Ashton Lane, one of the cobbled lanes in a trendy area of the city. 'Is Jinty's a favourite hangout of Karlie's?'

'No, she thought that she might meet some people who'd be involved in films. You know, with it being the West End and everything? She thought maybe she'd be spotted, like the way girls are sometimes spotted when they're out shopping and then they become models?'

Not at twenty-eight, thought Wheeler. 'And did she meet anyone at the pub, was she ever spotted?'

'No.'

'Does Karlie want to be a model?'

'An actress. She wrote to loads of folk asking for introductions, she sent an email to that group, the Kill Kestrels? She reckoned she'd been at school with one of them. Thought maybe he could help get her some exposure, seeing as how they're famous now.'

'Do you know which member of the group?'

'No, I'm not really that into their music. Karlie neither, it's just that she wants to be famous and she thinks that maybe he might...' Maureen pulled out a tissue and wiped her eyes.

'Does Karlie ever mention the Coach House bar?'

'No, I don't think so.'

'And you were meant to meet this morning for coffee, where?'

'The Murder of Crows café, but she didn't show and she never called to cancel. She's not answering her mobile.' Maureen's voice fell to a whisper. 'Karlie always answers her mobile.'

'Do you know where Karlie went last night? Did she mention meeting anyone?'

'We don't speak every day. I waited ages in the café for her, and then, when I saw on the telly that a body had been found up by Sandyhills...' Maureen appealed to Wheeler, 'I don't want it to be Karlie.'

'Does Karlie visit that area?'

'She never mentioned it. She sometimes goes into town and hangs about Princes Square. Maybe if she's feeling flush, she'd go for a drink – only a soft one, she doesn't touch alcohol – to that big place on Ingram Street. I forget the name of it, it's got statues and pillars outside.'

'The Corinthian?' said Wheeler.

Maureen nodded. 'Big posh place.'

The Corinthian was close to Wheeler's flat in the Merchant City and was one of the city's many stylish hangouts. 'Is Karlie seeing anyone?'

'No. She just isn't interested in men or in dating. Says it's a waste of time. She's ambitious.'

Wheeler heard the change in tone, the impatience. They should be out there looking for her friend, not sitting in the station, chatting. 'Does she live alone?'

'Yeah, she's got a flat in Glasgow Harbour Development. I've got her spare key.' Maureen rummaged in her bag. 'It's in here somewhere.'

Great, thought Wheeler. Had Maureen trampled over a potential crime scene? She thought of the SOCO Jim Watson and his complaint about the runner who threw up. *So a load of different footprints all contaminating the place. Have they never even seen an episode of* CSI? *You'd think they would have had more bloody sense.* Did that apply to Maureen too? Had she walked over a potential crime scene without thinking? What Maureen said next confirmed it.

'Karlie's not there. I went through the whole flat. Her bed hasn't been slept in – it looks like she wasn't home last night.' Maureen offered the key.

Wheeler took it. She would arrange for a thorough search to be done by SOCOs. She would also arrange to get CCTV from the area around Glasgow Harbour Development. 'Is she working?'

'Karlie does agency work for a photographer. His name's Gary, he's a wedding photographer—' Maureen faltered for a heartbeat '—but he's got a sideline in porn.'

'Go on,' said Wheeler.

'Karlie did a couple of porn movies for him. Small stuff. Nothing big that needs major distribution.'

'Does this Gary have a surname?' asked Wheeler.

'She never mentioned it. He has an office someplace in the East End, but I think the studio is out of town, out past Strathaven. Karlie sometimes goes into Strathaven for coffee, some really old-world coffee shop. She said it's a lovely place. She likes going to different places for coffee. It's her thing. We're going there for coffee next week.'

Ross continued taking notes.

'What about family?' asked Wheeler.

'Her parents are dead, but she has a cousin, Beth, I think that's her name.' Maureen took out her phone and scrolled through her messages. 'Wait. Hold on. I do have a photo of Karlie. She sent me this a few months ago. Beth had contacted her, out of the blue, to tell her about her new exhibition in some trendy gallery in town. Later, she sent on a box of old papers and photographs belonging to Karlie's father. Anyway, Karlie went into the gallery and started messing around taking selfies and an old guy told her to stop, said it was interfering with him enjoying the exhibition. They had a bit of a slanging match. She told him to fuck off, it was her cousin's work. She said it was a right laugh.'

Wheeler waited while Maureen went into folders, swiped through two months of information, until eventually she found it. 'Here it is. I knew I had it somewhere.'

Wheeler took the phone, studied the picture. It was definitely their victim. Karlie Merrick was grinning and making a daft face. In the background was a painting, an image of a woman with large, haunted eyes. Wheeler took in the details of the gallery. The space was familiar; she'd been there many times over the years. The CCA. The Centre for Contemporary Arts was located on Sauchiehall Street and was one of Glasgow's best-known institutions. Wheeler checked the date – the photograph had been sent at 11 a.m. on Saturday 10 May. The atmosphere in the room had changed; she guessed Maureen felt it too. This was now a murder inquiry with Karlie Merrick at the centre. Wheeler handed the phone back to Maureen.

'It's her, isn't it? It's Karlie? I saw your expression. You recognised her.'

Wheeler gave the tiniest nod and watched Maureen's face dissolve. The tea had finally arrived and a uniformed officer placed the tray down and quietly exited the room. Wheeler put a mug of tea in front of Maureen, watched while she tried to compose herself. Waited a moment before asking, 'Do you know of anyone who wanted to harm her?'

'No.'

'We need a list of Karlie's friends, her Facebook account, Twitter, Pinterest and any other social media. Anything and everything you can give us would be of help.'

Ross slid a piece of paper and pen across the table to Maureen. 'And also if you could jot down any passwords you know. Anything you can remember.'

'And I'm going to need to take her laptop,' Wheeler said gently.

Maureen began to cry again. 'Can I use the loo?'

'Of course.' Wheeler grabbed her notebook, escorted Maureen to the toilet. Waited outside in the corridor. Called the CCA, identified herself and asked to speak to the manager. Quickly explained why she was calling and what she needed. 'I don't know if the artist was part of a bigger exhibition or if she had a solo exhibition. Her name's Beth and the exhibition ran on Saturday tenth of May.'

She heard the woman tap the information into a computer. 'OK, here it is. Yes, I thought it would probably be Beth Swinton. She had a solo exhibition, "Eyes Wide to the World". It ran from third to the twenty-fourth of May.'

'Do you have contact details for her?'

More typing. A pause, then, 'Right, here they are, she's over in the Southside.' Wheeler flipped open her notebook, scribbled down an address in Queen's Park and a phone number. She thanked the manager and killed the call.

A few seconds later, Maureen reappeared, looking washed out and exhausted. Grief and shock had hit her. Wheeler led her back to the room. Scottish law stipulated that a formal identification of the body needed to be done by two people, and Wheeler wondered if Maureen would be one of them. But that was for later. A family liaison officer would be sent to her home and the FLO would talk Maureen through the process. 'I'll arrange for you to be driven home and also for someone to come and visit you.'

'And you're positive it's her?'

Wheeler heard the desperation.

'You might have made a mistake?'

Denial. Part of the bereavement process.

Maureen appealed to Ross. 'Can you just double-check the information you have? I mean it would be helpful to get a second opinion?'

Bargaining.

Wheeler kept her tone gentle. 'I'm sorry, Maureen.'

Later, in the Incident Room, Wheeler crossed to the board, noted down the information as she spoke. 'Our girl is Karlie Merrick. She was twenty-eight and lived in a flat in Glasgow Harbour Development. The SOCOs are on their way there now. Karlie's next of kin is Beth Swinton. Ross and I are going to visit her over in the Southside. We'll get to the flat and also check in with the band, the Kill Kestrels. It's a long shot but she tried to contact one of them.'

'Her and every other fan in the country,' muttered a uniformed officer.

'Karlie worked for a wedding photographer,' Wheeler continued. 'Boyd, I want you to find out which one, goes by the name of Gary. His office is in the East End but he has a place either near Strathaven or in the town itself. Also runs a porn business on the side. Get on to it. Can't be too difficult to find him.'

'Not for a genius like me.' Boyd fired up his computer.

'And there's some old-world café in Strathaven. Our victim went there, so get on to them too.'

'Got it.'

Wheeler addressed two female officers in uniform. 'I want you two to hit the social media sites used by our victim, see what she put on Facebook, Twitter, Pinterest, find out who she was friends with, who liked her posts and anyone who either trolled her or posted negative comments. The lot. Here are the details Maureen gave us and the passwords Karlie used. Our victim liked coffee bars. Get in touch with as many as you can in the city, find out if she was a regular. Maureen said Karlie went to the Corinthian and Jinty's, so get on to them.' She continued updating the team and issuing orders for a few minutes, until everyone knew what their particular task was. She was halfway across the room when she spoke to Ross. 'Let's go see the cousin. I'll arrange for an FLO to meet us there.'

Chapter Fourteen

The Gang

Mason

Mason Stitt fumed at a corner table in the Cockroach. His dark hair was cropped close to his skull, his T-shirt tight over muscled biceps. His eyes were dark and heavy with revenge as he stared at the picture of Brando. What would he do at a time like this? Mason gulped his beer. The deaths of Davie and that runt Chris Wood should've been avoidable; it should never have happened. And now the Southside police had arrested the two boys who did it and were sniffing around looking for more information. It was all Owen fucking McCrudden's fault. Strategic planning was supposed to have been in place. They were supposed to have had the edge. Instead, they'd been ambushed, the other gang had half a dozen more members, drafted in at the last minute. Owen had fucked up again, there was no place for him in the organisation. But Mason knew that it was he who had committed the first cardinal sin as a leader. He'd shown sympathy, he'd felt sorry for the homeless fucker living in his shit van.

Knew that Owen had been flattered when they'd sworn allegiance. 'I'll do anything. Steal anything, fight anyone.' He'd seen the desperation in Owen's freaky husky eyes. Knew the gang was all Owen had. *The weakest link in the chain.* Mason forced himself to slow down and sip his pint. Think this through. What if there was one more thing Owen could do for him, one more piece of action that would allow Mason to move up in the world? Mason knew that he would need to leave the gang behind, even after things died down with the police. His reputation as a street fighter was good, but this was boys' stuff and he was ambitious. He wanted to join the grown-ups, the drug men. Except that there wasn't an opening. Unless he made one. Ian Bunyan. Mason thought of Bunyan's stupid clown grin, how his face contorted when he smiled. The ridiculous affectation of covering his mouth with a savaged hand which looked like a devil's hoof. Mason knew that he had no chance going up against the cunt, but a germ of a plan began to form, a whorl of an image snuck its way into his mind. He waited, watched it grow, saw it form. Fact – Owen McCrudden was no match for Ian Bunyan. If they went head to head. But Owen was always boasting about his shitty van – 'This here weapon weighs three tons of metal.' Fact – Bunyan was only five seven and slight, maybe 135 pounds. Went everywhere on his motorbike. What if they did go head to head but on the road? Mason sat back, took a long slow drink of the cool liquid. Owen was desperate, would do anything to re-ingratiate himself with Mason and the gang and, given Owen's crap life, what did he have to lose? Mason smiled, watched his cousin, Andy Carmichael, cross the room.

'Mason.'

'Andy.'

'How're things?'

'They were shite, but I think they're improving.'

'I heard about the two boys who got killed, how'd that even happen?' said Carmichael.

Mason wasn't in the mood to discuss failure. 'It happens. I heard the filth have been sniffing around?'

'Two cops, Wheeler and Ross. But they're gone. They never mentioned the gang fight, they were looking into the murder of some lassie who got killed.'

'Right.'

'You know anything about her murder?'

'No.'

'You sure?'

'Fuck's sake.'

'OK, all right. What are you going to do about the gang?'

Mason sipped the dregs of his pint. 'That, Andy, I need to decide. Revenge, obviously, but I need to look at the crew, who needs promoted and who needs to be let go. But mainly I need to consider my future. It's not with the gang, long term.'

'You're not getting any younger, gang fights are a boy's game.'

'Agreed, so I need to think of my career.'

'Which direction?'

'Drug supply.'

'Not in this area, Ian Bunyan has it covered.'

Mason drained the last of his pint. 'Maybe we'll wait and see about that.'

Chapter Fifteen

The Kill Kestrels

Josh

He'd instructed the driver to bring the car around to the side entrance of the hotel. The Range Rover had darkened windows so it was the easiest way to get around the city without being recognised. While he waited, Josh replayed the argument with the guys. He hadn't been bullshitting Lexi, he had vividly remembered the day Dougie had brought a copy of the *Glasgow Chronicle* to rehearsals. The manager had been delighted with the two-page spread and that they'd used the promotional photographs taken by Paulo Di Stefano. They'd even made reference to 'Super-manager Dougie Scott'. Dougie had loved it, but that's not why Josh remembered that day by a long shot. And that's when he'd contacted Cutter Wysor.

During a break in rehearsals Josh had flicked through the newspaper, glanced at the 'What's On' section, some artist was curating an exhibition to raise money for the local hospice. He'd stared at the photograph that accompanied the article. Susan Moody was sitting on a chair, her smile weak. She was emaciated, her face heavily lined and her hair was almost gone, but it was definitely her. He'd scanned the article twice then googled the name of the hospice. He had the phone number in seconds and that's when the chase had gathered pace. He'd called the hospice and was told that the patient had deteriorated and had been moved to the Royal Infirmary. Two short phone calls later and he had Susan Moody's room number.

He heard the text come through. The Range Rover was waiting.

Twenty minutes later, the Royal Infirmary came into view. The original building dated from the late eighteenth century, but over the years a series of architectural hybrids had been added. The hospital sprawled across acres of the city and could accommodate a thousand beds and numerous outpatients. To Josh it looked like a small, architecturally malformed hamlet. Which was exactly the kind of a place to house the bitch. He was dropped at the main entrance, took the stairs to the second floor and turned into a long corridor. A solitary nurse sat behind the desk, she was on the phone, sounded harassed. 'I'm sorry Mr Simpson wasn't changed quickly enough yesterday. We had an emergency in the ward and . . .' She paused. 'Yes, of course, I do understand that he was soiled but—' She saw Josh and put her hand over the receiver. 'Can I help?'

'I'm looking for Susan Moody? I called earlier, room eight if I remember correctly?'

'The end of the corridor, last room on the right. If you wait for a moment, I'll tell her you're here?'

'It's fine, thanks,' he lied, 'she's expecting me.'

The nurse went back to her call. 'No, of course I'm listening to you, Ms Simpson. Yes, but we are short staffed and . . .'

Josh made his way down the corridor, reached for the door handle.

Inside, despite the open window, the room was muggy, the air thick and heavy with sickness. Susan Moody was slumped in a chair, her eyes closed. One wrinkled hand cradled the electric call bell. Josh moved quickly, snatched the bell and placed it on top of the cabinet, out of her grasp. He dragged a plastic chair across the room, sat facing the woman. The noise woke her. If the nurse had witnessed it, Susan's gasp could have been interpreted as surprise or delight. Josh knew it was neither.

The old woman fumbled frantically for the bell.

'I've put it over here for safe keeping.'

'No. Want it.' Her eyes wild with panic. 'Give it to me.'

He ignored her. 'Susan, good to see you after all these years and I'm delighted that you still recognise me, so we can have a nice chat undisturbed. It's such a shame we lost touch so soon after the fire, wasn't it?'

'I want the nurse.'

His voice hard. 'Wasn't it, Susan?'

'Don't want . . . to see you.' Her voice a thin rasp of air.

'I'm sure that's not true, Susan. And do you know why I'm sure? Because I read in the papers that you were distraught. If I remember correctly, the reporter from the *Chronicle* wrote, "The distraught foster carer Susan Moody was inconsolable and was taken to the Royal Infirmary where she was sedated." And now all these years later you're back here in the Royal. Full circle, eh?' Josh watched the woman. 'Distraught and inconsolable,

Susan,' he repeated. 'You were sedated. They made it easy for you, didn't they? The doctors made it all go away.'

'I told the polis the truth that night.' She shifted in her chair.

'Liar. They didn't tally, did they, your version of events and mine?'

'The polis knew that I told them the truth.'

'They had no reason to doubt you, had they?'

'I want my bell.'

'I want the facts.' Josh perched on the hospital bed, watched her try to pull herself out of the chair. Saw that she was too frail, saw her fall back, pain etched on her face. He felt all the old animosity resurface, understood that he despised the woman in front of him, knew that he always had.

'I want the truth, Susan,' he said.

'The truth is she—'

He spoke quickly. 'Her name was Amber.'

'I told them, Amber must have snuck into the living room and knocked over a candle.'

'And set the curtains alight?'

'It was an accident. She must have run back to her room.'

'She was fast asleep in her room all of the time and you weren't even in the house.'

'I only stepped out into the garden for a minute, for a quick smoke.'

'Liar. That's what you told the police.' Josh kept his voice steady. 'You went out that night.' More of a statement than a question.

Silence.

'Who else was in the house?'

'No one.'

'I heard raised voices.'

'You were asleep. I told you at the time, you must have been dreaming.' The old woman stared at the floor. 'You can't remember all those years ago, your memory's flawed.'

'See, that's where you're mistaken, Susan. Recently, the memories have been flooding back.'

The woman gave a small, stubborn shake of her head.

He carried on talking. 'I called the hospice when I saw your picture and, from what they told me, you haven't got long.' He let the silence stretch.

She attempted a shrug.

'So I'm giving you the opportunity to clear your conscience and tell me what really happened that night.'

She tried to talk but instead of words a gurgle of saliva escaped from her lips.

He leaned closer to her, smelled the stench of sickness. Death and decay were almost upon her.

'Whoever you were protecting can't get at you now. Just give it up, Susan, give it up.'

Again, the woman tried and failed to speak. Tiny flecks of spit fell from her mouth. She struggled to sit up. Failed again.

He leaned in closer.

Finally, he heard her, although it was only a whisper on her breath. 'Piss off.'

Josh stared at her for a second before whispering, 'You'll rot in hell, you fucking bitch.' He closed the door quietly behind him and made his way back along the corridor.

The nurse was still behind the desk. 'Doctor Rashid will be round in a few minutes, if you wanted to hang on and speak with her?'

'No, that's fine, thanks. I'll get on. Has anyone else been in to visit Susan?'

'Not that I know of.'

'Cheers.' He walked down the corridor and turned left, took the stairs. He was alone on the stairwell and spoke aloud. 'Another dead end but that's OK, bitch, I'll just keep digging.' He made his way to the car park, to the air-conditioned Range Rover and the anonymity of its blacked-out windows. He had one more visit to make before heading to the photo op.

Chapter Sixteen

The Winners

'Come on, Ellie. I'm going to be late. I need to get to work after I drop you two off.' In her semi-detached house in Dennistoun, in the East End of the city, Marisa Adamson stood at the bottom of the stairs and tried to keep the impatience out of her voice. She could hear the water running in the bathroom, knew her daughter probably couldn't even hear her. Marisa sprinted up the stairs and rattled the door handle. 'Ellie, we need to get going. I've got to get to work.' Heard a muffled, 'In a minute, Mum.' She listened at the door, knew if Ellie caught her, another row would ensue. She hoped that her daughter was putting on her make-up and not, as she suspected, quietly disposing of the contents of her stomach. She couldn't be certain that her daughter was bulimic, but since winning tickets to meet the Kill Kestrels, Ellie had dramatically trimmed down. She'd never been big but at just under nine stones on her five eight frame, she'd complained that she could lose a bit. Marisa had vehemently disagreed but Ellie had point blank refused to get on the scales in front of her. She knew Ellie weighed herself before breakfast every day, so one morning Marisa had listened outside the door for the robotic announcement, but the door had flown open and a furious Ellie had confronted her.

Marisa quickly went back downstairs to wait by the open door. She glanced out and saw Ellie's pal, Isla, chatting animatedly to Morag next door. Isla's hands were moving as fast as her mouth, both running away with excitement. She'd be telling Morag how much she LOVED the Kill Kestrels and how Skye Cooper and Josh Alden wrote songs that made her feel that they were written just for HER. Marisa had listened to their incessant chatter since they'd won the prize, had heard them squabbling childishly about who was the best-looking band member. Marisa grabbed her handbag and rummaged for her hairbrush, crossed to the mirror and tried to calm the mass of frizz that her hair had recently become. She studied the lines on her face. She'd just turned fifty, but in the past few years everything had changed. Fine lines had grown deeper and more entrenched and her hair had gone coarse and wiry and refused to be controlled. The colour had faded and fighting the grey had recently become more of a battle. And now the hot flushes had arrived. 'Whoop. Whoop,' she said to her reflection before asking, 'So how come I still feel nineteen inside?' She wished Jay were alive to see his daughter become a beautiful young woman. That he was here to see Marisa and her unruly hair. She heard the bathroom door open and Ellie step down the stairs in her new, ridiculously high heels. Their daughter had Jay's colouring and his large grey eyes. Marisa's heart flipped. How did Ellie get to be so gorgeous? Marisa knew that it wasn't just a mother's bias; Ellie was an ethereal beauty.

Tall and blonde, she made it look effortless. The heels, the make-up and the hair, which she'd taken an hour to blow dry, after having had it expensively highlighted, all for some boy in a band who would never see her again. We all have our heroes, Marisa reminded herself; it was human nature to need them.

Ellie stood in front of her. 'Do I look OK, Mum?'

She heard the tremor in her daughter's voice. 'You look fabulous, love. Just fabulous.'

'You'd say that anyway.'

Marisa smiled. She couldn't win.

'Where's Isla?'

'She's outside, no doubt boasting to Morag about you two meeting the Kill Kestrels.' That brought a smile to her face.

'Yeah, she's quite right too, Mum. It is cool. This is the coolest thing I'll ever get to do.'

She gently propelled her daughter out of the front door and locked it behind her. 'I very much doubt that, Ellie, you're only nineteen.'

'But I'm not smart like Lachlan.'

Lachlan Grieves again. Ellie was constantly comparing herself to her cousin who was studying medicine at Edinburgh University and had just won an award for sportsman of his year at the rugby club. Handsome, intelligent and athletic, Lachlan too was without a father, but for a very different reason.

'You've a whole life ahead of you to do cool and smart stuff.'

'You didn't, Mum. You hate your job.'

'Yes, and it pays the bills, but your father did a lot of cool things and you're his daughter. You'll be fine.'

In the car, she listened to them rehearse their questions. They were each allowed to ask the band up to four each. The girls and their friends had gone over which ones would be best. They were to be with the band for thirty-five minutes, including time for photographs. The letter had described the Kill Kestrels as being on a very tight schedule.

'I've got to ask Josh about "Death of an Angel".'

'I think it's about an ex-girlfriend.'

'I know, but it might upset him.'

'And we need to ask Skye about "My Desire For You". "And it was the best that ever was . . . the best that's ever been . . ." It must be about someone he loved and lost.'

'I can't wait.'

'I'm so nervous.'

Ten minutes later, Marisa pulled up at a red light. They were still debating. 'What if she's not an ex and what if she's there?' she asked.

'OMG, no, do not say that, Mum. None of them are dating. It said so on the website. They're all too committed to their music.'

'And to their fans, they said so, Mrs Adamson.' Isla was adamant. 'They would say if they had girlfriends or wives.'

'Skye would never lie to his fans.'

'No, Josh said the same, said his fans were the most important thing in his life.'

'Yeah. Mum, don't ruin it.'

'Sorry.' Marisa kept her own counsel. She knew that everything released about the band had probably gone through their manager or most likely a PR person, but she wasn't going to spoil it. This was Ellie and Isla's big day.

She waited for the light to change, saw a poster of the group on the bus in front of her. She studied the photograph. Josh Alden looked like he had anger issues; there was darkness in his smile, but the lead singer Skye Cooper's eyes were the coldest. Handsome as he was, Marisa couldn't help but be uneasy about his expression; there was something beyond the pretty-boy look. Something sinister. She shook herself, she was fantasising. They were just four boys in a band. Good luck to them. She'd drop the girls off, they'd have their time with the band and no doubt both girls would dine out on the experience for years. The light turned amber, then green, and Marisa drove on. She was looking forward to hooking up with her sister, Maggie, later for a drink. Knew that Maggie was beside herself with pride because of her son's award.

Chapter Seventeen

The Unknown Son

Across town, in her flat in Hillhead, Maggie Grieves pulled out her ironing board and hauled the plastic wash basket full of clean laundry out from the cupboard. She toyed with the idea of texting her sister Marisa who was ferrying her daughter Ellie and a pal to meet the Kill Kestrels, but she resisted. Marisa would have enough on her plate. Besides, they were meeting up later, she'd hear all about it then. She switched on the television and made a start on the ironing. The news report cut to a breaking scandal. Hugo Ponsensby-Edward, MP, the son of Mark Ponsensby-Edward, QC, had called for the resignation of Nathan Whatley, MP, who had been caught with a rent boy. At the sight of Hugo, her stomach soured. Her mobile rang, and the screen saver illuminated Lachlan's photograph, which was apt, seeing as the call was from her son.

'Lach, how are things?'

'Just giving you the heads-up to keep the fifth of September free. It's the rugby club do.'

'You getting the award then?'

'Yeah.'

'I am so proud of you. We all are. Auntie Marisa was just saying that—'

'Gotta go, Mum.'

'Love you.'

'Yeah. Keep the day free?'

'Will do.'

'And Auntie Marisa and Ellie too, there are extra tickets.'

'Will do,' she repeated. 'Love you.' Two little words. Love. You.

The line went dead before she could say, *Well done, love, congratulations on winning*.

She watched Hugo Ponsensby-Edward on screen. Hugo had been at Glasgow University when her son had been conceived. The man shared Lachlan's DNA but she would never refer to him as his father. Since then, she had studiously kept them apart. Lachlan's teachers at school had pressed him to apply to Glasgow University but she had persuaded him to go to Edinburgh. She thought of the night he was conceived. She'd been drinking with friends at a student bar close to the university. Hugo Ponsensby-Edward and his friends were at the next table. Even then she had known that his lines were well rehearsed, that he was high on drugs. Also where her flirting would lead. She hadn't fooled herself, she heard the public school accent, knew the encounter for what it was. For her, a casual hook-up, for him downmarket sex. Back at her bedsit, things had escalated quickly. He'd assured her that he'd stop if she felt uncomfortable, but then his hand was tight around her throat. She'd passed out. When she came around it was over. 'I feared that you wanted it to stop but too little, too late, eh? What did

<hr/>

119

you expect when you give a man the come-on?' And then the practised smile, the hand that swept through his hair, the boyish glance. All bravado. 'You're not going to tell anyone about this. Understand?'

She watched Hugo on the television, his wife and children flanking him. 'I stand firmly for family values, which is why, given the emerging scandal, I call on Nathan Whatley to resign after his despicable behaviour . . . I stand for what is right and moral and good . . . I am proud of my family values and of my faith. They underpin my every ethos and always have done. They bring an inner strength with which to lead . . . Nathan Whatley must stand down. It is a difficult decision but sometimes we have to be strong and make difficult decisions . . . I believe that as a strong upholder of family values, I am uniquely qualified to demand that Nathan Whatley resign with immediate effect.'

She'd been told that she could never have children. Had no idea that she was even pregnant.

Lachlan had been 8 lb 5 oz when he was born.

Hugo smiled into the camera, swept his hair back with his hand. A boyish gesture.

She felt her hand tight on the iron.

Her son Lachlan, six foot two. Hugo, six one. Same hair, same eyes. Same mannerisms. Identical, some might say, had they been looking, had they known where to look. A young student in Edinburgh, a married politician in London. Too disparate. She turned the sheet, folded it, pressed hard on the iron. Separate was how she was going to keep them. Hugo smiled into the camera. 'I am here to give you my word that— '

She flicked to another channel.

'And the two gang members who died, Davie Ward and Chris Wood . . .'

The newsreader had used an abbreviated form of their names. Touching intimacy, how they would have been known to their family and friends. Not David and Christopher, but Davie and Chris. She ironed a pillowcase, a small domestic warmth, a triumph over the chaos out there in the world. Davie and Chris, two boys who'd taken a wrong turning somewhere in their lives. It could have been Lachlan. It couldn't have been Lachlan. She would have done anything for it not be Lachlan. Sold the house. Moved countries. Whatever it took. She would have done it. The mother of Davie was crying, her eyes had the lost look, as if they couldn't find a focus; grief had blindsided her and she was quietly imploding. She pleaded for an end to the violence. 'Two boys dead,' she repeated, 'two dead and for what?'

Maggie reminded herself that her world hadn't been torn apart by violence. Lachlan was at university, right now he was on holiday, travelling with a group of friends through Italy. Facebook pictures of Milan, Lake Como and Venice had made her want to visit the country again. She had loved backpacking when she was a student, had loved Rome, Florence and Venice. Knew Lachlan would also be going to Sicily. She'd never made it there. It would be fantastic for him, and she wished him nothing but love and happiness. She pictured the way he pushed his hair back with his hand. The boyish glance. She thought of the man she never wanted him to meet.

Chapter Eighteen

The Graveyard

'Christ, we're running out of time, can't you just fucking floor it?'

'I'm doing my best, sir. I can't speed in a built-up area. I'm sure you realise that.'

They were stuck at another red light. Josh glanced at his watch – if they didn't move it, he'd be late for the photo op. 'Fucking useless.'

Eventually, they pulled up outside the shop and he bolted inside. Thankfully, the place was empty and there was no flicker of recognition from the middle-aged assistant. 'I need some flowers. Fast.'

'I have some already made, or I could make up a bunch for you?'

'Fast.'

She led him to a shelf of bouquets. 'These are in cellophane and water and are in gift bags already, so the recipient doesn't need to bother with vases or food.' She turned to him. 'Did you have any particular blooms in mind?'

'No.'

'Are they a gift?'

Josh ignored her, looked at the display, recognised roses, of course, and chrysanthemums, but fuck all else. He grabbed the largest bunch. The flowers were predominantly pink, Amber's favourite colour. 'These are fine.'

The woman took him to the counter, rang up the sale. 'Oh these are lovely, aren't they? You've got roses, the double flowering lisianthus, stocks, statice, alstroemeria and freesia. It's a beautiful bouquet, don't you think?'

'How much?'

'Forty-eight pounds, sixty-five.'

He paid in cash. The flowers gave off a heady perfume and, outside, he dropped them into the boot of the car.

'Where to now?' The driver's usually friendly tone had moved down a notch.

'Mosspark Boulevard.' Josh settled into the back seat. From behind the darkened windows, he watched two young women wearing Kill Kestrels T-shirts walk past. He smiled, money in the bank. Twenty minutes later, the car turned on to Paisley Road West and then into Mosspark Boulevard. They carried on through the wrought-iron gates and on to the back of the cemetery. 'Just here's fine.' Josh grabbed the bouquet from the boot of the car.

The place was deserted, the graves he passed were well tended; there were plots with fresh flowers, others with small teddy bears resting on the headstone and some festooned with balloons. As if death was a celebration. On another, a heart-shaped wreath rested on the soil. Reminders to the living maybe because the dead were already too long gone. He knew it was stupid but he'd done the same when buying the flowers. Finally, he reached the plot. The gravestone was a sleeping cherub carved into marble, its face resting on the stone.

> Sleep with the Angels
> Amber Ellen Ellis
> Born 20 March 1986
> Died 3 September 1994
> Rest in Peace

He hoped his sister was resting in peace, because she hadn't had any fucking peace when she'd been alive. When Josh was eight and Amber six, their mother's latest druggie boyfriend Mikey had finally had enough. After he left, their alcoholic mother had decided that booze and drugs were her two best friends and had gone with any-one who might provide them. The night she'd died, hunger had driven him and his sister out of the house. He'd walked on ahead, had seen the orange glow from the street lights above him. It had calmed him and he'd found comfort enough that he'd taken Amber's hand and told her stories while they walked. A police car had slowed to a stop and they had been picked up and taken back. The policemen had found his mother's body; they wouldn't let them go back into the house. They were quickly taken to an emergency foster home. Social services had become involved. The following day, they were told their mother was dead, her vodka had been contaminated with a clean-ing chemical. She must have been drunk and disorientated. There was no one else in the house at the time.

Later, a court decided that it was in their best interest to be fostered. And so it had begun, moving from placement to placement, both unable to settle. He had remained quiet, angry and withdrawn, but Amber had suffered from night terrors which left her exhausted. She had tantrums, lashing out and biting and swearing. She developed faecal incontinence and none of the strategies offered by the foster carers could change her behaviour. Then they were placed with Susan Moody.

'But that didn't work out for us, did it. Amber?' He spoke to the gravestone. 'That was the worst fucking thing that happened.' He put the flowers on the dirt. 'The shop assistant told me the name of these but I can't remember them; you've got roses and some other shit. At least they're your favourite colour.'

Above him, gulls, which had flown in from the River Clyde, cried and shrieked. He closed his eyes and tried to remember being ten years old and living in Susan Moody's house. He recalled the smell of fried food, the greasy square sausage for Sunday breakfast, the smell of boiled potatoes, cabbage and mince at dinner time. He often tried to remember the night Amber died, but the elusive images were nothing more than a shattered mirror, unreliable shards lacking cohesion.

The night of the fire, he had been sleeping fitfully, dozing on and off, and had woken to hear two unfamiliar voices, a woman and a man, shouting. Had he gone back to sleep? Were the voices part of the dream? Was Susan Moody right? His memory slid, as it always did, away from that night, to take refuge elsewhere. The white cat that belonged to a neighbour, a dog barking in a garden across the road. The fragments returned, splinters that haunted and teased him. Violence. Anger. Threat. The smell of smoke. A scream. Silence. Then nothing. The image he needed refused to reveal itself.

Josh felt the familiar anger rise, and he cursed the sunlight and the gulls which circled above him. Finally, he consoled himself with the fact that he had found a way forward, that progress might be slow, but it was progress. He turned back towards the car, took a minute to compose himself, to distance himself from the angry and troubled Joshua Alden who grew up in care. Took time to re-establish Josh Alden, founding member of the Kill Kestrels, one of Scotland's most successful indie bands. He took a pair of reflective aviator sunglasses from his pocket and slipped them on. 'Ready to go,' he said to the empty graveyard. A few seconds later, he opened the door of the Range Rover, spoke to the driver – 'The Golden Unicorn.' He would work on his memory of that night later on. For now, though, he needed to get his shit together. As the car pulled out of the cemetery and joined the line of traffic, Josh spoke aloud, 'We're rolling.'

Chapter Nineteen

The Cousin

Beth Swinton lived in a blond sandstone building in Queen's Drive, Southside. Wheeler pulled up outside the flat.

The FLO was waiting for them. Wheeler recognised Helen Downie, wondered if she was going to be at least civil. 'Morning, Helen.'

The FLO ignored her, turned to Ross. 'Morning, DI Ross. All set?'

'As always.'

'Good to see you again, Ross.' The FLO kept her back to Wheeler.

Wheeler rang the bell. Waited. Turned to looked into Queen's Park. It was busy with families having picnics, people sunbathing, others jogging or walking their dogs. Just like in Kelvingrove Park that morning, Glaswegians out enjoying the sunshine and warmth of the day. She knew the area where the gang fight had taken place was on the other side of the park and was still sealed off. She thought of the two dead gang members and Karlie Merrick, three bodies lying on cool slabs in the dark of the mortuary.

'The park looks mobbed,' said Ross.

'At least it's getting used in a good way, not with raging gang fights,' said the FLO. 'Folk out and about on a lovely sunny day and here's you and me, Ross, being the harbingers of doom and gloom.'

Wheeler said nothing.

The door was opened by a small woman in her mid-fifties. Her black hair was cut into a severe bob and she wore a blue artist's smock. In her hands she held a red and white striped tea towel.

'Beth Swinton?' asked Wheeler.

'Yes.' Caution in her tone.

'We're police. I'm DI Wheeler, this is DI Ross.'

The FLO's voice was soft. 'I'm Helen Downie, Ms Swinton. We'd like to come in for a word.'

Wheeler saw apprehension slide over Beth Swinton's face as she stood back. They followed her through a vast hallway and on through to the living room. One wall was covered with paintings similar to the one Wheeler had seen on Maureen Anderson's phone. The female figures all had large, troubled eyes. None of them was smiling.

Beth stood in the middle of the living room and twisted the tea towel between her fingers.

The FLO moved towards her. 'Would you like to sit down?'

Beth gave a tiny shake of her head.

'I understand you're related to Karlie Merrick?' asked Wheeler.

'Karlie? Yes, we're cousins, well first cousins once removed to be accurate. Karlie's the daughter of my cousin Mary.' She paused. 'There are very few reasons for police to come to my door and ask me to take a seat. Something's happened to her, hasn't it?'

'A woman's body was found this morning in the East End which matches Karlie's description,' said Wheeler. She heard Beth's sharp intake of breath, saw her pallor fade.

The FLO crossed the room. 'Have a sit down.' She led Beth to the sofa.

Wheeler and Ross sat opposite.

'I saw on the news that a body was found. I can't believe it's Karlie.'

'Do you know why she might have been in the Sandyhills area?'

'I've no idea, but then I haven't seen Karlie in years. I'm afraid we never got on well.'

'Then perhaps you could tell me a little about her? Just in general terms, it would really help to build up a picture of who she was,' said Wheeler.

Beth's voice was soft. 'Well, her background was quite distressing. My cousin Mary married John Merrick and they had Karlie. Mary passed away when Karlie was very young. It was an awful shock. Mary had a lot of, well—' she glanced at Ross '—female problems and finally went in for a hysterectomy. After surgery, she contracted MRSA, there was a lot of it about then, she never recovered. Then, a few years later, John was murdered. I mean,' Beth beseeched Wheeler, 'how much tragedy can one family take? And now this? The whole family gone.'

Wheeler sat forward. 'Karlie's father was murdered?'

Beth continued to wring the tea towel through her fingers. 'Battered to death in his own home. Karlie was about eight, so twenty years ago. No one was ever charged, but then things changed during the investigation. I'm not sure . . . the will to find the killer was . . . well, the police had other cases, other priorities. They searched John's house and found . . .' Her voice trailed off.

Wheeler waited while the woman got lost in her memories.

'They found a collection of porn, some of it related to teenage girls—' Beth swallowed '—underage girls. It was very distressing. And, of course, there was no one to look after Karlie. She was supposed to go into care and then eventually be fostered. I don't know if, on reflection, she would have preferred that. It may have worked out better for her. But I offered to take her. I had a job and this flat and I thought we could make a go of it, but I made a bit of a dog's dinner of it, I'm afraid. I was in shock. John had been murdered, then his cache of filth uncovered, revolting given an eight-year-old was in the house. You can imagine the rumours; people believed he had, well that he had . . .' Her voice trailed off.

The FLO quietly sat down beside Beth.

'And were other agencies involved with Karlie?' asked Wheeler.

'Initially, a psychiatrist, then later a couple of child psychologists. Karlie said nothing, refused to even speak to them. They asked me, but I'd barely known the man. She was physically examined by a doctor and she hadn't been . . . you know.'

'And the last time you talked to Karlie?' asked Wheeler.

'It was over a year ago. We had an argument. I wanted her to stop obsessing about her father's death. I lost my temper and shouted at her, told her to live in the present. It was awful for her to lose her parents and I knew that her dad's murder was a nightmare for her, but I wanted her to live her life. To try to be happy. She got annoyed with me and slammed down the phone. We can both sulk for Scotland, I'm afraid.' Beth blew into the tissue. 'But then in March, I texted her about the new exhibition at the CCA. I thought we might have a coffee. Maybe build some bridges. She never replied. Later, I sent her a box of her father's belongings, just old photographs I found at the back of a cupboard. I think I might have more in the attic. But again, no reply.'

'What was it about her dad's death that she wanted to explore?' asked Wheeler.

'Karlie was very ambitious. Like a lot of young people today, she wanted to be famous. She wanted to star, her word, in a true-life re-enactment of her dad's murder. She had an idea that it would be her road to fame, that she'd get other acting roles. She told me that she was an actress and I quizzed her, then she mentioned glamour and I knew without her having to tell me directly that she was doing seedy work. Mary would have been horrified. Perhaps it's better that she died when she did.' Beth cleared her throat. 'Anyway, Karlie wanted to walk a film crew through the house where John's body had been found and then she'd take them outside into the surrounding area. I thought it was macabre; to have lived through it once was traumatic enough but to actually want to take part in a re-enactment was just too grisly for me. I asked her if she intended to include the images the police found? I was very honest with her.' Her voice dropped to a whisper. 'I regret that now. Perhaps I could have been kinder.'

'I know it was a while ago but when you last spoke, did

131

she ever mention that she was scared or that someone had threatened her?'

'No. My God, it's awful.'

'A friend of Karlie's told us that she tried to contact a member of a band, the Kill Kestrels?'

'Never heard of them.'

'Did she ever mention someone called Gary?'

'Not that I recall.'

'He's a wedding photographer – she did some work for him?'

'No, she didn't tell me much at all.'

'What about boyfriends, did she have a boyfriend or any friends that you could tell us about?'

Beth sighed. 'She was very attractive physically, she took after Mary in that way, but she never mentioned boys or asked about sex. If I had to name it, I'd say Karlie was asexual, but then she only lived with me until she was sixteen. She found both me and my home stifling and I thought her too demanding. We were both relieved when she moved out. She was very wilful and needed to create chaos, whereas I need calm to function well and for my work.'

'Chaos?' asked Wheeler.

'It's not that her father hadn't left her money, it's just that there was a grasping quality to her.' The shock hit Beth and she began to tremble.

The FLO quickly went through into the bedroom and brought back a blanket. 'Put this around you.'

Beth breathed deeply before she continued. 'Karlie loved attention. It started when she was still quite young. She went through phases of lying, and would lie to me about the tiniest little thing, even when it was obvious.

For example, she'd finish the last biscuit from the tin and then say she hadn't. It didn't make sense. I mean she wouldn't have got into trouble, she just needed to tell me so that I could buy more biscuits. But she would always lie. Even at school. At the time, I put it down to the trauma. Her father's case had been tainted because of those images the police found and every now and again we'd get nasty calls from perverts. But for Karlie, it was like a circus, it was as if fantasy was more exciting than everyday life. In the fourth year at school, she concocted this whole story that she was being bullied and taunted about her father's death. She accused a group of girls from her class. There was a huge investigation by the head teacher and the girls were interviewed and eventually it escalated and their parents were summoned to the school. Karlie was in pieces and went to the doctor, who suggested anti-anxiety pills, but she told him she wanted to "tough it out". She went back into school and was allowed to change class and the girls were all made to apologise to her. One girl refused; she stuck to her guns, said it didn't happen. She was suspended for a bit and then she transferred to another school. I heard later that she'd taken an overdose. The poor girl died.

'A few weeks later, Karlie and I were watching television and she calmly told me that she'd made it all up, said that she'd wanted to be the centre of attention, that creating that situation had made her feel special. Told me that she'd felt like a star and had created an audience. Well, of course, I had to go back to the head teacher and explain everything and Karlie was asked to go in and give her version of events. But she didn't go back, she dropped out of school. The head teacher was devastated about the girl who overdosed. The whole situation was an absolute mess.' Beth wound the corner of the tea towel around her forefinger. 'This is a horrible thing to say, but around that time I had a big exhibition and I was very busy, there were interviews to be done and the *Chronicle* had devoted two pages to my work. Just when I was getting some serious attention, Karlie kicked off.' Beth sighed. 'I can't believe this is happening. There are monsters out there. All Karlie wanted was to be famous, for people to know who she was, and now this.'

She's got her wish, thought Wheeler.

Beth looked at Wheeler, blinked hard before asking, 'Will you need the body identified?'

'Yes.'

'It's the least I can do for her.' Beth wiped tears from her cheeks before repeating, 'The least I can do.'

'Is there anyone you'd like me to call?' the FLO offered.

'No, no one.'

'Anything I can get you?'

'A glass of water would be helpful, thank you.'

When the FLO had left the room, Beth turned to Wheeler. 'I don't know how you can do this work. How can you face it every day?'

'It's my job,' said Wheeler quietly.

'I suppose I need to start thinking about the funeral.'

'Because of the nature of Karlie's death,' said the FLO, returning with the water, 'I'm afraid there will have to be a post-mortem.'

'Then I'll arrange it for afterwards.'

'That might not be possible, just yet. There might be a second PM at some point in the future. If the case goes to trial, the defence have the right to their own PM.'

'Let me get this straight. Karlie was murdered and her body won't be released for burial until you find whoever did it, make a case against them and charge them?'

Wheeler heard the anger in Beth's voice.

'This is some kind of nonsense, surely? And all this delay to accommodate the person who murdered her? I take it there will be no need for another one if whoever you charge admits to the murder? I mean sometimes they do confess, don't they?'

'Yes,' said the FLO, 'sometimes they do confess.'

'I don't remember this happening when John died. I could be wrong, but I don't remember any delay at all. Maybe I'm confused, maybe my memory isn't right?'

'There's nothing wrong with your memory. Defence post-mortems came in recently,' said the FLO. 'They're a comparatively new consideration, so it's something we're all getting used to, including the police.'

'I don't think they sound like a good thing.' Beth picked savagely at the threads in the tea towel. 'How can carving her body up for a second time be anything other than disrespectful? Karlie's been murdered and then a post-mortem violates her again. And then later, another one? I mean, I watch crime movies on the television and the post-mortems look very invasive. Parts have to be removed and then, oh my goodness, it seems so gruesome. Just the idea of it makes me feel sick.'

Wheeler stood. 'We need to be getting back to the station. If you can think of anything else that might be helpful, please get in touch.' She offered Beth her card, watched her accept it with a trembling hand.

Outside, Ross breathed deeply. 'God, but that was claustrophobic, wasn't it? She was really going into tunnel

135

vision about the PMs, I felt queasy just listening to her.'

'The mum dies, the dad's murdered, then underage porn is found. Later, his daughter goes into the same profession. What the hell was going on in that family?' Wheeler headed for the car.

'Abuse? But Karlie was seen by a psychiatrist and psychologists. And was examined physically. Beth seemed to rule it out.'

'Families are often in denial. Your take on Beth Swinton?'

'They obviously didn't get on and I think she regrets it now, but—'

'But?'

'Karlie sounds as if she was hard work.'

'Both parents dead,' said Wheeler. 'How do you even begin to process that at such a young age?'

They reached the car.

'You and Helen Downie not talking?' said Ross.

Wheeler shrugged. 'Breakdown in communication.' No point in going into detail. She'd had a one-night stand with Helen's ex-husband Jamie. At least Jamie had told her they'd separated. Turned out Helen thought they'd been on a trial separation to work through their issues. As far as she was concerned, they were still very much married. The one and only text Helen sent her was three words.

WHORE. BITCH. SLUT.

'Fancy coffee and a sandwich?' said Ross.

'You're hungry after hearing all that? Have you got worms?'

Five minutes later, they settled at a table in a café, ordered and continued their discussion.

'I'm positive the two deaths are related,' said Wheeler.

'It's a hell of a coincidence that two members of the same family were murdered, outside of a crime clan.'

The waitress brought their order, and they waited until she had gone before continuing.

'Why was Karlie Merrick dumped in the Sandyhills area? A meaningful place for her?' asked Wheeler.

'Or a meaningful place for her killer?' said Ross. 'Or just a fucking quiet, convenient spot to dump a body?' He sipped his coffee. 'Do you remember John Merrick's murder? It must have been in the papers.'

'Not offhand. Twenty years ago, I had no idea I'd even be in the police force. I was thinking of the army. What about you?'

'My parents' relationship was beginning to implode. I was considering the police force, but primarily I just wanted to get away from their constant arguments, home had become a battleground. It wasn't a great time.'

Wheeler thought of the tensions in her own family. She heard the bitterness in Ross's tone when he mentioned his parents, and thought about the animosity that had existed between Beth Swinton and Karlie Merrick, of John Merrick who'd collected underage porn when he had an eight-year-old in the house. 'Fucking families,' she muttered before starting on her sandwich.

Chapter Twenty

The Photo Shoot

The Kill Kestrels, Dougie thought to himself as he entered the hotel, were just like a family, albeit a dysfunctional one.

The Golden Unicorn was a small, luxury boutique hotel located at the corner of Byres Road and Great Western Road. Stationed at the entrance were two liveried doormen waiting to assist guests with the opening of doors, parking, directions and anything else with which they might struggle. Inside the foyer, four crystal chandeliers glittered and the reflected light from them danced across the polished wooden floor.

Dougie approached reception and waited in line, glanced at the etching that hung behind the desk. Steven Campbell's, 'Natural Follies at Bee Junction'. In it, a bearded figure stood in front of a tent, another lay on the ground, close by a beehive and a swarm of bees. The image of the insects made Dougie itchy, and he scratched absent-mindedly at his cheek. He thought of the meaning of the word 'folly', a stupid act, an act which would have a costly outcome. Christ, he hoped it wasn't a portent of what was to come with the Kill Kestrels. He waited behind a guest who was checking in, heard the accent, the tone of entitlement. Dougie would have booked the Unicorn for the band but for a few reasons. One, they couldn't afford the whole place. Two, he couldn't guarantee the absolute discretion of the staff in the way he could at the Braque. Although he knew the manager, Harry Franklin, from way back in the day, the hotel had only been open a year and had yet to prove its worth regarding the privacy of its guests. But for a photo shoot, it was perfect. Even the press boys couldn't complain about the location or the bar – the hotel had a designated cocktail lounge filled with drinks named after the musical heroes of the resident mixologist.

Finally, it was his turn.

The receptionist's smile was purely professional. 'How may I help?'

'Dougie Scott.'

'Yes, sir, your party is in the Long Hall.'

'Cheers.' He listened to directions, made his way towards the Hall and was immediately put at ease. The walls of the corridor were filled with framed black and white photographs of the band. He reached the Hall and was similarly impressed – whoever had staged the room clearly really got the Kill Kestrels and what they were about. Their latest album was playing and Skye's voice soared around the room. Dougie heard Josh on bass, Joe on keyboard and then finally Lexi's drum kick in. It was just loud enough to have the rock and roll vibe without causing his ears to bleed.

A waiter appeared carrying a tray. Buck's Fizz. Dougie took one. He hated the tiny glasses. Granted, he knew the shape was something to do with preserving the bubbles, but he found they held such a small amount of alcohol that by the time he was halfway around the photography display, he was on his second glass. Without having eaten anything, the alcohol went straight into his system. Not necessarily a bad thing. He felt the tension leave him, but reminded himself to slow down. He walked around the room, admiring the photographs, pleased they had used the ones he'd sent over. Paulo Di Stefano's shots were the best he'd ever seen of the band. Di Stefano was obviously heavily influenced by Anton Corbijn's black and white photographs of the Stones, Springsteen and Morrissey amongst others. Dougie studied the images – Skye looked moody and sensitive, Josh earnest and engrossed. Dougie wondered about the guy who'd appeared at the hotel the previous evening, Cutter Wysor. He didn't like the man's vibe at all, but whatever shit Josh was up to, he wasn't sharing it with his manager. He glanced at photographs of Lexi and Joe. Di Stefano had added a hard edge to their portraits. No need to add hardness to either Josh or Skye's portraits – they already had it. All to the good, thought Dougie, as he felt the reverberation from Josh's bass thunder around the room. He passed a console table with newspapers and glossy magazines, glanced at the headlines – a gang fight had left two dead. There were pictures of the two boys, Davie Ward and Chris Wood. They looked like wasters, their gaunt faces and haunted expressions screamed drugs to him. Dougie kept moving, and his thoughts returned once again to the longevity of the band. Last night's scrap was nothing compared to some of their full-blown arguments, but he could see a pattern emerging that he had to squash; the soul of the band was decaying and he couldn't let that happen. He thought of recent break-ups by mega-stars in the US. There seemed to be a reluctance to admit the truth and instead to dress it up in some kind of denial, calling it extended sabbaticals, instead of what they were, fucking split-ups.

A man in his thirties with dark curly hair and a tailored grey suit came into the room and made towards him. Harry Franklin. Dougie offered his hand. 'How goes it, my friend?'

'It's all good, Dougie, the press guys are upstairs in the bar having drinks. Are we just doing the photo shoot and a quick meet and greet with the two girls?'

'Yep, Ellie something and her pal Isla. And Paulo Di Stefano, the guy who did these photographs, is coming to take some shots for the next album cover.'

'What's next?'

'The O2 Academy on Saturday night.'

'How many does a place like that hold?'

'Give or take, two and a half thousand. The next step up is the SSE Hydro. This time next year, I want the Kill Kestrels to be there. Holds a smidge over the ten thousand mark. I think the boys can do it.'

'I'm impressed.'

'It is actually achievable, Harry, if they manage not to fall out big time. The band could conceivably hit this trajectory and then, after it, well, maybe we could crack America? Every other successful band in the world knows the score, knows that it's a business. But me? I'm fighting against the rhetoric of "you don't treat my family of fans like you're trying to make a profit out of them". I think one of them has had too much fucking liberal socialism in their childhood and not enough reality.'

'You didn't manage to talk them all round to the VIP arrangement then?'

'I told Lexi it would create a very memorable day for the fans. Not just these two lassies who won the tickets. I really tried to sell it, but would he have it? Would he shite.'

'But everyone has a VIP package for their shows, from early entrance, to signed merchandise, to meeting the band, a complete smorgasbord of the stuff.'

'It's normal currency. What Lexi forgets is that the Kill Kestrels are a product, that the band is together purely to make money, and if they want to go global and reach out to an international fan base, then he's got to at least start playing the game.' Dougie finished his drink, reached for another.

'Rant over?' asked Harry.

'Sorry, but I know that riding high doesn't always last. The screaming girls who love you today have moved on by tomorrow. When groups are on the up, they mistakenly think that it's a one-way street. It's not. I've been at this gig long enough to recognise the key points, when to cash in and take the money and when to soldier on. I've had other groups with this same attitude as the Kill Kestrels and they've lived to regret it, namely the Grimsdales and Stations of the Cross. They valued their integrity over making a buck.'

'How'd that go for them?'

'They got new management then parted company with their labels. Fast-forward a year and they're still not signed, so they sacked the new guys. The last I heard, they were playing pubs for beer money.' Dougie let out a shrill bark of a laugh. 'But at least they still have their fucking integrity.'

Harry steered the conversation back to business. 'Is the room OK?'

'The room looks great. Cheers for doing it. I love the photographs and the soundtrack is perfect.'

'I got my girlfriend, Adrianna, to do it. She's a big Kill Kestrels fan.'

'You got the complimentary tickets for the gig?'

'Yes.' He made for the door.

'One last thing, mate,' said Dougie, 'I thought we'd ordered food?'

'You did, a buffet to be served when your guests arrive.' Harry checked his watch. 'But they're not due for another half-hour.'

'I thought that there might be a sandwich or something laid out a bit earlier?' said Dougie. 'Only I'm peckish, haven't eaten yet. And this—' he raised his glass '—is going straight to an empty stomach.'

'You want the usual?'

'I'd appreciate anything.' Dougie sipped his Buck's Fizz.

Harry returned a few minutes later carrying a platter with a selection of mini pies – macaroni, cheese and onion and traditional mince. 'I've included a bowl of complimentary fries. You think this will see you through until your guests arrive?'

Dougie reached for a mince pie. 'Breakfast's the most important meal of the day. Cheers, Harry.'

He'd just finished the last pie when his mobile rang – the girls were waiting at reception.

He met them in the foyer. 'I'm Dougie Scott, the Kill Kestrels' manager.'

'I'm just dropping these two off, I'm Ellie's mum. This

is Ellie and her friend, Isla. They've suddenly come over all shy.'

Dougie waved her away. 'Come away in, girls. No need to be shy. Skye and the rest of the boys are upstairs.'

For the next half an hour he made sure the band made a fuss of the two girls and that the drinks kept coming. The band dutifully posed for pictures and answered questions. When asked about their lyrics, both Skye and Josh had been creative with the truth. Dougie had already warned them, 'Wee lassies need to think it's all about love and heartbreak.'

Dougie watched the girls blush, saw Skye drape a casual arm around Ellie. Saw her blush deepen. Saw Isla capture it all on her mobile. Then they swapped places.

Then it was Skye taking Ellie off to the side while Isla was busy chatting to Josh. Dougie watched Skye expertly manoeuvre the tipsy girl through the door and into the corridor. Heard a text come through – Di Stefano was at reception.

Dougie went into the corridor. Empty. Two signs: turn right for the conference room, left for private dining. Dougie took a sharp left, shoved open the door. The noise stopped Skye from going any further. Again, thought Dougie. Fucking again. *Keep it in your fucking pants.* 'Time out, you guys. Skye, the photographer's here.'

Ten minutes later, the girls had been dispatched home in a taxi and Di Stefano had suggested an outdoor shot.

'The roof garden?' Skye's words were beginning to slur.

Dougie led the way. 'Maybe some fresh air will do us all good.' He knew that through Di Stefano's filter the sunny day would be transformed into a series of shadows and the creases on the faces of the four band members

144

would be emphasised. He heard Skye talking to the photographer.

'Why portraits?' Skye asked, as they made their way up the stairs.

'I started out doing landscapes as a hobby, then I did a degree in psychology and got into portrait photography. A photograph of a landscape represents the real world, but for me portraiture is more complex. Sure, a good representation of a landscape is interesting and I knew how to grab the viewer's attention, but to be really successful, I want to shoot people, to be able to show something of the true identity of the soul of the person.'

'Their soul?'

'Yes, if I can capture some of their spirit or their soul then the photograph transcends its medium in a way and becomes more than just a photographic representation. It captures the essence of the person.'

'And makes them immortal? Never ageing, never changing? Make me immortal,' Skye demanded, as he raised his arms and ran around the roof garden like some demented windmill. Di Stefano began snapping. Dougie watched Skye turn on the charm. Skye smiling, kohl-rimmed eyes glassy. Dangerous, sexy, bad-boy Skye, giddy with fame, quickened the momentum, running and pouting and posing. Dougie watched. Too close to the edge, a hell of a drop on to a concrete pavement below, but Skye kept racing, dancing, posing in a world of his own.

'Fuck! Be careful!' Dougie grabbed him, ushered him roughly away from the edge. Probably secure enough but no point in taking any chances.

'Make me immortal, Paulo!' Skye repeated, as he raised

his arms, looked to the heavens, drank in the bright sunshine.

Dougie smiled thinly. The band were going to go stratospheric and Di Stefano's photographs would be part of the journey. The Kill Kestrels would be up there with the Stones and the Who. He watched the photographer capture the moment as Skye ran around the space as if it were a huge arena and he was the only one on stage.

Dougie settled into the photo shoot. After a few minutes, he saw Harry walk into the shot followed by a tall blonde woman and a dark-haired guy. They were both holding police ID. Dougie glanced at Skye, muttered under his breath, 'Fuck's sake, what now?'

He approached them, hand outstretched. 'I'm Dougie Scott, the manager. What's this about?'

'Dougie, the police are here to have a word with the band.' Harry glanced at Wheeler. 'Of course I'll ask my staff if they remember the dead woman being here, but, as I said, I'm sure they've all seen the news on the television and radio and would have come forward by now if they knew anything.'

Wheeler addressed Dougie. 'We believe that a woman who was murdered had recently contacted a member of the Kill Kestrels.'

'Go on.'

'I'm not sure who she emailed. As far as we know it was via the online forum.'

'The guys never see that,' said Dougie. 'I have a part-time assistant who does all the web stuff.'

'I think our victim was at school with one of the band, Langside Academy?' said Wheeler.

146

'Guys, any of you go to Langside Academy?' asked Dougie.

'I did, for a short while,' said Josh.

Wheeler held up a photograph.

'Never seen her before.'

'Her name's Karlie Merrick. She would've been two years behind you at school.'

'Oh, yeah, I heard about her,' said Josh. 'Didn't she lie about being bullied and got some kid kicked out of school? Then the kid OD'd?'

'Yes.'

'I'd left by then but I heard about it. Sounds like Karlie Merrick was a complete fucking brat.'

'She was murdered,' Wheeler reminded him.

'Still can't help you,' said Josh.

'And before you ask, Inspector, we were all together in our hotel last night, all night,' Dougie lied. 'I can vouch for all of my boys.'

Skye looked at the ground, said nothing.

Wheeler looked at Josh. 'And you're sure you never met her?'

'Positive. And we never even see the fan shit. It's all done in-house.

'Look, Inspector,' said Dougie, 'we're in the middle of a shoot. And time is money. Do you mind?'

Wheeler turned to go. 'They're all heart,' she muttered to Ross.

Chapter Twenty-One

The Mortuary

Beth Swinton sat in the waiting room and felt her mouth too dry to speak. Reminded herself that what she was about to do was merely duty. Told herself that there would be no surprise, that she would not be ambushed by shock, she already knew that it was Karlie. She told herself this over and over, as if the refrain might make it better. To her right, Maureen Anderson sat grey-faced and silent; to her left, the FLO, Helen, who had explained the process to her in sensitive, gentle tones. In the Scottish system, identification must be attended by two people, and the FLO had suggested that the process be done via a video link. 'No,' Beth had told her. 'This is the final time I shall actually see her. I want to say goodbye, properly. You told me yourself, there may be a long delay before she can be buried.'

The FLO had reluctantly agreed and explained some of what to expect. Beth had been surprised to learn that they wouldn't be alone at the mortuary, that others would be there, so many protocols, so many rules and instructions. She'd heard terms and abbreviations she'd never heard before. It felt like there was too much to remember. She looked around the room. It was cool and she could hear the air-conditioning unit hum quietly. She'd been grateful for the FLO's support, especially around the press. She replayed one of the conversations they'd had when Graham Reaper had called for the fourth consecutive time. The phone had been ringing constantly since Karlie's name had been released.

'How did they even get my number?'

'They would have been digging from the moment her name was released. It's what they do. DI Wheeler should have warned you this might happen. But remember, if you want me to deal with the press, I can take over. Reporters and journalists can be very persistent and, in some cases, invasive. And in the case of Graham Reaper, he can be completely tactless. This whole process, between myself and DIs Ross and Wheeler, is all about supporting you. I realise too that DI Wheeler isn't always the most sensitive person around bereavement. She can be a little abrupt.'

'Maybe. Just doing her job, I suppose.'

'If you did think she was a little too sharp, you can always offer a feedback comment. I'm happy to facilitate it for you.'

'I can't really remember much of what she said.'

'Have a think later on,' the FLO said smoothly. 'You tell me and I'll contact DCI Stewart. You know, sometimes it can be really helpful to get feedback, however negative it may sound. Makes them better cops in the long run. Kind of doing them a favour. And, of course, I'd have a very discreet word.'

Beth looked up as an attendant came into the room.

'We're ready now.' Her voice, soft, low. Respectful.

Beth stood, felt the sweat on her palms. Wanted for a split second to turn and walk away. To keep walking and to get as far away as possible from the horror of what she was confronting. She thought of earlier that morning, before the police had arrived, of how simple her life had been. She'd been thinking about her recent exhibition at the CCA, how well it had been received. Simple, happy thoughts. And now darkness and evil had bled into her life. An uncharitable thought about Karlie came into her mind. When things were going well for Beth, Karlie would kick off. Now this. The exhibition had been a triumph but Karlie had somehow stolen the show. Beth hated herself for thinking it.

She allowed herself to be led through to a room with a glass window. On the other side, the blind was drawn. The assistant left them. 'Are you sure you're ready?' asked Helen. Beth nodded, felt her heartbeat quicken. Watched while the blind was raised.

Karlie's eyes were closed and she looked at peace. As if she were only sleeping. A white sheet had been drawn over the body, and only her face was visible. 'Yes, it's her. That's Karlie.' Beth stared at the body, remembered going to the chapel of repose and viewing her cousin Mary's body. Karlie looked so like her mother. Beth's memory flashed back to John's funeral. Now there would be another gravestone to be engraved. Too many deaths, too much loss. She stared at Karlie's face, saw it morph into Mary's and then John's. Beth felt herself sway. She thought of how Karlie had wanted to be on the television, for her name to be known, for her to be famous. She had achieved in death the fame that had eluded her in life. Beth closed her eyes. A slide show of Karlie's life began as if it needed to exist in the final moments before her body disappeared: Karlie at secondary school, smiling slyly; Karlie casually throwing a brick at a duck in the pond in the park; Karlie leaving school at sixteen, triumphant and grinning. Beth shivered, felt the damp of sweat on her back, on her scalp. She felt faint. She opened her eyes in time to see Helen move towards her but she collapsed on to the cool of the floor. Then, welcome darkness.

Chapter Twenty-Two

The Reporter

Graham Reaper finished one story.

CARNAGE!

Fatal Gang Rampage Leaves Two Dead
and Four Fighting for their Lives

But the two losers were no longer on the front page; Reaper slotted them into third. Southside police had arrested two men in their twenties in connection with the deaths and there was an ongoing investigation into the other gang members. Nothing more he could do to sex it up. Instead, Reaper concentrated on the story for the first page.

After leaving Sandyhills that morning he'd returned to his office at the *Chronicle* and selected four photographs to run with the article: one of the police cordon, two of the SOCOs scouring the area and one of the mortuary van containing the body, being driven off, DIs Wheeler and Ross in the background. Readers needed to get a flavour of the crime scene and a few photographs hooked them in. Later, the cops had released a name – Karlie Merrick – but they'd been tight with any other information. No matter, he'd done his own digging and the updated headline was more specific. Then he'd added a strategically cropped shot of a naked Karlie Merrick on the front page, not clear nudity but enough to suggest that somewhere just out of shot she was starkers. A further trawl through the online archives had given him a rich seam to mine – the victim's father had also been murdered and some very dodgy porn discovered in his home. The story would run for a bit now it had legs. Now it had been sexed up. Reaper typed quickly.

BRUTAL SLAYING OF SULTRY PORN STARLET

The body of the twenty-eight-year-old porn star was discovered this morning by members of the public. The gruesome discover was made by four friends out for their morning run. Ms Merrick's body was found in a secluded area in Sandyhills Road and police have confirmed that they are treating her death as murder.

Detectives from Police Scotland are anxious to ascertain the final movements of the porn star. DCI Craig Stewart, from Carmyle Police Station, said: 'We are appealing to anyone who may have known Karlie Merrick, or who may have any information about her movements over the course of the past few days, to get in touch. It is extremely important that we trace her final movements. Did you know Karlie, or did you see someone acting suspiciously in the Sandyhills area of the city? Was there a car near the scene? Did you see or hear anything that might be helpful? If so, please contact us immediately.'

Reaper continued typing:

Sandyhills Road remains cordoned off while police search for further evidence. Police Scotland did not supply information about either Ms Merrick's injuries or reveal how she was killed.

DCI Stewart added, 'The area around where the body was discovered is particularly well used by runners and dog walkers, and the nearby sports field is well attended. There is also a golf course and a local pub nearby, both of which are often busy. I would urge everyone who was in the area yesterday to think back. Did you see anything at all that may help us? Any information, however small, may help us piece together Karlie Merrick's final hours.'

At the time of going to press, officers have also cordoned off the entrance to a flat in Glasgow Harbour Development.

Reaper added another picture of Karlie, pouting provocatively at the camera, and then continued typing:

A grisly twist in the tragedy is that Karlie Merrick's father was also murdered, twenty years previously. No one has ever been charged with his death.

Reaper finished the article and sat back in his chair. There was enough out there to sate interest in the Merrick story. He needn't add the detail about the father's porn stash until later. Drip-feed the readership the salacious detail. Keep them happy. Sex. It always sold.

He glanced again at the photographs of the two dead gang members, Davie Ward and Chris Wood. They looked like losers. They'd been killed in a stupid gang fight over what? Disputed territory, one of the gang had told him. Did they not realise the council owned all of the territory? It had fuck all to do with them and their petty, imaginary boundaries. Already the public was losing interest in them.

Reaper felt the tremor in his hand. Christ, he needed a pint. His divorce had come through that morning and he'd been on Tinder all last week. He was hooking up with a woman called Jacqui later. He checked his watch; they were due to meet at the Victoria Bar in the Bridgegate in an hour. If he left now, he could get in early, have a couple of pints beforehand. If she didn't work out, he could always call a halt early and cross over to the Scotia for a couple more. He wavered for a spilt second before he reached over and shut down his computer, grabbed his jacket, headed out.

Chapter Twenty-Three

Braveheart **Ducks**

The man stood at a safe distance from the red sandstone building and watched. Karlie Merrick's flat was on the second floor of Glasgow Harbour Development, situated on the banks of the River Clyde. He saw the police cars, the cordon. He'd watched the SOCOs and assorted personnel go in earlier and now the two detectives had arrived. The man knew that they would be combing the flat for his DNA. Perhaps they were looking for signs of forced entry? There were none. Karlie had opened the door to him just after midnight. He'd been casually dressed, gloved hands in pockets. All smiles. She'd turned back into the hallway. It wasn't until the last minute that she'd been aware of the belt. She hadn't had time to struggle. At only five foot four and certainly under a hundred pounds, it had been one of his easier tasks. Inside, the cops would find a sterile flat with pathetic images of the dead woman, lifeless ghosts haunting the place, unable to repeat what they saw that night, forced to stare mutely into eternity. The man turned away and began walking towards the city centre and the crowds and welcome anonymity.

Inside the flat, Wheeler and Ross found a modern, open-plan arrangement. In the living room, light from three full-height windows flooded the space. Professional photographs of Karlie lined the walls.

'She certainly had enough images of herself,' said Ross.

'There's no sign of a struggle,' said Wheeler. 'If she died here then she let the killer into the flat. She knew him or her. I've ordered a copy of CCTV from the entrance; there's nothing covering the back. Uniform are still interviewing the neighbours.'

In the kitchen each of the surfaces was clear, the chrome taps shone and the wooden floorboards were highly polished. On the wall was a canvas print of flowers, around their petals, glitter. She walked into the bedroom – the bed was made up, with the duvet cover and pillowcases neatly aligned; the curtains were open and light filled the room. 'Everything's white,' said Wheeler. 'The bedlinen, the curtains, the carpet. All white. The monochrome photographs of Karlie are the only contrast.'

'It's sterile,' said Ross. 'Soulless. There's no personality, no colour.'

'Clinical, I'd say.' Wheeler pulled on a pair of gloves and opened a drawer. It contained matching sets of expensive-looking underwear, all neatly paired and folded. A second drawer held jewellery, neatly boxed or stacked. Karlie had favoured loud, statement jewellery.

Ross peered at it. 'She liked her bling, but why did someone with a bit of money even go into this sadomaso-chistic stuff? Why not wait for mainstream roles?'

'Beth insisted that Karlie was ambitious. Maybe she thought she'd make a fortune? Some of the big porn stars do get rich, so perhaps she thought it was a way in and that she'd get exposure? If the documentary about her dad was ever made that might've been the transition to mainstream.' Wheeler opened the wardrobe. On the top shelf was a collection of old dolls, stained and ragged. She carefully took one out. 'Look at these, they're grubby and stained, they don't reflect the OCD feel of this place.'

'Which tells us what?'

'They might be symbolic of the cosiness of her childhood before it all got very messy? And OCD tendencies could have been a way of Karlie trying to control her surroundings when her reality was very painful or out of control. I wonder if the lack of a relationship was about control too?' Wheeler glanced at the photographs of Karlie, saw the pout, the provocative pose.

Ross flicked through the stack of DVDs. '*Geordie Shore, Keeping Up with the Kardashians, Made in Chelsea, The Only Way is Essex* – she wanted to be a reality TV star. There are no bookshelves, no magazines, no newspapers – she wasn't much of a reader.'

'And no CDs or anything about the Kill Kestrels,' said Wheeler. 'Then again, Maureen said that Karlie hadn't been a fan, that she'd only contacted the group to further her ambition.'

'Their manager has them covered for the night she died.'

'Your take on the Kill Kestrels?' Wheeler asked.

'At the very top of their game, so why fuck it up?'

Wheeler crossed to a shelf. On it were three small bears dressed as pipers. They wore tartan and held bagpipes. A blue and white Saltire was printed on one foot.

The bathroom was equally clinical, the only exception

being a row of plastic ducks. Ducks that were also decked out in tartan.

'*Braveheart* ducks,' muttered Ross.

In the hall cupboard Wheeler saw the opened jiffy bag. 'This might be what Beth sent.' She saw a series of old photographs – one of them had Karlie Merrick as a small child, standing between her parents, holding hands. She was grinning, not a care in the world. Unaware of how her life would unfold. Beth had been right – Karlie was the spit of her mother. Wheeler walked to the window, glanced out, saw the neatness of the communal garden, and, beyond, the River Clyde meandering through the city.

Ross stood at her shoulder. 'A peaceful idyll.'

'Yes,' said Wheeler. 'Until she opened the door to her killer.'

Chapter Twenty-Four

The Team

Wheeler strode into a bustling CID suite. Officers were on the phones, working at their computers, reading case notes or writing up their own. 'Right, while we're all here, let's have a quick update. Karlie Merrick's PM is first thing in the morning. Ross and I will be attending.'

'You two get all the fun,' said Boyd.

'How did you get on with the cousin?' Stewart stood in the doorway. 'Get me up to speed with the new developments.'

'Beth Swinton hadn't seen our victim in years, but she did tell us that Karlie had speculated about doing a true crime programme about her father's death. Beth suggested Karlie was hungry for fame and that would've been a way to get noticed.'

'Bit cynical since she's just died?'

'Not necessarily, boss. Karlie Merrick seems to have been good at manipulation – she lied about being bullied at school, resulting in another pupil OD-ing. Also, our victim's father was murdered.'

'You're kidding me?' said Boyd.

'No, John Merrick was battered to death at his home twenty years back. Over in the Temple area.'

'Anyone done for it?'

'No one.'

'Christ, and now his daughter's been killed.'

'A cache of underage porn was discovered at his home,' Wheeler continued. 'Beth Swinton says there was no proof of him having interfered with his daughter, but she was seen by a psychiatrist and a couple of psychologists. She said nothing, kept schtum.'

'Tell me something turned up at Karlie Merrick's flat?' said Stewart.

'No signs of a struggle. Everything's neat and tidy, no sign of a break-in. Her silver Volkswagen Golf's been parked outside all night according to a neighbour. Forensics are working on it now.'

Stewart scowled. 'Nothing untoward in the flat, no defence wounds on the body. We've got sweet FA to go on. Did uniform get anything from house-to-house in Sandyhills?'

'Nothing useful, boss,' said Wheeler. 'Ross and I went to see the group, the Kill Kestrels. Turns out it was Josh Alden she attempted to contact.'

'And?'

'Her email only got as far as the online system. Alden claims he never knew her. He'd heard rumours about her while she was at school, but nothing else.'

'Alibi?'

'The manager says they were all together at the hotel. All night.' Wheeler felt the tension in the room increase. Too many dead ends. 'I think we need to be looking at any link with her father's murder, so I've requested the files.'

'A twenty-year-old case,' said Stewart. 'Has there been any new evidence?'

'Not that I know of, but it's got to have some relevance, surely? It's too much of a coincidence.'

'I hear what you are saying, but keep an open mind.'

'Will do, boss.' She looked around the room. 'Anyone know who the SIO was on the original John Merrick case?'

A uniformed officer spoke. 'If my memory serves me well, the senior investigating officer was Eddie Furlan.'

'The Bulldog?' asked Robertson. 'I've heard about him.'

'Yeah, that was his nickname,' said the officer. 'He was extremely tenacious, would keep at a case until he got a result. And generally he did. He was a bit of a local legend in the force; the guys at his station had a lot of respect for him.'

'Is he long retired?' asked Wheeler. 'I'd like to have a word with him.'

'A few years now. He lives out Newlands way. I heard his wife recently passed away.'

'Maybe not an ideal time,' said Stewart.

'I only want a quick word,' said Wheeler. 'I'll be very sensitive. It might give me an insight into our victim, who she was growing up. I'll do it in my own time.'

'You know as well as I do, that the first twenty-four hours of a murder inquiry are crucial,' said Stewart. 'Right now, we have nothing. You start looking backwards and you're liable to miss something important.'

'Eddie Furlan might give me something useful, although the surname makes me want to retch.'

'Because?' asked Ross.

'I knew a Paul Furlan back in my army days. Let's just say we didn't get along.'

'A love–hate relationship?' said Ross.

'Certainly the latter. If I never run into him again, it'll be too soon.'

'Wheeler—' Stewart made for the door '—I don't need you wasting time on personal details. First, you come in dressed like you're on route to the bloody coast, now you're having a tête-à-tête about your past. Get back to work.'

Boyd slammed down the phone, high-fived an imaginary friend. 'Yes! Capture the Dream. I've just bloody nailed it. I've tracked down Gary Ashton, the wedding photographer – he's got an office in Duke Street.' He scribbled the address and brought it over to her desk.

Wheeler quickly gathered her paperwork together and crammed it into her tray. 'Forget I mentioned Paul Furlan. Ross, get yourself together and let's get over to meet this photographer.' She was out the door and striding down the corridor by the time he'd grabbed his jacket.

Chapter Twenty-Five

Capture the Dream

Gary Ashton's office was on the first floor of the tenement building. A brass plaque announced the business. Wheeler saw a Kawasaki motorbike parked outside. She pressed the intercom. 'DIs Wheeler and Ross from Carmyle Police Station.'

They were buzzed in.

Inside, Wheeler saw that the furniture was cheap and the carpet worn. Around the walls were portraits of weddings. She saw churches and registry offices. Many photographs had Kibble Palace in the background, with a marble statue she recognised – 'Eve', by the Italian sculpture Scipione Tadolini. The noise from the road outside travelled in through the old sash windows. By the looks of things, Ashton's business was just about covering costs; it certainly hadn't propelled him into the higher echelons of society. 'Mr Ashton?' she asked, flashing her ID.

'Gary Ashton, professional wedding photographer.' He held out his hand. 'This is about Karlie, right? I just saw the news that she's dead. Dreadful. I feel awful at the thought of it. I mean, you don't ever think it'll happen to someone you know, do you?' He sat down at his desk. 'She was only young.'

'We need to ask you a few questions, Mr Ashton,' said Wheeler.

'Of course.'

'When did you last see Karlie?' Wheeler took out her notebook.

'Yesterday. We were out at the studio filming.'

'Where's the studio?'

'It's outside of the city. Out at Brookes Farm, in Strathaven.'

'We'll need access to the place,' said Wheeler.

'Why? Karlie wasn't killed there.'

'Really?' Wheeler paused. 'Do you know where she was killed, Mr Ashton?'

'I didn't mean it like that.'

'What did you mean?'

Ashton sighed. 'The farmer, Rory McFee, has a spare key to all the containers.'

Wheeler took down the address. 'What time did she leave?'

'Around two-ish.'

'Any ideas where she went?'

'No.'

'When you say "filming"?'

'We were shooting a couple of videos.'

It was like pulling teeth, thought Wheeler. 'Can you elaborate?'

'I have an offshoot from the wedding photography business. I make a little bit of porn. Small stuff, more of a hobby really. I do it for the love of it.'

'And what was Karlie doing? Exactly?' asked Wheeler. She wasn't about to mention the ligature marks to Ashton and it had been kept out of the police statement. Only the killer and the victim had known what happened that night.

Ashton sighed. 'This is so difficult.'

'Take your time.'

'First up, Karlie and Will Reid. It was just regular role play, you know, the sexy secretary being disciplined for getting it wrong?'

'Go on.'

'Then, in the second video, there was a little bit of asphyxiation going on. You know, dungeon and chains? The usual, I mean, there was nothing kinky. It was mainstream stuff, just a leather collar and a lead. Nothing dangerous. It was taut around her throat and Will yanked it a few times. It's standard practice.'

'She had a leather collar around her neck?' said Wheeler.

'That was it, really. It was all very tame. She just had to look fearful and turned on. Pain and fear, it sells.'

'And the customers who buy your videos?' asked Ross. 'Do they like to see a bit of fear on someone's face?'

'I'll take it that you never watch porn, Inspector? Then you're very much in the minority here in the UK, not to mention the rest of the civilised world. Porn is a main-stream industry now, everybody's in on it.' Ashton's voice rose. 'And when Karlie pretended to look fearful or com-pelled, she was only acting. It was her job. And despite what you're implying, this is legal shit. I'm not taking a snooty tone from you lot. My taxes pay your bloody wages and presumably you have no leads or you'd be out chasing whoever did it, instead of coming over all sancti-monious with me.'

166

'When Karlie left the farm yesterday, was she alone?' Wheeler asked quietly.

'Yep, Will was waiting for a ride home with me. Johnny was putting away the props.'

'I'll need a list of everyone on site and their contact details.'

'Fine.'

'Did she ever mention the group, the Kill Kestrels?' asked Wheeler.

'No.'

'What can you tell me about her?'

'I assumed that she was active in the BDSM scene, that she probably dipped in and out. She did the role play in our films accurately. I imagined that she dabbled, but she didn't say. We didn't chat much. It was purely a professional relationship.'

'Did she ever mention a boyfriend?' asked Wheeler.

'No, but obviously she could have had anyone. Good-looking girl, hot body. She'd be able to pick and choose who she dated. A guy finds out she knows all the tricks and he'd love it. A bit of bondage, a bit of gasping and she knew how to rock a ball gag.'

Ross stared at him.

'In my experience, most normal blokes are into this kind of stuff, but maybe you're a little bit inhibited, Inspector?'

'You were one of the last people to see her and she acted out being fearful while being strangled,' said Ross. 'Now she's dead, you can see how awkward it looks.'

'Her role play was consistent with the S&M scene. Thousands of folk work in the industry. Most of us are professionals. Karlie certainly was.'

'Who else would she have worked with? I mean, whose DNA do we have to eliminate?' asked Wheeler.

'No one recently, it was just her and Will.'

'And the collar, would it have chafed?' asked Wheeler.

'Usually, if Will was a bit rough, but the welts would have gone down after a day or two. Hazard of the profession. That and burn marks from cheap carpet. Other than that, there are no risks.'

'Where's the collar now?'

'Should still be at the studio.'

'And how did Karlie seem? Was she anxious or worried? Was there anything on her mind?'

'No, she was her usual self. Karlie wasn't the most outgoing of people – she came in and did her job. Didn't want to socialise with us, no going out for a drink after work. Just straight up, came in, got changed, got on with it. Left.'

'What about online punters?' asked Ross. 'Anyone fixated or obsessed with her?'

'She never mentioned anyone in particular.'

'You were one of the last people to see her alive, Mr Ashton,' said Wheeler. 'Take a moment. Is there anything else you can tell us?'

'Nothing much, I'm afraid. She was very much alive when she left the studio. She was doing what she loved. Perhaps she had been a little preoccupied with her future prospects.'

'Because?'

'The government's thinking of pushing through legislation trying to stop us showing certain sex acts. It'll just about close us independent film makers down. She was worried that the money might dry up in the UK. She talked of us going to the US together.'

'As a couple?'

'Professionally. If we got the right break, that's where the serious money is.'

'And she only worked at the farm?'

'There were other venues. We used empty hotels that are on the market.'

'So,' said Ross, 'you book out the hotel and do the video, but the owners have no idea they're being ripped off?'

'No one gets hurt, it's a win-win situation,' said Ashton.

'Who supplies the properties?'

'Terry McAvoy, he works for Turner Estate Agents in Milngavie.'

'We'll need Mr McAvoy's details too,' said Wheeler.

'So your mate Terry gets you the keys to the property he's showing and you have it for a couple of hours?' said Ross.

'Yep, we always tidy up and take away our props, used sheeting and throws. Keep the lighting subdued and the owners never guess it's their place, not for certain. And it's a bit of a long shot anyone ever coming round – Terry only uses properties when their owners are out of the country.'

'Classy,' said Ross. 'We'll need a list of the locations Karlie used.'

'Some of the properties have already been sold. I don't want to get Terry into trouble.'

'Not our problem,' said Ross.

'You go sniffing around these places and it'll drop him in the shit.'

'If you could email them to me ASAP, I'd appreciate it,' said Wheeler. 'We'll try to be as discreet as possible, but you can understand that a murder investigation takes precedence. Can I ask where you were last night?'

Ashton's eyes narrowed. 'You don't think I had anything to do with it?'

'We'd like to eliminate you from our inquiries, Mr Ashton,' said Wheeler. 'It's purely routine.'

'I was on another shoot.'

'Where?' asked Wheeler.

'The George Hotel in Milngavie.'

'Can anyone corroborate this?'

'Yes, the team were there. Laura McCormack, Will Reid and Johnny Pierce.'

Wheeler jotted down their names. 'Do you have contact numbers and addresses for them?'

Ashton reached for his phone, scrolled down and read out the numbers. 'Laura lives in the East End, out by Greenfield, but she flew out to Amsterdam after the shoot for a short break, back Friday. Johnny's out in the sticks and Will lives with his girlfriend, out by Tollcross Road. Hold on.' He went to his desk and took out a folder. 'Here are their addresses.'

'That your bike outside?' said Wheeler.

'Yeah, so?'

'Do you know the Coach House in Sandyhills?'

'Yeah, I know the manager Andy Carmichael.'

'Did Karlie ever go there?'

'Not that I know of. I never heard her mention it. She wasn't a biker, so unlikely.'

'Thanks for your time, Mr Ashton.' Wheeler gave him her card.

They made their way to the car.

'Ashton thought more about him being dropped in it,

than her being dead. Didn't see much sign of grief,' said Ross.

'None at all.'

'You reckon he would have called us later?'

'Not a chance.' A breeze meant that the air was, thankfully, cooler. 'I'll get Boyd and Robertson to pay them a visit.' She made the call.

Chapter Twenty-Six

The Confession

Johnny Pierce lived in an ancient caravan which was parked on rough standing on a farm. A small motorcycle was parked beside the pickup truck.

'This is some kind of shit-hole.' Boyd guided the car off the dirt track and on to the concrete. A few hundred yards away, cows were being herded into the field and, in their wake, they'd left the usual farmyard slurry behind. 'Pierce did time for assaulting his ex-partner.'

'Yep.'

Boyd parked the car. 'Now we need to wade through shit and piss and fuck knows what else.'

'Stop complaining, it's our job,' said Robertson, but he eyed the yard with distaste. Great steaming mounds of fresh shit lay across their path. 'This guy certainly lives the high life.' He closed the door and they picked their way carefully across the yard. It was impossible not to get it on their shoes and splashed on to their trousers.

'See, this is why I've always lived in the city,' muttered Boyd, as they approached the caravan.

When a small, skinny man with deep-set wrinkles

around bloodshot eyes opened the door, Boyd could smell it – marijuana. Weed. Dope. Cannabis. Call it what you will, the place stank of it. 'Johnny Pierce?'

'Who wants to know?'

They flashed their IDs.

He sniffed, brought a hand roughly across his eyes. 'I can guess why you're here.' He didn't move. 'No need for you coming inside.'

'We're not here to discuss the merits of personal use,' Boyd reassured him.

'I'm staying here.'

'We're investigating—'

'I know what you're investigating – that body found over by Sandyhills was wee Karlie. I heard it on the radio.'

'When did you last see Karlie?'

'Yesterday at the studio.'

'At Brooks Farm in Strathaven?'

Pierce nodded.

'My colleagues are out there now speaking with the farmer,' said Boyd. 'Did she leave alone?'

'Yeah.'

'Have you any idea where Karlie might have been going last night? Did she mention any plans?'

'Nope.'

'And what was Karlie's mood like? Did she seem upset or anxious about anything?'

'She was fine, she seemed OK.'

'Do you know why she would be out in Sandyhills?'

'No.'

'Did she ever mention the pub, the Coach House, to you? Do you know it?'

'Yeah, I've been there a few times and no, I've never

heard her mention it. Me and Gary are bikers. We hang out at the bars.'

'But not Karlie?'

'Karlie wasn't a biker, and she didn't drink or smoke. She was a great girl. Friendly and chatty.'

'What did she chat about? Did she every mention a group name of the Kill Kestrels?'

'Nope. She talked about her parents, mainly her dad. She said she wanted to get a programme made about how he was killed. A kind of a re-enactment to jog folks' memories. Get herself some publicity and maybe get someone convicted of his murder.'

'Did she ever mention that she was frightened or scared of anyone?'

'Never.' Pierce swallowed hard. 'I don't know who would do anything to harm her. She was a good girl.'

'You were close?'

'You could say that.'

'You were involved with her?'

'We were pals. I liked her a lot. If you're looking for a confession, that's about it. I loved her.'

'Was it reciprocated?'

'What do you think? This here—' Pierce jerked a thumb at the dilapidated caravan '—this is all I've got. She was twenty-eight and beautiful and there's not a hope she'd have gone for a wreck like me. I knew that, so I never even told her. And, before you ask, I was filming with the crew last night at a hotel in Milngavie. Later, I was here all night, but if you're looking for an alibi, you need to talk to them.' He gestured to the field of cows. 'It was just me and Sam.'

'Sam?'

'My dog.'

'How did she get on with the other people she worked with?'

'Fine.'

'No arguments?'

'The usual banter. Karlie wound Gary up, said she was going to drop him in it with his missus if he didn't up her wages. The missus doesn't know about his sideline.'

'And how did Mr Ashton respond?'

Pierce shrugged. 'Listen, I know how this sounds . . .'

They waited.

'Gary said he'd kill her if she did, but he was only pissing about. It was cheap talk. He was full of it.'

'You did time for assault?'

'So?'

'Care to tell me what that was about?'

'Domestic. I was set up. Ex-girlfriend called the cops, said I punched her. Her word against mine. The cops believed her. The bitch was lying.'

They carried on for a few minutes, but Pierce gave them nothing, no insights.

Back in the car, Boyd started the engine and coughed. 'Fuck's sake, this car stinks now.' They had carried the shit on the soles of their feet and now the car did indeed give off a strong odour.

'How come Wheeler and Ross get all the good stuff and we get the duff visits?'

'Promotion,' muttered Robertson, vainly trying to sponge some of the wet from his trouser leg with a scrunched-up tissue. Finally, he gave up and tossed it out of the window.

'Where to now, Batman?' asked Boyd.

'Will Reid's next up. What do you reckon about Ashton's cheap talk?'

'I don't know,' said Boyd, turning the car back towards the road. 'Could be nothing. Could be she meant it and was blackmailing him. As far as motives go, it wouldn't be the first time.'

'You have Johnny Pierce for a suspect?'

'Maybe.'

'The assault? Says he was set up.'

'They all say that.' He switched on the radio.

'Earlier today, Hugo Ponsensby-Edward responded to the dramatic resignation of disgraced MP, Nathan Whatley. Mr Whatley said it was with a heavy heart that he'd made the most difficult decision of his life . . .'

Chapter Twenty-Seven

The McIver, Moroccan Room

Difficult Decisions

The empty champagne bottle was resting in a silver ice bucket on one of the low side tables. A half-empty glass stood beside it. Hugo Ponsensby-Edward was thrilled that he'd delivered such a resounding speech on family values. To stand firm, one had to make difficult decisions, he'd told them. He'd completely nailed it. Nathan Whatley had resigned two hours ago, complaining that he had suffered from a moment of temporary weakness and it was a difficult decision. Well, they all had difficult decisions to make. Even his own wife, Octavia, had had to make one. Understanding that he had 'immensely important work to do', she had returned to London with their children and tomorrow would give an interview with local television about their shared family values. Hugo would return to his constituency soon, but for now he was free to celebrate his moral victory. He knew that Nathan Whatley would also need to resign from two lucrative consultancies, Saffar and Reid

Woodstock. Hugo had already approached them, money in the bank.

But now to the question in hand. Bath or shower?

The redhead was naked and lay on the mosaic floor. The tiles were bright and glittered in the gentle lamplight. She was bound by her ankles and wrists. Hog-tied. Secure, safe. Only her mouth was fixed open. Golden baths or golden showers, call them what you will, they were about humiliation and degradation and he couldn't get enough. He felt the warm stream pass from him towards her. Replayed the image of Nathan Whatley resigning. Heard the redhead gag, kept going. Revelled in it. The warmth. The smell. The power.

Chapter Twenty-Eight

Erotic Asphyxiation

The anger in the CID suite was almost palpable. Stills from Karlie Merrick's porn videos had been splashed across the papers, and there was no doubt that the appeal for information had taken a different turn. Images of a sultry, sexy woman pouted out at them, and veiled references to prostitution had been made.

'The online edition now mentions her father's underage porn stash,' said a uniformed officer.

'I pity Beth Swinton,' said Ross. 'The poor woman's being bloody harassed.'

'The press has been calling, asking the usual shitty questions about Karlie's personal life. If she was on the game? Or if John Merrick's collection of porn included pictures of his eight-year-old naked? I mean come on!' the officer fumed.

Wheeler sipped her coffee. Karlie Merrick's death had indeed become a bloody media circus. A few of the tabloids had suggested that she'd been a sex worker and had been in a dangerous situation. Wheeler knew that the police needed the media coverage, but she was troubled by the way the reporters were twisting the story. Karlie had gone from a twenty-eight-year-old murder victim to a dead porn star, and crudely pixelated pictures of her naked body had been published gratuitously alongside information about her murder. Two former pupils at her school had sold their story to the *Chronicle*, citing that the Karlie they'd known had been a manipulative liar who garnered attention at any cost. Mention had also been made of the suicide of the classmate falsely accused of bullying. 'The mechanics of a twisted mind' was how one girl had described Karlie's behaviour.

Stewart strode to the front of the room. 'What's been the response to the appeal?'

'Five folk called in, boss.'

'Anything?'

'Bloody time wasters. Jake Munro confessed to killing Karlie Merrick.'

'Jake confessed again?' asked Boyd.

'Must be a record,' said Stewart. 'That's four now. He's desperate to be famous and this is his route in to what he considers the hall of fame.'

'Bloody nutter,' muttered Ross.

'I've seen the news,' said Stewart. 'Karlie Merrick has morphed from tragic victim to scintillating porn star slash sex worker, complete with nude pictures. Let's ignore the media's take on our victim and concentrate on solving the crime. In real terms, what do we have?'

Boyd spoke. 'Johnny Pierce witnessed Karlie threatening to drop Gary Ashton in it with his missus.'

'Go on.'

'Said he'd kill her if she did.'

'Bring Ashton into the station,' said Stewart. 'If our victim intended to blackmail him, I want him in here.'

'Pierce reckoned it was just banter, that Karlie used it as leverage to try to get a pay rise.'

A uniformed officer updated the board.

'Even so,' said Stewart. 'Anything else?'

'Pierce had a thing for her, said she didn't know,' said Robertson.

'Did he now? Jealous type?' said Stewart.

'Said he never told her, but he's got previous for assaulting an ex-girlfriend.'

'Your take on Pierce?' asked Stewart.

'Bit of a waster,' said Robertson. 'No alibi.'

'Anything from Karlie's flat?'

Wheeler spoke. 'No sign of a break-in or struggle. If she was killed there, she let him or her in. Ordinary flat, usual detritus. Loads of DVDs – our victim was a big fan of reality TV shows. Nothing about the Kill Kestrels. And there was nothing erotic in the flat,' said Wheeler. 'No sex toys, nothing kinky. It doesn't reflect what Gary Ashton told us, that our victim was involved in the S&M scene.'

'What do we know about it?' asked Stewart.

'Pretty much just the clubs in the city centre. Leather and Lace, Pump It, The Tiger and Bondage Inc. That sort of stuff. Uniform are out there now doing the rounds. Nothing so far.'

'Has anyone come forward claiming to be her boyfriend or partner?' asked Stewart.

'No one, boss.'

'What about this guy Will Reid? Anything on him?'

'Not as much as a parking ticket,' said Robertson.

'Seems a very sensitive guy. He seemed genuinely gutted about Karlie's death.'

'A front?'

'Very much doubt it.'

Boyd spoke. 'Does anyone remember the Marcus Newton case from a decade ago?'

'Vaguely,' said Stewart. 'Why?'

'Newton was part of the whole BDSM scene in Glasgow. He was eventually done for killing a woman named Amy Dawson.'

'I remember reading about the case in the *Chronicle*,' said a young female officer. 'I'd never heard of strappado before the case.'

'Strap what?' asked Ross.

'Strappado. Apparently it's some kind of BDSM practice,' said the officer. 'The *Chronicle* had a follow-up article a few months after Marcus Newton was put away. He'd started to get more fan mail than any other prisoner. Women wanted to date him or marry him, and there was some sort of an altercation with the other prisoners who reckoned they should be getting their fair share of the fan mail.'

'For fuck's sake,' Ross muttered. 'Who writes to killers? Is it some kind of nutter syndrome?'

'There are a few syndromes,' said Wheeler. 'The one that you're referring to is hybristophilia.'

'Right,' said Ross. 'It actually has a name, for when folk are complete nut jobs. That's a consolation.'

'Its when someone is turned on by the idea of being with a person who has done something wrong,' said Wheeler.

'Like rape or murder?' asked an officer from the back of the room.

'Exactly,' said Wheeler. 'So I guess it's the condition Marcus Newton's fans suffer from, but there are a number of other choices.'

'Christ, this just gets better.' Ross sipped his coffee.

Wheeler continued, 'Asphyxiophilia or erotic asphyxiation, which we think Karlie was involved with.'

'Breath control during sex,' said Boyd. 'It's when you choke your partner and they get a massive high and go on to orgasm in a great way.' He looked around the room. Realised that the team were all staring at him, stopped right there.

'Go on,' said Ross.

'I mean, it's just me and the fiancée but it's great. She's a real fan because of the depth of the orgasm and—'

'Just stick to the facts,' said Wheeler.

'Right,' said Boyd. 'Because of the lack of oxygen to the brain, the orgasm is more powerful. Believe me, it's effective.'

'And alone?' said Robertson. 'If it was just you by yourself, maybe when the fiancée's out?'

'Alone, it's fantastic. It's called auto-erotic asphyxia. It's phenomenal, all you do is—'

The room was silent. Boyd got it. 'Fuck you lot. I was just trying to be helpful.'

'And you were,' said Wheeler, 'if a little too enthusiastic about the subject. Is this Marcus Newton still in prison or out?'

'No idea,' said Boyd.

'Then get on to it and find out,' said Wheeler. 'But realistically, though, how much do we really know about the porn industry?'

'You mean, apart from Boyd and his fiancée's foray into erotic asphyxiation?' said Ross.

183

A cheer went around the room.

Boyd gave him the finger.

'I mean, not as consumers,' said Wheeler. 'What happens to the people involved?'

Silence.

'I thought so, so we need to get ourselves up to speed. Go to it.'

Chapter Twenty-Nine

Downtime

Wheeler's flat was in the Merchant City. The Italian restaurant across the road was just closing and the night air was heady with the scent of flowers.

'God, but that plant's strong,' said Ross.

'Night-flowering jasmine,' she told him. '*Cestrum nocturnum*, if you want to know its Latin name, though it's not actually jasmine.'

'And you know all this, because?'

'The owner of the restaurant told me; he's crazy proud of those plants.'

Inside her flat, it was cool. Wheeler crossed to her CDs, selected John Coltrane's *Blue Train*. The title track filled the room. 'Pinot Gris OK, Ross?'

'Yep, anything to be honest.'

In the kitchen, she checked the fridge for food. There wasn't much – a pot of olives, some cheese. A bag of cashews in the cupboard. She located a couple of options in the freezer. Tried to ignore the headache which had returned. 'Looks like it's got to be pizza and garlic bread.'

'Fine.' Ross got to work, tipped the olives into a bowl, the cashews into another, and put them on a tray with the wine. 'I'll take these through.'

A few minutes later, they were settled on the sofa. Wheeler sipped her wine and felt the knot of tension in her shoulders begin to relax. 'You reckon Ashton is our killer?'

'He struck me as a complete sleazeball.'

'You two certainly didn't hit it off.'

'He's a heartless git; all that talk about the business and how the new legislation might affect his profit margins, while a friend or, at the very least, a colleague's body lies cold and silent in the mortuary. It creeped me out.'

'Yes, he doesn't get my award for person of the year, but do you think he's capable of murder?'

'He did threaten her.'

'Stewart had him back in. Ashton claimed it was just banter.'

'Hell of a coincidence.' Ross grabbed a couple of nuts.

'Certainly, I think he might be capable of being exceptionally detached, but his alibi stacks up – he was filming until late and then went home to his partner.'

'She could be lying to cover him?'

'He was being inauthentic in some way; the upset bit didn't ring true.'

'Could just be he's just a heartless bastard?' said Ross. 'And Johnny Pierce had the hots for her and he'd no alibi.'

'Unless you count the cows. Motive?'

'Unrequited love?' Ross sipped his wine, reached for the olives. 'What about the dolls and the teddy bears? And the *Braveheart* ducks? A bit childish for a woman of twenty-eight.'

'A lot of women like stuffed toys,' said Wheeler.

'What about Newton?'

'Marcus Newton's still inside, so there's one suspect we can cross off our list,' said Wheeler.

'And Ian Bunyan was at an overnight party, so he's out of the loop.'

'Doesn't mean it wasn't him,' said Wheeler.

'True, he could have ordered her killing,' said Ross.

'Nothing sticks to Bunyan.'

'I know, Tefal-coated.'

'Josh Alden?'

'I reckon he's in the clear.'

Finally, after the pizza and garlic bread were finished and they'd found themselves going in decreasing circles, Wheeler broached the subject. 'Are you going for the advertised DI post?'

'I haven't decided yet.'

'You've got acting experience, Ross. You could do it well enough.'

'Thanks for the vote of confidence, Wheeler. Damned by faint praise.'

'That's not what I meant. I think you'd be a great asset to them.'

Ross leaned forward, refilled their glasses. 'It would mean leaving the station.'

'It's your career.'

'You trying to get rid of me?'

'What's the problem?'

Ross glanced at her. 'How would you manage without me?'

'True, I'd have to depend on Boyd and Robertson.'

'And that way leads to a nightmare scenario.'

'Seriously, Ross, are you going for it?'

'I'm not sure I'm ready to leave our team.'

'Because?'

He drained his glass. 'I'm off. See you in the morning.'

After he left, she loaded the dishes into the dishwasher and took her coffee through to the living room. Changed the CD to Thelonious Monk's *Brilliant Corners*, selected track three and sat back as 'Pannonica' began. The night felt warm. Karlie Merrick's life had been extinguished far too soon, but by whom? Who had killed her and why? Wheeler spoke out loud. 'Why did your life end in this way? What happened?' She sipped her coffee, closed her eyes against the pounding headache and listened to the music. Something would shift in the upcoming investigation, she knew it. She just had to wait and see what the shift exposed. Her mobile chirped a text.

'You around? Jamie xx'

Jamie Downie, Helen's ex or present, depending on your point of view. She texted him.

Helen thinks you're still together.

She's living in fantasy land. You up for a nightcap?

Wheeler wasn't looking for a relationship, but maybe she should let him come up? Decided against it.

It's a school night. In the middle of a case.
Maybe after it's over?

No reply.

Then fuck you, Jamie, thought Wheeler as she went to bed.

* * *

The man approached the deserted Italian restaurant, stood outside and enjoyed the scent from the flowering jasmine. He was doing nothing more than taking a late-night stroll through the Merchant City. He glanced up, saw the light in Wheeler's flat extinguished. He would take his time; it was a beautiful night and there was no rush. He wondered if the inspector was thinking about the case. Would it haunt her nightmares? His work, was she in awe of it? Intimidated? They would see. In time he would know if she was a capable adversary.

The Campsie Fells, volcanic hills located to the north of the city. Owen parked up. Glasgow was spread out beneath him, the lights from the city glittered in the darkness. He looked up at the sky and saw a pale, cold moon shine over the city and it seemed that the darkness clawed at his heart. A galaxy of a billion stars glittered their farewell. Mason had called, told him that the hit was scheduled for Friday evening. Bunyan had a regular delivery in the West End. Owen sipped tepid water from the bottle, stared at the birthday card, wondered if there was a galaxy of stars in the forest, just out of sight of the horses. Stars that might light his way through eternity? He hoped so. If the forest was to be his final home and he knew that it was, then a galaxy above him would be a comfort. He nestled into the seat, closed his eyes. Felt the familiar pain in his hand begin again, yet somehow it was a comfort too. Owen fell into a deep sleep. In his dream, the carousel of horses began to move, the music played and he was seven years old again. The horses surrounded him and he knew that he was loved and that he would be protected. He smiled in his sleep. For the first time in his life, he was content.

Chapter Thirty

Thursday 10 July

The Post-mortem

The sun was bright and the drive across the city had been smooth. Despite this, Wheeler felt ill. Her headache from the previous night had, if anything, got worse. Again, she'd started the day with coffee and painkillers. They still hadn't kicked in.

Ross pulled into the car park, killed the engine. 'I told you we'd be too early.'

'Stop whining.'

'Do we know who's doing the Double D?'

A double doctor post-mortem was one of a number of post-mortems which could be ordered by the procurator fiscal, so-called as it enabled two pathologists to corroborate evidence.

'Callum Fraser, and I think the second will be Karen Simmons.' Wheeler stepped out of the car, flipped on her sunglasses, began walking towards the mortuary.

Ross caught up with her. 'Karen's a bit much with the saw, isn't she? Talk about going at it with gusto.'

'She's certainly very thorough.'

'I can't imagine doing that every day for a living.'

'Since it takes stamina, perseverance and a brilliant scientific mind, I can't imagine you doing it either.'

'Any idea who's coming from the procurator fiscal's office?

Wheeler knew that in addition to the two pathologists, there would be various other personnel in attendance. 'No idea. Why all the interest in who's going to be inside?'

'I just hope it's not Sharon Begg.'

'Because?'

'You don't want to know.'

'Oh, but I do.'

'She private messaged me on Facebook last Friday night. Late on.'

'And?'

'She sounded upbeat, she was really flirtatious.'

'Drinking?'

'I mean, she was really chatty. The gist of it is that she reckons I'm quite good-looking.'

Wheeler looked at him, took in the dark hair, the pale blue eyes, long lashes. He was six foot three of gym-honed muscle. 'Poor woman, she must have been drunk? Surely? Severely impaired thought process. Delusional, by the sound of it.' She tutted sadly. 'She's more to be pitied than mocked.'

'She asked me out on a date.'

'You're kidding! Is she not out of your league?'

'Suggested we meet up for a drink.'

'And?'

'I dodged it.'

'Why?'

'It would've been embarrassing since we work together but now it's been left hanging, so I think it's better if I don't bump into her. Let it quietly die off.'

'I wouldn't worry. Even with you being so irresistible, there's not much opportunity to get romantic at a PM.'

'But she might hang around afterwards and suggest a time and place.'

'Are you that worried?' said Wheeler. 'Just go for a quick drink with her.'

'And then try to extract myself from an awkward situation?'

'You're overthinking this.' But Wheeler knew what he meant; she'd worked with Sharon and knew her to be both tenacious and dogged, which were admiral qualities for her work in the procurator fiscal's office, but maybe not so much in the romance department. 'By way of reassurance, you know she has a black belt in karate?'

'Lucky me.'

'Sharon's a strong, disciplined and determined woman. Once she's decided on something, it's only a matter of time, like a hunter with its prey, and, right now, Ross, it looks like you're the prey.' Wheeler patted his arm. 'I'm sure if it comes to it, she'll be gentle with you.' She strode on in the sunshine, sunglasses reflecting the strong rays.

Five minutes later, they were in the welcome cool of the mortuary. As usual, Wheeler was impressed with the quiet efficiency of the place. All staff observed a strict protocol, dealt with the bodies in a scientific manner, yet never lost sight of the fact that they were dealing with human remains. Each corpse, whether killer or victim, was shown the respect it deserved. She saw that the attendee from the procurator fiscal's office was Michelle

Barratt, Helen Downie's sister, so no Sharon to complicate things for Ross. She glanced at Ross, met his gaze, saw the smirk. She gave a small shake of her head, mouthed Pathetic. Ignored the filthy look Michelle gave her. No doubt her sister Helen had given her side of the story. Just as long as she didn't start with the whore, bitch, slut, slur.

They waited as Callum Fraser busied himself with the final preparations. From experience, Wheeler knew that the pathologist would begin with an external examination of Karlie Merrick's body and later an internal one. Wheeler thought of Beth Swinton and how she had railed against the notion of a second PM being performed on her cousin's body.

Callum switched on the recorder and began. He gave the date, time and a full list of those present in the room. He named the victim and gave a detailed description of the clothes Karlie was wearing.

Wheeler stared at the corpse. Karlie looked very much younger than her years, her dark hair shone and her skin was blemish free. But it was the rich red of the varnish on her finger and toe nails which appeared to be most incongruous in the sterile setting. She looked small and delicate, the dark bruises around her throat in sharp contrast to her pale skin. The other attendees were silent as Callum and his team worked around the body, accurately measuring and recording every detail.

When the photographer stepped forward and took shots, Wheeler once again thought of the waste of life and wondered about the link between Karlie's murder and her father's. Wondered about Josh Alden. She'd found out that he had been brought up in care. He had a sister, Amber, who'd been killed in a house fire. He'd had a bit of trouble as a kid, fighting mostly. Nothing much. Then he'd formed the band.

As the PM progressed, Callum provided more details. 'And there is extensive bruising around the throat. Strangulation had occurred . . .'

Wheeler saw Ross avert his gaze, saw him study the tiled floor, heard him quietly clear his throat. She whispered across to him, 'You need to back off for a sec?'

He responded likewise. 'It's just a bit warm in here.'

'It is a very warm day, Inspector Ross,' said Callum. 'Why don't you step to the side for a few minutes and join us later when you've taken some air?'

Wheeler was concerned. She knew that Ross absolutely loathed this part of the job. None of the team actually welcomed it, but it was part of the deal. Wheeler wasn't immune to the tragedy of death but she was never going to let viewing a corpse interfere with her ability to analyse the case. Dissecting a body provided valuable information, which, in turn, often helped secure a conviction. It was a crucial part of the process. Ross was a good detective, but was he beginning to let his squeamishness interfere with his work? His face was grey and, despite the cool of the mortuary, beads of perspiration had formed across his top lip and his forehead. He had to rein it in, he had to get a grip. She wondered if this was the reason he wasn't going for promotion. Was he considering leaving the job? And should he be?

Eventually, when it was over and they were about to leave, Callum smiled at Ross. 'I'm pleased to see that your colour has returned.'

The pathologist was being kind – Ross was still grey.

Outside, Wheeler took the keys. 'I'll drive.' A few

minutes later, she pulled out of the car park. 'Karlie Merrick was strangled but not with the killer's bare hands. And she'd had anal and vaginal sex. Both consensual.'

'I missed that bit, I kept zoning in and out. I was feeling a bit rough, think I'm coming down with something.'

'There was no internal bruising or damage, which there would have been if she'd resisted.'

'Then the sex ties in with her job?'

'Looks like it.' She glanced at him. 'You're weren't looking too good back there.'

'Think it might be flu.'

'Seriously, Ross, you need some time out?'

'I'm fine.'

She drove on. Eventually, she said, 'You need to sort this out.'

'Sort what out?'

'This whole sensitivity shit. Post-mortems are part of our job and if you are struggling . . . ?'

'I'm not.'

'You think you're in the wrong job?'

'Do you?'

'I hope not, because, let's face it, what the hell else could you do?'

'That my motivational pep talk over?'

'For now.' Wheeler switched on the radio. The Kill Kestrels' 'Death of an Angel' was just finishing. She heard the DJ enthuse, 'The group's return to Glasgow has been triumphant. These four guys are on fire right now. Give us a call here at the station if you're one of the lucky fans who'll be going to their sold-out gig at the O2 Academy on Saturday night.' It cut to the news. 'Disgraced MP Nathan Whatley, who recently announced his resignation, has been declared bankrupt. Earlier, Hugo Ponsensby-Edward who had led calls for Whatley to step down had this to say . . .' She switched stations. 'The mother of one of the murdered gang members has called for an end to the violence and was in tears as she implored other gang members to . . .'

Wheeler switched off the radio. Glasgow. City of dreams.

Twenty-five minutes later, she was at her desk struggling to decipher a note that had been left for her. Unfortunately, it was in Boyd's handwriting. She scrutinised the bizarre hieroglyphics for a few minutes before she gave up and called across the room, 'Boyd, did you even go to school? I can't read your scrawl. Just tell me, who rang in?'

'A guy name of George Bellerose, about half an hour ago. He's been in London. Had no idea Karlie Merrick was dead until he saw one of the appeals.'

'Who's Bellerose?' asked Wheeler.

'A therapist. Life coach, I think he said. Either way, Karlie Merrick was seeing him for help with her career. "Goal setting" is the phrase he used.'

'So our victim had a therapist,' said Ross. 'Why am I surprised?'

'He offered to come in for a chat,' Boyd continued. 'He's on his way over from Hillhead. I can see him if you like?'

'You're OK.' Wheeler turned back to her computer. Another person in Karlie Merrick's life was coming into the frame. Another little bit of the jigsaw. But before George Bellerose's arrival, she had a call to make. She dialled the number. It was answered on the second ring.

'Mr Eddie Furlan?'

'Yes.'

'DI Wheeler from Carmyle Police Station. I'm sorry to bother you, but I wondered if you remember Karlie Merrick?'

'Indeed I do. I was horrified to read that her body had been found. Out by Sandyhills, wasn't it? I worked on her father's case many years ago.'

'And now I'm working on Karlie's, it's painful what happens to some families. I wonder, if it's not too intrusive and you have a few minutes, if I could have a quick chat with you about the John Merrick case?'

'I'm afraid it's not a great time. I lost my wife recently and I'm waiting for a charity to come by and collect her clothes.'

'I'm so sorry to hear that.'

'Thank you, grief is a very difficult emotion to bear.'

A pause.

'Is there a more convenient time?'

She heard the sigh.

'If you insist. Why don't you come over this evening and I'll have more time to talk to you? It'll also give me a chance to try to remember the details. It was a long time ago.'

Wheeler grabbed a pen, scribbled down an address in the Newlands area of the city.

'Make it around seven-thirty.' His voice weary.

'I appreciate it,' said Wheeler. The line went dead.

Chapter Thirty-One

The Hypnotherapist

The large wooden sign read 'Anne Marie Reeves, Registered Clinical Hypnotherapist. MBSCH, DHyp'. Underneath, a mobile phone number. Josh walked around the side of the house and up stone steps, then made his way through neat flower beds and took his place in the waiting room. Another door led directly from the consulting room itself, which meant clients arrived and left without encountering others; the hypnotherapist was big on confidentiality. Josh thought of the foster carer, Susan Moody, and felt the anger rise in him. He picked up a magazine, flicked through it, saw an interview with Skye. As usual, he looked like he was either just recovering from, or on his way to, a party. The dark kohl around his eyes was smudged and the photographer had captured his air of distraction. It was as if Skye was never fully present, there was always part of him somewhere else. Skye was entitled to live his own life, but for a band who travelled and played together, they lived completely separate lives. They were at their best when they were on stage working; left alone for too long and the cracks began to show in their relationships. The other three were not guys Josh would choose to hang out with. They were merely work colleagues, despite what Dougie fed to the press. But colleagues who were losing focus. He knew Dougie was anxious about it, knew that he was worried that, somehow, they'd blow it. Josh closed the magazine, picked up a dog-eared hypnotherapy journal, flicked aimlessly through it. Thought briefly about the visit from the two detectives, Wheeler and Ross, who had asked about Karlie Merrick. Finally, the door opened and he was ushered in.

The therapy room was cool, the air full with the smell of lavender. Comfortable chairs had plump cushions. Everything in the room had been chosen to create a sense of relaxation. Josh settled himself on one chair, and the therapist sat facing him. Her voice was soft. 'Take a moment to arrive, to really come into the room and be present . . .' She paused. 'Do you want to tell me a little about how you've been since your last appointment?'

'I'm making progress. Things have been busy with the band, we've got a big gig at the O2 on Saturday night.'

'I read it's sold out. Congratulations.'

'I've been thinking about what you said in our last session, about me suffering from post-traumatic stress disorder and maybe that being the reason I can't remember what happened that night. Makes sense. PTSD seems to fit.'

'It's certainly worth considering. As a rough guide, when we experience a traumatic event—'

'Like Amber's death in the fire?'

'Yes, the death of a loved one in traumatic or distressing circumstances may trigger a substance called glucocorti-coid, which helps our brains to cope with the trauma, while the central part of our memory system, the hip-pocampus, stores the event in our long-term memory.'

'And this all kicked in the night she died?'

'In short, it's a coping mechanism. Too much trauma may overwhelm us, so the brain has a way of shutting it out or storing it elsewhere.'

'So, I can't recall the details of that night because it was too much for me to deal with?'

'Josh, you were ten,' the therapist said gently. 'It would have been a terrible shock for you. And you had already experienced the loss of your father when he walked out, then subsequent violent boyfriends of your mother's and, finally, her horrific death. You suffered a large amount of loss from a very young age. Even before the night of the fire.'

'I can hardly recall anything at all about my childhood, very few details of when we lived with Mum or anything much about our house. No favourite games or anything about what we did as children. At least I couldn't prior to coming here.'

'It's safe here, your subconscious knows that you are not alone, that there is someone helping you to remember, so the images and memories become more accessible and available.'

'I need to remember it to understand my background. I was talking to one of the guys who grew up near the home. Cutter Wysor. He can't remember anything from his childhood either. Except maybe a bit about school. Nothing about his home life.'

'It's extremely common. For example, it can be very difficult if his home life was challenging. He may have buried the memories.'

'Maybe he should come to see you?'

'Does he want to remember?'

'Fair point. Probably not.'

'Hypnotic regression allows you to go back and access the memory you want to recall.' She paused. 'Are you ready to begin?'

'Yeah. Hope I don't drift off.'

'It doesn't matter if you do. You'll remember what you need to when you awaken. We can establish some of the facts. We don't want the whole night to come flooding back to you and overwhelm you; just a detail here and there, until we have the whole picture. You'll reclaim your memory of that night, piece by piece.'

'It's bloody frustrating that I can't just remember what happened.'

'Be patient, Josh, you have a big weekend ahead. You have the concert and you really don't want to be upset and potentially reliving grief, bereavement and shock at such an important event.'

'I was just at Amber's grave and the old feelings of letting her down resurfaced. I just want to find out the truth. I don't believe what Susan Moody says happened that night.'

'Because?'

'I'm sure I heard voices.'

'How sure?'

Josh stared at the wooden floor, followed the contours of the bumps and tiny cracks and tried hard to remember. Finally, he admitted, 'Not certain. Maybe I was dreaming, but I thought that I was awake. It felt real.'

'So today—' she checked her notes '—you wanted to concentrate on remembering the name of your next-door neighbour?'

'Do you think it's possible to remember everything?'

'If we are gentle with ourselves and do it in a supportive, guided way, it's incredible what can be released. Remember it's little by little, until we have the whole picture.'

Josh crossed to the therapy couch, lay down and closed his eyes, let his mind float as he heard her talk him through the script, guiding him into hypnosis.

'You can remember with ease what happened that night . . . Your memory is perfect . . . just relax . . . and trust that it will provide everything that you need . . . You can recall whatever you want . . . every little detail is there for you to uncover . . .'

She continued talking, leading him back into the past, reminding him that he wasn't alone, that it was safe to remember.

He felt himself fall into a dream-like trance, heard her voice from far away.

'Tell me, what do you remember? What can you see?'

He saw Susan Moody. She was angry. Amber had soiled the bed again. Susan was shouting. Amber was crying and screaming. Susan's voice changing to a low threatening growl. But then the memory faded and the old one returned. His mother's house. 'No,' he muttered. His heartbeat quickened, his hands slippery with sweat. 'No.'

'What do you see, Josh?'

'Mum's house, she's lying on the couch, she's drinking. I'm scared.' He saw flickers of the memory. The kitchen with its filthy cupboards. Him searching for food. The memory swirled, dark and unpleasant. An inner voice told him not to go there. Get. Out. Now. He forced himself to open his eyes. 'Wrong house. Wrong memory. It's the foster carer's house I want to remember.'

'All memories surface in their own time.'

'No.'

'Perhaps you should just go with the process?'

'That's not what I'm paying you for. I want you to direct my memory to that night.' He closed his eyes.

'Just relax . . . Your memory of that particular night is coming back now, the details will come to you . . .'

'I can see Susan Moody's house, I'm on the street with a boy from school.'

'Go on.'

'I asked him why Susan took in foster kids. He said it was for the money. I knew she didn't like us but she changed when the social worker or the woman from the agency came around. I used to wish that she'd die . . . that we'd go back into the home.' He felt himself drift, images of the other house, his mother's, curled around the edge of his memory. He ignored it, forced himself back to Susan Moody's house.

'And that night, Josh, what do you remember from the night of the fire?'

'The cat. Next door's cat had come in through the open window. It was a tiny cat. It was white and its eyes were weepy, like they needed a good clean. Amber loved that cat. We talked about when we'd get a forever home, we'd ask the owner if we could take it with us. It was called Willow.'

'Can you remember the name of the neighbour? Can you remember who owned Willow?'

Memories flooded his mind. His mother's house again. The kitchen. Him sitting on the floor, his mother unconscious on the couch. The darkness swirled around the images, the feeling of dread giving way to anger. He balled his hands into fists, forced the memories down.

Back to Susan Moody's house. He battled through fog until he had it. 'Mrs Free. Adele Free.'

'Was she there that night?'

'No, but two others were. A man was shouting at a woman.'

'What was he shouting?'

'He was swearing at her and she was crying and asking him something.'

He continued with the session for a few more minutes, but he'd lost the thread and couldn't recall anything else. The session ended.

'You seemed to be struggling with the memories of your mother's house. Is this something you'd like to explore?'

'Old news.' He stood. 'Let's hope that Adele Free's still alive and that she remembers that night. Same time next week?' He made for the door.

'Take it easy, this is a big week for you,' she called after him.

He walked to the car.

Half an hour later, he was back in his room at the Braque Hotel. He fired up his laptop, typed 'Adele Free' into the search engine. If his memory was correct, she had been kind to both himself and Amber. Josh felt the adrenaline flow. He wondered about the two voices. Bit by bit, it was all coming back. He had a good feeling about this. If Adele Free was out there then he would find her. He looked at the results, saw references to Adele the singer come up on screen. He typed in 'A. Free. Glasgow' and waited. Great, now he had all the links to the Scottish Referendum. Josh crossed to the minibar, took out the bottle of white wine, poured a glass, gulped down half, topped it up. Helped himself to the tub of peanuts before returning to his computer. This was going to take longer than he thought.

Across town, George Bellerose was coming down. It wouldn't take long, he reasoned, as he made his way into a café. He had a bastard of a hangover. He had to get it sorted before he went to the police station to talk about Karlie. Karlie being dead. Murdered. He rubbed his forehead. Fuck it, the hangover was his own fault; he'd been up half the night. Later that evening he'd get drunk and hurt Angie. He'd texted her earlier, told her to wear the fetish gear. Told her to rest up, it would be a long night. Instead, she'd suggested that they go to the cinema. There was a film she wanted to see, said her friend Jenny at the café had suggested they go together but the stupid cow had refused, said she'd wanted to go with him. Afterwards, they might go somewhere nice for a drink. He'd texted back, told her that what he was intending doing to her couldn't be done in a cinema. He'd added a cheeky face and a wink. Keep up the script, he told himself. Keep her sweet, let her dream her dreams about future kids, a house and a bloody white picket fence. Let her have her fantasies. And then, because of the hangover and the impending visit to the police, he texted her again:

> Maybe you need to look into losing a bit of weight? You won't be the first chunky monkey I've dated but I know you mentioned something about being self-conscious. Only, if the weight is an issue for you, I'm happy to support you trying to shift it? I want you to be happy with how you look and be the best person you can be.

He added a smiley face. Thought of how she would crumple when she got the message. It was a little slap in the face. He pressed send.

He sipped his double espresso, felt the smooth of the liquid calm him. A blonde, middle-aged businesswoman approached the counter, ordered and waited. The hair a stiff helmet, the neat tailored suit. The bag with a logo. Prada. He tried for eye contact. She glanced at him. He smiled. She looked straight through him, paid for her coffee, made her way to a seat. Stuck-up bitch. He drained his cup. Fish at the bottom of the pool, he reminded himself as he let the door slam on the cool of the café. He started up his pale blue Suzuki motorbike and turned towards Carmyle Police Station. With Karlie dead, he needed a replacement. He had a problem.

Chapter Thirty-Two

Families

'No, that's not a problem.' Wheeler put down the phone. George Bellerose was running late. Half an hour to forty minutes. An unforeseen hold-up. She fired up her computer. It wasn't like she didn't have anything to be getting on with in the meantime. She heard Ross take a call; there was something peculiar in his tone. She saw his hand go to his forehead, watched him rub a spot just above his eyebrow as he carried on talking. Talking and rubbing and not glancing up. She crossed to the kettle, switched it on, grabbed a couple of mugs, scooped in coffee granules. Read the expression. Waited until he had finished the call. 'Important?'

'That was Francesca Miller, my dad's neighbour up in Pittenweem.'

Wheeler heard the tone, registered the body language, made an educated guess. Waited.

'It's my dad. Francesca found him an hour ago. He was on the floor, looks like he'd been getting dressed. Sounds like a heart attack. The paramedics have just left.'

'Ross, I'm sorry. What can I do to help?'

'I need to drive across there . . .' He shook his head. 'I need to get organised. He began randomly sorting through the paperwork on his desk, pilling it into haphazard stacks and stuffing them into trays.

'Leave that. Boyd can pick it up later.' She filled two mugs with boiling water. 'Here.' She thrust one towards him. 'At least have a drink before you go.'

He accepted the coffee.

'Take a minute.' She dragged a chair over to his desk, sat opposite him. They were alone in the room and for that she was grateful. At a time like this he needed to process the news of his father's death. She knew him, knew that he would want to talk about it. Wheeler's parents were both dead. She had a sister, a brother-in-law and a nephew who were based in Somerset, but she was no longer in touch with them. Essentially, she was alone in the world and it suited her.

Ross began to talk. 'I was going to try to get over and see him soon, maybe go see some football at the beginning of the season. It's not like it's far.'

'How long's the drive?' Bland, mundane conversation that masked the emotion.

'Under two hours if there are no hold-ups. Do you know Pittenweem?'

'I've heard of it. A small fishing village on the tourist trail?'

'It's a nice place. He was originally from Elie, but he'd moved around a lot over the years. He was in Glasgow when he met Mum. After they split, he moved to a few other areas, but eventually he settled back in Fife.'

'What age was your dad?'

'Sixty-nine. No age at all.'

'Did he have a history of heart trouble?'

'No, but the drinking wouldn't have helped. He drank more than he ate. Not outrageously drunk or anything, he'd too much dignity for that, but steady drinking, if you know what I mean. Steady and committed.'

'When did you last see him?'

'A few months ago. It's not that we weren't close, it's just that he was a very private person. He'd got a bit lost, what with the booze. We'd already had a falling-out over it. I wanted him to move on. Mum certainly had. I told him that he ought to stop drinking and start dating. I actually thought that he was going to hit me. I probably wasn't as sensitive as I could have been.'

Wheeler could imagine. Ross wasn't known at the station for his tact and diplomacy. 'When did they divorce?'

'Years ago. I was out of the house. They just quietly divided up the contents, sold the house, split the money and separated. A couple of years later, Mum filed for divorce and that was it. Nightmare.'

'Their separation wasn't amicable?'

'Not even close. Mum's still with the guy she left Dad for, Frank Brogan. He owns a number of hotels in Ireland. Galway, Dublin, Cork. Apparently they're very luxurious and loads of famous folk go there to get married. Not that I've ever been. They've invited me over but I've just never found the time.'

'Do you still see your mum?'

'When she's back in Glasgow, we'll meet for a coffee. Maybe at a push, lunch. But only if it's somewhere she likes, the Rogano or the Ubiquitous Chip. Even then, I feel like we're really only making small talk. Killing time.

Going through the motions until she can leave. We're pretty much estranged.'

'But you were close to your dad?'

'We used to go to the games together, years ago. He used to go to Stark's Park regularly, Raith Rovers' home ground. He was a big fan, growing up in Fife, which is why I support them. That wasn't easy growing up in Glasgow. But then the drinking kicked in and he stopped being so interested.'

'I'm sorry, Ross.'

'Yeah, me too.' He finished his coffee and stood. 'I'd better get going.'

'Take as long as you need, we'll cover everything until you're back. And if there's anything I can do to help . . .' She paused. 'What about the mutt? She'll need walking.'

He put on his jacket. 'I'll need to see if my neighbour Mary can take her full time while I'm away.'

'If you're stuck, you want me to take her?'

'Would it be a problem?'

'Not at all,' she lied. 'I'd love to have her.'

'Thanks, Wheeler.'

She watched him leave. No matter which way round you spun it, family and parents could always bring you some sort of pain. It was certainly true for her, and it sounded like Ross too. She thought of the strained relationship between Beth Swinton and Karlie Merrick. Of the underage porn found in John Merrick's house. Families. Was it the same for everyone? There were no guaranteed happy endings. What was that line from the Philip Larkin poem?

Chapter Thirty-Three

The Hero

She'd just finished updating the team about Ross's situation when the phone rang and the desk sergeant told her that George Bellerose had arrived. Wheeler stood. 'Right, Boyd, you and me downstairs, let's go and chat to the life coach.'

George Bellerose was pacing in the waiting area when they arrived downstairs. She saw that he was about thirty-five, had a broad suntanned face, dark eyes and thick, shoulder-length hair. He was wearing a leather motorbike jacket, helmet in hand.

'I'm DI Wheeler and this is DC Boyd.'

'Thanks for meeting with me.' His words tumbled over themselves. 'I'm still in shock. I don't know if I can be of help in any way but I wanted to come in and speak to you. Have you any suspects yet?' He caught himself. 'So sorry, I know you can't say anything. I'm just not thinking straight.'

Wheeler gestured to the interview room. 'Let's go through here, Mr Bellerose, it's more private.'

'Yes, of course. I'm just back from a conference in

London on Carl Jung's twelve archetypes. His theories about the universal characters that are present in our collective unconscious are fascinating, aren't they?'

'Through here, please,' said Boyd. The man hadn't budged.

Wheeler knew about the archetypes. If she had to guess, Bellerose was the caregiver. Their goal in life was to help others. On the flip side they hated ingratitude and were prone to martyrdom. Everyone had a shadow side. She wondered about Bellerose. There was something about the man she didn't like.

'But then, when I returned from my London trip,' his voice faltered, 'and I saw that Karlie had been murdered.' He stared at the table, shook his head in disbelief.

'That's OK, Mr Bellerose, just take your time. Please, have a seat.'

'And I know that everything we discussed was confidential and, if she were alive, I wouldn't dream of talking to you, but since she's dead, I thought it might be helpful? I don't know, maybe you've spoken with others about her and you don't need anything from me?' He paused. 'Have you any leads?'

Wheeler ignored the question, let them get settled around the table before she spoke. 'At this stage of the investigation everything may be helpful. We would like you to tell us whatever you know about Karlie Merrick.'

'She came to me for help. I believe that the work she was doing with me would have been truly life-changing, if it had been seen through to its conclusion. I work primarily with women to goal set and progress their careers. I'm very successful.'

'Life-changing?' prompted Wheeler.

'We all have the capacity to experience our potential. I work in such a way as to allow people to access that fully and, if I do say so myself, I get impressive results.'

Bellerose saw himself as a hero. As far as Wheeler was concerned, she'd wait and see.

'When was the last time you saw Karlie?'

'Ten days ago. She was in what she felt was a dead-end job and she wanted to make as much money as she could to launch herself in the States. We made a detailed plan, did a cost analysis of where she was financially and where she wanted to be. We identified the spectrum of potential earnings available to her. She worked with a guy called Gary Ashton, making porn films. Quite a small concern, Karlie made it sound a bit hokey. Shipping containers or empty hotels, usually a commercial property that was up for sale. She was ashamed of how small the operation was, saw it merely as a stepping stone. She was incredibly ambitious and craved fame. For her, the whole Gary outfit was really just a small step in a greater journey. Her job didn't pay as well as she'd expected, and she said she found it meaningless. She'd show up for shoots and just role play, but she didn't rate him as a producer. She said it was more difficult not to make money from porn. She thought that he should have been better off financially, be able to afford a decent lifestyle and to up her salary.'

'Money was important to her?'

'Fame was most important but money she saw as security.' His voice wavered. 'I'm sorry, it's just so shocking. You see, security was important because of her horrible childhood. You know that her father was murdered?'

'Yes.'

'Did you know about her home life? I gather her father

214

was her hero and after his murder things were very difficult for her. The police found some rather incriminating porn. Underage. I wondered if he'd ever . . . if they'd ever . . . if he'd? You know?'

She heard a ribbon of excitement weave its way into his tone.

'It's just . . . it would have been terrible. I mean just the thought of it . . . the very thought.'

'Did Karlie talk about her father's murder?'

'Not very often, just in vague terms. I often tried to get her to talk about their relationship but she just clammed up.'

'But she mentioned the porn?'

'Only because it was out there already, the papers had reported it. I was concerned. I felt that she had come through such a lot, at such a tender age. I just wanted to explore it fully with her. I was very sympathetic to her challenges.'

Wheeler heard how rushed the sentences were. There was barely a pause. Bellerose was talking a lot but telling them very little. Other than about himself. She wondered how professional his interest in Karlie had been. 'Is there anything you can tell me about Karlie's involvement in the BDSM scene or clubs she might have frequented?'

'She wasn't involved.' A firm statement.

'You're certain?'

'Positive. She would have told me. She told me absolutely everything.'

'But not about her relationship with her father?'

Silence.

'Was Karlie seeing anyone? Did she have a boyfriend?'

'No.'

'How can you be so sure?'

'She'd never dated at all. Ever. She'd had sex obviously at work but no relationships outside of work. Karlie was firmly asexual.'

Which tied in with what the cousin had told them, thought Wheeler.

'Wasn't that unusual?' asked Boyd. 'A porn actress who doesn't have sex?'

'Some people don't have a need for emotional intimacy. I thought, as a professional, you might be aware of that. Karlie saw sex as work. It's what she did, the same way you come in here every day. Christ Almighty.' He slammed his fist on to the table. 'You people just don't get it, do you?'

Wheeler watched as Bellerose paused, saw his fist retreat to the safety of his lap, watched while his composure was refitted over his countenance like a straitjacket. Saw the slick, professional smile being pasted on as he continued. 'Sorry. It's just that it's a difficult time for me.'

Wheeler glanced at his motorcycle helmet. 'Did she ever mention the Coach House?'

'Karlie had never been there as far as I know. I've been in a few times.'

'Did she ever mention the group, the Kill Kestrels? She tried to contact one of them.'

'No.'

'Do you have any idea where she might have been going the night she died? Anyone she could have been meeting?'

'Sorry.'

'And how did you feel about Karlie, Mr Bellerose?'

'My work with her was intensely solution-focused.

The main goal we set was for her to pull together a portfolio of images, and we made a list of the type of companies in the States that she wanted to target.'

Wheeler repeated herself. 'I asked you how you felt about her, not what you did together.'

George Bellerose stared at the table, blinked hard.

Wheeler passed the box of tissues to him, saw his eyes flit to her and away again. Saw his expression harden.

'This is very unprofessional.'

'Everyone gets upset at some point,' said Boyd.

'I don't mean the upset!' snapped Bellerose. 'I mean being attracted to a client. It's so unprofessional to develop feelings, it shouldn't have happened. We have a code of ethics in our profession. When I knew that I was developing feelings for her, I should have terminated the relationship. I am usually very in control of myself.'

Wheeler observed that Bellerose had moved from caregiver to rebel by breaking the rules and falling for the person he was meant to help. Had he crossed to his shadow side?

Bellerose repeated, 'I am always in control of myself.'

Again the use of the word 'control'. Did he like to control women? thought Wheeler. Did he try to control Karlie? 'But in this case you weren't and your feelings for Karlie, were they reciprocated?'

He took his time answering. 'I don't know. I never told her how I felt. I don't know if she ever guessed.' He sat back, steepled his fingers. 'And now it's too late. I had wondered, during our last session, whether or not to tell her, but I decided against it.'

'Did she talk about her friends, what she did outside of work?'

'No, she was there to focus on getting to the States. She sent some photographs to a half-dozen US studios, got a couple of lukewarm replies. They told her if she was ever over there to make an appointment but nothing that she felt was concrete enough to warrant the expense of the journey.'

He may have come in with the best of intentions but he had nothing specific for them. 'Is there anything else you can remember, Mr Bellerose?' said Wheeler.

'She mentioned another place. Not by name. It was somewhere she said paid well for role play but she had to sign a confidentiality contract agreeing not to talk about it.'

Wheeler leaned forward. 'A confidentiality contract? Because?' Karlie's flat had been well furnished and worth nearly two hundred thousand. Wherever she had made her money, it wasn't through her arrangement with Gary Ashton. Then again, Beth Swinton had alluded to an inheritance.

'I've no idea. She only mentioned it a couple of times. She was pretty reticent about it.'

'It would be very helpful if you could remember anything at all. It may help us get closer to the person who killed her.' She watched him trawl through his memory.

'She mentioned once that she had been driving home thinking that she'd made some decent money for a change. I asked why she was there and she laughed and said it involved soap.'

'Soap?'

'Yeah, I know. It sounded nuts but then she clammed up.'

'Driving back home from where?'

'She didn't say.'

'And you didn't press it?'

'Why would I? I would be prying.'

Again the quick look, the sharpness of expression. Whatever he was telling them it wasn't the whole story.

'If this one last thing helps in any way, then I will have been of assistance. I mean, she was the victim of such a sorry childhood trauma.'

The victim/hero, thought Wheeler. 'Can you tell me where you were on Tuesday night?'

She saw him bristle, the mask slip again.

'I was at home.'

'Alone?'

'Yes, I live alone and the last time I looked that wasn't a crime. And no, no one can corroborate that. No friend called round. No neighbour popped in to borrow a cup of sugar. Nothing so convenient for your investigation, I'm afraid. I had a takeaway meal and was online for most of the evening, then I read until eleven – Carl Jung's *Psychology of the Unconscious*, if you're interested. I had an early night. I was booked on the 7.15 a.m. flight to London the following day and I don't like the inference here.'

Wheeler kept her voice steady. 'There's been no inference, Mr Bellerose. I was only asking a question.'

'Right, well, I think I've done my civic duty, now. May I leave?'

Wheeler stood. 'Of course. Thank you for your time.' Heard him grunt a goodbye.

Once he had gone, she turned to Boyd. 'Your take on our Mr Bellerose? You think he planned to go to the US with her, like Gary Ashton did? And he was in love with her, as was Pierce.'

'His attitude changed quickly from lovelorn therapist to snappy controlling type.'

'And he said "civic duty",' said Wheeler. 'Bellerose wants to be seen to do the right thing in the community. I'm not sure that I believe him that he didn't tell Karlie about his feelings. All that code of ethics stuff was laid on a little too thick for me. And yes, the word "control" popped up regularly.'

'You think he told her and she rejected him?'

'I don't know why he was lying, or what about, but I'm certain that he was. But yes, he could have told her about his feelings for her and been rejected. It wouldn't be the first time someone's had the red mist descend, especially if they'd built up a fantasy that it was all going to end well. Karlie went to him asking for his help and he wanted to rescue her.'

'She was the victim?' said Boyd.

'Initially, until she no longer needed rescuing.'

'It's classic, isn't it? Woman rejects man, man gets angry and takes revenge. What about the no sex other than at work? It chimes with what the cousin said.'

'Yep, it's unusual. I wonder if Bellerose fantasised about taking her away from the porn industry and having her settle down with him. I think we keep an eye on Bellerose. It might be nothing; maybe he was just in love and didn't express it. Or maybe he did and there were consequences. But the reference to soap?'

'You've lost me there,' said Boyd.

Thirty minutes later, George Bellerose turned into Kersland Street in Hillhead and parked in front of his flat. The first-floor, three-bedroom flat was spacious. His home was also his clinic, but Bellerose passed through the waiting area quickly, ignored his treatment room and the living room and walked along the corridor to his bedroom. Closed the door behind him. He could feel the sweat on his back, and his hair was damp. It had been a mistake to go to the police – that fucking bitch Wheeler had twisted everything he said. He had wanted to tell her that Karlie had gone to him for help, that he had made her life better, but the police-woman had tainted his words. She had made him feel dirty and out of control. He took off his shirt, scrunched it into a ball, chucked it into the corner of the room. Fuck it. He had tried, as usual, to do the right thing and it had been misconstrued. His efforts had been entirely misinterpreted by that bitch. He was a professional, he rescued women and helped mould and bend them into being the best they could be. He never fished at the bottom of the pond with his patients. He was their hero, their fucking hero. His heartbeat thundered. He had been Karlie's hero – why couldn't that cunt Wheeler see that? And her lying about Karlie having contacted a member of the Kill Kestrels. Karlie would have told him. She told him everything. Wheeler was a bitch. He checked his watch; he had a couple of hours yet before he had to see clients. Only had two appointments. Emma Bailey would want to work on her plan to open a deli in the West End. Joyce Wilkie wanted to look at retraining as a consultant and working in Europe. Bellerose didn't feel at all like working, but at £150 an hour he wasn't about to turn them away. He felt his heartbeat calm, felt the tension abate. He had enough time. He grabbed his laptop and moved to the bed. Around the room, Karlie Merrick stared out from dozens of images. The stills from the video had been printed off on his top-of-the-range printer. She was naked in all of them. In some, she was kneeling in front of the camera. In others, she lay on her back. Behind her there was darkness. In the original videos, Will Reid had featured, but Bellerose had edited him out. It was to be just him and Karlie. Bellerose opened his laptop, saw that Angie was online. He ignored her; he didn't need that amateur shit right now. He down-loaded Karlie's final video. Watched her walk into shot and felt his arousal begin. Felt himself get hard. It had been the same after every session with her, he'd been left want-ing more. Always more of the patients he was drawn to, that had become his pattern over the years. And he'd had to satisfy it.

Chapter Thirty-Four

The Grieving Son

Ross drove into Pittenweem. The dog lay on the back seat of the car – he hadn't bothered to ask his neighbour Mary to look after her, nor had he taken Wheeler up on her offer. He was glad of the company. He'd spoken to Francesca Miller again before setting off, and she'd told him his dad's body had been taken to the mortuary and there may have to be a post-mortem. Ross thought of Karlie Merrick's post-mortem and how ill he'd felt, of the times he'd joked about the noise from the Stryker saw to Wheeler. He thought about the work Callum Fraser did, weighing corpses, measuring them, recording every detail before slicing into them to extract organs. He thought of his father's heart giving out and how a post-mortem was suddenly different. Double standards.

He parked up, looked out to the water. No matter what the season, the view was always stunning. He grabbed the lead and got out of the car. 'Come on, you.'

The sun was warm on his face, the breeze gentle. The area was busy; tourists passed him clutching maps and taking photographs. Incongruous. The beautiful day, the sun-dappled water and the happiness on the faces of the holidaymakers, juxtaposed with the death of his father. Ross felt weary as grief hit him. He walked towards the High Street. A poster told him the arts festival ran from the second to the tenth of August. He recognised one of the names – the late Steven Campbell; his father had been a fan. Ross tugged gently at the dog's lead and they trudged through the crowd. His father had been a part of this community, had made friends, built a life here. Ross remembered him talking about a proposed memorial to the women historically accused of being witches, which had divided the town. The eventual vote was split and the council had decided not to go ahead, but his father had disagreed with the decision. 'Torturing twenty-odd women and killing a good many of them, surely should be remembered in some way, Steven?'

Ahead, two tourists. As he passed, one asked, 'Can you tell me the way to St Fillan's cave?' An American accent, maybe New York. 'Is it true that he was the patron saint of the mentally ill and that people were locked in the cave overnight to be cured?'

'So I've heard,' said Ross.

'Are you from around here?'

'Glasgow.'

'Oh, we're visiting Glasgow tomorrow.' She smiled up at him. 'Is it as violent as they say?'

Ross thought of the women of Pittenweem who had been killed in the witch hunts, of the mentally ill people who'd been abandoned in a dark cave. He thought of Karlie Merrick's murdered body on a slab at the post-mortem. Of Davie Ward and Chris Wood, the two dead gang members. Of his dad. Every place had its darkness. 'Glasgow's a great city. You'll love it.' He pointed them in the direction of the cave. Walked on. Above him, gulls rose and swooped while the dog trotted obediently beside him. At this stage, she was the closest thing to family he had. Or at least family he got on with.

His father had a three-bedroom detached house on the High Street. Inside, the dog's nails clicked on the oak floor. The room was filled with light; the furniture had been kept to a minimum, allowing plenty of space for paintings, prints and small sculptures. Ross crossed to the kitchen, put on the kettle. Saw the glass in the sink, the almost empty bottle on the worktop. He hoped his father had had a peaceful night, that he'd sat contentedly with his whisky, his art and his view.

Ross made coffee, forced himself to focus. Knew it was time. Made the call. It rang for several seconds before it was answered. 'It's me.' He paused. 'I've got some bad news.' He gave her the brief details, thought that it was unlikely that she'd want to attend the funeral, heard himself ask anyway.

'I don't think so, Steven, it's been too long.'

His mother, ever the sentimental one. 'Thought you might want to pay your respects.'

'I do, honestly I do, and, of course, it's terribly sad, but we need to be realistic.'

'Is it unrealistic to think that maybe you'd want to come over for his funeral? You were married to the man for years.' They were getting into their old pattern.

Her voice sharp. 'I'm well aware of that, Steven. However, Frank and I have our business here in Galway and summer is our busiest time. There are a number of high-profile weddings coming up, one or two of which may be prominently featured in the press.'

'Sorry, is this inconvenient? You reckon maybe he died now out of spite?' Old patterns.

Her tone hostile. 'Don't you dare try the guilt trip again. Your father and I have lived separate lives for years and it's worked out perfectly well.'

'Apart from the alcoholism.'

'That was his choice and he was drinking before I left. In fact, his drinking was a major contributing factor to my leaving, as you bloody well know.'

'Maybe it was his way of coping?'

'Steven, you are doing what you always do, taking your father's side. I have done nothing wrong and I refuse to listen to you demonise me.'

He heard her trying to justify her position, knew that she was right, that she had every right to leave his father. On the one hand, but on the other? 'All I'm saying is—'

She cut across him. 'Hold on one second, my other mobile's ringing. I'll pass you over to Frank.'

He heard a muffled explanation and then Frank Brogan came on the line. 'Steven, your mother just told me about your dad. It must have come as a hell of a shock for you?'

Ross listened to the platitudes, knew how these conversations usually ended. Heard the usual refrain: 'You're welcome here, anytime. You know that, don't you?'

'I've been busy.'

'We're all busy, but you're missing out. We have the Galway Races coming up. Are you a betting man?'

Ross thought of the bet he'd lost to Wheeler, which had cost him breakfast – that was the extent of his gambling habit. It seemed a lifetime away.

'And the fishing season's going great guns. Why don't you come over for it?'

Ross knew that Frank Brogan was, yet again, attempting to forge some kind of a bond between them. He wondered what it was his mother had fallen for; what was it that Frank Brogan possessed that his father hadn't?

Then she was back on the line. 'Steven, dear.'

She had never called him 'dear' and now it felt manipulative, as if they were playing happy families. 'If you let me know the date of the funeral, we'll send flowers.'

Did she even know the man? 'Dad wouldn't want flowers.'

'Then a donation to his favourite charity or whatever it is he wanted. Is it to be a burial or cremation?' She didn't wait for an answer, kept on talking. 'I heard Frank inviting you over. Now I really think that you should come; we are family and this is a time for us all to be together.'

'Together,' agreed Ross. 'Just not at the funeral?'

Silence.

'I wouldn't want to distract you from business. I'll let you know when I've got a date.' He ended the call. He would have to start making arrangements but he'd never had that conversation with his dad. When would have been a good time to ask, 'So, Dad, about your funeral? What would you like? To be buried or cremated? What do you fancy? What feels best?' The dog rubbed her nose against his leg and he leaned down and stroked her. He would deal with the practical issues, but not just yet. He saw a text come through. His mother. He ignored it. Went to a drawer and pulled out a roll of plastic bin bags. He would make a start with the clothes. Knew that something had ended without a goodbye. Without a fucking goodbye.

227

His father had kept one of the bedrooms for him. On a shelf, a photograph of Ross as a child, kitted out in his Raith Rovers strip. He was holding his father's hand and smiling into the camera. The other shelves held his old vinyl and CD collections. Most of the albums he'd converted to MP3s, but he had recently started buying vinyl again. He flicked through them. Belle and Sebastian. Teenage Fanclub. The Bathers. He selected *Kelvingrove Baby*. Heard the opening bars of 'Thrive'. He wandered over to the bookcase. His collection of books. Kurt Vonnegut's *Slaughterhouse 5, Cat's Cradle*. Alasdair Gray's *Lanark*. Iain Banks' *The Wasp Factory*. On the top shelf a catalogue for the Steven Campbell exhibition he and his father had attended. Ross flicked through it. When he'd been a teenager, his father had a habit of taking him into Glasgow's city centre for the day. One time, they'd had lunch at the Third Eye Centre and later had wandered in to see the Campbell exhibition. His father had been a huge fan. His mother was supposed to have been with them but after yet another explosive argument had decided to stay home. Ross wondered if Frank Brogan had already been on the scene. In the gallery, Ross had been transported to a surreal world of ink drawings and massive paintings. He remembered his father and himself sitting on the hard wooden benches borrowed from the Kelvingrove Art Gallery and Museum.

The sound of his mobile cut through the memories. Wheeler.

'Just wanted to check that you're OK?'

'I'm going through his stuff. There's probably going to be a post-mortem, even though they're sure it was a heart attack. The weird thing is, when it's . . .' He drifted.

'Personal?' she prompted.

'Yeah, it's different. I hate to think of Dad going under the saw. I know it sounds like I'm complaining.'

'But since that's unknown . . .'

'I've told Mum and made a start on the house.'

'Anything I can do?'

'Update me. How's the case going?'

'Obviously very slowly without your genius.'

'Boyd, Robertson and the team bumbling along?'

'They do their best. Karlie was seeing a life coach, George Bellerose. He came into the station today. I'm not sure about him, Ross. I don't like him.'

'How did he present?'

'He wanted to appear as the caring professional, but he fell for her, and later, when he was talking, the façade slipped. He did mention that she'd worked in a club where she had to sign a confidentiality contract, meaning they are gagging people who work for them. That in itself is suspicious.'

'A lot of clubs and even local councils have contracts, Wheeler. It's standard. You reckon it's an S&M club?'

'Could be. He also mentioned soap.'

'Soap?'

'Think it might be some kind of fetish. For now, we're concentrating on clubs in and around the Glasgow area. So far, no one is admitting to having known her.'

'Next step?'

'I'm on my way over to see Eddie Furlan, the SIO in the John Merrick murder, to try to get a bit of background from a cop's point of view.'

'I wish I was back there.'

'You need to be getting on.'

'I'm sitting here listening to my old albums and looking through an old exhibition catalogue. Steven Campbell at the Third Eye.'

'"On Form and Fiction".' More of a statement.

'You saw it?'

'Our Art teacher, Mrs Dowling, was very into Campbell, Howson, Currie and Wisniewski. The whole New Glasgow Boys thing. She took us to exhibitions once a month. She bloody insisted that we needed to get out of the classroom and see art in a gallery setting. I think she was stir-crazy at school. We spent hours at the Kelvingrove too.'

'I'll wrap things up here ASAP.'

'There's really no need.'

'I need to, for my own sanity.' He ended the call. Walked through to the kitchen. He'd have another coffee and then head back to Glasgow. Staying in this house felt like sitting with his ghost. His dad was gone. Ross thought of Karlie Merrick, decided that the dead in Glasgow needed him more.

Chapter Thirty-Five

The Bulldog

Wheeler drove, listened to the radio. Hugo Ponsensby-Edward was still banging on about his moral victory.

'. . . and what I'm saying is this, that firm family values are the bedrock of our society and I firmly believe that I have the strict moral code with which to serve . . . I called on the disgraced Nathan Whatley to resign and, finally, reluctantly, he did . . . It was the only moral thing to do in the circumstances . . . We all have to make difficult choices and decisions. I know this myself from experience . . . but I have the moral backbone necessary to . . .'

She knew that there had been a scandal. Nathan Whatley MP had been found with a rent boy. He had now resigned as an MP and also as consultant to two large companies. And the icing on the cake was that he was now bankrupt. Wheeler thought of the politicians she'd heard on the BBC and at Westminster – Hugo Ponsensby-Edward sounded just like all the rest of them. She switched it off.

Eddie Furlan lived in a detached house in Fernleigh Road in Newlands. She knew the houses went for close to four hundred thousand pounds, wondered briefly how he could afford to live there. She rang the bell. Waited. The man who opened the door looked a good decade younger than his years. He was tall and broad with a bushy moustache and a distinctive boxer's nose. But it was his eyes that held her attention. They were the colour of jade. The Paul Furlan she'd known in the army had the same nose and the same unusual eye colour; he was the absolute spit of the man in front of her. She hoped to God Paul wasn't waiting inside, as she fixed a smile on her face and extended her hand. 'Mr Furlan?'

He shook her hand. 'It's Eddie, come in.'

She followed him through the hallway and into a large sitting room. Everything was neat, ordered. 'Tea or coffee, DI Wheeler?' He was halfway to the kitchen. 'I've boiled the kettle.'

'Kat. And a coffee would be great, thanks.' Wheeler perched on the sofa. The room was immaculate to the point of obsession. Two side tables were aligned exactly. On one, the remotes for the television were at perfect angles. On the other, two glass ashtrays. In the bookcase, the books had been arranged by size, except for the bottom shelf where they'd been arranged by colour. Wheeler liked order, but there was something obsessive about Eddie Furlan's place.

He returned carrying a tray, gestured to the ashtrays. 'Would you mind clearing a space?'

Wheeler moved them.

He put a plate of biscuits before her. 'Dreadful news about young Karlie Merrick. Do you have any leads?'

'Nothing yet.'

'And her body was found up by that pub, what's it called?'

'The Coach House.'

'That's the one; it has a bit of a reputation. You think someone from the pub was involved?'

'Too early to say.' Wheeler sipped her coffee.

He reached for a biscuit. 'So you want a bit of background about the John Merrick case?'

'Yes, anything you can recall may be of help.'

'Karlie Merrick must have only been about eight or nine when her father was killed. I remember thinking what terrible bad luck the wee girl had. First the mother passed away – some type of superbug, I think?'

'MRSA. We spoke with Beth Swinton, Karlie's cousin, yesterday. She filled us in about the Merrick family.'

'John Merrick was murdered in his own home. Karlie wasn't there at the time, thank goodness, or God knows what might have happened. And, of course, it wasn't good what we found at the crime scene.'

Wheeler waited.

'Very explicit porn. Violent images of underage girls. Shocking stuff.'

'Did you trace the source?'

'No, we never found out where they came from. Revolting images, given that his eight-year-old daughter was in the house and could have discovered them.' He paused. 'And maybe did. She was interviewed by a psychologist and a whole team of folk, but she gave nothing away. Her father wasn't a good man but she was loyal to him.'

'Abuse?'

'Not that we could prove. The family lived in the Temple area and we did a massive amount of house-to-house, spoke to everyone in the community. No one had any suspicions but then that's often the case. Me and a couple of the boys really dug in hard, but nothing came of it.'

'You and the boys?'

'The whole team was involved but I'd say it was myself, Gerry Dolin and Willie Lester who did the majority of it. Gerry died a year later. Tragic. But Lester, the Old Coyote, kept at it. We were thorough.'

The Old Coyote and the Bulldog, thought Wheeler; they certainly liked their nicknames. She wondered if there was too much reassurance from Eddie. What if Beth Swinton was right, that enthusiasm for the case had cooled? 'Where's Willie Lester now?'

'We lost contact. I think he went off to the country someplace, probably to fish, knowing him.'

'And when you were doing house-to-house, what did you find out about the family?'

'That John Merrick had been a very secretive man who didn't socialise much. Outside of the family a bit of a loner. After the death of John's wife, from what some of the neighbours told me, Karlie became a bit of a handful. But then, after what we found, who knows what was going on in that family.' He reached for another biscuit. 'You got kids?'

'No.'

'I've two sons. The eldest is abroad. He's doing great, he's a credit to me. My late wife adored him too. But kids can be bloody difficult. The youngest, Paul, was a bit of a nightmare, used to swear at his mother. Jean as good as washed her hands of him and let me tell you she was a damn patient woman. He'd real anger management issues, that one, till the military sorted him out. Still, he never made as much of himself as he could've. Certainly he's not done as well as his brother, James.'

She wasn't going to go there. 'Did you have any suspects in the case?'

'It was gang related, I'm sure of it. There were a lot of drugs doing the rounds in those days. A load of heroin arrived and flooded the city. There were a couple of young guys who ran in the local gangs. Nothing changes. I see gangs are still killing. Anyway these two, they thought they were right hard men.' He paused. 'I can't remember their names now. Wait. Give me a sec. One of them was Keith Sullivan, can't recall the other one. I was sure it was one of them or both but there was no evidence to link them to it. My gut instinct said they were the culprits and I know as a cop how accurate gut can be. About a week before the murder, John Merrick's house and a couple of others had graffiti sprayed on the side. It was a gang logo. It was like they were identifying specific targets. A week later, Merrick was dead. Of course we hauled both boys in for questioning. Keith Sullivan was off his face and the other one was a gobby git as usual, giving it the old verbals.'

'And what happened?'

'Eventually, we had to let them go, we'd nothing on them. Nothing at all.' Eddie sat back and sipped his coffee. After a while, he continued. 'They were both around sixteen at the time and I was of the opinion that it was only a matter of time before the good folk at Barlinnie Prison made their personal acquaintance. They were horrible boys, sleekit, feral gang members. Nasty, nasty stuff. No idea if they're still around.' He put his empty cup on the table. 'Wait, I've got it. I remember the gobby one's name, it was Cal Moody.'

Wheeler sat forward. 'There's a Cal Moody works at the pub in Sandyhills, the Coach House.'

'Well, if it's the same guy, I'd get on to him.'

'I'll get to him, Keith Sullivan too. What would've been their motive?'

'Theft, intended burglary. Both Moody and Sullivan were addicts. A lot of teenagers back then were out of their faces on heroin, sedatives, glue. Maybe they thought that, being a therapist, John Merrick would have access to medication. Who knows what went through their drug-addled minds?'

'And Karlie, did she have any ideas about who killed her father?'

'No, as I said she was just a kid at the time.'

'Were any of John Merrick's clients implicated?'

'None. All fine. We contacted all of them and there was nothing suspicious. Mostly folk wanting to lose weight or get over their fear of spiders, flying, heights. The usual list of complaints. We waded through all of them. There were quite a few cancelled appointments, quite usual for a therapist. Lines scored through names, but we tracked them all down in the end, everyone was accounted for. There was a list of clients and we worked through them all.'

'But after all of this, you came up with nothing?'

'I just said that, didn't I?' Furlan sat forward. His tone had changed. 'We did a thorough investigation, Inspector. Believe you me, we covered everything.'

Wheeler recognised the flash of anger, the narrowing of the jade eyes. She'd seen it before. It looked like Paul Furlan had inherited his anger issues from his father. 'I'm sure you did, Eddie, I'm not for a minute suggesting that—'

'I don't like your tone.'

'Eddie, honestly, I'm just—'

'I did everything I could. You saying maybe I missed something?'

'Absolutely not. All I mean is that it's frustrating when they get away. I wasn't implying anything.'

'Of course you weren't.' The bitterness of tone.

'I'm just saying that—'

'I'm just bloody frustrated. We all feel like this when we can't finish the job, when some bastard walks away from a murder scot-free.'

Wheeler changed the subject. 'The cousin told us that Karlie went to stay with her.'

'I remember she was taken in by a relative. She was a singer or an artist or something.'

'A painter,' said Wheeler. 'Did Karlie ever contact you after the investigation?'

'No, I never saw her again.'

'Karlie wanted to take part in a re-enactment of the night her dad was murdered, to have it broadcast on the television.'

'Did she now? I suppose re-enactments can be helpful, but it's twenty years ago now. If anyone was going to come forward, I reckon they would've done so. The case was well documented, it was in all the papers and it got a fair bit of television coverage. We did a massive house-to-house and numerous appeals to the public. But nothing. Lots of folk telling us how much they wanted to help but had nothing concrete to give us. Still, the DNA database is always expanding, so who knows?'

'Beth told me she had a couple of falling-outs with Karlie over the years.'

'I'm not surprised; it happens with kids. I've had a couple of real kick-offs with my sons when they were teenagers, especially the youngest.'

'Beth felt that Karlie had become obsessed with her father's death.'

'Understandable since she didn't have any real closure, but sometimes you just have to try to move on. Life goes on. I struggled when my wife died, but you have to find a way to look forward.'

'I'm sorry.'

'It's only been a month, it's still very raw.'

'Did Karlie ever mention a boy a few years above her at school, Josh Alden?'

'Not that I remember.'

Wheeler finished her coffee. 'I should go now, Eddie. Thanks for taking time to see to me.'

'Believe me, we all wanted to get whoever did John Merrick, but there was just no evidence.'

In the hallway he held the door open for her. 'Do you think the two murders are linked? Maybe it's worth you hauling Moody and Sullivan back in?'

'Certainly it's worth talking to them.'

'The cold case guys will have all the original files from the case, including a full client list.'

'I've already requested copies of everything, and they sent them over.'

''Course there could be another reason the killer wasn't caught.'

'Go on,' said Wheeler.

'Maybe the killer got a dodgy mix of drugs. Happened a lot in Glasgow. They mixed heroin with all sorts of substances.'

'You think the killer overdosed?'

'Either that or someone in the community took things into their own hands and sold them a toxic dose. It wouldn't be the first time a neighbourhood has regulated itself, and the Temple area was very tight.'

'I won't bother you again, Eddie.'

'Keep me up to speed and let me know if I can help.'

Wheeler heard the door close behind her as she made her way through the carefully tended garden, past heavily scented roses and out to the car. She'd begun to feel suffocated in Furlan's presence. He had the same intensity as his son. She'd known that there was a possibility; Furlan was a fairly unusual name, but seeing the green eyes and the boxer's nose had meant that her stomach had soured. The mention of Paul Furlan had brought back memories that she'd buried years ago of a much hated army colleague. Wheeler pushed the images to the back of her mind. She had work to do.

Her mobile rang. Ross.

'I've made the rest of the calls. On my way back to Glasgow. You going over the case?'

'When I get home. I got a couple of names from Eddie Furlan that I need to check out. Cal Moody and Keith Sullivan.'

'Want company?'

'Take some time off.'

'I need to be working.'

'If it would help.' Wheeler knew that, if she were in his position, she would do the same. 'I'll organise some Italian food. See you back at the flat later?'

Their old pattern.

Chapter Thirty-Six

Pirates

Maureen flicked on the television, watched a news segment. A reporter stared into the camera. It was as if he were speaking directly to her. Karlie's face filled the screen.

'Beth Swinton, the cousin of murder victim Karlie Merrick, released this picture of her today in a bid to help stir memories in the community, while police at Carmyle Police Station continue to study CCTV footage of the area where her body was dumped. The detective leading the hunt for Karlie's killer is here with me now. DCI Stewart, can you update us on what's happening with the case?'

The camera cut to Stewart.

'We believe that Karlie was killed at another location and her body moved to the scene. We are asking anyone who saw or heard anything suspicious to come forward.'

'What about possible motives for the killing?'

'We are keeping a completely open mind. Karlie Merrick was a bright, hard-working woman who was also very ambitious. We need members of the public to come forward with any small detail, regardless of how inconsequential they think it might be. The last confirmed sighting of Karlie was when she left Brooks Farm, Strathaven, on Tuesday around 2 p.m. Her car was driven to her home and parked outside, where it remained overnight. Was Karlie driving or someone else? Where did she go after leaving the farm? We need to find out where she went, who she was with. We're asking everyone to think back. Were you on that road that day? Were you in the area? Did you see or hear anything?'

'I believe that you also have a statement from Beth Swinton?'

Stewart read the statement: 'I am distraught that my cousin has been taken in such a horrendous way and would plead with everyone to search their memory and their conscience for any information and to come forward. Someone knows who did this horrendous crime. Please, I beg you to come forward.'

The camera cut to the Sandyhills area as the reporter continued. 'Floral tributes to the victim have been left at the scene where her body was discovered and a Go Fund Me account has been set up by local wedding photographer, Gary Ashton, in order to help Karlie's family. Earlier today, the photographer said that he just wanted to do something to help.'

Back to Stewart.

'We would like to thank all of Karlie's friends and colleagues for their help in building a picture of who she was, but we still need more people to come forward. We are working our way down a list of information received from the public. If you have any information at all, please contact Carmyle CID on 101. Or you can call Crimestoppers on 0800 555 111 where information can be taken in confidence.'

They had nothing, thought Maureen. The screen changed and a reporter in the television studio told her that Police Scotland was struggling with cutbacks and that resources were stretched to breaking point.

Maureen thought of Karlie, of what she'd said about the old man in the care home. Maureen had laughed about it at the time, but what if there was something in it? She made the call, grabbed her bag, locked the door and headed out. She'd check it out herself. It probably was a waste of time, but better to waste her time than that of the police.

Twenty minutes later, she pulled into Fullarton Avenue and parked in front of a long, single-storey building. Fullarton Care Home. When she'd called they'd said they would let Steve Penwell know to expect a visitor. Maureen walked into reception and gave her name to the nurse behind the desk.

'He's in the day room, three doors down on your left.' The nurse paused. 'Are you a relative?'

'A friend of a friend.'

'Have you visited Steve recently?' The woman's voice was low. 'I need to advise you that he can say things that are a little unusual.'

'I know that he's schizophrenic.'

'It can be upsetting to see a change in behaviour or hear unusual comments.'

'Is he capable of knowing what's real?'

'There are moments when he's lucid but at other times he hallucinates. This morning, for example, he was convinced that he was captain of a ship and that the ship was in danger of capsizing.'

'Really?'

'He was most insistent. People with schizophrenia can sometimes suffer from hallucinations. Steve is one of them.'

'Did you explain to him that he wasn't on a ship?'

'No, I reassured him that it was going to be fine. It's not always helpful to continually contradict and undermine him. If I had done so, Steve would only have become agitated and distressed.'

'Right, so if he's talking like this to me, I should just go along with him?'

'I've just been in to see him. He isn't hallucinating at present, so it should be fine. But if he does start, just try to be supportive and calm. At this point it's all about his quality of life. I'll take you through.'

'I think I've changed my mind.'

'Oh dear, I do hope I haven't put you off?'

'It's just that I need to ask him something and to know if it's factually true. From what you tell me, it sounds like he might not know.'

'Just a quick visit? He's already been told to expect you, he'll be glad of the company.'

Maureen caved. 'OK.' By the sounds of it, the visit would be a waste of time.

'Let's pop along now. I'm sure he'll be delighted. His children phone every week but they live in the States.'

The day room had been painted bright yellow and the sofa and curtains were pale blue and there was only one person in the room. Steve Penwell was sitting on the sofa.

'Steve, you have a visitor.' The nurse turned. 'I'll leave you to it.'

Maureen saw a thin shell of a man; his eyes were rheumy, his cheeks sunken. She sat on a chair facing him.

'I'm Maureen, I'm a friend of Karlie's.' Prayed that he already knew, that he'd seen the news on the telly.

'Where's Karlie?'

How was she supposed to tell him? Maureen worried that the news might send him into free fall and he'd start to hallucinate again. She wished she'd turned back after she'd spoken to the nurse. 'She's . . . Karlie's not that well.' She swallowed.

'How not well?'

'Not well at all, Steve.'

He stared at her. 'Will she be coming back to see me? I told her something important.'

There was no other way of saying it. 'Karlie's dead.' She spoke quietly. 'She was murdered.'

'Christ, no?'

'They found her body up by Sandyhills Road.'

'What was she doing up there?'

'Don't know, that's where they found her.'

'They ken who did it?'

Maureen shook her head.

'She tell you we talked?'

'Yes.'

'She tell you what about?'

'A man you saw the night her dad was killed.'

'My eyesight was always good. Not now, mind you, but it was, years ago. I should have gone to the polis back then.' He stared at the curtains. 'There, over there in the curtains! Can you see a face? Someone's listening!'

Maureen looked at the curtains. 'There's nothing there.' Immediately regretted contradicting him.

'Only I don't want spies or pirates to hear me. They're everywhere, but I'm going tell you the same thing I told her.' He leaned closer, his voice dropped to a whisper. 'The night of the murder, I saw a man running. He had a patch over one eye.'

'A patch?'

'Aye, a patch. Like a pirate! I can't remember if it was his left or right eye.' Steve scanned the room. 'But it doesn't matter, does it?' he whispered. 'If you're a pirate.'

'No, it doesn't matter, Steve.'

'You believe me?'

Maureen nodded, remembered not to contradict him.

'You going to tell the polis?'

'I don't know, Steve. Why didn't you?'

He sat forward. 'I was supposed to be at work, but I was with the girlfriend when I saw him. The wife would've left me and taken the kids. I couldn't let her do that.'

'But now?'

'The wife's dead and I'll follow her soon.' He glanced at the curtain. 'There's that face again. I tell you, he's watching me!'

'Did your girlfriend not recognise the man, seeing as how she lived in the area?'

'Never got the chance to ask her. It was the next day before I found out someone had been killed. I tried to call her but she wasn't having it, never returned my messages. Chucked me. I told myself the guy was running for a bus or late for work.'

'Could be, Steve, that would explain it.'

'Then I've been helpful?'

'In a way,' she lied. What was she supposed to tell him? That she'd go to the police station and tell them that an ill man, who thought he was on a capsizing ship, had seen a man wearing a patch, just like a pirate, running from the scene all those years ago? She was glad she hadn't bothered the police. 'I need to get going.' She made for the door.

Steve continued to stare at the curtains. 'You'll come back and visit me?' he called after her.

She turned. 'If I can.'

Once out in the corridor, she took a deep breath. So much for trying to help.

Chapter Thirty-Seven

The Self-Harmer

Cal Moody had been picked up and was waiting in the interview room.

Wheeler made her way briskly along the corridor.

Boyd was beside her. 'And he's happy to talk to us?'

'I wouldn't say he's happy, Boyd, but he's agreed to it, so let's get in there before he changes his bloody mind.'

'How'd you get on with the Bulldog?'

'Eddie Furlan wants to be kept in the loop.'

'Still sees it as his case?'

'I think so, a little bit,' said Wheeler. 'I guess he just wants Cal Moody nailed for it, if he's guilty.' She knew from experience the frustration of knowing who the perpetrator was and not being able to prove it. Gut instinct counted for a lot as a cop, and there were times she'd had to walk away from an unsolved case knowing the culprit had got away with it. Stewart had mentioned Ian Bunyan, the drug dealer, as an example of someone who'd got away with the attack at the Cockroach. Whoever had worked that case would have had to park their frustration. She knew that some crooked cops would plant evidence to back up their theories, but Wheeler had never met one. Others allowed the unsolved cases to eat away at them, destroying their chance of a peaceful retirement. She'd known a few of those over the years, wondered if Eddie Furlan was one of them. 'What about the other guy Eddie had in the frame, Keith Sullivan? Did you find him?'

'Sullivan's dead,' said Boyd.

She turned to him. 'How'd he die?'

'Overdose. Heroin. Eighteen months ago.'

They reached the doorway. Wheeler was first through. She knew that Cal Moody was thirty-six, but the man sitting at the table looked twenty years older. Whatever life he had led after John Merrick's death had left its mark on him. His gaunt face was deeply pockmarked and one hand was heavily bandaged.

Wheeler and Boyd sat opposite him.

'Thanks for coming in, Mr Moody,' said Wheeler.

'This about the Merrick lassie?' Moody eyed them warily.

'Yes, it is,' said Wheeler.

'Well, before you ask, I was working at the Coach House the night she got done.'

'Until when?'

'Till I cut myself in the kitchen.'

'How'd you manage that?' Wheeler thought of the man who'd been previously stabbed at the pub, but, despite the place being crowded, no one had seen anything. And now Cal Moody was cut so badly that he'd ended up in hospital. Whatever else the Cockroach was, it was a hell of a blind spot for self-harming.

'I'm clumsy. I was trying to cut up frozen sausage meat.'

He held up his bandaged hand. 'Ended up at Accident and Emergency at the Royal Infirmary.'

That tied with what the pub manager, Andy Carmichael, had told her. 'And when was this?'

'I can't remember the exact time, but it would be about eleven I did it, around midnight when I was at the Royal.'

It would be easy enough to check the records at the hospital. Karlie had been killed between midnight and 2 a.m.

'Did Andy Carmichael not tell you this when you went to see him?' said Moody.

'Best to hear it from you. Where did you go after the hospital?'

'I went to my pal Davie's. You can phone him if you like? I've got his number here, waiting for you.' He held out a scrap of paper. 'Lives up by Shettleston.'

Wheeler took the paper. 'Thanks, Mr Moody, very organised of you.'

'I don't trust you lot. Call me paranoid but I reckon I'm getting stitched up here.'

Wheeler watched him fidget, wondered what he was hiding. She spoke calmly. 'I'm not here to stitch anyone up, Mr Moody. I just need to find out, for the process of elimination, what you and Davie were doing that night.'

'Gaming. We pulled an all-nighter.'

'Is that right?'

'Aye. "Call of Duty". It was fucking great.'

'Was it just the two of you? All night?'

'Yep.'

'Had Karlie Merrick been in the Coach House?'

'Not as far as I know.'

Again, the fidgeting. Cal Moody didn't know what to

do with his hands. She watched him eventually lace his fingers together, saw the white of knuckle on one hand. The bandage covered the other.

'Are you sure?'

'Definitely.'

'Did you know Karlie?'

'No.'

'I got the impression from Inspector Furlan that you did.'

'Aye well, ages ago, when she was a kid. She was only young. I only knew her to see her.'

'She was eight when her dad was murdered.'

'So I was sixteen then. What are you saying? That I'm some kind of a pervert?'

'Not at all. I'm asking if we could have a bit of a chat about her dad's case?'

'She moved away right after he got killed. Never saw her again.'

'If you could remember anything at all.'

'Can't help you there.'

'Why not?'

'I've got some kind of a condition, brain fog. It affects the memory.'

She saw the trace of a smile develop into a smirk. 'Oh that's fine, Mr Moody. I understand.' Wheeler stood. 'I'll just leave you here for a couple of hours, maybe a rest will help jog your memory? Funny how these things can sometimes help.'

Moody sat back in his seat. 'OK. Fuck's sake. I was only young at the time. I ran with the gang. The Temple. Me and Keith Sullivan. He's dead now. Wee bit too much in the needle. It's the way he'd have wanted to go though.'

'I'm sorry to hear that. You were telling me that you got into trouble when you were younger?'

'A bit. Mostly stupid stuff – thieving, graffiti, gambling – and then I took a bit of a nosedive. Got into drugs. Smack mostly.'

'You were a heroin addict?'

'I just said that! I needed to make some quick money, so did a couple of stupid jobs. I was only a boy. A daft boy. Didn't know any better. My ma and da had split up and me and my sister went to live with the auld man. He's gone now and I hear that my ma's in the Royal Infirmary, dying.'

Wheeler cut through the sob story. 'Do you remember the night of John Merrick's murder, Mr Moody?'

'We were out with the gang, scoring drugs. Furlan wasn't like you two are, sitting here calling me Mr Moody. The last time I was called Mr Moody, I was up in court.'

'This when you were a daft boy?' asked Wheeler, although she already knew the answer.

'It was a while ago now. Got done for resetting a couple of fridges.'

Wheeler knew that there had been a lot more to it, but she wasn't here because of stolen property. Maybe the Cockroach was where he got rid of the stuff? She made a mental note to keep an eye on both the pub and its manager, Andy Carmichael.

'But back then it was a different story. And Furlan? He was old school.'

'In what way?'

'He'd just stop the car and pick you up in the street in front of your pals. Just to embarrass you or try and pretend like you were a grass and feeding him information.'

Moody warmed to the subject and became more animated. 'He gave me a bollocking for smoking one time. Like it had any fucking thing to do with him. He'd try to pressurise us into saying we did stuff that we never did. He was all about clearing the crime rate for his district. He'd stop you in the street for a pretend chat and then have a real go at you. He'd try to trip you up when you said anything by contradicting you and calling you a liar. He was a right twisted bastard.'

It wasn't the first time Wheeler had heard an ex-con mouth off about the police procedure. 'About the night John Merrick was murdered?' she prompted.

'Me and my pals were round the back of the car park. We were getting wasted. Merrick got done that night. First I knew of it was when the polis cars came screeching round the corner and Furlan hauled us into the station. Made us sit there for hours, going over our movements for that night. Next thing we knew, Furlan starts telling us we were fucking suspects. It was way out of order, he was just on some mad fucking mission to get someone banged up for it and he reckoned we'd do.' Moody sneered at her. 'It was Furlan who put you on to me, wasn't it?'

'Inspector Furlan mentioned your name but I just wanted us to have a quiet chat. He's not working this investigation.'

'Thank fuck for that or he'd be in here trying to twist my arm into confessing to this one an' all.'

'Karlie Merrick?' prompted Wheeler.

'I only knew her from being around. She was just a young lassie back then. They never got the guy that did her da, did they?'

'Not yet. Any ideas?'

'I can't help you. Besides, I'm not a grass.'

'But you have some idea who it might have been?'

'No.'

'Anyone in the community have a vendetta against the Merricks? Someone who killed the father and now the daughter?'

'I never heard anything. Read the papers though – seems he was well into porn. The hard stuff.' Moody looked at her. 'You reckon he was grooming Karlie? I read in the paper she was a porn star.'

'What about the drugs? Was there a bad batch around at that time?'

'Not that I remember.'

'Nothing deadly?'

'No.' Moody studied his bandaged hand, absent-mindedly picked at the dressing. 'I think I'm going to get set up.'

'Why would I set you up?'

'You've got my DNA from way back. I know it's on file. The swab?'

'When you were arrested, the police had a right to take a DNA sample.' A mouth swab was standard practice.

'Where's it kept?'

'It's stored in the Scottish DNA database.'

'And you can pull it out now and make it fit the crime.' Moody spat. 'And I get blamed for something some other fucker's done? Furlan couldn't get me for auld Merrick's murder, so you're going to stitch me up for the daughter's.'

Wheeler saw his expression, the wide haunted eyes. Cal Moody was either very guilty or very paranoid. Or both. She knew that any DNA found at Sandyhills on Karlie Merrick's body would have been collected and would be run through the system. 'Is there any reason your DNA would be at the crime scene?'

'I just told you. If it's at the scene, it's because you lot have it already.'

'Do you know anything about Josh Alden from the Kill Kestrels?'

'I've heard of them. Don't know them, though.'

Wheeler asked a few more questions but Cal Moody's increasing paranoia meant that he made little sense. She ended the interview.

'Paranoid or what?' said Boyd outside in the corridor. 'He sounded like he was going into meltdown. Does Moody know what happened that night and he's not saying?'

'And the twitchy body language,' said Wheeler. 'I don't know if he killed Karlie Merrick but he's bloody terrified of something or someone. And no one seems to know anything about Josh Alden.'

Chapter Thirty-Eight

The McIver, Swedish Room

There was the inevitable comedown. The emptiness. He needed the next high. The last time had been OK but way too tame. This time Skye knew that he needed total control.

He was always careful, made sure that it was safe. His experience of the McIver had been good so far; the girls were fine but he needed more. He needed to tailor it to his own exact needs. His preference was erotic asphyxia, and he knew that as he tightened the scarf, his sexual excitement would increase. The high it gave him was more extreme than anything he'd felt. It felt dangerous and scary and sexy. He knotted the scarf. She would only be about three or four inches off the floor. He flicked through the magazine, found a favourite photograph. He'd not known a woman could be bent at such an angle. At least not without extreme pain. He took the magazine and laid it on the table, left it open at his chosen image. Opened the laptop, set up the video.

She came through the door. He watched while she stripped. She had green eyes and her long blonde hair lay smooth and flat. He liked that. She had a tiny scar above her top lip. An imperfection.

He fastened the restraints securely. Slipped the scarf around her neck and adjusted it. Watched the action on the screen, glanced at the photograph, tightened the scarf. Held it steady. No point in going too fast. Kept himself engrossed with the screen, forced himself to think of the production. It was good. Premium rate. The women were beautiful, that was the difference. With cheap porn, the women were so obviously flawed. Never beautiful but sometimes just the right side of depraved. Or really fucked up. A glance at the photograph, the painfully contorted body. Pain. Sex. Beauty. Pain. Sex. Slow down. Slow it down.

Death. It was present in the room with them, its nearness was intoxicating. So close, so close. He couldn't go there. Not here. But it was so fucking tantalisingly close. Hands damp, he worked quickly. He placed the ball gag into her mouth, strapped the collar around her jaw and secured it behind her head. It was breathable; tiny holes were visible in the metal ball, so oxygen could flow through. It was adjustable so he could control how much or how little air she could access. He would be God. He was a rock God. He was immortal. His hand trembled as he closed it. He heard her gasp. Watched her nostrils flair in an attempt to breath. He peered at her, reached over and placed his thumb and forefinger on either side of her nose, squeezed. 'No,' he whispered, 'no air.' He watched her thrash, her head twist and jerk. Ignored the guttural noises. Sat back.

He felt his arousal, moved towards her again, adjusted the ball, let her breathe fully, heard her suck air before he closed the ball again. He leaned back, felt his heart hammer. Took his time, delayed the moment. Forced himself to look away, to study the room, to really notice the detail. The predominant white of the room, the exposed brickwork. Back to the rush. Pain. Sex. Beauty. Pain. He pulled the scarf tight around her neck. Felt his body respond. The increase in pleasure was sublime. A little more. The action on screen intensified; he mirrored the intensity and the vigour. Tightened the scarf further. The photograph. The woman's contorted body swam in front of his eyes, his vision blurred. So close, so close. The scarf was taut. He leaned forward. Forward. Forward. He was dizzy. Disorientated. Strained to breath. Gasped. Sucked on jagged mouthfuls of air. His head felt like it was ready to explode. He came hard. Shuddered. Gasped. 'Fuck!' Opened his eyes. Felt his heartbeat return to normal. Took a deep breath. Calm. Calm. Reached across and released the ball gag.

Nothing.

She wasn't breathing.

Shit, it had only been three or four minutes.

He had a fucking problem.

Chapter Thirty-Nine

Old Patterns

Wheeler hoisted the box of files out of the boot of the car and hauled them up the stairs to her flat. Thought about Eddie Furlan's conviction that John Merrick had been murdered by either Cal Moody or Keith Sullivan. She wondered about Moody's paranoia. And Keith Sullivan? What if he had murdered John Merrick, and, now that he was dead, it may never be proven? But her gut instinct told her that John and Karlie Merrick's murders were connected somehow. And were the Kill Kestrels involved? Once inside the flat, she dumped the box on the coffee table in the living room. Put on a CD. *Straight, No Chaser* by Monk.

Ross arrived as 'Between the Devil and the Deep Blue Sea' started. She collected plates, cutlery and carried them through to the sitting room. Ross opened the wine, poured two glasses. Old patterns.

'Sure you don't want to talk about things?' she asked as the buzzer sounded.

'Positive.'

She went to the door, took the food delivery, brought it through. Spread the contents on the table.

'What are we having?'

'Italian.'

'From the place across the road, with the jasmine plants?'

'Yep.'

They both began with the bruschetta.

'Get me up to speed on the case,' Ross said before sipping his wine. 'Anything more about the group?'

'Nothing. I dug into Josh Alden's background. He grew up in a home, a bit of minor trouble. Nothing on the others. Looks like they're all clean.'

'What did Eddie Furlan say about the John Merrick case? Are you still convinced they're related?'

'There's something in it, Ross. It can't be coincidence. Eddie thought John Merrick's killer was drug and gang related; heroin cocktails were around – cocaine and heroin, or cocaine and morphine. Folk were injecting heroin with very erratic combinations of other drugs, like sedatives and painkillers.'

'He thought it was a robbery gone wrong?'

'He suggested that the killer was a druggie who was desperate. In particular, he had two guys down for it – Cal Moody and Keith Sullivan. Both guys were users. Sullivan's dead. I had Moody in earlier.'

'Let me guess, he denied it?' said Ross.

'Of course. Furlan had another theory, that someone in the community decided not to bother reporting the killer.'

'And let them overdose on a bad batch cut with something fatal?' said Ross. 'That would do the trick. What about the other gang members?'

She read through the notes. 'Apparently they had all been shooting up.' She sat back. 'Furlan's notes are meticulous. He asked all the right questions and complied with standard operational procedures.'

'You sound surprised.'

'There's something about him, Ross. I don't like him. At one point he got very bloody irritable. He bristled when he thought I was somehow questioning his work. It reminded me of the Paul Furlan I knew in the army, who could turn from reasonable to vicious in a heartbeat.'

'Are they related?'

'Definitely, they're the spit of each other. Plus, Eddie mentioned a son, Paul, who had anger management issues, and Eddie certainly has a short fuse.'

'He's probably still angry that the killer got away. You know from experience, it happens. Then you go around and bring it all up again. His failure. He might've been more annoyed with himself than you.'

'He was pissed with me.' She made a start on the pizza. 'I've seen that expression before.'

'Care to enlighten me about Paul?'

'He's a fuckwit.'

'Charming.'

'He was an absolute bully.'

'Towards you?'

'No, but we were under a lot of pressure. There was this younger guy, Colin Jenkins, he was doing his best but was obviously struggling. Furlan just kept at him. Kept repeating that he had to man up, man up, like it was some kind of a fucking mantra. He just kept up with the sarky comments and I could see that it was badly affecting Jenkins. It wore him down and he got depressed, but Paul Fucking Furlan just wouldn't give it a rest.'

'What happened?'

'On the second last day of the tour Jenkins was killed.'

'I'm sorry.'

'It was a tough time. Anyway, it's over. We need to concentrate on the case, forget Paul Furlan.'

'What else do we have?'

'These.' Wheeler looked at the copies of the images found in John Merrick's home. Teenage girls, all naked, stared back at her with large, soulless eyes. They lacked the vibrancy of their years, had probably been drugged. She understood Beth Swinton's belief, that after finding these disturbing images, the cops had lost some of their energy to find the killer. She held them up to Ross.

'Revolting,' he said. 'Was Karlie groomed by her father? No wonder the police went on a go-slow to find his killer. What sort of a man looks at filth like this?'

Wheeler lifted photographs from the two post-mortems. 'John Merrick's attack was frenzied, his face bruised and beaten. Other than the ligature marks around her neck, Karlie looks like she's sleeping.'

'Frenzied attack versus a contained approach. A different killer?' asked Ross.

'Or a different approach,' said Wheeler.

'Suspects?' asked Ross.

'For Karlie? Pierce, Ashton, Reid. Someone she worked with? Someone she knew vaguely? Someone she'd never met? One of the Kill Kestrels? At this stage, bloody everyone.'

'Ashton certainly has a temper.'

'He threatened to kill Karlie. And Pierce had a thing for her. Unrequited. He'd no alibi.' She reached for another slice of pizza. 'Bellerose, the life coach, was rankled when asked where he was that night. Had a thing for her and also no alibi.'

'Could be any of them.'

'CCTV came back from Glasgow Harbour Development showing Karlie going into the front entrance to her flat at 7.15 p.m.,' said Wheeler. 'She didn't come back out again, at least not by the front.'

'Car still out front?'

'All night.'

'Back entrance?' asked Ross.

'Not covered.'

'You reckon she knew her killer?'

'You saw the flat, there was no sign of a struggle or a break-in, she opened the door to whoever killed her.'

'What about neighbours?'

'We've taken statements from all of them. No obvious suspects yet.' She brought out the list of John Merrick's appointments. 'But, look here, see these cancellations. All these clients just didn't turn up for their appointment on a regular basis. I don't know, it feels like there's something wrong.'

'Clients get to cancel,' said Ross.

'But every week? Eddie said that he'd checked out all the clients, but—' she shook her head '—there was something about his defensiveness.'

'You think he's holding back information?'

'I don't know.' She stared at the crossed-out appointments. 'Some names have been completely obliterated. There's something about the desk diary, something's amiss.'

* * *

It was late when Ross finally left, but she couldn't sleep. Talking about Paul Furlan had brought it all back. She thought that when she'd left the army, she had successfully buried the memories. She thought of Colin Jenkins and his death, of Paul Furlan and his continual taunts. She knew that she needed to let the memories go, but when she closed her eyes she was back in the army, watching Furlan bully Jenkins. Heard him use his most often repeated phrase. Man up. Just man the fuck up. She felt the bile rise in her.

Chapter Forty

The Security Guy

Paul Furlan had arrived in minutes. He quickly closed the door behind him. Locked it. Recognised the signs. Knew that Holly Lithgow would have fought for breath, but the restraints had been secure. Her mind and lungs would have scrambled furiously to search for a source of oxygen. Any at all. Any way of breathing. She had died from suffocation. Erotic asphyxiation had its downside. He opened his bag, took out the tarpaulin, put it to one side. Took out the fresh bar of soap, unwrapped it. The medicinal smell hit him and he was instantly transported back to the family house, his mother complaining to his father about him. His father reaching for the soap. His mother turning away, symbolically washing her hands of him. He crossed to the body, double-checked for a pulse. Nothing. But she was still warm. He removed the restraints and the ball gag. Her eyes were open, her long blonde hair was damp and lay in disarray. The scar above her top lip quivered as he sat astride her, opened her mouth, pushed the bar of soap inside. Began working it into a lather. Felt his arousal begin. He'd take his time, there was no rush, he had all the time he needed. 'Don't we, Jean?' he asked the corpse. 'What do you say, Jean?'

When he'd finished, he spread the tarpaulin over her body. Wrapped it. Tied it securely. Threw what was left of the bar of soap into a bin bag. Heard her mobile ring, glanced at the screen, the name *Nikki* flashed up. He shoved it into his pocket, locked the door securely behind him. He'd be back later.

In the Braque Hotel, Skye reached for the bottle of Merlot, opened it. Didn't bother with a glass. Put the bottle to his mouth and took a long, long drink. He was on fire. Felt immortal. He carried the bottle to the desk, sat.

Began with the lyrics.

'We were meant to be together . . . a love so strong, you couldn't speak . . . so much between us . . . so much to say . . . I wanted to tell you that us being together . . .'

He picked up his acoustic guitar, fingered an open C chord, strummed, let the notes ring out. Tried a couple of melodies for the first line, 'We were meant to be together . . .' Carried on composing. This was what he was meant to be, this was who he was.

This was his destiny.

Chapter Forty-One

Horses in the Forest

Owen had never had the money to have it properly framed. Thought he'd wait until he had a wall to hang it on. The cardboard backing he'd put in place to keep it upright was now buckling and the plastic cover was peeling. He stared at the card, willed the fairground horses to move. Knew that they were trying but the poles that should have connected them to the carousel, connected them instead to the darkness in the forest. The branches of the trees wove around them, kept them stationary as they tried to prance. The tiny horse, now he was looking closely, looked more like a little pig. It looked off into the darkness, ready to run to its death. The horse in the foreground, the one with the pink saddle— Oh for fuck's sake! Why hadn't he seen it before? What was wrong with him? The big horse, its pink mane long and flowing, a pink tail, three golden stars on her rump, pranced and dominated. He could see it now. The horse with three stars had a horn. It wasn't a horse. It was a unicorn. It had a long tail and a horn in the middle of its forehead. A fucking unicorn. The other horse, the one with the blue saddle, was stepping out, legs high. A purple plum on its head. A male? No stars on its rump, only a series of circles, nine in all. Did they mean something? Where they runes? Could they tell Owen his future? Above the horses, strung through the trees, were lights to illuminate the darkness. But how long would they last before the darkness would engulf them? If there was music, would that help? Carousels always had music. They needed music. He reached forward, switched on the radio. The Kill Kestrels' 'Death of an Angel' was being played.

His hand throbbed. The pain seemed to reverberate to its own internal rhythm. It was a physical reminder of his cowardice; he'd been caught by a sharp blade while running away. Running away! Owen peeled off the filthy bandage and the odour hit him. The wound had blackened and smelled like liver that had gone off. A scent that whispered of maggots and decay and death. He clumsily rewrapped the wound. The song ended and he switched off the radio. Touched the card. His birthday card. His talisman. Suddenly, he felt clear and certain. He knew that he was going to die in this collision. He let the knowledge settle around him like a cloak. All the fear and frustration and anxiety about the world, the fucking world that he had never belonged to, left him. In death there would be a quiet dignity. This would be his last move on earth. The one gift which would convince Mason that he had been a faithful foot soldier. That he was to the end brave and true and good. That's the way he would be spoken about, it's how Mason would remember him. A fitting epitaph his grandfather had often said when reading the obituaries of his friends. This would be his fitting epitaph. Owen glanced again at the picture, was startled and delighted to hear the horses and the unicorn snort, saw them paw the ground. Impatient, they wanted to get going, for their journey into the underworld to begin. He heard the organ music in the distance. There had never been music in the picture before, the forest had always been silent. But now it was transformed, the stage was set. The horses moved rhythmically, the unicorn to the fore, the music getting louder and louder until it surrounded him and all he could see and smell and hear were the dancing horses. He felt the heat from a myriad of coloured light bulbs. The scene sucked him in. If he could make it to the forest after the crash, he would be home. Finally, he would have a home.

Paul Furlan parked the car and began to haul the tarpaulin, which contained Holly's body, out of the boot. There was nowhere he could conceivably dump it. It would have to be the river. He'd driven her car from the McIver Club and parked it in long-term parking at Prestwick Airport. His mobile chirped a text.

His father.

> Where the hell are you? We were supposed to meeting for a nightcap. I'm waiting here in the bloody bar.

'Shit.' He started texting.

> Sorry, Dad, have to work late at the club.
> An emergency. Lunch tomorrow as arranged?

> Bloody useless, I could have met up with one of the guys.

> See you tomorrow?

> Be sharp.

Furlan stuffed the mobile back into his jeans, heaved the tarpaulin over his shoulder and began the journey. The area was deserted, the night air warm and pleasant. He reached the riverbank, hauled the package to the edge. Slipped it into the water, watched it sink. Threw her mobile in after her. Not ideal, he knew, but time was short.

Chapter Forty-Two

Friday

Laura McCormack

Wheeler met him halfway down the stairs, 'We're off out, Ross.'

'I haven't bloody arrived yet.'

She kept walking.

He caught up with her at the door. 'Where to now?'

'Laura McCormack, Karlie's colleague, has a place in Greenfield. Her flight from Amsterdam landed at eight this morning. I'll drive.' She paused. 'How are you feeling?'

'Better now I'm back on the case; might need to make a few calls en route though.'

And he did.

On the way she heard him talk to the funeral director, heard the change in tone. Glanced at him, saw him kill the call. Saw the tears threaten.

He took out a pair of reflective sunglasses, slipped them on.

'That your Hollywood look?' said Wheeler.

'Yeah. Difficult to imagine that I could look even cooler.'

'It's a struggle.'

'George Clooney or what?'

'I'd have to go for the "or what".'

'You're in denial.'

'You need a hand with anything? Are you going back to Pittenweem?'

'The house needs to be cleared, but I'll wait until after the funeral. I took a load of his clothes and books to the charity shop, and the bigger stuff, the artwork and sculptures, can wait. I'm not sure what to do with the house.'

'You wouldn't want to keep it?'

'As a holiday home?'

'Either that or maybe let it?'

'Not sure.'

'Don't make any rash decisions. These things take time.' She turned the car into Lightburn Place. Laura McCormack lived in a semi-detached house midway down the street.

'Anything turn up on Karlie Merrick's social media accounts?' he asked.

'Not yet. Robertson and the team have gone through all her posts, Facebook, Twitter and Instagram. Mainly selfies. Lots of likes and retweets. So far no obvious flashpoints.' She parked the car. 'And the clubs we've visited have turned up negative.'

The woman who opened the door to them was physically very different from their victim. While Karlie had been petite, with dark hair and delicate features, Laura was tall and broad with blonde hair and strong features. She'd obviously been crying. 'I can't believe wee Karlie's dead. I just can't believe it.'

They followed her into the living room.

'I mean, I just don't feel safe any more . . . I look at Gary, Johnny and Will and wonder would they be capable? Of course I know they wouldn't. But still . . .' Laura began to cry again, then to hyperventilate.

Wheeler spoke calmly. 'Deep breaths, Laura, that's it, nice deep breaths.'

'I'm sorry, I just got scared. The thought of poor Karlie being left out all night in the pitch dark terrifies me. I mean, her lying there on her own all night.'

'You were talking about Gary, Will and Johnny?' said Wheeler.

'I just look at every man now and wonder what he could be capable of. It's scary.'

'Go on.'

Laura was wide-eyed. 'Oh no, I don't mean that they really could be capable of doing anything, well, definitely not Johnny or Will.'

'But Gary?' said Wheeler. 'You're not so sure of him?'

'Gary shouts a lot; he's got a hell of a temper but . . . I don't think he could ever do that. Not really, no. He just gets angry.'

'What does he get angry about?'

'If you don't face the camera properly or you don't move the way he wants you to. It's not like we don't try, but sometimes he expects us to be mind-readers. *Move this way, no, I meant the other way.*' She mimicked him.

'Did Karlie and Gary ever argue?'

'No more than the rest of us with him. He can be an absolute prick sometimes. Karlie would get pissed off about the poor lighting or the lack of script or the fact that there's no bloody washing facilities, the usual stuff. She often tried to develop the storyline, to be more

272

professional, but Gary just wanted her naked and moaning. He didn't care about dialogue.'

'Did she mention anyone else? Was there anything she was anxious about or anyone who wanted to harm her?'

'No.'

'What about the group, the Kill Kestrels. Did she ever mention them?'

'No.'

'Think, Laura,' said Wheeler. 'Was there anything at all? It could be really helpful for the investigation. What about a club. Did she ever mention a club?'

Laura was silent for a few seconds. 'Yes, she did once. We were at my cousin Sandra's twenty-fifth birthday party. Well, her birthday and her divorce day combined. It was at the Sandy-Shack; do you know it?'

Wheeler gave a brief nod. The Sandy-Shack was a complete dive, which had a reputation for attracting a rough crowd. It was known as the Shit-Shack.

'Karlie didn't drink, but some idiot put something in her Diet Coke. Spiked it. She was staggering about like she was really drunk. The guy was watching her and laughing. Well, I knew exactly what he was up to. I quickly got her out of there and into a taxi and brought her back here. My cousin was pissed off that I'd left so early, but I thought Karlie needed taking care of.'

'And the guy who spiked her drink?'

'Never saw him again. I asked my cousin but she says he came with a friend of a friend, she'd no idea who he was. Karlie was babbling, talked about her mum and dad and stuff and how she missed them. It all got muddled up together.'

'But the club? What did she say about it?'

273

Laura took her time. 'She said she'd had to sign a confidentiality thingy at the club.'

'A confidentiality agreement?'

'Yes, that she wasn't supposed to talk about it, but that it felt odd to have to sign an agreement. She said she went to the unicorn and then she started laughing and said that she thought that maybe it was a good omen. I'd never seen her like that.'

'The Golden Unicorn, the hotel in the West End?'

Laura shrugged. 'I didn't know what she was talking about; it was as if she was drunk. She said it was the view from the unicorn that did it for her. It was when she was talking about the club.'

'Not the view of the unicorn?'

'I'm sure she said the view *from* the unicorn because I thought she was on a horse or some type of unicorn on a carousel, like they have at the carnival? She said she loved the view and that it was historic.'

'Was there a carnival here at the time?'

'Not that I know of, and when I asked her the next morning she denied saying any of it, said she made it up for a laugh.'

'You didn't believe her?'

'I wasn't sure what to think. Maybe she didn't want me to apply to work at this club. Karlie was great in lots of ways but she was really competitive, she liked to think of herself as a star. She was a bit of a diva.'

'Can you think of anything else about this unicorn place? What made it historic? Could it be the Kibble Palace at the Botanic Gardens? It's across from the Golden Unicorn Hotel.'

Laura paused, thought for a few seconds. 'She said it

was a historic monument. Sorry. Believe me, if I knew anything else, I'd tell you.'

'This is very helpful, Laura,' said Wheeler. 'And, just to be clear, as far as you know, no one had threatened her or implied that they wanted to harm her?'

'No, she wasn't involved in anything dodgy. She had a normal life.'

'What about Cal Moody or Keith Sullivan?'

'Never heard of them.'

'Boyfriends?'

Laura shook her head. 'I feel like I haven't helped at all.'

Wheeler tried again. 'Did she ever mention soap?'

'Soap?'

Wheeler nodded.

'Not really, no. She was pissed that there were no washing facilities at the farm, but not specifically soap.'

They left their card and thanked her. 'If you think of anything else, Laura, no matter how small, will you call me?'

Laura followed them to the door. 'I don't feel safe with the killer out there. I mean, what if it's someone she knew, someone we both knew?'

'If you feel threatened at all, please get in touch. Straight away. Promise?'

'Promise.'

The door closed and Wheeler heard the lock being turned. 'This place, the Unicorn, if it's the hotel, is diagonally across from the Botanic Gardens. You reckon the historic monument Karlie talked about was the Kibble Palace? There's a marble statue of Eve in the Kibble, by the Italian sculpture Scipione Tadolini. Remember it featured in a load of Gary Ashton's wedding pictures? Let's get over to the Golden Unicorn, see if they remember her. And the Kill Kestrels were also at the hotel. Karlie wrote to them, tried to get in touch with Josh. I'll get on to the café in the Botanic Gardens. She may have been there since coffee shops were her thing.' On her way to the car, she continued. 'It had to be a bloody unicorn; they're everywhere, being Scotland's official animal.'

'I thought it was the lion rampant?' said Ross.

'It's the unicorn. Used to be used on Scottish heraldic symbols. Think of all the unicorns dotted about the place. The Lion and the Unicorn staircase at Glasgow University? Mercat Cross, Edinburgh? The UK coat of arms?'

'Can't say I've really noticed.'

'You're driving; I need to make a call.' She spoke with the manager of the café at the Botanic Gardens, listened to her agree to talk to the staff, heard her reiterate that they'd all seen the report of the murder in the papers and also the television coverage and she was certain that if any of her staff had seen Karlie, they would have mentioned it. But yes, of course, she would speak to them all again, but she'd already put the poster with Karlie's photograph and the appeal for information on the noticeboard. Wheeler thanked her and ended the call.

'Any joy?' said Ross.

'Not yet, but the unicorn is a breakthrough.'

'I hope so, Wheeler.'

'I can feel it.'

Chapter Forty-Three

The Old Neighbour

Downfield Street, in Glasgow's East End, was a mixture of housing, mainly semis and flats. Adele Free lived in a housing complex for the elderly. Josh rang the bell, waited. A few seconds later, he heard a voice. 'Out of the way, Barney, get out of the way.' The door opened and an enormous ginger cat shot past him. Adele Free stood in the hallway. She was the same as he'd remembered her. She'd always looked like an old lady, with her white hair and an old-fashioned apron tied around her waist. 'Adele Free? You won't remember me, but I used to live a couple of doors down from you. Susan Moody fostered me and my sister for a while in 1994?'

She peered up at him. 'Give me a minute. Who'd you say you are?'

'Joshua Alden. I was ten at the time. Susan Moody fostered me and my sister, Amber.'

'I recall that Susan fostered a lot of kids.'

A long pause.

'There was a fire when we were there.'

'Oh my God, I remember the fire, and yes, there was a wee girl that was killed, poor thing. It was awful.'

'I just wanted to have a bit of a chat about it, if that's OK?'

'How did you get my address?' Suddenly suspicious.

'A friend of mine asked around. He knew some folk from our old scheme. He's a PI.'

'A what?'

'A private investigator.'

'Would I know him?'

'Cutter Wysor?'

'Hell of a name.'

'Yeah, it's unusual.'

'Means nothing to me.' She opened the door fully. 'It's as well you managed to find your way here. My son Ricky only lives down in Bridgeton, but can he make it over here to see his old mother? No chance. My four girls make the effort to see me though.' She ushered him into the living room. 'Sit down. Mind you don't get covered in cat hair. Barney's a big boy and he moults everywhere and you're dressed all in black, the hairs will show. That's what young folk tend to wear, isn't it, black, even in this heat? In my day it was different. And your ear lobes! What on earth have you done to them? There are holes straight through them.'

'I've stretched them. It's the fashion.'

'Looks painful.'

'It's fine.'

'Would you like a cup of tea or coffee, son?'

Josh sat on the sofa. 'I'm OK thanks, Mrs Free. I just wanted to ask you a couple of things about when we stayed with Susan.'

'I bumped into old Agnes last week down at The Forge shopping centre. She told me Susan was poorly.'

'Yeah, I went to see her in the hospital.'

'I don't go near those places, I'm feart that I'll not come back out again. How did she seem to you?'

'I don't think she'll be coming out.'

'See. Telt you. Stay away from hospitals, folk die in them. What with them superbugs and the other sick folk coughing and sneezing germs all over the place.'

'Were you friends with Susan?'

'No, we weren't really friends exactly, just neighbours. We went to the bingo a couple of times together. Not that I went out a lot, what with the kids and all. Maybe a couple of times a month, I'd see her at the bingo hall if there was a big prize.'

'Was Susan at the bingo the night of the fire?'

'I can't remember. She moved away soon after, said she couldn't stay in that house. Don't think anyone blamed her. The wee girl who died, you say she was your sister?'

'Yeah. Amber Ellis.'

'I'm awfully sorry, you two hadn't been there long, had you?'

'Only a few weeks.'

'It was a tragedy, a right horrible thing to have happened.'

Josh let the silence stretch, allowed the old woman to remember the night. It had happened in her housing scheme, to her neighbour, and it would have been in all the papers. 'Had Susan lived in the house for a long time?'

'About four or five years if I remember rightly. Mind you, although they rehoused her the day after the fire, it took them a good few months after that to do up the house. I moved away not long after.'

'She lived alone, didn't she? I mean other than the kids she fostered?'

'That's right.'

'Only I was wondering if she had anyone around that night, maybe someone she asked to babysit?'

'Did you not ask her when you visited her in the hospital?'

'I did.'

'And what did she say?'

'She denied it. But I don't believe her.'

Mrs Free stared him. 'Why would she lie?'

'I don't know.'

Silence.

He broke it. 'Can you remember anything else about her, Mrs Free? Anything at all?'

'Give me a minute.' The old woman closed her eyes, frowned in concentration. Eventually, she spoke. 'She had kids, they would've been older than you and your sister, but they didn't live with her. She'd only ever had the two. I wondered if that was why she fostered; maybe she'd wanted more kids but couldn't have them? Or maybe it was just because things hadn't worked out between her and her man?'

'The kids weren't there when Amber and I lived with her, not that we were there that long. But she never mentioned them.'

'They lived with their dad. I think it all went sour around the time of the divorce. The kids sided with their dad and the three of them moved to the Temple area. Susan said she hadn't seen them much afterwards, said it was like a kick in the teeth to her. A bit like me and my son, Ricky. I've not seen him for five years and even then it was at my cousin's funeral. His youngest will be eighteen now. It happens in families. Folk take sides against other folk.' She paused. 'You have family?'

'No. After my mother died, it was just me and Amber.'

'I'm sorry, I just open my mouth sometimes. I thought that you might've had kids of your own.'

'Maybe one day,' said Josh. 'Right now I'm concentrating on my career.'

'What is it that you do?'

'I'm in a band, the Kill Kestrels.'

She blinked, her expression blank. 'Then good for you, here's hoping you make the big time, eh?'

Josh sat forward on the sofa. 'Susan's kids, what were their names?'

The old woman thought for a long while. 'I can't remember now, I never met them. She only moved in after her divorce. Susan usually called them "the kids" when she was ranting about the divorce and the falling-out. She was really angry with them. There was a rumour from one of the other neighbours who knew the dad, think she was maybe seeing him on the fly, that the son got into drugs, heroin it was. That stuff was everywhere back then. Thank God none of my kids ever touched it. Give me a second, that's right I remember now, the neighbour said the son's name was Cal. I think that was it. Not sure now. But I can't remember what the daughter's name was. The neighbour said there was a bit of a stand-off between Susan and the daughter, something about a boyfriend Susan didn't approve of. Wait, I think the daughter's name was Lynn or Lyndsay. Susan wanted her kids to come about the house more – not sure if they ever did though.'

'A boyfriend?' *He had heard a man and woman shouting. The daughter and a boyfriend? Or the son and daughter?*

'Aye. Susan said he was applying for the forces or the police or something. She thought he was going to go off and the daughter would be dumped, probably left holding a baby.'

'Can you remember his name?'

The old woman took her time. 'The neighbour mentioned the boyfriend's name and it was the same as our minister's name. What was the minister's name? Furness or Furlan? Give me a minute. That's it. It was Furlan.'

'First name for the boyfriend?'

'Sorry.'

'No worries, it's a start. And you had no way of knowing I'd pop up after all these years.' Josh stood to leave. 'Thanks very much, Mrs Free.'

She followed him into the hall. 'It was my pleasure. I'm sure your mum is looking down on you and is really proud of you being in a band and all.'

He doubted it.

'And wee Amber will be reunited with her; they'll be together now.'

He certainly hoped the fuck not. He knew the old woman was just trying to be nice, that she was speaking in platitudes uttered by the well-meaning, however inappropriate. Perhaps that's why her son stayed away? Families could be toxic; his certainly had been.

When Mrs Free opened the door, the cat meandered in and sat at her feet.

'You used to have a white cat. Willow. I remember it.'

'Oh, you've a great memory. Willow was a gentle wee thing, not like this big bruiser.' She bent down and stroked the cat's head affectionately. 'He eats me out of home and habitation. Still, he's great company. I'm sorry I couldn't be of more help, son.'

The door closed behind him and he walked to the car. The old woman had given him names and so the next piece of the puzzle. He could feel it; this was important.

The internet was his friend in these matters. And if he couldn't find Susan Moody's son Cal or her daughter Lynn/Lyndsay or the Furlan guy, something told him that he could count on Cutter Wysor to do so. Josh felt optimistic about the chase. He pulled out his phone, typed 'Furlan Glasgow' into the engine, got a couple of hits.

First up an article about a cop. DI Edward Furlan had retired from the police. Josh read on. Adele Free had mentioned that the boyfriend might have been in the forces or the police. Age wise, Eddie Furlan would have been forty at the time? Presumably, given Susan's age, the daughter would have been a lot younger. Was that why Susan Moody didn't approve, or was it another Furlan altogether?

Next up was a death notice from the *Chronicle*. Eddie Furlan's wife had died a month previously.

Furlan

Jean Dorothy, peacefully at the Royal Infirmary
on Thursday 12 June, aged 60. Devoted wife to
Eddie, much loved mother of Paul and James.
Funeral service to take place at Cathcart Old
Parish Church on Friday 20 June at 11 a.m.

Josh punched the numbers into his mobile.

'Cutter? I need your help. I need to find Susan Moody's son, Cal. And her daughter, Lynn/Lyndsay and her ex-boyfriend. I think the guy's name is Eddie, James or Paul Furlan.'

'Don't know any Furlans but there's a guy name of Cal Moody works out at the Cockroach. Give me a bit of time to check if it's the right person and I'll get back to you.'

Chapter Forty-Four

Memories and Meetings

Josh knew that the work he'd done with the hypnotherapist had uncoiled parts of his memory. He thought about
the policewoman, Wheeler, who had asked him about
Karlie Merrick. His memory didn't include her. She had
never figured in his life. He closed his eyes and was back
in his mother's house. He felt the familiar resistance to go
there; ignored it. Finally, he let the memory flood his
mind. The night she'd died, his mother had passed out.
He was kneeling on the kitchen floor, looking through the
cupboards for food, when she'd woken up and begun
screaming at Amber for crying, for her own lack of drugs,
for the whole sorry mess that was her fucking life. He saw
his ten-year-old self take out an old bottle of drain cleaner,
pick up a half-empty bottle of vodka and pour the drain
cleaner into it. He'd shaken the bottle well, mixed the two
liquids thoroughly. Heard his mother slap Amber, saw
her stagger through to the kitchen, grab the bottle and
begin to drink the liquid. The vodka alone might have
killed her; she drank it like Coke. But even back then he'd
known what had happened, had understood somewhere

deep in his psyche that it would kill her. Finally, he'd heard her retch. He'd ignored her and had quietly taken Amber's hand and they'd left the house. Began walking. He understood completely that his mother had been dying. The images came flooding back, sharp and clear as ice. He crossed to the minibar, opened the bottle of white wine, poured a large glass, began drinking. He would wait for Cutter to call.

Cutter parked outside the Cockroach.

Inside, the manager Andy Carmichael nodded to him. 'Cutter, what brings you out?'

'Need a quick word with one of your staff.'

'That right?'

'Cal Moody.'

'What's he been up to then? It's not his week. He had a bit of a mishap the other night.'

'So I heard, he was clumsy with a knife, ended up in A and E.'

'Correct.'

'Interesting that Ian Bunyan was in the kitchen with him at the time.'

'Purely coincidental.'

'I'll bet.'

'This anything to do with Bunyan's gripe? Only, he's on his way over for a drop-off?'

'No, personal business. Just need a bit of information, a couple of names and addresses.'

Carmichael stood aside. 'Moody's in the back. Help yourself, I'm sure he'll tell you whatever you need to know.'

'He'd better,' said Cutter.

Twenty minutes later, Josh's mobile rang and he listened to instructions. 'Meet up at the Coach House in twenty.'

Josh texted for the Range Rover to be brought around.

Soon they were parked behind the pub.

'I don't like the look of this place, not one bit,' said the driver. 'You sure this is the place?'

Josh sat in the back seat of the car. 'Cutter said it was here.'

The driver tapped a finger on the wheel. 'It doesn't look too salubrious, Josh. Maybe you can meet this guy back at the hotel? This place looks very fucking dodgy.'

'We're staying.' Josh watched a black Honda pull in and park. Saw the driver pull off his helmet.

'Shit,' said the driver. 'That lunatic there is Ian Bunyan. A creep and a sadist. Believe me, you don't want to be hanging around with people like him.'

'He's not the one I'm here to see.'

'Christ, if you get into a barney inside, Dougie'll kill me.'

'No worries, I'm meeting Cutter and he can handle himself. Not that I can't.'

Five minutes later, and they were in the back room.

Cal Moody tried and failed for a smile. 'All right, guys?'

Cutter sat opposite him. Josh stood.

Andy Carmichael approached. 'Listen, Cutter, I don't want any trouble. If Moody's fucked up, take it outside. I've already had the filth crawling over the place and Bunyan's just left. Talk about trying to keep this place under the radar.'

'Just need a quiet word, Andy.' Cutter smiled.

'You want a drink? On the house?'

'Absinthe for me.' Cutter turned to Josh. 'You?'

'Vodka.'

'Right it is then, gents.'

Moody spoke. 'I'll have a—'

Carmichael ignored him, made his way to the bar.

Josh looked around the place. It was a low-rent dive of a bar and, from his perspective, Cal Moody looked like hell. He was shaking and his hand was bandaged. But he was also the image of his dying mother, Susan. Things were looking up.

Chapter Forty-Five

The Birthday Lunch

The McIver was busy, the atmosphere loud and convivial. Lunch at the club, often a boozy affair, was served in the Oak Room. A smattering of members were dining alone. Some were talking discreetly into mobile phones, making deals, organising meetings.

Paul Furlan strode into the room. He led as usual with his shoulders. He wore a grey linen Ted Baker suit, a pristine white shirt and a teal tie. An expensive stainless-steel diver's watch was just visible on his left wrist. He nodded to an ex-MP who was lunching with one of the city's leading barristers.

A waiter approached him. 'Your guest's already here, Paul.'

He could see his father had been seated at his favourite corner table. 'Fine.'

Furlan saw Mark Ponsensby-Edward at a table. Ponsensby-Edward's white hair and moustache were in stark contrast to his black suit. Paul approached the table, heard the boast, 'It was heaven.' Mark raised his wine glass to his guest. 'Honestly, Mauritius was sublime, the hotel was magnificent . . .'

'Enjoying your lunch, Mark?' said Paul.

'Paul.' Ponsensby-Edward smiled. 'The lamb heart is excellent.'

'Glad to hear it.' Paul continued on to his father's table. 'Hey,' he greeted him. 'How goes it, birthday man?'

'You're late, you always were. It used to drive your mother mad.'

'Sorry, Dad.'

'And what the hell happened to you last night? We were supposed to be meeting for a nightcap. I was left in the bloody pub alone.'

'Apologies, I had to stand you up. I was working late.'

'What was so important that you had to do it last night?'

'Forget it, it's all sorted now, Dad.' Paul tapped the menu. 'This new menu looks great, doesn't it? I can't decide between the pig's ear or lamb heart. What says you?'

'The lamb heart followed by steak tartare. Mark recommended it. If it's good enough for Mark Ponsensby-Edward, it'll do me fine. I've just had a quick word with him; he was telling me how well Hugo's doing. He's a real success, with a beautiful wife and kids, not to mention a stellar career. He has his constituency in London and is a rising star in the Tory Party. And now that Nathan chap has resigned. You could do worse than to look to Hugo as a role model. What do you think?'

Paul studied the menu. 'I think I'll have the pig's ear.'

A waiter approached. 'Would you like to order?'

Paul recited his father's order, added a main course of venison for himself and glanced quickly at the wine menu. 'What do you fancy? I'd settle for the Côtes du Rhône. It always does the job.'

'Brilliant, why don't we *settle* for it, there's no point in overdoing it on my birthday.'

'Christ, Dad, you said you didn't want a fuss.'

The waiter jotted down their order, returned a few minutes later and poured the wine. Left them to it.

'Cheers.' Paul raised his glass. 'Happy birthday.' He slid a package across the table.

Eddie opened it, took out the stainless-steel diver's watch, frowned. 'It's the same as yours.'

'You said you liked my watch.'

'Why would I need a diver's watch? I barely swim at the local pool.'

'It's—'

'Never mind, it's fine.' Eddie put the watch back into its case, snapped it shut and pushed it aside.

'You said you didn't even want a present,' said Paul.

'Not on your salary.'

'I'm doing all right.'

'Not in comparison with your brother James or Hugo Ponsensby-Edward.'

'No one makes their salaries—'

'They do.'

'Dad, I'm well thought of here. I'm respected.'

'You only got this job because Mark Ponsensby-Edward put in a good word for you. You owe him big time. He did it as a favour to me and don't you ever forget it.'

'Mark owes us!'

'Me, not you. You did nothing but fuck up. Remember?'

The starters arrived. They ate in silence.

Eventually, Eddie broke it. 'The good news is I get to play golf at Gleneagles tomorrow.'

'That right?'

'Your big brother's very generous. I told him I didn't want a fuss, but there we have it. It was very good of him. He must have spent a fortune, but he knows how to do it in style.' Eddie sipped his wine. 'I had an interesting visit from a detective.'

'That right?'

'An officer from Carmyle Station. Wanted to chat about an old case. Twenty years back. John Merrick.'

Paul stared at him. 'I see. Why did they come to see you?'

'John Merrick's daughter Karlie was murdered. Her body was found over in Sandyhills Road on Wednesday morning. She was only twenty-eight. Bad luck runs in some families.'

Paul paused. 'She did some work here at the club but she wasn't here the night she was killed.'

'What did you tell the police?'

'I haven't contacted them. No point in dragging the McIver into a murder inquiry. It has nothing to do with the club. What did this guy want?'

'It was a female officer, DI Kat Wheeler.'

Paul put down his knife and fork. 'Tall, blonde?'

'She was tall and blonde, a good-looking woman. Why, are you interested? I think you'd be punching above your weight with her.' He paused. 'What the hell's the thunder-face for?'

'It might not be the same woman, but there was a Kat Wheeler in the army with me. I suppose she was attractive enough physically, but if it is the same Wheeler, she caused real problems for me. It's fair to say we never hit it off.'

'You can be quite the acquired taste; even your own mother struggled with you.'

Their plates were cleared and the mains arrived. They waited until the waiter had moved off before resuming their conversation.

'Wheeler had a real problem,' said Paul. 'She wore her feminism like some jagged badge of honour and—' he stabbed his forefinger in the air '—men were in the wrong with her, purely because they were male.'

Eddie took up his cutlery, drew his knife through the food on his plate. 'Eat something,' he instructed his son. Waited until Paul had eaten a few mouthfuls before he spoke again. 'So you and Kat Wheeler had a falling-out?'

'One of our squad, a wee squirt name of Jenkins, was mouthing off and he and I had a bit of a go at each other.'

'As in fisticuffs?'

'Nothing serious, just a bit of verbal.'

'Your anger management issues again?'

'Wheeler reckoned I was hassling the wee scrote. She got into the whole "this is bullying" shit.'

'Watch your language.'

'She was never off my back about it. Felt that I couldn't open my mouth if Wheeler was in the vicinity. She tried to poison a few of the lads against me, but they weren't having it, told her where to go.'

'Sounds like it was personal.'

'That's what Wheeler does; she makes it about the person, not the situation. If the bitch takes a dislike to you, it colours her judgement completely. I mean, we were part of the same squad and she turned on me.'

'And this Jenkins lad?'

'He got killed.'

'Sorry to hear that.'

'And rather than be relieved the rest of us got out alive,

Wheeler started muttering that Jenkins had been depressed because I was bullying him, that he wasn't on the ball because of me. That, basically, my relationship with him had made him so unnerved that he couldn't function properly. She accused me of tormenting Jenkins to the point that he didn't know what he was doing – "psycho-logical turmoil" was the phrase she used. In her crazy mind, I'd bullied the guy into a nervous breakdown and he couldn't do his job. He made a mistake and got himself killed; it was nothing to do with me.'

'Did Wheeler take it further?'

'She definitely wanted to but she couldn't prove it. Where was the evidence? She had no one to back her up. But you know what divisive tactics can do to a team, and Wheeler was a fucking stirrer. She made it really tough for me and things were tough enough in the army.'

Eddie put down his knife and fork. 'Christ, it was your bloody job! What in hell is wrong with you? You were always one for complaining, right from when you were a kid. Your brother just got on with things but you were always the oddity. And your language, even in front of your mother. You mind the times I had to wash your mouth out with soap?'

'I'm just saying, Dad, I didn't need an enemy from within.' Paul's voice fell to a whisper. 'It's like she was always sniping at me. But, listen, I don't want to put you in the middle of this, I know she's a cop and you're loyal to your own.'

'I'm a professional, but maybe you need to try, just for once in your life, to man up?' Eddie Furlan chewed thoughtfully. 'And perhaps DI Wheeler still has issues with you?'

'Apart from Colin Jenkins, everyone else got back alive. Wheeler probably still blames me for his death.'

'You're paranoid. Always were. Your mother was right about you. Not right in the head was what she said, although she meant it in a good way. She was concerned about you, how you'd cope with life. She understood that you weren't wired properly.'

'Wheeler's a loose cannon. It wasn't my fault.'

Eddie took a long drink of his wine. 'Christ, I just told you, man up and deal with it.'

Paul spoke quietly. 'Yes, Dad.'

Chapter Forty-Six

The Golden Unicorn

Wheeler strode down the corridor, past the row of black and white photographs of the Kill Kestrels. Wondered again if Josh Alden had known that Karlie Merrick had been trying to contact him. Did he know more than he was letting on?

'Mr Franklin,' she said, as the manager of the hotel approached them.

'Back again, DI Wheeler? Should I be getting worried? Perhaps you now suspect a member of staff or myself? Or perhaps a member of the band?'

She heard the defensive tone. Obviously a second visit from the police wasn't what he wanted his hotel guests to see. 'We know that Karlie Merrick frequented a place that had a unicorn and a monument, and we wondered if you could shed any light.'

'Other than the name, obviously, we don't have any monuments here.'

'Have any of your staff mentioned that she'd been in?'

'None. I double-checked after your last visit as I promised I would. Of course my staff were fully aware of the woman's death. They'd heard the television and radio appeals, but no one recognised her. As I've already assured you, they'd have come forward if they could help in any way. I spoke again with Dougie – he's apologetic but there's nothing the band can offer by way of help. I'm so sorry, it looks like your visit has been a waste of time.' He glanced at Ross. 'Perhaps I can offer you a tea or coffee? On the house, of course.'

She declined for both of them.

'Then I'll leave you to it.'

'Bloody waste of time,' muttered Ross when the manager had gone.

'What about this area, Ross? The Kill Kestrels were here.' She stared out of the window, across to the Botanic Gardens. 'The Kibble Palace isn't a monument, but there's the marble statue of Eve; it was in some of the photographs Gary Ashton took. Let's go.' Wheeler made her way to the car park. She felt energised. Maybe this was the breakthrough they'd been waiting for? Maybe the net was now closing in on the killer?

Five minutes later, she stood in front of the manager of the café in the Botanic Gardens and felt her energy dissipate and the net evaporate. 'No, as I mentioned on the phone, I've never seen her. At least I don't think so; she could have been here but we get so many people coming in for coffee over the summer months, it's impossible to remember all of them.'

'CCTV?'

'It's broken, I'm afraid. It's due to be repaired soon.'

After a few more questions, Wheeler thanked her, and made her way to the marble statue of Eve.

'I've never really noticed it,' said Ross.

'It's by the Italian sculpture Scipione Tadolini. It was in lots of Gary Ashton's photographs.'

'And you know the statue because of your art teacher at school, the one who took you to the Campbell exhibition?'

'Mrs Dowling. Yes, she told us about this.' Wheeler pointed to the relief on the pedestal. '"The first family" and "The expulsion from the Garden of Eden".'

'Karlie Merrick's first family would have been John Merrick and his wife. But the expulsion from the Garden of Eden? Family life destroyed?' said Ross.

'It was for her.'

'What was Eden? A time before sin? A time of innocence? Bellerose said Karlie didn't have sex other than for work.'

'Eve ate the apple and they had sex? Eve – responsible for the fall of Adam and their expulsion from paradise?' said Ross. 'Was Eve seen as a sinner or a seductress?'

'Depends on your perspective,' said Wheeler.

'So, was Karlie a sinner or a seductress to her killer?' said Ross.

'The cousin said she was asexual and Bellerose confirmed it.'

'You reckon she was here?'

Wheeler sighed. 'I don't know. I feel like we're just clutching at straws.'

'Then let's take some time out, grab a coffee and rethink?'

A few minutes later, Wheeler settled herself at the table and sipped her latte. 'Was this a meaningful place to her?'

'But the club,' said Ross, 'where is it? We've contacted every private members' club in Glasgow. No one recognised the name, but all have a policy of casual contracts,

298

cash in hand and zero hours' contracts and employ a number of people depending on fluctuating business needs.'

'Fucking zero contract hours,' said Wheeler. 'And lots of cash in hand, so very hard to trace.'

'No one at the Golden Unicorn or here at the Botanics has recognised her. No one has come forward. It might just mean that she wasn't here,' said Ross.

'So we start over.' Wheeler grabbed her phone, opened the search engine, punched in 'unicorn', found 98 million references in 0.51 of a second. 'Great. Just great,' she muttered. She refined the search. 'Scottish unicorn' – 408,000 references in 0.45 of a second. 'Christ Almighty.' She tried 'Unicorns Glasgow' – 411,000 references in 0.43. References to the staircase at Glasgow University, historical Glasgow Cross. She typed in different permutations, scoured the results, which included a history of the unicorn. Tried 'Monument unicorn'. Scrolled through more pictures of the Lion and Unicorn staircase at Glasgow University and the Mercat Cross in Edinburgh. She took a gulp of coffee. 'What about the unicorn at the Mercat Cross, in Edinburgh?'

'It's in Parliament Square and close to St Giles' Cathedral. It's in the Old Town,' said Ross. 'You think Karlie went through to Edinburgh? Are we looking in the wrong bloody city?'

'Maybe.' Wheeler refined the search, tried 'Unicorn Monument' . . . information told her that Stirling Castle had a fourteen-year tapestry project, the biggest in a hundred years . . . it would be finished next year . . . Stirling Castle had a café called The Unicorn . . . and close by was the towering Wallace Monument.

Stirling. Unicorn. Café. Wallace. Monument. She stared

at the screen. Maureen was sure that Karlie had said the view *from* the unicorn not *of* the unicorn. And the monument was historical. This had to be it.

'Ross, I think I've got it. The club Karlie worked in isn't in Glasgow. It's in Stirling. You're right, we've been looking in the wrong place. Stirling Castle has a café called The Unicorn. Guess what's nearby?'

'The Wallace Monument.'

She rang the station, spoke to Boyd. 'Get me a list of clubs in and around Stirling: bigger clubs, where there's a shitload of money. Get as much as you can on them. Anything interesting, get back to me ASAP.'

'Stewart's looking for you. He wants you to put out an updated appeal. The press is having a field day, what with Karlie Merrick being a porn actress. He wants you to refocus public perception.'

'You do it.'

'The boss wants you.'

'I won't be back in time.' She rang off, drained her coffee cup and made for the door.

She had just fastened her seat belt when Stewart called. 'Why aren't you back at the station?'

'We have a strong lead, boss. Karlie's colleague, Laura McCormack, mentioned that Karlie's drink was spiked one night, and while she was drunk she let slip about a club. Also, she mentioned something about a unicorn and a monument.'

'Narrow it down for me.'

'Stirling Castle has a café called The Unicorn and the Wallace Monument is close by.'

'And?'

'And what?'

'That's it?'

'It's all I have.'

'There are dozens of cafés, unicorns and monuments, Wheeler. This is historic Scotland, for God's sake.'

'Her drink had been spiked, boss. She'd no control over what she was saying. And our victim liked cafés, it was her thing to go out to nice coffee shops. She only went to the bigger pubs on the off chance of being discovered by a scout, but coffee shops were her thing. They were what she loved.'

'It's not much, Wheeler. Tentative at best.'

'We've been looking in the wrong city, boss. It wasn't Glasgow, it was Stirling, and we're almost halfway there, no point in turning back now.'

'You should have headed back to the station, Wheeler.'

'You're cracking up, boss, I can't hear you.'

'I said, you should have—'

'You still there, boss? Only the reception's not that great out here in the country.' She killed the call.

'Halfway there?' said Ross.

'Let's go.'

They pulled out of the car park.

Forty-five minutes later, Stirling Castle came into view. The castle sat on top of Castle Hill, had steep cliffs on three sides and had a reputation for being haunted. They went straight to the Unicorn café, stood on the rooftop patio, looked across to the Wallace Monument.

'Bloody lovely,' she said. The tower, built to commemorate William Wallace, stood over seven hundred feet high. 'This is it, Ross. It's a perfect fit.'

'Looks like it.'

She raced into the cool of the café and spoke to the

manager, explained why they were there, heard the familiar refrain.

'Oh absolutely, the poor girl could've been here, but we have a lot of people coming through our doors. The castle has close to a half-million visitors a year; it's impossible to say for sure if she was one of them. I don't recognise her from your photograph but that doesn't go for much. I saw the appeal on telly and I'm sorry, I've wracked my brains but it just doesn't ring any bells.'

'What about clubs in the area? Businesses which use casual staff?'

'There's Stirling University, they have clubs. Gleneagles take on staff for catering, waitressing and suchlike. Other than that I can't really help you. I only work here; I live in Glasgow.'

Wheeler thanked her, called Boyd quickly with the update. 'See what you can find out about these places.' She hurried into the shop. Stopped.

'Ross, look at these.' The little bears were dressed as pipers. They wore tartan and were holding a set of bagpipes, a blue and white Saltire on one foot. 'The same bears that Karlie Merrick had in her flat in Glasgow. And over here.' She pointed to a row of plastic ducks, decked out in tartan.

'The *Braveheart* ducks,' said Ross. 'This was the place she came to for coffee, saw the monument and bought the merchandise.'

Wheeler heard the ring tone. Boyd.

'Apart from the golf club at Gleneagles, there's a place called the Ford Club, another called the McIver and one called Wright's.'

She heard him type.

'The Ford Club has just recently reopened after refurbishment. By the looks of their website, pole dancing and burlesque nights – stag dos, I reckon. The McIver is a private gentlemen's club. Wright's, in Bridge of Allan, also do mainly stag and hen dos. There are a few clubs at the university.'

'I'm looking for serious money. Get details of who runs the clubs.'

'Give me a sec.'

She waited.

'The Ford and Wright's both have a general enquiry number to call. The McIver's a bit harder to find anything on. A few names on their website – Alastair Brodie, Anton Melville, Jeffrey King. But nothing much about what they offer. Looks very exclusive.'

'So big money?'

'Yeah, their fees aren't advertised on the site, so I'd imagine it must be big bucks; the others have a list of their joining fees. Any of this any good? You want me to keep looking?'

Wheeler grabbed her notebook. 'Yep, give me all the details, but start with the McIver.'

'Oh, and it's an all-male preserve.'

'Right.' She started to jot down the details. 'For that reason alone, they don't get my vote.'

A few minutes later, they were back on the road. 'Ross, call the Ford Club and Wright's, see if they knew our victim.'

Ten minutes later, he updated her. 'If they did know her, they're not admitting it.'

Chapter Forty-Seven

The McIver

The beauty of the landscape was lost on her as she raced through the countryside. She ignored the fields, hedge-rows and the ancient gnarled trees, until a fox shot out in front of her and she slammed on the brakes.

'Christ, Wheeler, take it easy.'

'It's got to be the McIver, Ross.'

'Because it's not the other two? We haven't explored everything yet.'

'The McIver reeks of money, the way they don't even need to advertise their fees, the complete lack of detail on their website, the close proximity to the Unicorn Café and the Wallace Monument.'

'Open mind and all that, Wheeler.'

She drove to the perimeter wall, stared at it. 'Looks more like a fortress.' They followed the high stone wall that surrounded the grounds.

'A big old estate,' said Ross. 'Certainly wealthy.'

The intricate wrought-iron gates stood over seven foot, and beyond there was a stone gatehouse. An intercom system meant that they were forced to announce their arrival. Wheeler pressed the button, kept her finger on it. Noticed a small glass eye, a camera – they were being filmed.

A voice answered. 'Yes?'

'DIs Wheeler and Ross.'

'I'll need to see identification.'

'Whatever.'

'Did you hear me?'

'I did. Now open the gates.'

'I need to see your ID. There's a camera above the intercom.' They held their IDs in front of it. The gates opened and they drove through. A uniformed security guard met them at the gatehouse. 'I've called ahead to the Club House. Drive to reception, someone will meet you there.'

'This place is more secure than Barlinnie,' said Ross. 'And this driveway – how bloody long is it?'

'It reeks of money,' said Wheeler, 'and power.' She took in the beautifully manicured lawns, the peacocks which were grouped around a lily pond.

'A flock of peacocks,' said Ross.

'Not a flock, a muster or an ostentation,' said Wheeler. The noise from the engine hadn't made them fly off; their wings had been clipped. She saw the walled garden, the wooded area off to the right. Ahead the grand building itself. 'Scottish Baronial architecture,' she muttered. 'Impressive building.'

Inside, the huge reception area was an expanse of oak, brass and glass. The polished marble floor was pristine. The smell of beeswax hung in the air and mingled with the scent from the vases of roses.

'And guess what?' said Ross.

She followed his gaze and saw Sir Brian Sutherland,

chief executive of the huge Sutherland haulage business, leaving reception. Beside him was Malcolm Ray, who'd just won Entrepreneur of the Year after he'd bought and rebuilt a failing IT company. She'd recently read that he was worth £24 million. She glanced down the corridor. 'Is that Mark Ponsensby-Edward?'

'Yep. This place certainly attracts money.'

Wheeler turned away, saw signs for the supper club, the restaurant, the snug and the sauna. Her mobile rang. She glanced at the number. 'Boss?'

'Boyd's just updated me, you're at the McIver Club. It has quite a reputation.'

'Karlie worked here, in some capacity. I'd bet on it.'

'Step lightly.'

'I'm on official business.'

'Do I need to spell it out to you, Wheeler? One, you're not in your own jurisdiction, you're a Glasgow cop, remember? Two, that club is frequented by the great and good, people who not only uphold the law, but who actually make it. Am I making myself clear?'

'Crystal.' She kept her voice low. 'I'm not unaware, boss. I just passed Sir Brian Sutherland in reception. And it looks like Mark Ponsensby-Edward is a member.'

'Go easy.'

Fucking outrageous, she thought. Kept her voice calm. 'I'm not here to make a point, this is my bloody investigation.'

'Then mind you keep it that way.' The line went dead.

She turned to Ross. 'You heard that, right?'

'I heard enough. Stewart telling you to be diplomatic around these fragile rich folk in case you upset them. I'm surprised at the boss, he's usually up for a confrontation.'

306

'It's not like him,' agreed Wheeler. She wondered what was going on, what did Stewart know that she didn't? Through the glass door she watched a man saunter along the corridor towards them. 'OK, here we go. Let's see who's been sent to meet us.'

'Although, it's maybe for the best that I'm here too,' Ross muttered.

'Because?'

'Because you lit up like a beacon when you heard that it was an all-male club.'

It was all that she could do not to hit him. 'Are you fucking serious?' she hissed before turning towards the man approaching them.

He was tall, wore a dark suit, a silk handkerchief in the breast pocket, and a bow tie. His oiled hair was neatly parted to the side. He adjusted his cufflinks as he approached. His smile was confident, assured.

'I'm DI Wheeler and this is my colleague, DI Ross.'

He held out his hand. 'Alastair Brodie. I'm club secretary. My colleague at the gatehouse informed me that you were here.' He offered his hand.

Wheeler shook it; it was limp.

Brodie continued, 'Please come through and have a seat. Shall I order some tea, coffee perhaps?'

'We're fine, thanks.' They followed him through to one of the smaller bar areas.

He closed the door behind them. 'How may I be of assistance?'

'We're investigating a murder. A woman's body was discovered in the East End of Glasgow on Wednesday morning.'

'Oh dear. How awful.'

'And we believe the victim may have worked in this area,' said Wheeler. 'Her name was Karlie Merrick.'

Brodie considered it for a moment. 'The name isn't familiar but I wouldn't necessarily know all the staff; we have quite a few temporary and casual contracts. Our general manager, Anton Melville, is on holiday at present. As is our admissions secretary, Jeffrey King.'

'Then maybe you could call them?'

'I'm afraid not. They've both gone off on a trekking holiday in Nepal. They're uncontactable. I could speak with housekeeping?' Brodie offered. 'They use a number of casual staff.'

'I'd appreciate if you could check your records.' Wheeler crossed to a chair, sat.

'Of course. In the meantime, I've asked our head of security to join us; he's aware of everyone who comes and goes in the club.'

He keeps the secrets, thought Wheeler.

'Paul may be more up to date with those individuals who are here on a temporary basis.'

Wheeler held up a photograph of Karlie Merrick. 'Perhaps you recognise her, Mr Brodie?'

Brodie glanced at it. 'No, I'm afraid not. As I said, I don't recall the name and I certainly don't recognise the woman.'

The door opened and Wheeler looked at the man entering. Felt her stomach contract and the acid form in her mouth. Watched Paul Furlan use all of his six foot three physique to make an entrance. His suit was tailored to emphasise his muscles; a large watch just visible. Jade green eyes and a boxer's nose. The bastard. She forced herself to swallow down the phlegm that had gathered in her mouth. She saw Alastair Brodie visibly relax.

'Paul, I do hope your father had an enjoyable birthday lunch?'

So Eddie Furlan was in the building too, thought Wheeler.

'Yeah, he had a great time, thanks.'

'Allow me to introduce DIs Wheeler and Ross. They are investigating a murder; some unfortunate woman has been killed.'

'Wheeler and I are old army colleagues.'

'I see.' Brodie turned to her. 'Perhaps you knew that already, Inspector?'

Wheeler ignored him, addressed Furlan. 'Karlie Merrick worked here, didn't she?'

'She did a couple of shifts.'

'And you never thought to call it in, when we were appealing for information?'

Silence.

'When was the last time she was here?'

'I can check our records.' Brodie stood.

She stared at Furlan. 'In the meantime, just from memory?'

'She was here a few weeks ago.'

'What was her job description?'

'Erotic dancer.'

'She was a stripper?' asked Ross. 'I didn't think the McIver was that kind of a club.'

'Nothing quite so vulgar,' spat Brodie from the door. 'Our clients are extremely respectable, professional gentlemen who wouldn't dream of attending those types of places.'

'And you have a list of the clients Karlie danced for? These respectable gents?' asked Wheeler.

'We don't keep specific records. A client will put in a request for us to arrange a dance and then it's arranged.'

'So you have no record of who asked for the dance?' said Ross. 'Why not?'

'A request form is left in the office. It doesn't need to be signed, just the date and the time. We don't monitor our guests, Inspector Ross. They are free to attend a dance appointment, just like any other club. I'm sure if you go to a less exclusive club, the lap dancing clubs you alluded to, you are not monitored. Your name and details aren't recorded if you partake in a dance, are they? Or if you were clubbing? Would you expect management to record the details of everyone you'd danced with? Then, why on earth would we inflict this on our clients?' The question was obviously rhetorical; Brodie didn't bother waiting for her reply. The door closed softly behind him.

'Have any of our clients been linked to this death?' asked Furlan.

'Process of elimination.'

'Presumably for the night she died, Tuesday? I've already told you, she wasn't here that night.'

Wheeler recognised the edge in Furlan's voice. Knew that it preceded a violent outburst. Despite the slick suit, the expensive watch and the air of superiority he tried to project, Furlan was the same bully she'd known in the army.

'Where were you on Tuesday night?'

'Up to your old tricks again, Wheeler?'

'Don't make me ask a second time.'

'I was here until midnight, then I went to a party at Ronald McMasters' country house.' He scowled. 'I stayed over.'

310

'Can anyone corroborate this?'

'They don't need to, I'm telling you.'

'How well did you know Karlie Merrick?'

'Hardly at all, I only saw her in passing.'

Brodie returned with a printout. 'Our gatehouse entry has Karlie Merrick arriving at 8 p.m. on Friday 20 June and leaving at 11 p.m. She returned on Friday 27 June and was on the premises from 9.30 p.m. until 11 p.m. These are the only times she was at the club.'

'I'll need to talk to those staff on duty that night.'

'Dancers are ushered in and out via the side entrance; they don't walk through the club itself. Therefore, only security see them.'

'And the client obviously.' Wheeler addressed Furlan. 'Did anything unusual happen when she was here?'

'Nope.'

She didn't expect that he'd tell her anything. She tried Brodie. 'We've had to look long and hard to find that she worked here.'

'Our members are not involved in any way, so do try to be discreet, Inspector.'

'Why so secretive and why did she have to sign a confidentiality agreement?'

'It's nothing ominous, DI Wheeler, merely that a great many of our clients are extremely well known. All employees, myself and Paul included, sign the confidentiality contract. Clients need to be assured that when they come here to relax, no one is going to sell their story or talk about them to the press. If details were made public, it would contradict the whole ethos of a private members' club. Surely you can't think we're doing anything that other private clubs don't?'

'I'll need to see where she worked.'

'Of course, we've nothing to hide.' Brodie checked the records. 'Both evenings she worked in the Moroccan Room. Paul, could you show our guests downstairs?'

They walked in silence to the large, windowless room. The seven large lamps were lit and the room was cool and relaxing. The brightly coloured tiles in the mosaic floor glittered, and on the low leather sofas, plump cushions were neatly arranged.

Wheeler made for the hoist. 'What's this?'

'Some of the girls use it as a prop, most theatre acts have them. It's been specially adapted and fitted so there's no way they can hurt themselves. Health and Safety tested. Nothing sinister, Wheeler. You always were one to jump to conclusions.'

'Did you meet Karlie outside work?' she asked.

'No, it's against the rules for staff to hook up. I only saw her here at the club. And I didn't see her the night she died. Now, if we're done here, I'm off.'

Wheeler stepped forward. 'This is a *murder* inquiry, in case you don't quite grasp the significance.'

Furlan's voice was low. 'I know more about life and death situations than you'll ever experience, Wheeler. I'm telling you we're done.'

She didn't move.

Ross touched her arm. 'Let's go.'

'I would be wary of dragging the McIver or its members through the mud of a murder investigation, if I were you. Karlie Merrick was only here a couple of times on a casual basis.' Furlan paused. 'Then again, you never were good at holding boundaries.'

Upstairs, Brodie stood in the corridor. 'This is a very

distressing time. If you need anything else, please don't hesitate to contact me.'

'A few more questions if you don't mind,' said Wheeler. More of a statement. She didn't know how much more access she was going to get to the club, but, judging from Brodie's tone, very little. 'Tell me about the club. How do prospective members join? Are they vetted?'

'They must be proposed by a current member, and that, in turn, must be seconded by another.'

'And then they're in?' said Ross.

'Then their application is heard by the committee. Finally, if that is successful, there is an interview.'

'Who sits on the committee?' asked Wheeler.

'A number of our distinguished members, for example Mark Ponsensby-Edward and Judge Storey rotate, depending on work commitments. Our accounts are held in our central office in Edinburgh.'

'There doesn't appear to be much information on your website,' said Wheeler.

'There's nothing unusual about that, Inspector. We don't need to advertise. We provide a private members' club of such distinctive calibre that we attract a first-class membership. Here our gentlemen can relax in the bar or dine in the restaurant, where they can do business over lunch or dinner.'

'When's chucking-out time?' asked Ross

Brodie winced. 'We do not chuck our members out. They leave when they are ready. Mostly their chauffeurs are waiting to whisk them home around midnight, perhaps a little later, certainly, no one is here after 2 a.m. Alas, we have no overnight accommodation. Our club is very well attended. Edmund McIver founded it in 1854 and, of course, it was a much smaller establishment then. However, we've grown considerably over the years.'

'Why not admit women?' asked Wheeler.

'Tradition.'

'And you need such a high level of security that Paul Furlan is employed to run it?' she said.

'Some years ago there was an attempt to kidnap one of our most high-profile members, a prominent judge who was presiding over a controversial case. Thankfully, the attempt was thwarted and the men in question arrested and charged, but it was decided then that we needed to employ a professional to run security. We have to protect our clients. Without going into extraneous detail or breaching confidentiality, I can say that the majority of our members have high-profile professions. They are sometimes the target of maliciousness because they are either upholding the law at the highest echelons, or, frankly, they are making it. Adequate security is necessary in today's climate.' Brodie peered at her. 'Surely you of all people must appreciate this, Inspector Wheeler? You strive to keep the streets of Glasgow safe; why would we be any different here? We keep our members safe, and in that regard there is very little difference between you and Paul Furlan.'

'I'm a detective, committed to public service. Paul Furlan is a security consultant, committed to private service. I think there's a difference.'

Brodie dismissed her with a flick of his hand. 'Allow me to show you out.'

'Can you tell me where you were on Tuesday night, the night she died?'

'I was attending a birthday party for Hugo

314

Ponsensby-Edward on Nicholas Watson-Dunbar's estate in Perthshire.'

She might have bloody guessed. Hugo Ponsensby-Edward, son of Mark. And Watson-Dunbar, a top QC, who was presently defending in a high-profile case. He was also one of Scotland's biggest egos.

Brodie smiled stiffly, his voice cold. 'Please do feel free to bother Nicholas Watson-Dunbar with a call, Inspector Wheeler. I'm sure he would be only too pleased to drag himself away from the trial. He'd be delighted to answer your *obviously very important questions* as to our whereabouts the night the poor unfortunate woman was murdered. I'm curious why you seem to view the club with such suspicion; perhaps you are a little biased? Goodbye, Inspector.'

Outside, Ross started the car, indicated and pulled out. 'Well, that went well. I think you won them over by dint of your sunny disposition.'

'It's not my job to win anyone over.'

'Just as well.'

'They're arrogant pricks.'

'You didn't cut them any slack; you went in guns blazing.'

'All that about "important questions", Brodie might have just said "from the little lady". Patronising git. And comparing me to Furlan.'

'Of all people.' Ross tried for a smile.

'It's not the same though, is it? Our Code of Ethics reflects the values of our police force and demands that we show integrity, fairness and respect. I know from experience that Paul-fucking-Furlan is completely lacking in integrity.'

'You've memorised that whole document, haven't you?'

'Didn't you?'

'No, I got the gist of it and obviously I agree with it, but I think your take on the McIver may be influenced by Paul Furlan. The tension between you two was palpable.'

'The tension wasn't between us, Ross. It was in the room. I was aware of it too. He's hiding something. He didn't inform us that Karlie worked there.'

'He didn't want the club involved. Other than that, concrete evidence?'

'None yet. And as for Brodie, what's your take on him?'

Ross pulled up at a red light before he replied. 'A bit of a throwback, but if you can get by that, he seemed OK. He offered a rational explanation about the club and its history. Also, it made sense about why Paul Furlan's employed. There are nutters out there who will try to get at a judge if they have a gangland boss who's going down; you'd need security to be tight.' The lights changed and he drove on. 'The McIver is expensive and exclusive, so you've got a load of rich, influential guys in one place; they're sitting targets. The club can't have the security letting it down. You've got to agree, Wheeler, don't you? You saw who was at the bloody reception.'

She said nothing, stared out of the window.

'But that doesn't suit your argument about Paul Furlan, does it?' said Ross.

'I don't need arguments; I deal in facts.'

'You two have unresolved issues and maybe—'

She cut him off. 'I'm a professional, Ross.'

'All I meant is that you have a bit of a grudge against him. Don't let it get in the way of the investigation.'

Wheeler waited until a huge HGV rumbled past before she answered. 'I might not like him, but it doesn't mean I've lost my ability to be analytical.'

'Be careful, Wheeler. Paul Furlan might make this look like your problem, that you have a personal vendetta against him.'

'Furlan's a bully and a bullshitter, Ross. He always was.'

Inside the McIver, Paul Furlan closed the door to his office. Made the call.

Five minutes later, Mark Ponsensby-Edward entered the office. 'I hear we have a problem.'

'We've had a visit from the police.'

'About the girl's death?'

'Yes.'

'Purely routine?'

'They know she worked here.'

'I see.'

'The cop in charge is an old adversary of mine, she means to make trouble.'

'Then we'll need to deal with her, Paul. Won't we?'

Chapter Forty-Eight

The DCC's Office

An hour later and the informal meeting had already begun. The Deputy Chief Constable, Gregor McCoy, was seated behind his desk. Across from him, Mark Ponsensby-Edward relaxed into a chair and smiled at his friend. 'Gregor, I do hope you don't think I'm interfering in this investigation?'

'Of course not.'

'I'm just concerned that one of your officers is a bit of a loose cannon at present, and what with you being in line for—'

'Let's keep that between ourselves and these four walls for the time being.'

'Oh, of my absolute discretion you can be assured. Presumably when you get the nod you can publicly throw your cap into the ring?'

'If and when I get the nod.'

'Come, Gregor, don't be so modest. I had dinner with Judge Storey last week. He spoke very highly of you.'

'He's not the only one involved in the selection committee.'

'You're absolutely the best candidate. I've known you long enough to be certain of your integrity.' He paused. 'Which is why I'm so concerned about this blowing up in our faces at this very sensitive time. I'm afraid that your DI Kat Wheeler is becoming a liability.'

'Are you making this official?'

'Absolutely not, there's no need. Paul Furlan and the other members of the McIver understand the type of investigation she's running and they are all committed to supporting her. Indeed, no one understands the stress she's under more than Paul and he's at pains to be both supportive and sympathetic towards her. They served in the army together and unfortunately, like many of our heroes, they came home bearing the scars of what they'd seen.'

'I imagine they did.'

'For good or bad, the army creates a bond, it's like a family. Maybe a little dysfunctional but there we have it. However, a good friend of DI Wheeler's, Colin Jenkins, was tragically killed while on duty and she was naturally deeply affected by his death. She felt responsible for him, and his death left her feeling guilty and angry. Her way of dealing with the loss was to hit out at Paul and a number of other army personnel for not supporting Jenkins.'

'Classic grief and bereavement response – anger.'

'Absolutely, and of course no one blamed Wheeler, she just needed to take some time out to decompress. But you know what she's like, she's extremely driven and didn't give herself time to adequately deal with it. I believe that she's now experiencing delayed grief and she's hitting out again by targeting Paul. I spoke with Eddie Furlan, whom Wheeler insisted on meeting up with, despite his recent bereavement. Eddie believes that she's obsessed with solving both Karlie's murder and John Merrick's murder, so utterly convinced is she that they are connected. My concern is that she believes that somehow the McIver is also complicit. Gregor, it's dangerously flawed thinking.'

'You're suggesting that Wheeler can't be objective?'

'I think her meeting up with Paul again has triggered a lot of old resentment and frustration about Colin Jenkins' death. Paul mentioned that yesterday was the anniversary of Jenkins' death. Paul also told me that Wheeler and Jenkins were far more than merely colleagues. She's been through a lot and is in a raw, vulnerable state.'

'DCI Stewart thinks very highly of her.'

'I don't for a moment doubt that, but in this instance she's too emotionally unstable. Wheeler is churning up old ground, old issues that bear no relation to the case, and, speaking on behalf of the McIver, I would respectfully ask that a stop be put to her behaviour. Not only because of the reputation of the club but also the sensitivity around your career. What you don't need is a formal complaint being lodged when your imminent promotion should really be the focus.'

'Do they all agree that Wheeler's out of control?'

'She has a vendetta.'

'All our officers are required to be impartial.' Gregor paused. 'But you're convinced that Wheeler's impartiality has been compromised in some way?'

'Completely. All we want to do is to safeguard the force from official complaints while also supporting Wheeler. Also, I have it on good authority that Wheeler is having an affair with a colleague's husband, one of the family liaison officers working on the Karlie Merrick case, Helen

Downie. Again another boundary issue. It seems Wheeler's ruffling some feathers. I don't think that she's in a good space, either emotionally or psychologically.'

'I'll have a quiet word with DCI Stewart.'

Ponsensby-Edward smiled, offered a bony hand. 'Excellent. We all knew that you would be extremely professional and act with integrity. It's no wonder you're tipped for a great future. Gregor, you have my support.'

The DCC shook the offered hand. 'And you mine.'

Ponsensby-Edward paused at the door. 'She doesn't know about the earlier discrepancy.'

'There's no way she could find out.'

'Eddie may get cold feet.'

'Stop worrying.'

'You weren't promoted at the time, Gregor. You've a lot more to lose now.' Ponsensby-Edward closed the door gently behind him.

Chapter Forty-Nine

The Boss

The door of the station had barely closed behind her when the desk sergeant spoke. 'Stewart wants to see you in his office. Immediately.' He glanced at Ross. 'Just Wheeler.'

'Christ, I'm hardly in the door,' said Wheeler.

The desk sergeant had already returned to his paperwork. 'Don't shoot the messenger.'

Wheeler nodded for Ross to go on upstairs. A few minutes later, she stood in front of DCI Stewart's desk. 'You wanted to see me?'

'Take a seat, Wheeler. Tell me, how did you get on at the McIver Club?'

'We spoke with two employees: Paul Furlan, who is head of security, and Alastair Brodie, who is the club secretary.'

'Excellent.'

'It turns out Karlie Merrick was employed there.'

'Doing what exactly?'

'Erotic dance. She was employed on a casual basis.'

'Go on.'

'She'd done a couple of shifts.' Wheeler checked her notebook. 'She arrived around 8 p.m. on Friday 20 June and left at 11 p.m. She returned on Friday 27 June around 9.30 p.m. and left around 11 p.m.'

'These are the only times she was at the club?'

'Yes, and they were pretty reticent about how well they'd known her. Brodie implied that casual staff, like the dancers, are secreted in and out by a side entrance.'

'He actually said "secreted"? Sounds pretty sinister.'

She caught the tone. 'It was my choice of wording. What Brodie actually said was "ushered".'

'Casual staff use a side door? It's not that unusual.'

'I think we need to keep a close eye on the place.'

'Because?'

'They employed Karlie Merrick.'

'As did Gary Ashton, although not as a dancer. The work he offered was a little more physical.'

'I don't think Ashton's our man, boss.'

'What about the Kill Kestrel guy, Josh Alden?'

'Nothing to specifically link him to her, but the club . . .'

'I'm waiting.'

'Gut instinct is that it's at the heart of the murder.'

'Evidence?'

'Nothing at present, but the McIver is connected in some way. I felt the tension in the room when I was talking to Brodie and Furlan.'

'So I heard.'

'Paul bloody Furlan called you, didn't he? Or was it Alastair Brodie?'

'Neither. It was Gregor McCoy,' said Stewart.

'Christ, the Deputy Chief Constable called you because I went to a private members' club?'

'I told him that you were doing your job and that I fully support you.'

323

'Good.'

'However, the DCC is also concerned about boundaries and your emotional state.'

'Why?'

'An affair with Helen Downie's husband.'

'Jamie told me they were separated; they'd spilt for good.'

'The DCC is well aware of the McIver and its sterling reputation and apparently you took a somewhat adversarial approach to questioning not just Alastair Brodie but especially Paul Furlan.'

'Rubbish.'

'The DCC was at pains to remind me that Paul Furlan is the son of Detective Inspector Eddie Furlan.'

'As a retired officer, Eddie Furlan would know that I was doing my job; he'd back me fully.'

'I'm afraid not. He found the timing of your visit to see him at home somewhat tactless, given that his wife had recently died. The DCC also reminded me that Paul Furlan is an army veteran and that following a distinguished career in the armed forces—'

Wheeler snorted. 'Listen, boss—'

Stewart held up his hand. 'No, you listen. Paul Furlan's an ex-army colleague of yours, whom you seem to have unresolved issues with. He now assists in running a private members' club. Humour me, Wheeler; can you take a wild guess who some of the other members might be?'

'Brodie mentioned he'd been at a party for Hugo Ponsensby-Edward at Nicholas Watson-Dunbar's estate and I saw Mark Ponsensby-Edward at the club too. No doubt they're all members.'

'I did warn you to go easy, Wheeler. These people are

way above us in the pecking order. We're talking men who head up our profession. The DCC was playing golf with Judge Storey last week.'

'Good for them, so now we know that the DCC is a big fan of the McIver.'

'You can cut the sarcasm, Wheeler, because he is indeed a fan and he's distinctly unimpressed with your aggressive approach towards the victim's former colleagues. Paul Furlan and Alastair Brodie worked with Karlie Merrick and must be given time to grieve. As should Eddie Furlan for his wife and Paul for his mum. The DCC also intimated that the club may make a formal complaint. We all want this case solved, but annoying Eddie and Paul Furlan and pissing off Alastair Brodie, to the extent that he complains and Gregor McCoy gets involved, means that we are all now fully aware of your clumsiness. Congratulations, you did all this in a single visit.'

Shit travels downhill fast, thought Wheeler. 'It's a murder investigation, boss. I have a right to find out about Karlie's Merrick's last known movements.'

'Of course you do, but not to go in there like the proverbial bull.' He paused. 'What are your concrete leads?'

'None, other than Karlie worked at the club, but I need to find out more about the McIver. Who did she dance for? There's something sinister about that place, I can feel it.'

'Feelings, Wheeler? Good police work is based on concrete evidence, not feelings.'

'I believe that there is something sinister about the place.'

'Perhaps you need to take a step back and reassess the situation?'

Wheeler leant on the desk. 'I disagree, boss, I think that—'

'You're not listening, Wheeler. You need to let whatever it is you have against the club go. I know you're not a fan of the all-male preserve, but it's a reality and you not liking it isn't going to change it.'

'I think it's bloody sinister that you were even contacted; that right there is a problem for me. And the whole old boys' network—'

'Sinister's a bit harsh, Wheeler. A casual employee was murdered and you think all roads lead back to the McIver. You and Paul Furlan have had previous. You're a good detective, but I head up this team and I won't have you firing off about old grudges which have nothing to do with the here and now. Your job is to find Karlie Merrick's killer. Got it?'

'Yes, boss.' Her headache returned, a familiar shooting pain.

'In the meantime, since you've given me the update, I want you to go home early. You don't look too well.'

'I'm fine.'

'Ross mentioned you've been having recurring headaches. Think about getting to the doctor.'

'Bloody hell, for a headache?'

'A recurring headache, Wheeler. It could be something that needs checking out.'

Wheeler had to remind herself that Stewart's wife had died unexpectedly. 'Fine.' She fought the urge to slam the door behind her. She would go home and work on the case. As she strode along the corridor, she thought of Paul Furlan and of the bile that rose in her throat when he walked into the room. She detested the man but it wouldn't stop her working the case. Surely Stewart knew that? But she also knew that Stewart was going for promotion and no doubt her pissing off the DCC wouldn't go in his favour. And as for bloody Helen Downie . . .

In the CID suite she grabbed her jacket from the back of the chair.

Boyd stood in the doorway. 'I'm off out to get some coffee and rolls. You want anything, Wheeler?'

'No, I bloody don't.'

'Christ, I'm only asking.'

'You OK?' said Ross.

'Apparently I need a bit of downtime.'

'Now, in the middle of a case?'

'Seems like it. And Ross?'

'Yeah?'

'Cheers for dropping me in it about the headaches.' She let the door slam behind her.

Chapter Fifty

The Café

'You got a picture of this George Bellerose then?' demanded Jenny McLoughlin.

Angie fished her phone out of her pocket, scrolled down the photographs until she found the best one, held it up to her friend. 'He's gorgeous, isn't he?'

Jenny glanced at the image, saw that he was mid-thirties, had dark eyes and his thick hair was shoulder length. 'If you like that sort of thing. A big reunion later then?'

'Yeah, it'll be great to see him, he's been busy since he came back from the conference.'

'What did he get you for your birthday?'

'I think he brought something back from London.'

'You still want it to be a ring?'

'Maybe.'

'Got a date in mind?'

Angie sighed. 'No, but this guy's for keeps.'

'Never seems to take you out.'

Angie heard the sarcasm. 'It's just that he's very busy with his career.'

'And you believe him?'

'Of course.'

'Damned if I can see any good reason for not taking you on a date.'

'George says it's just a matter of timing.'

'George says a lot, doesn't he? You lost the power to talk?'

'Of course not. I'm just telling you what it's like.'

'What I'm hearing is someone who's being dominated. He sounds very fucking controlling if you ask me.'

'He's not controlling and I wasn't asking you.' Angie opened the dishwasher and stood back to let the whorls of steam rise. 'Anyway, how are you getting on in your hot pursuit of your policeman?'

Jenny looked through the hatch into the café. 'Talk of the handsome devil, he's just come in.' She smoothed her hair and shot through the door. Angie watched her friend move like a missile towards DC Alexander Boyd. Watched her pretend to clear a table and stop, saw her smile and begin to chat. Watched her laugh and try to hold eye contact. Subtle she was not. Angie began stacking the cups and saucers on the shelf, wondered what would happen if she was to flirt with someone, like Jenny was doing. If she did it in front of George, would it make him appreciate her more?

Jenny was soon back with the policeman's order. 'Two takeaway coffees, both with milk, and two fried egg rolls.' She dropped her voice to a whisper. 'Who's the other one for? You think he's got a girlfriend?'

'How would I know?' Angie crossed to the cooker, cracked the eggs into the pan. Felt nausea rise. 'Here Jenny, can you cook these? I don't like being around food. Feeling queasy.'

'Are you kidding me and miss out on five minutes with him out there? You're on your own, Angie.' She disappeared through the swing door.

Angie turned back to the pan, swallowed down the acid and began to cook the eggs. She crossed to the hot water urn, grabbed two takeaway cups, put a scoop of coffee into each and filled them, put the cups on the tray, made sure the lids were tight. A customer had scalded herself last week and Maria had been furious with her for not putting the lid on properly. She put the rolls into paper bags, dumped in two thick napkins and went through.

Jenny was in full flow, practically wriggling with excitement. 'So, you being police and everything, do you get to investigate all the big cases? I mean that poor soul who was killed up in Sandyhills Road, are you involved with that? Any leads?'

Boyd said nothing.

'Of course, you can't say too much about it, can you?'

'That's right.'

Angie handed him the coffees. 'You taking these back to the station?'

'Yeah, working late.'

Once he'd gone, Jenny turned to her. 'I think he maybe has a girlfriend.'

'I've seen him a few times with a tall, blonde woman, think they might work together.'

'That was awful about that dead woman, Karlie Merrick, wasn't it?'

Despite the heat, a chill came over Angie and she shivered. 'I'm so glad George's back, I can't wait to see him.'

'And I can't wait until the lovely policeman comes to his senses and notices me.'

'I don't think he could miss the show you gave him.'

Jenny's face spread into a huge grin. 'It's nothing to the show I'd give him in private if I ever get the chance. And at least with me, the guy would have plenty to hold on to, unlike you, skinny. Why isn't your guy feeding you up?'

'He does OK.'

'You're losing too much.'

'It's just the excitement of being in a new relationship, you know how it is.'

'No, I don't know. I was a beefy bride the first time around and I'm sure as shit not going to slim down if there's a second time. If someone wants me skinny, they're with the wrong woman, they can jog the fuck on.'

'It's just that George likes to play games and being slim suits these games.'

'What sort of games?'

'Role play, a little bit kinky.'

'As long as you're into it?' said Jenny.

'I'm trying to get into it. I said I'd put on some fetish gear later, but—'

'But what?'

'It doesn't matter. George says I'm just being a prude.'

'George says a whole lot. If you don't want to do it, don't be talked into it.'

'But he loves it and I want him to be happy with the sex side of things. I know that anything he says, anything at all, is just to help me be a better person. It's what he does, he's a life coach.'

Jenny eyed her. 'What else does this nut tell you?'

'Forget it.'

'He's a nice-looking guy all right, Angie, but is he a nice guy? They're not the same thing.'

'He's lovely.'

'Give me an example.'

'Don't be ridiculous.'

'Tell me what he does that's so lovely.'

Angie glanced around the café, found what she was looking for. 'Table five needs clearing. I'll get it.'

At the next table, Maureen Anderson sipped her coffee. Open in front of her was the *Chronicle* and the appeal for information. Maureen ran through what she had. Was it worth sharing with the police? She sighed. Took out a card. She'd call that DI Wheeler, who'd told her to call with anything, no matter how small or insignificant it seemed. Well, thought Maureen, this piece of information was tiny. But was it important or useless? Either way, it was all she had. She punched the numbers into her phone, heard it ring. Heard the automated voice tell her to leave a message.

Chapter Fifty-One

Peace Offering

Wheeler let herself into her flat, fished her mobile out of her pocket, saw that it was out of charge. Shit. She plugged it in, waited. A few seconds later it spluttered into life. Three missed calls. Two from Ross and one from an unknown who'd left a message. Wheeler left the phone charging while she listened to Maureen Anderson hesitantly describe her visit to Fullarton Care Home where she'd spoken to someone named Steve Penwell.

Wheeler hit call-back and it was answered immediately. She took notes. Thanked Maureen for the information, agreed that it may be nothing. Certainly the fact that Steve Penwell was suffering from schizophrenia meant that what he told them might be compromised. She ended the call, rang the care home.

'I'm afraid Mr Penwell has deteriorated, he's in no fit state to communicate with anyone at present, he's hallucinating badly.'

'When will he be well enough for a visit?'

'I'm not sure, these things take their own time. Perhaps

I could call you if he improves later tonight? Or in the morning, after he's had a good rest?'

Wheeler left her number. In the living room she put Coltrane's *Blue Train* on low, pulled the pile of notes on Karlie Merrick's case into the middle of the table.

The intercom sounded. 'I was just passing,' said Ross. 'You fancy company?'

She buzzed him in. 'Coffee?'

'If that's all that's on offer.'

'Red or white?'

'White; need to keep a clear head.'

'Chardonnay OK?'

'Yep. Need to focus.'

'Then don't drink it like it's water.' She poured two glasses. Realised she hadn't eaten for hours.

'Brought this,' he said. 'Korma.'

She took the bag, peered inside. Indian food. Samosa, two curries, nan bread.

'I'm sorry that I even mentioned the headaches to Stewart – it was just that we were chatting and you know the way he can casually elicit information and then use it against you? It's a fucking nightmare.'

'Forget it.' Wheeler spooned the food into bowls. Just the smell made her salivate. 'I've just spoken with Karlie's friend, Maureen. A guy name of Steve Penwell contacted Karlie a few days before she was killed, told her about a man he'd seen running past the window on the night her father was murdered.'

'And he didn't come forward?'

'He was having an affair – he was with his girlfriend and shouldn't have been in the area at the time. Also, he wasn't sure the guy wasn't just running for a bus. Penwell didn't want to risk his marriage and then find out it was nothing sinister.'

'No name?'

'Just a description. He was wearing an eye patch and that's the problem.'

'Because?'

'Steve Penwell's schizophrenic and fixated on pirates, sees them hiding in the curtains. He can be very confused at times,' said Wheeler.

'Is it even worth seeing him?'

'It's always worth following up a lead, Ross. But he's not well – the nurse says tomorrow might be a better bet.'

'Stewart thinks you went in a bit too heavy at the McIver Club.'

'It's bloody sinister they didn't call it in that she worked there. And that the DCC contacted Stewart.'

'Stewart thinks you have issues around the club being an all-male preserve.'

'Not enough to interfere with this investigation. She worked there,' Wheeler repeated.

'She worked with Ashton too and he threatened her. Pierce and Bellerose both had a thing for her. Plus, she tried to contact Josh Alden. Besides, we don't know if her death is linked to any of the places she worked or her colleagues. It could be a neighbour, a stranger, anyone. I warned you that it might look skewed, like you're harassing the Furlans just to settle an old feud.'

'I think the Furlans are involved in some way.'

'Eddie's just lost his wife and Paul his mum. They're grieving, Wheeler.'

She heard the sadness in his voice. Maybe now wasn't the best time to argue with him about grieving for dead parents. 'Anyway, let's look at these again.' She spread the photocopied pages out over the table. 'Notes from John Merrick's appointments diary. His desk diary. Eddie Furlan spoke to every client; they all checked out, but in his mind he had Cal Moody and Keith Sullivan down for the murder, not a client.'

'You think he didn't look at the client list closely enough?'

'Look at these lines. Names have obviously been crossed out. That was the system Merrick used when a client cancelled. A line was put through the name and the time of the appointment and a small "c" in brackets for "cancellation".'

'So?'

'Look at the thickness of the lines. They're identical. You can just about make out the initials of the clients. And they have a "c" beside each. And they tally with the client list. But look at these.' She pointed to others. 'These are far darker and the lines are much thicker.'

'He used a different pen some days, a biro versus a felt tip? Relevance?'

'The initials have been completely obliterated, plus, there's no "c" for "cancellation" beside them. What if the diary was falsified later? There are two appointments per week for ten weeks, twenty appointments in all. What if they weren't cancellations but appointments that were obliterated?'

'Did you ask Eddie about this?'

'He said he'd provided a complete list of clients, that these were only cancellations. But what if they weren't? What if the appointments were deleted after the murder? Merrick used one way of recording a cancellation, then a completely different system altogether. Why would he do that? Why have two ways of recording cancellations? Everyone has their own particular system. Think of the way you do your paperwork. It's always the same. Always.'

'Tenuous, Wheeler.'

'But possible that someone else deleted these appointments?'

'Meaning there are other clients unaccounted for?'

'Who haven't come forward,' said Wheeler.

'But if the killer was a client, why not just take the diary?'

'Because then it would point directly to the client list.' Wheeler took a sip of wine, reached for some curry.

'You're questioning the thoroughness of Eddie Furlan's investigation?'

'I'm saying he bloody missed something. If he hadn't, John Merrick's killer would be in jail.'

'You'd need to be very sure of yourself and of the evidence. You don't have much to go on.'

She couldn't contradict him.

After Ross had gone, she sat at the table and reread the notes again. She was positive that the Furlans were somehow involved in the case. All she had to do was prove it. She knew that the tension in the room at the McIver hadn't all been about her. She sifted through the photographs from Karlie's flat, returned to the desk diary. John Merrick couldn't have a large diary with him all the time. What if there was another diary, a smaller daily diary he carried with him? Would he have used a smaller one for making initial appointments, perhaps when he was on the phone or away from the office? Did he keep the space when offering clients the choice of potential appointments and only transfer them to the office diary when they had been confirmed? She would contact Karlie Merrick's cousin Beth and ask her if there was anything at all she still had, relating to John Merrick's hypnotherapy practice. There had to be something else, some missing part of the picture. All she had to do was find it.

Chapter Fifty-Two

The Reunion

George Bellerose was biding his time before his meet-up with Bunyan. He made for the bar. He'd recovered from the fucking police ordeal with Wheeler. With Karlie Merrick dead, he needed to move on, find another one, someone he felt the same way about. One who'd occupy his thoughts. He ordered another drink, one for the road before heading to Angie's. After that, a meet-up with Bunyan at the Kibble Palace in the West End. Right now, he'd have a whisky, just the one. He watched the bartender serve it. Christ, the amount that trickled through from the optics in these places, it was hardly worth counting as a drink. Still, he was beginning to come down. He needed to leave work and the visit to the police station and all that shit behind him. He sipped his drink, felt the smoothness of the liquid calm him. A brunette approached the bar, ordered and waited. He tried for eye contact, no point in missing an opportunity. The brunette ignored him.

He knew Angie would be wearing the fetish gear and would be excited about their reunion. Let her fucking wait.

***

Later, when he parked his pale blue Suzuki motorbike outside her flat, he had the overwhelming urge to turn around and go home. Knew somehow that he wouldn't see her again after tonight, that this was the end. It was over. He wasn't one for premonitions but there was something dark about his mood, something unforeseen. He was about to turn back when Angie opened the door and smiled. 'Welcome back.' She kissed him, walked into the living room.

He made his way to the bedroom. 'In here, Angie. Now. Move it.'

'I thought we could just have a chat. I'm worried. That poor woman who was killed out in Sandyhills, she was called Karlie Merrick and—'

'In here, Angie.'

'George, I want—'

'Kneel.' He unbuckled his belt.

Ten minutes later, he was still trying to get started. He heard himself grunt, a low guttural sound, as he rutted her like an animal. Couldn't get hard. Couldn't do it. It was her fault. She wasn't Karlie. He pulled away. 'I'm out of here.'

Angie turned. 'You don't need to go, we can have dinner. I bought—'

'What do you think you're doing?'

'I'm sorry, George, I thought maybe we could—'

'Master.'

'Sorry, Master.'

'You're not fucking sorry.' He spreadeagled her, pinned her to the bed, brought his face close to hers. 'Karlie is dead and you know what? She was a fucking million times better than you.' He released her.

340

'George.' She reached for him.

He pushed her away. 'You want it rough? You'll get it rough but not from me.' He peered down at her. 'You little bitch, you've been stuffing your face, haven't you?'

'No, George, honestly.'

'Greedy little sow.' The slap left a reassuring palm-sized print on her cheek. He got himself together. Left.

Chapter Fifty-Three

The Meet-Up

George Bellerose let all thoughts of Angie go as he turned his Suzuki motorbike in the direction of the Botanic Gardens. He was meeting Bunyan behind the Kibble Palace. At the thought of the white powder, his stomach clenched and he began to salivate. He gripped the handles of the Suzuki. Christ, hold it together. He'd meet with Bunyan, ignore the clown-like grin, the disfigured hand clawing at his face. Ignore all that. Get the bags. Take them back to the privacy of his bedroom and put on Karlie's videos. He felt his phone vibrate. Probably fucking Angie. He couldn't be arsed. He needed to cut her loose. Get someone who was really into pain. He waited at a red light, checked his mirror. Fuck, that shitty white van was all over the place. Watched it pull in behind him. Glanced at the driver, young guy, sunken cheeks, looked wasted. Hand on the wheel bandaged with something filthy, ripped T-shirt. Christ, was the loser actually crying?

* * *

Behind Bellerose, in his van, Owen scanned the area for Bunyan's black Honda. Nothing yet. Took a minute to register that the noise was his mobile. 'Yeah?'

Mason's voice. 'You in place?'

Owen felt himself calm and emboldened at the same time. He wiped away the tears. ''Course I am. Why the fuck wouldn't I be?'

'I need you, Owen. I'm depending on you.'

'I know.' He was back with the family. He felt the pain in his hand spread. It was as if his whole being was throbbing, pulsating. His mouth was dry. He glanced at the plastic water bottle. Empty.

'Only, I don't want you to fuck this up.'

'I told you, I'm on it.'

The line went dead. Owen waited at the red light. A pale blue Suzuki motorbike was in front; the driver was staring in his mirror at him. What the fuck was he looking at? Owen gave him the finger. Tosser. Fucking Bunyan had to be arriving soon, he needed to be alert. But the windscreen swam in front of him. He opened the glove compartment, grabbed the painkillers, popped the tinfoil, swallowed two, took the other four for the hit. Tossed the empty packet into the back of the van. Glanced at the picture, willed the scene to become animated again, for him to hear the music. Then it began, just as he wished. The horses and the unicorn began to move and he could hear music. Party music. They were holding a birthday party for him. The lights changed and the cunt in front turned left. Owen followed. Bunyan would be coming down the road soon. It would be easy, a simple feat. It had been difficult to drive with his hand bandaged but he'd managed it. He heard the engine purr in agreement; this

343

wasn't the dummy run. He would make it look like an accident. 'Random,' Mason had said, 'So there's no fallout on me.'

Owen drove on, listened to the sound of the carousel in the brightly lit forest, glanced again at the horses – they were all moving in unison, as if by magic. He smiled, it was all coming together. He would kill Bunyan and be reunited with Mason and the gang. In death, he would belong again. Bunyan would be dead and Mason would be proud of him. He'd be a hero. Owen closed his eyes for a second, listened to the music. It was beautiful. Haunting and sad. He let it wash over him. Then he snapped his eyes open. Ahead, a black Honda motorbike turned into the road.

It had to be that bastard Bunyan, it had to be his bike. Owen heard the music get louder, saw Mason smile at him; he'd be made an honorary lieutenant in the organisation. Him a lieutenant, that would show his fucking mother that he'd made something of his life. He watched the black Honda move into the road, overtake the pale blue Suzuki. Now was his time. He smiled at the horses. Soon he would be in the forest with them, the lights, the music. He would be home. Home. He stared at the Honda, closed his eyes. Hit the accelerator. Floored it. 'FUCK FUCK FUCK!' Heard the squeal of shattered steel.

Chapter Fifty-Four

A Trio of Endings

One

It was 1.30 a.m. and Fullarton Care Home was in darkness. Wide awake in his bed, Steve Penwell watched the pirate hide in the folds of the curtains and felt the numbness begin in his left arm, before it spread to his left leg. He kept himself still. Quiet. He knew what was happening. The headache had woken him an hour earlier and now it was intense. Beside him, the bell. He ignored it, refused to summon help. He wondered fleetingly about Maureen, wondered if she would go to the police. Knew that he would never know the outcome of his action. What if the man with the patch had only been running because he was late for work or needed to catch a bus? Too many 'what ifs'. He would never know. Maybe he should have come forward all those years ago. But he would have lost his family. He thought of his two grown-up children on the other side of the Atlantic Ocean, who never visited him. It was too late now, too late for any of it. He felt the numbness spread across his body, the pain from the blistering headache increase until, finally, a door closed, first on his vision, then on his life.

Two

The excited voice of the reporter as he stared into the camera. 'In the West End of Glasgow police and ambulance have attended the scene of a road traffic accident.' Behind him, lights flashed around a police cordon. The reporter continued. 'The accident has left one man dead and another fighting for his life when a white Transit van collided with a motorbike. Witnesses at the scene said the van drove straight through a red light and into the motorbike. The driver of the van has been taken to the Royal Infirmary with injuries that are said to be life-threatening and remains in intensive care. The driver of the motorcycle, who has not yet been identified, was pronounced dead at the scene. His decapitated body was found in the road by horrified resident Mr Michael Campbell.'

'I rushed out to see what had happened and it was so terrible. It was like in the movies, when I picked up the helmet, I didn't know the head was still inside . . .'

'Meanwhile, neighbour Anna Westborne had this to say . . .'

'I was driving home and I had right of way and then this white van shot out and straight into the motorcyclist, it was as if he didn't see him. It was the worst thing I've ever seen. The poor motorcyclist. I feel traumatised even to have witnessed it.'

Three

When she returned from Blackpool she went straight to her sister's flat. Nikki opened the door and knew immediately, without even having to put on a light, that it was empty and had been for some time. It was the sense of a departure, like walking through a graveyard of recently filled graves. She switched on the light, took in the neatness of the living room. In the bedroom, she saw that Holly's bed hadn't been slept in. In the kitchen, a single upturned mug was on the draining board, a solitary plate beside it. Nikki walked back into the hallway and closed the front door behind her. She would go to the police station, no matter the time. There would be someone on duty, someone who would record that her sister Holly was now missing.

Thirty minutes later, she stood at the front desk in Carmyle Police Station. 'I want to report my sister, Holly Lithgow, missing. It's been twenty-four hours since her neighbour saw her on the stairs. I've been away but now I'm back. I just checked her flat. Empty. Her bed hasn't been slept in. And before you begin to tell me she might be with friends or at a party or somewhere safe, she hasn't replied to my texts and I know my sister. This isn't like her. You have to do something. You need to listen to me.'

The desk sergeant reached for the paperwork, began to ask questions, record details. Build a case.

Chapter Fifty-Five

Phone calls

Wheeler had completed her run, had showered and was making coffee by 7 a.m. She listened to the news report. The motorcyclist killed in the West End the previous night had been identified – George Bellerose, Karlie Merrick's life coach. The driver of the van, a guy name of Owen McCrudden, was in intensive care in the Royal Infirmary with life-threatening injuries. Wheeler wondered what had actually happened.

By half past seven, she'd made the first call. Fullarton Care Home. Explained why she was calling.

'I'm afraid Mr Penwell passed away last night.' After a short conversation, Wheeler put down the phone. Thought about what Maureen Anderson had said, that Penwell had seen a man with an eye patch. At least she still had that. The second call on the list was a 01786 code. Bridge of Allan was where Willie Lester, the Old Coyote, lived. It was close to Stirling Castle, the Unicorn Café, the Wallace Monument and the McIver. She was certain the answer to Karlie's murder lay in that geographical area. Certain that the McIver and some of its staff were involved, wondered if the Old Coyote was too. She punched in the numbers. Waited. Finally, it was answered. 'Mr Lester?'

'Yes?'

'DI Kat Wheeler from Carmyle Police Station. I'm investigating the Karlie Merrick case.'

'I've been keeping up with it via the television. Dreadful. And you're having a lot of gang trouble in the city too. Plus, that horrific motorcycle accident – the poor man was decapitated, wasn't he?'

'I've been reading the notes on the John Merrick case.'

'That's right, I worked the case with the Bulldog.'

'I wonder if you'd mind a quick meet-up? I could drive up this morning if you're free?'

'Anytime you or any of your colleagues need to have a chat, come on up. I'd be happy to help. To be honest, I wish I was back on the force, retirement's no kind of fun.'

'What time suits?'

She jotted down the address, finished the phone call. Rang the station. 'Boss?'

'Good morning, Wheeler.' She heard the coolness in his tone. 'I just heard about George Bellerose.'

'Me too. I just wanted to update you. Karlie's friend Maureen spoke with a man name of Steve Penwell, who saw someone running past his window on the night John Merrick was killed. Penwell was with his girlfriend not his wife at the time, which is why he didn't come forward.'

'In that case, have Mr Penwell brought into the station.'

'That's not possible. He died last night, although he had been ill. He was in Fullarton Care Home. Karlie had

349

gone to see him and then later Maureen. He told them both the same thing.'

'Go on.'

She sighed. 'He was schizophrenic and suffered from hallucinations. In particular, he had a fixation with pirates. He saw them in the room and the man he saw the night John Merrick was murdered was wearing a patch. And, boss, I think the appointments scored out in John Merrick's diary weren't cancellations but deletions; at least one name, if not two, has been obliterated. I want the original diary from John Merrick's case to be re-examined and his clients re-interviewed. I'm concerned that some of the entries were altered after Merrick was killed.'

'You think Eddie Furlan missed crucial evidence?'

'I'm saying that there are areas of the investigation that need to be revisited, in particular the diary. I want to get this information out there to the public, see if we can contact the other clients. I'm just about to call Beth Swinton and ask her to search for anything she may still have belonging to John Merrick.'

'Eddie's one of us, Wheeler. Accusing him of a balls-up, with as yet bugger all evidence seems a bit harsh, given what's recently happened. Just concentrate on solving the Karlie Merrick case, rather than pointing the finger at another cop and their work from two decades past. Particularly one you've recently upset.'

'Fine.'

'Wheeler, this is looking like a grudge against the Furlans.'

'Boss, you need to trust me.'

'You need to be damn sure of your facts. Are you?'

She ended the call. Quickly rang Beth Swinton and left a message on her answering machine, if she could please double-check if she had anything still relating to John Merrick's hypnotherapy practice. Wheeler recalled that Beth had said earlier that there might be more in the attic.

Chapter Fifty-Six

The Old Coyote

Her mobile rang again as she approached Bridge of Allan.

Ross sounded harassed. 'Where are you?'

'About to meet up with the Old Coyote. I think Eddie Furlan had some questionable practices, just like his son.'

'If the DCC's on the case, you need to be careful, Wheeler.'

'I'm certain that the Furlans are connected somehow. I need to find out what this Coyote guy knows.'

'You're sounding weird.'

'Because I'm following a lead?'

'You're going off at a tangent. I warned you, Paul Furlan is making this look like your personal vendetta, first against him then against his father.'

'You need to trust me.'

She ended the call. Was this what it was coming to? Asking Stewart and now Ross to trust her? Did she even want to be a cop anymore? She started the car, heard her mobile ring again. Ignored it, let it go through to voicemail. She thought about what Ross had said, reasoned that since the DCC was breathing down Stewart's neck, it had to come from the McIver Club. In which case, she was definitely on to something.

Five minutes later, she found the bungalow. The door was opened by a thick-set man in his early sixties. His shirt was open at the neck, exposing an object that she hadn't seen for a long time, but there it was, nestled in the grey chest hair – a silver medallion. She saw the flash of a name bracelet. Country music drifted through the doorway; she heard Tammy Wynette imploring women to stand by their man.

'Mr Lester, thanks for agreeing to see me.'

'You make it sound formal. It's Willie. Come in and have a seat.'

'I just wanted a quick word about the John Merrick case.'

'So you said on the phone, but it's all in the files. I told Eddie this when he rang.'

'Eddie called you?'

'Yesterday. Told me his wife Jean had died. An awful shame. Eddie's a hell of a bright guy, did most of the reports, paperwork was never my forte.'

'Mine neither.' So Furlan had known how to contact his former partner. *We lost contact, I think he went off to the country someplace. Probably to fish, knowing him.* Wheeler wondered what else Eddie Furlan had kept from her. So much for them all being on the same side and him being so fucking concerned about her.

'Are you a member of the McIver Club?'

'Never heard of it.'

'It's in Stirling. Eddie and his son, Paul, are members.'

'Again, not on my radar. What kind of a club is it?'

Her mobile rang again; she ignored it.

'You need to answer that?'

'It's fine. Can you tell me about the John Merrick case?'

'Well, me and Eddie worked the case but it was one of the ones that got away. Eddie had Cal Moody and Keith Sullivan up for it but we'd no evidence and their alibis stacked up. It was a real pity.'

'Did all of the team feel so committed to finding the killer?'

Lester sighed. 'Maybe a few of the guys back at the station lost focus. I'm not saying they didn't want to find the killer, it's just the sickening material we found. On the surface, John Merrick appeared to have been a family man, clean as a whistle, but the stuff we uncovered was just shocking. I think it changed the tone of the investigation.'

'Less of a priority?'

'He wasn't one of the good guys any more, he was a sleazeball. But, believe me, Eddie and I were still completely thorough.'

'John Merrick went from innocent family man to pervert?'

'We had other cases. It crossed our minds that it might have been one of the community. Maybe someone who knew that he had the images, suspected he was a paedophile? There are vigilantes out there.'

'Do you think that some of the details in Merrick's diary could have been changed post murder?'

'That couldn't have happened.'

'Because?'

'Eddie was very thorough.'

'What if some of the appointments were deleted?'

'Did you ask Eddie?'

'I'm asking you.'

'Then I'm telling you no. Poor Eddie's just lost his wife. He's not what he was, I could hear it in his voice.'

'Eddie's wife, what was she like?'

'Jean? She was a blast, went off like a wee rocket.'

'Happily married?'

'They had their challenges. I know that it was rocky for a while but they got through it.'

'When you say "rocky"?'

'They argued; what couple doesn't? I argued a lot with my ex-wife Gloria. You married, DI Wheeler?'

Wheeler thought of the ashtrays in Eddie Furlan's house. 'Did she smoke?'

'Like a chimney.'

'She ever try to stop?'

'No idea.' He paused. 'Oh, I get it, you're trying to link her with John Merrick.'

'Is it possible that she went to see him?'

'Eddie would have mentioned if Jean had gone to see Merrick and it would have been in the diary.'

Wheeler waited.

'You think he deleted Jean's name? Why would he do that? What in hell is wrong with you? Subtle you're not, Inspector. So what are you saying, that Jean went to see Merrick and then what? They fell in love, had an affair? She threatened to leave Eddie and, being a well-respected cop, his first instinct was to go over and batter Merrick to death in his own home? You know what? You're in the wrong job, you need to be writing fantasy books.'

Wheeler stood. 'I'd best be off. I don't want to take up any more of your time.'

'You be careful what you're doing out there, DI

Wheeler.' More of a warning than advice. 'You don't want to go stirring up trouble. Stay on track with your new case. Eddie and I were thorough in the John Merrick case.'

'Then why is it unsolved?'

'Some cases just are, you must know that.'

'I have concerns that crucial evidence may have been altered.'

'For what end?'

'I don't know yet.'

'You can see yourself out.'

Wheeler closed the door behind her. As she made her way back to the car she went over and over it in her mind. Who were the missing clients? And if Eddie Furlan had deleted their names, why? If it had been Eddie's wife, why bother? There was no scandal around smoking. She rubbed her forehead, thought of her mother's words before her death. 'If you start getting regular headaches like these, go and get tested.' A week later, she was dead. Wheeler slipped a packet of painkillers out of her bag, took two, swallowed them dry. Played the *what if* game. What if Jean Furlan had been having an affair with John Merrick? There's motive. Or what if Merrick had discovered something while a client was under hypnosis? Something illegal, something he'd be duty bound to report to the police? What if he'd threatened to go to the police and report it? Client confidentiality only went so far. The therapist had to encourage the client to go to the police. If not, it was their duty to report criminal activity. What if a client had revealed something incriminating whilst under hypnosis and John Merrick had threatened to reveal it? Whose names had been deleted and why? Wheeler knew that there was something just out of the picture, something about the case that didn't add up. Lester had said that he and Eddie Furlan had been thorough, but the discovery of underage porn had changed the perception of the team's investigation. Another *what if* presented itself. What if the porn had been planted to discredit the victim? She checked her phone, one message, Beth Swinton would search her attic. Wheeler reached the car. Felt the pain behind her eyes increase. Thought of calling the GP's surgery. Instead, turned the car back towards the city.

Beth Swinton called as she approached the city boundary. She'd found a small diary and a couple of old wedding photographs. Wheeler made the detour. An hour later she'd known it was worth it.

Chapter Fifty-Seven

Nikki

Despite the weather Nikki Lithgow shivered, exhausted by the sheer effort of believing that Holly was still alive. She was on the same bridge Rachel Dawson had stood on, a decade earlier, watching and waiting while the police divers searched the River Clyde. Like Rachel, Nikki had been assigned a family liaison officer to support her and who'd explained what Police Scotland could offer by way of specialist resources. Nikki recognised the signs, knew that the police were now searching for the body a horrified tourist had reported seeing an hour earlier. Nikki knew that, given the description, the police had a strong suspicion that it was Holly. That she was dead.

Nikki knew that up ahead a pack of rubberneckers and press was watching to see if the corpse would reappear. Nikki stared at the Clyde. She had always thought that the river was so integral to the city, a ribbon of water softly meandering through, on its way to the Firth of Clyde. Not now. Now she saw it as a multi-armed monster with suction fronds to grasp and pull underwater innocent victims. She thought of Holly, of her confidence, her long blonde hair and her ambition. Then she thought of a body being dredged from the river.

Nikki offered a silent prayer to a God she didn't believe in, promised Him anything, *anything* for Holly not to be dead. Like Rachel a decade earlier, Nikki had provided the police with a recent photograph. Holly had been smiling into the camera, long hair framing her face. A whole life ahead of her. Nikki closed her eyes, felt hot tears swell and fall. She hadn't felt this vulnerable since their mum had died. She spoke to Holly out loud. 'Please get in touch. I love you.'

It was an hour and fifteen minutes before Holly responded.

Nikki stood at a distance, beyond the police cordon, recognised the change in behaviour, knew by the flurry of activity that the police divers had found a body. She sent up another silent plea to the unknown God, pleaded that it not be Holly.

It's one of life's truisms that the dead, when their body is disposed of in water, will resurface to ascertain their place in life. Holly Lithgow's body did just that. As her body decayed, gas had formed in the tissue. Thanks to a combination of the warm temperature of the water, the low fat in her tissue and the bacterial action, she rose quickly and floated on the surface of the River Clyde, gently ebbing and flowing in a macabre aquatic waltz.

Chapter Fifty-Eight

Good News

'Boss, we definitely need to be looking at the John Merrick case. Information in the main diary was deleted.'

'I'm listening.'

'The deletions were to hide at least one name. Look.' She put the small diary in front of him. 'I've just collected this from Beth Swinton. There was a long-term client – HPE. I think it could be Hugo Ponsensby-Edward.'

'Indeed it could. And it could be other names. Why jump to conclusions that it's Mark's son? Is this to do with the McIver, Wheeler?'

'The name was deleted.'

'And Merrick deleted it?'

'I think it was deleted after Merrick was murdered.' She paused. 'And not many people had access.'

'You're accusing one of the team?'

'You have to admit it's a possibility. Willie Lester said Eddie Furlan handled all the paperwork.'

'Motive?'

'I don't know yet.'

'Evidence?'

'Gut instinct. I'm certain that—'

'A retired police colleague, Wheeler. Think about what you're saying. You've already pissed off everyone at the McIver and now, for good measure, you're taking another potshot at Eddie Furlan? Yet you have no evidence and no motive. This whole business with his son Paul has put you out of sorts.'

'I know there's something amiss.'

'I don't agree.'

'Look, I'm telling you that—'

'Drop the attitude, Wheeler. The DCC told me about the loss you experienced while serving in the army, about Colin Jenkins.'

'How does he even know this information?'

'He was acting in your best interests.'

She very much doubted it.

'They all are.'

'They?'

'Mark Ponsensby-Edward and Paul Furlan too.'

'You've got to be fucking joking, Paul bloody Furlan is—'

'Watch your language, Wheeler! You haven't been yourself recently, what with these bloody headaches and now all this. You need to rest.'

'Are you taking me off the case?'

'Of course not, but I want Ross to lead the investigation for the next couple of days, give you time to reflect.'

'This is garbage.'

'You can close the door on your way out.'

Back at her desk, Boyd updated her. 'Holly Lithgow's body has just been pulled from the Clyde. Early indications suggest that she didn't fall in accidently.'

Wheeler knew that a woman named Holly Lithgow had been reported missing. She felt the tension in the room rise. Whoever Holly Lithgow was, she'd now gone from missing person to victim.

'Her blue Micra's turned up in long-term parking at Prestwick Airport. It's been there since Thursday night,' said Boyd. 'Forensics are on their way.'

Wheeler's phone rang. She answered it and listened: 'We have some good news about the DNA recovered from the back door to Karlie Merrick's flat.'

'You've got a match?' said Wheeler.

'Not a full match, but is a partial good enough for you?'

'Tell me you've got a name?'

'Interestingly enough, the database did throw one up. That's the good news.'

She grabbed a pen. 'I'm listening.'

'Paul Furlan.'

Chapter Fifty-Nine

The Vendetta

They were barely four minutes into the interview and Paul Furlan was adamant. 'This is your personal vendetta, Wheeler.'

'Your DNA was found—'

He cut across her. 'My DNA was on the database because of a fucking motoring offence, years ago. And I've already told you that I had never contacted Karlie Merrick outside of the club, I didn't go to her flat and I didn't bloody murder her. You are wasting time, Wheeler, when you should be out finding the killer. You are on some twisted revenge fantasy over Jenkins' death; you were on it in the army and you're on it now.'

'How did your DNA come to be in the location of Karlie Merrick's flat?'

'That's for you to find out, isn't it? Do your fucking job. But I know one thing for sure. You had access to her flat. Now my DNA turns up. Convenient. I'm making an official complaint. You're not fit to serve.'

'Go ahead.'

'Your bizarre hounding of me is unhinged. I've already told you that I was at a party the night she was killed.'

The door flew open.

Stewart stormed into the room. 'I am terminating this interview.' He identified himself, gave the time and switched off the tape. 'DI Wheeler, outside now.' He shot a look at Boyd. 'I'll see you in my office later.' In the corridor, he rounded on her. 'What the hell do you think you're up to?'

'It's my case, I'm entitled to—'

'Ross was to lead, I told you.'

'It's my case,' she repeated.

'It's no longer appropriate for you to speak with Paul Furlan.'

'Because?'

'It may jeopardise the case. His father and the DCC have all complained that you are at best biased, at worst—'

'That's rubbish. You know it and I know it.'

'Certainly, I believe that your ability to be objective has been severely compromised,' said Stewart.

'Boss—'

He held up his hand, palm facing her. 'Wheeler, for God's sake, we're on the same bloody side. If Paul Furlan did kill Karlie Merrick then I need every step of this investigation to be transparent. I won't have this investigation compromised, either by past grudges or by your absolute surety that he's involved, despite having little evidence. Do you even get it? You've pissed off Eddie Furlan, the Ponsensby-Edwards and then, just to complete the hat-trick, the DCC. Now go home. That's an order.'

Wheeler waited in the corridor, shaking with anger,

saw Stewart go back into the interview room. Watched the door close in her face.

* * *

An hour later DCI Stewart escorted Paul Furlan to the exit. 'Thanks for being so patient while we double-checked you alibi. Ronald McMasters has indeed confirmed that you stayed overnight at his country house, the night Karlie Merrick was murdered.'

'Wheeler's unhinged. This was personal. You know it as well as I do, Stewart. Don't you?'

'Thanks for your co-operation, Mr Furlan.' Stewart opened the door.

'You need to rein her in, or face the fucking consequences.'

'Goodbye, Mr Furlan.'

The door closed.

Chapter Sixty

No. 195

Wheeler strode into the grand hotel. Mark Ponsensby-Edward's lecture, 'Upholding the Law – an ongoing challenge', was in a place swanky enough that it didn't need a name, only a number. The lecture had finished thirty minutes earlier. Through the open door, she saw Ponsensby-Edward standing at a lectern tidying some papers. A security guard blocked her as she approached. Wheeler flashed her ID. He blocked her again. 'DI Wheeler. Police.' She spoke loudly enough that Ponsensby-Edward glanced across.

'Police? Let her through, Wilkinson.'

Wilkinson glared at her but acquiesced.

'Thank you, sir. I'm DI Kat Wheeler, I just wanted to apologise.' She kept her tone the right side of ingratiating.

'Not at all, DI Wheeler.' He waved her apology away with a bony hand. 'There's really no need to apologise. We all know that you're upset.'

'DCI Stewart explained the whole scenario to me,' she lied.

'Good.' The smile; she saw the sharp incisors.

'Yes, I was rather too excitable at the McIver Club. I went stomping in with my size sixes.'

Ponsensby-Edward waited.

'Your son Hugo was seeing John Merrick,' said Wheeler.

He paused. 'Really? Was his name on the client list?'

'His initials were in an old diary. Karlie's cousin Beth Swinton gave it to me.'

'I see. And, to be clear, Hugo's name was actually in it?'

'His initials. HPE.'

'Hardly conclusive, could be anyone. Hugh Philip Evenson, perhaps Harry Pritchard Eavis, what about Harriet Pullman Egar? Oh dear, I do believe the permutations may be endless.'

'I think the diary entry was doctored after Merrick was killed.'

'How interesting. And you think Hugo was involved?'

'Was he a client?'

'My dear Inspector Wheeler, Hugo was nowhere near John Merrick's house the night he was killed. He was at a private party on our country estate that evening.' He turned to Wilkinson. 'Our guest is leaving.'

Wheeler watched him, knew that there were laws for some people in society, while others, like Mark Ponsensby-Edward and his son, Hugo, thought themselves above the law. That the rules which applied to the majority of folk simply did not apply to them. Wilkinson escorted her to the door. She turned back to Ponsensby-Edward. 'I'm asking you again, was your son Hugo a client of John Merrick?'

He smiled. 'My son didn't kill John Merrick. If you know what's good for you, you won't persist in this curious witch-hunt of yours, Inspector.'

Chapter Sixty-One

The Reprimand

'You couldn't let it go, could you?' said Stewart. 'I told you to go home but you went to see Mark Ponsensby-Edward.'

'I needed to find out what was going on.'

'I told you not take this line of inquiry any further.'

Wheeler said nothing.

'Did you hear me?'

She tried to keep her voice the right side of reasonable. Failed. 'I think Eddie Furlan falsified information in a police inquiry; even his partner Willie Lester didn't know. The initials HPE were in the other diary.'

'HPE isn't necessarily who you think it is. You know Mark Ponsensby-Edward and his son Hugo had nothing to do with the death of John Merrick, they both have alibis, so why are you trying to drag their reputation and the McIver's through the dirt?'

'Call me idealistic but—'

'I could think of other descriptions.'

'I believe transparency and accountability are important in police work,' said Wheeler.

'Well, idealism is all well and good, but as a savvy cop,

you need to hold the bigger picture. We don't work in isolation, we are part of the bigger community and, like it or not, there are whole layers of this community that operate at a more influential level.'

'It was in the interest of the case. There are clients unaccounted for; it must be relevant. Why didn't they come forward?'

'You think there are two clients missing? It could be just cancellations, Wheeler. I'm concerned that you are becoming obsessed with an old unresolved murder and not the task we have in front of us. Police Scotland do have a cold case team. Leave John Merrick's case to them.'

'Boss—'

'Wheeler, I'm telling you, for the last time, to go home.' He paused. 'Paul Furlan has a watertight alibi for the night Karlie Merrick was murdered. All night.'

'Then the DNA must belong to a family member. Eddie? Or Paul's brother, James? Familial DNA.'

'Christ, Wheeler, take a break from persecuting the Furlans. Paul has accused you of planting evidence. You had access to Eddie's house and later to Paul. And then to Karlie's flat. Can you see how this looks?'

'Boss, I want—'

'You need to go home.'

'You need to trust me.'

'It's not a request, Wheeler. I'm telling you to go home. Now.'

Chapter Sixty-Two

Small Details

Wheeler found an empty office at the opposite end of the station and fired up a tired, old computer. First off, she tried to call Hugo Ponsensby-Edward again. Got through to voicemail. Again. She left another message. She began wading through old newspaper reports, scanning them for details. She scrolled through years of information, worked steadily through every story, every reference, until her head felt like it was going to explode. Mark Ponsensby-Edward and Hugo at a myriad of grand parties. Then Willie Lester. Edward Furlan. Police. Glasgow. She scrolled through pages and pages of irrelevant information, constantly refining the search, narrowing it down. It was two hours and twenty-five minutes later when she saw it and froze.

A photograph of them together at a function. She reached forward and touched the screen. There they were, the Old Coyote and the Bulldog. Underneath the photograph were their names, Willie Lester and Eddie Furlan and two women, presumably their wives.

'Christ, it's taken a while to track you down.' Ross

stood in the doorway. 'What the hell are you up to? You're meant to be at home. You need to take a breather.'

'Look at this,' She gestured to the image on the screen. 'An old photograph of the two of them at a posh do.'

Ross looked at it. Got it.

She picked up her mobile, called Willie Lester, explained why she was calling.

'Yes, I remember Eddie had eye surgery and there were complications. He couldn't let any light get to it so had to wear a patch for a while. Is this important?'

'Thanks, you've been a great help.' She slammed down the phone. 'Eddie Furlan killed John Merrick.'

'What was his motive?'

'I don't know that yet, but I'll find out.' She printed out the photograph, sprinted through the corridors to Stewart's office, burst into his office. 'Boss.'

'Why the hell are you still here?'

'Eddie Furlan killed John Merrick.'

'Oh, for God's sake, Wheeler.'

'Hear me out. Look.' She gave him the printout. 'I found this photograph of Eddie from years ago. He had a patch over his eye. Steve Penwell said he'd seen someone running away from the area of John Merrick's murder. The guy had an eye patch. Like a pirate. I just checked with Willie Lester. Eddie Furlan had eye surgery and wore an eye patch for a while. Eddie killed John Merrick. I believe he killed Karlie too and that's why the DNA found at Karlie's flat was only a partial match for Paul Furlan. Eddie Furlan's will be a full match, I'm sure of it.'

Chapter Sixty-Three

Lyndsay Moody

Six miles south of Glasgow lies the village of Busby. Lyndsay Moody lived in an old stone cottage on the outskirts of the village. Through his casual chat with Cal Moody, Cutter had tracked down not just Cal's sister Lyndsay, but her ex-boyfriend too. Cutter knew that they had separated the night of the fire, knew too that the boyfriend was fucking liable for it. Cutter had dressed for the party. His five foot five frame was encased in motorbike leathers, his head freshly shaved, his hands balled into their customary fists. He parked his motorbike outside the cottage, watched Josh get out of the Range Rover. They walked together to the wooden door. Josh knocked.

A man in his early forties opened it, a mug of tea in his hand.

'We're friends of Lyndsay's,' said Cutter. 'And you are?'

'I'm her partner, Rob Vernon.' The man settled into the space he inhabited; five eleven, eighteen stones, he took his time expanding into the doorway.

'Right then, Rob,' said Cutter, looking up at him, 'you tootle back inside and we'll come in for a chat.'

Rob Vernon stared hard at Cutter, looked as if he was about to remonstrate. Took in the expression, the blazing eyes. The balled fists. Thought better of it. Instead, he turned and called into the hallway, 'Lyndsay doll, you've got visitors.'

They walked into the hall and were met by a woman who was a little over five foot in height. She was casually dressed in a white T-shirt and patterned shorts. She pushed her horn-rimmed glasses onto her hair and peered at Cutter.

'Good to finally meet you, Lyndsay.' Cutter smiled. 'I've heard all about you.'

The woman's smile was hesitant. 'Do I know you?'

'We have a couple of people in common. Paul Furlan and your mum.'

'I haven't seen Paul for years. How do you know Mum?'

'I know a friend of hers from way back, the time of the fire.'

'Get out.'

'Fuck, have you no manners?' Cutter tutted. 'There's a wee problem. Josh here believes that there's been . . .' He paused. 'How shall I put this? A miscarriage of justice. Now he's distracted from his work, which is a worry to me, so I thought it would be better all round if we come to an agreement.'

'I have no idea what you're talking about.'

'Glasgow Cross,' said Cutter.

'What about it?'

'You know it?'

'I grew up in Glasgow, but I expect you know that already?'

'There's a great wee saying carved on one of these buildings,' said Cutter. 'Do you know what it is?'

Lyndsay chewed at her bottom lip.

'I'm going to call the police,' said Rob.

Lyndsay put her hand on his arm.

'What's that, Cutter?' asked Josh.

'It says "Nobody provokes me with impunity." It means nae fucker messes with me, without getting fucked.'

Lyndsay bit her thumbnail. 'You better come through.'

They followed her through to a small living room with two sofas. Cutter and Josh took one, Rob and Lyndsay the other.

'Do you think maybe we can get a couple of glasses of water?' asked Cutter pleasantly. 'Only, it's roasting hot and we're parched.'

Rob went to the kitchen and returned with four glasses of water. They rattled on the tray as he brought them through. His and Lyndsay's remained untouched but Cutter finished his water before he spoke. 'I know how Amber Ellis died.'

'It was all in the papers.'

'No, I know how she really died,' he repeated slowly. 'And I know who did it.'

'I didn't do . . .' Lyndsay started.

Cutter glanced at her. 'Did I say it was you?'

Lyndsay was silent.

Rob turned to her. 'What's this about?'

'I don't know.'

'I think you do,' said Cutter.

'Lyndsay?' said Rob.

'It was twenty years ago; I was a very different person. There was an accident.' She looked at Cutter. 'I'm telling you the truth, it was an accident.'

'What accident?' asked Rob.

'It was the lies that came after that caused the problem, wasn't it?' said Cutter.

'What is going on here?' Rob demanded.

Lyndsay addressed Cutter. 'Look, Mum's dying, the doctor says it could be a few days, a week at the most.'

'Difficult to tell, these things; it's not like it's an exact science,' Cutter admitted. 'And then your junkie brother, Cal, got himself sliced up over at the Cockroach. Tut-tut. Careless.'

'It was Cal who told you where I was?'

'Yeah.'

'I just wanted to protect Mum until then. Afterwards, I'll go to the police.'

'No. That's not what's going to happen.' Cutter finished his glass of water and held it out to Rob. 'I'll have another.'

'Christ.' Rob got to his feet.

Cutter waited until another glass was in front of him before continuing, 'You're not just protecting your wee mammy, though, Christ knows, she doesn't deserve it. You're protecting the cunt that caused all this.'

When she spoke her voice was a whisper. 'We weren't even established as a couple really. I was a bit nervous around him. I didn't want to . . .' She glanced at Rob. 'I was eighteen and I didn't want to, you know. He was going off to the army and I just wasn't sure. Me and Cal were living with our dad, over in Temple. Mum and I never got on that well. We hadn't seen each other for ages but she was desperate to go to the bingo that night, some big prize. She rang and asked me to babysit, said it would be a big favour to her, help us build some bridges. She said the kids would already be in bed, it was just a matter of keeping an eye out. I agreed. Thought I'd ask Paul round while Mum slipped out to the bingo for an hour or so.'

'You didn't want to fuck him and he got pissed off?' asked Josh.

'Yes, I thought we were in love but—'

Rob got up and walked into the kitchen. 'I'll leave you to it.'

'When it came to it, I couldn't do it and he flipped. He got really angry, started yelling abuse, asking me what kind of a game was I playing? I was crying and trying to reason with him, but it just made him angrier. He grabbed the candle and threw it across the room. The curtains took hold but Paul just laughed, took out his lighter, threw it into the blaze. It exploded. He kept shouting at me, said some horrible things and then left.' She swallowed. 'And I didn't know what to do and then Mum ran in and screamed at me to get out. I was scared. I went back to Dad's. Mum told me later that she managed to get into the downstairs bedroom and grab you.' She looked at Josh. 'Upstairs was in flames, there was no time to . . .'

'And your mother stuck to her story,' said Cutter.

'She told them Amber must have snuck into the living room and knocked over a candle and set the curtain alight.' Lyndsay sniffed. 'What good would it have done if everyone had known what happened? It wouldn't have brought Amber back, would it? Mum said he would ruin my life if I told on him, that he would've gone to prison and you don't do that to someone like him. So, what would it have changed?'

'It might have helped Josh to get closure.'

She tried for the moral high ground. 'My mother went into a burning house to save you.'

'She was supposed to be looking after them,' said Cutter quietly. 'She was his foster carer. There's a duty and responsibility right there.'

'What is it you want from me?'

Cutter stood. 'Nothing much; just go to the polis and tell them the truth.'

'They'll ask me who else was there.'

'And you'll tell them the fucking truth.'

'And if I don't?'

'You'll have upset Josh, which in turn affects me. Do you know what that will make you?'

Silence.

'My enemy. Can you see where this might end? Folk who cause me any fucking inconvenience have got to understand that I'll inconvenience them. Understand?'

Lyndsay nodded, reached for her glass of water. Took a gulp.

Chapter Sixty-Four

Interview Room One

Stewart spoke. 'We have a full match, placing you at Karlie Merrick's house the night she died.'

Eddie Furlan smiled, tried for a bravado he didn't feel. Mark Ponsensby-Edward should have been in touch already. And why the hell was Gregor McCoy not returning his calls? 'You know I have nothing to do with any of this, you're making a grave mistake.' He continued, his tone authoritative. 'You've already been advised that Wheeler's on a witch-hunt.'

'Forensics have your DNA at Karlie Merrick's flat,' repeated Stewart. 'A complete match.'

'Crime scenes have been known to have been contaminated. Wheeler's out of control. Why don't you turn off the tape and we can have a chat?'

'Why don't we keep it on and you start talking? And, I repeat, your DNA was found at Karlie Merrick's flat. Let's begin there.'

Eddie swallowed hard. Looked at the floor. He knew what the lack of contact from the DCC and Mark Ponsensby-Edward meant. They had cut him loose; he was on his own. Well, if he was going down, he was damn sure he wasn't going down alone.

'Well?'

Eddie smiled. It was still early days. 'I've nothing to say.'

Two hours later, he'd had plenty of time to consider his options. Had tried to contact the other two, but to no avail. They were all fighting for their own lives now, establishing their own lies, making their own deals. Eddie knew, however, that he was at the bottom of the pecking order. Mark and Gregor could perhaps still pull in favours, threaten and cajole people in power. But he had nothing. Except the truth about what happened. It wouldn't save him, but it might ensure that they were brought down with him.

Finally, he returned to the interview room.

'You lied about you and Karlie not being in touch,' said Stewart.

'She'd pester me two or three times a year. She was always trying to solve her father's murder. I knew that she wanted to stage a reconstruction for television. She asked me to take part in it. As the original detective who'd worked the case, she thought it would bring a certain gravitas. Of course, I refused.'

'But then Steve Penwell got in touch and told her about seeing the man with the patch and she called you?'

'She said she had new evidence, insisted that she was going to take it to the police. I tried to discredit him, reminded her that Steve was schizophrenic and very sick, that it wouldn't hold up. But she wouldn't listen. She was desperate to make it public. The little bitch would have done anything to get on television, regardless of how many lives it ruined. I couldn't let that happen. I'd have been immediately connected to his murder. Everyone at the station had seen the patch. I'd taken a lot of ribbing about it. I told her I'd come over, that we'd discuss it.

'Why did you kill her?'

'Because she would have linked me to her father.' Furlan studied his hands. 'Twenty years ago, I'd made Paul go for therapy for his anger management issues. He had a dreadful temper, needed to get it sorted before he went into the army. Hugo Ponsensby-Edward was a client of Merrick's, recommended him. Hugo was an addict trying to get clean, but there had been a couple of rumours about rape allegations. Nothing formal. Hugo told Merrick everything and then got drunk at a party and confessed to his father, told him Merrick would have it all in his notes. Mark called me. He'd already spoken to Gregor McCoy. I feared that Paul's behaviour at Susan Moody's house would be recorded too. We all agreed that I would warn Merrick off. I reminded him about client confidentiality but it didn't wash. He was an arrogant prick, said he'd encourage both boys to go to the police and confess. If they didn't, he'd report them. He said that it would do them good to be congruent. He laughed in my face.' Furlan paused. 'That's when things got out of hand.'

Stewart waited.

'However flawed he is, Paul's the innocent in all of this. I can assure you, he's done nothing.'

They had continued the interview for another twenty minutes, teasing out information and gathering facts until, finally, Eddie Furlan was led to a cell.

Chapter Sixty-Five

The O2 Academy

It was nearly time. The four of them clustered backstage. Skye began his pre-show ritual, sank the tequila shot in one, listened to the noise of the crowd, stamping their feet, somewhere between expectation and impatience. He downed a second shot, walked through the door into the corridor, through another door. The others followed behind. Skye ran to the front of the stage, adrenaline coursing through his veins as he grabbed the microphone and yelled, 'Good evening, Glasgow!' Heard the roar, as the crowd surged forward to be met by the bouncers who'd lined up in front of the stage. One fan got through and leapt towards him. Bouncers raced in from the side and grabbed her. Lexi started on the drums, made them thunder. Josh kicked in on bass and then Joe came in on keyboards. The band was flying. Skye was on fire and fed off the energy of the crowd who sang every single word with him. He paused at the end of the song, let them carry the final few bars before he bellowed into the microphone, 'Thank you for the duet. I love you, Glasgow!' Heard the roar again. He felt the intense heat from the lights and amps. He was high on the energy.

Skye began the second song and the crowd responded, swaying as one. Tonight, he thought, I am immortal. I am a rock god. He watched a blonde-haired girl launch herself into the crowd and be lifted high and passed, hand over hand, towards the stage. A gift to the god. He knew that the crowd would support her, take care of her as she journeyed towards the stage. We are one, thought Skye, as she made her way towards him. As he sang, he moved towards the audience, caught the eye of the girl being passed to him. Smiled. Reached out his hand. A bouncer intercepted and grabbed her and she was rushed backstage. Skye knew that she would be run through the labyrinth of corridors and led back into the arena from a side entrance. He finished the song, listened to the rapturous applause. Began again. As he sang, he glanced at the rest of the band. Josh was bent over his Fender Precision; he'd found his own little piece of heaven. He paced the stage cradling his guitar, drinking in the vibes. Lexi smashed the drums, also in his own world. Joe sat behind the keyboards, frowning slightly, as he always did, as if, by deduction alone, he could unravel a great sound. Skye thought about their recent interview, how Dougie had insisted that the band were very tight, but Skye knew it was a lie; they all inhabited singular worlds, they just happened to share a stage.

Next up was 'My Desire for You'. It had been their first big hit and had been voted the perfect love ballad of 2013, an anthem for lovers across the country. The Kill Kestrels had been sent video links and messages from weddings, engagement parties and anniversary celebrations thanking them for the song. Smiling couples sharing the love. Skye remembered the woman he'd written it about;

she'd been a Slovakian sex worker and she had been the best he'd ever had; she'd been full on. He'd taken sex to the extreme with her, just as he had with the blonde girl at the McIver.

He finished the song – 'And it was the best that ever was . . . the best that's ever been . . . And you and me . . . a memory for eternity . . .' The lust of death. The pain. The knowledge. Nothing else mattered. Pain. Sex. Death. 'And you were the best that's ever been . . .' Perhaps this time next year the love anthem would be the one he was currently writing about the woman from the McIver. She hadn't been the best he'd ever had but she'd given her life for his pleasure. Something like, 'I gave you my all.' The fans would think it was about him being in love, they always did. He thought of the two girls who'd won the tickets. He couldn't recall their names; why would he? He'd never see them again. But knew that they would be out there in the audience, worshipping him. He'd nearly got the blonde's mobile number before Dougie had blundered his way into the room and disturbed them. Fat bastard. Once they'd really made it they'd dump Dougie and get some proper fucking management. Skye looked out over the audience, listened to the applause. Revelled in it. He was a God. A Rock God.

Chapter Sixty-Six

Party Over

The Incident Room was busy, information was coming in quickly and phones were ringing.

Stewart strode into the room. 'Update?'

'Holly Lithgow's body has been taken to the mortuary. Forensics are crawling all over her car,' said Ross.

'I'm checking through CCTV from Prestwick Airport,' said Wheeler. 'We have a clear window of time. CCTV puts the car being driven into airport parking around ten o'clock on Thursday night.' She scrolled through the grainy CCTV footage; people moved in awkward frame shots as they exited the car park. Slightly blurred, grey shapes, jerky movements. She was excluding families with children. Groups of young women. Her gut instinct told her she was looking for a man or men. She discounted an elderly man walking with a stick. The group of probably drunk men wearing Stetsons, deliberately pushing into each other. A stag do. Lone men hurried across her screen, carrying briefcases, rucksacks. She jotted down notes, freeze-framed the images. She stared at the screen. At ten past ten, a lone man walked through the exit.

He was wearing a fleece, hood up. Jeans and trainers. Hands in pockets. But it wasn't what he was wearing, it was his walk. Unmistakable. He led with his shoulders. They already had his DNA on the system.

She turned to Ross. 'Deoxyribonucleic acid, you've got to love it.'

'DNA,' said Ross. 'What do you have?'

'I'll bet money that this figure—' she tapped the image '—is Paul Furlan. Holly's car was parked at Prestwick Airport. Less than ten minutes later, he's leaving the airport.'

An hour later, in Interview Room One, Stewart faced Paul Furlan. 'You killed Holly Lithgow.'

'Rubbish.'

'CCTV has you parking her car at Prestwick Airport on Thursday night. DNA has been recovered from the vehicle and will be checked against yours.'

Furlan paused. 'I dumped her car, but I didn't kill her. It's not what it seems.'

'Go on.'

'That's not what happened.'

Stewart sat forward in his chair. 'Then tell me what did happen.'

At the end of the interview, Stewart sent out a command. Skye Cooper was to be arrested and brought into the station.

Lyndsay Moody was in Interview Room Two and the tape was running. 'I want to make a statement. On the night of 3 September 2004, I was at my mother, Susan Moody's house. I was there with my boyfriend at the time, Paul

Furlan.' She paused. 'It's a long story, but, in essence, we had an argument. He got mad, grabbed a candle and threw it across the room, and the curtains took hold.'

'Then what?'

'Paul laughed, took out his disposable lighter, threw it into the fire. Like it was some kind of game. It exploded, the fire was out of control.' She buried her face in her hands. 'It all happened so quickly. I was upset, I wasn't thinking straight. Mum rushed in, shouted for me to go home. Paul vanished. There were two kids asleep in the house. One of them, a little girl named Amber, died.'

Boyd let her talk, heard all about the fire and the subsequent lies and the fear of confronting Paul Furlan. The fear of holding him accountable.

Across from him Robertson sat, listening. He was silent.

Forty-five minutes later, Wheeler witnessed the tears and self-pity. Watched as Skye's kohl-rimmed eyes filled with tears. Wheeler knew that the pity had little to do with Holly Lithgow and everything to do with Skye himself. Paul Furlan had told them the full extent of Skye Cooper's involvement in Holly Lithgow's death.

She began the interview.

Chapter Sixty-Seven

Survival

Dougie sat in the bar and monitored the Facebook and Twitter accounts, which had gone stratospheric. The UK newspapers had clamoured for interviews and Paulo Di Stefano's photographs had been splashed across the UK press, particularly the one of Skye taken on the hotel roof garden, arms outstretched like a modern-day Christ. Under the photographs, the sound bite from Skye, 'Make me immortal.' Christ, but this was a fucking nightmare. Dougie gulped the Jack Daniel's. Because of Skye's monumental fuck-up, the rest of the band needed careful handling, if they weren't to go down the proverbial drain. On the upside, and fuck knows how this had happened, sales of 'Death of an Angel' had soared. Their fans had rallied. From what he could gather, Skye's fans were in complete denial that their hero could have done anything wrong. This was simply a mistake that would be cleared up soon. The others all wanted to protect the remaining members from the fall-out and were anxious for the band to continue.

Dougie watched Josh come into the bar. Saw Cutter Wysor hover in the doorway.

Dougie looked at Josh. Handsome guy, sensitive. 'You want to front the band? I could get someone to step in for a bit? Let you make up your mind, but I think you'd be great.' Watched him consider it. Gave him time to visualise himself in Skye's shoes, the adulation, the adoration of the fans. 'Remember, we don't want to let the fans down, to disappoint them when they are in such turmoil. This might help them through a tough time, that's all I'm concerned about. All those young folk who looked to the band for inspiration? You could help them through this. What do you think? I'm thinking of Ellie and Isla, the two wee lassies we had over for the photo op. They'll be gutted.'

'I had something I've been trying to resolve for a long time.'

Christ, now what was coming? 'OK, I get it. That's why he's here.' Dougie glanced at Cutter. 'What is it?'

'A personal matter. It's resolved, it's with the police now. Let me think about fronting the band.'

'Take your time.'

'Skye's really fucked this up.'

Dougie watched him leave. Ordered another drink. Watched his hand shake as he lifted the glass. Christ, what a fucking mess. Without careful handling, his retirement fund was going up in flames. In fucking flames.

Chapter Sixty-Eight

Old Patterns

'I'm bloody starving.'

'Is there ever a time when you're not?' asked Wheeler.

'When I'm asleep.' Ross studied the menu. 'Have you come into money? An inheritance you never mentioned?'

'I'm feeling generous.'

'Always a first time, I suppose.' He sipped his wine. 'This place is expensive.'

She didn't contradict him.

The waiter approached. Wheeler ordered the sea bass with potatoes.

'I'll have the salmon.' Ross hesitated. 'And frites.'

After the waiter left she turned to him. 'You couldn't not order chips, could you?'

'See, that right there, is where you're wrong, they're frites.'

'They're potatoes and oil and salt.'

'Different shape altogether from chips,' said Ross. 'Besides, a place this posh, they'll be more of a garnish. Anyway, we're celebrating the case.'

'It all started when bloody Mark Ponsensby-Edward

pulled rank so his precious son would be removed from John Merrick's client list,' said Wheeler.

'And then Eddie Furlan planted the porn at Merrick's house to discredit him and influence the investigation.'

'Talk about bloody entitled,' said Wheeler. 'A policeman and a QC trying to pervert the course of justice. And the bloody DCC was in cahoots with them. The DCC knew about it from the off. He wasn't promoted at the time and Mark Ponsensby-Edward had had him in his pocket. Afterwards, Ponsensby-Edward helped to get McCoy promoted. It's all rotten. I hate that they were all part of our system.'

'But, now they're all fucked, Wheeler.'

'Completely.'

'Furlan dumped the body close to the pub to incriminate Cal Moody,' said Ross. 'He just couldn't let go of his hatred for Moody, could he?'

'No.'

'Stewart was shamefaced at the briefing. Difficult for him that it was our own.'

'It happens, Ross. Maybe we need to be more open to it? If we had been we'd have cracked it sooner.'

'Do you think that we'll ever get to know who else was putting pressure on the boss?'

'Doubt it.' Wheeler sipped her wine.

'The DCC, Mark Ponsensby-Edward, Eddie and Paul Furlan and Skye Cooper. Quite a haul, Wheeler. And the McIver's been closed.'

'For the time being. I think they'll reopen. Distance themselves from "rogue members" and carry on. Alistair Brodie's already given an interview intimating as much.'

Their food arrived.

'What happened, do you think?' said Ross. 'Guys like Skye Cooper who had everything. Fame, fortune, a great future. Why do you think he threw it all away?'

'It's a compulsion, an obsession. It began with the Marcus Newton trial all those years ago. Bloody Ponsensby-Edward was the defence QC.'

'And George Bellerose being killed in a RTA,' said Ross. 'Seems the driver of the van, Owen McCrudden, was part of the bust-up over in Queen's Park. Glasgow gang culture, the gift that keeps on giving.'

'I know.' Wheeler started on her food. It was only days since she and Ross had met in the park for breakfast. It seemed much longer. She felt the headache begin again. Rubbed her forehead.

'You going to get to the GP?'

'I've already been.'

'And?'

'She reckons it's nothing suspicious.'

'Hope you're not going to die on me?'

'I doubt it.'

He raised his glass. 'To Glasgow.'

'To Glasgow,' said Wheeler. 'City of Dreams.'

Acknowledgements

Thanks to my agent Jane Conway-Gordon, Krystyna Green and all at Little, Brown.